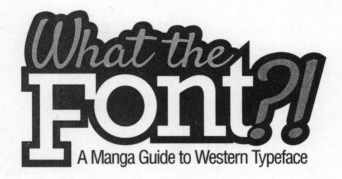

A Manga Guide to Western Typeface

written & illustrated by
Kuniichi Ashiya

editorial supervision:
Masayuki Yamamoto

Seven Seas Entertainment

What the Font?!

A Manga Guide to Western Typeface

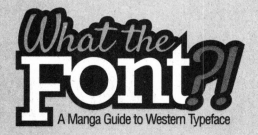

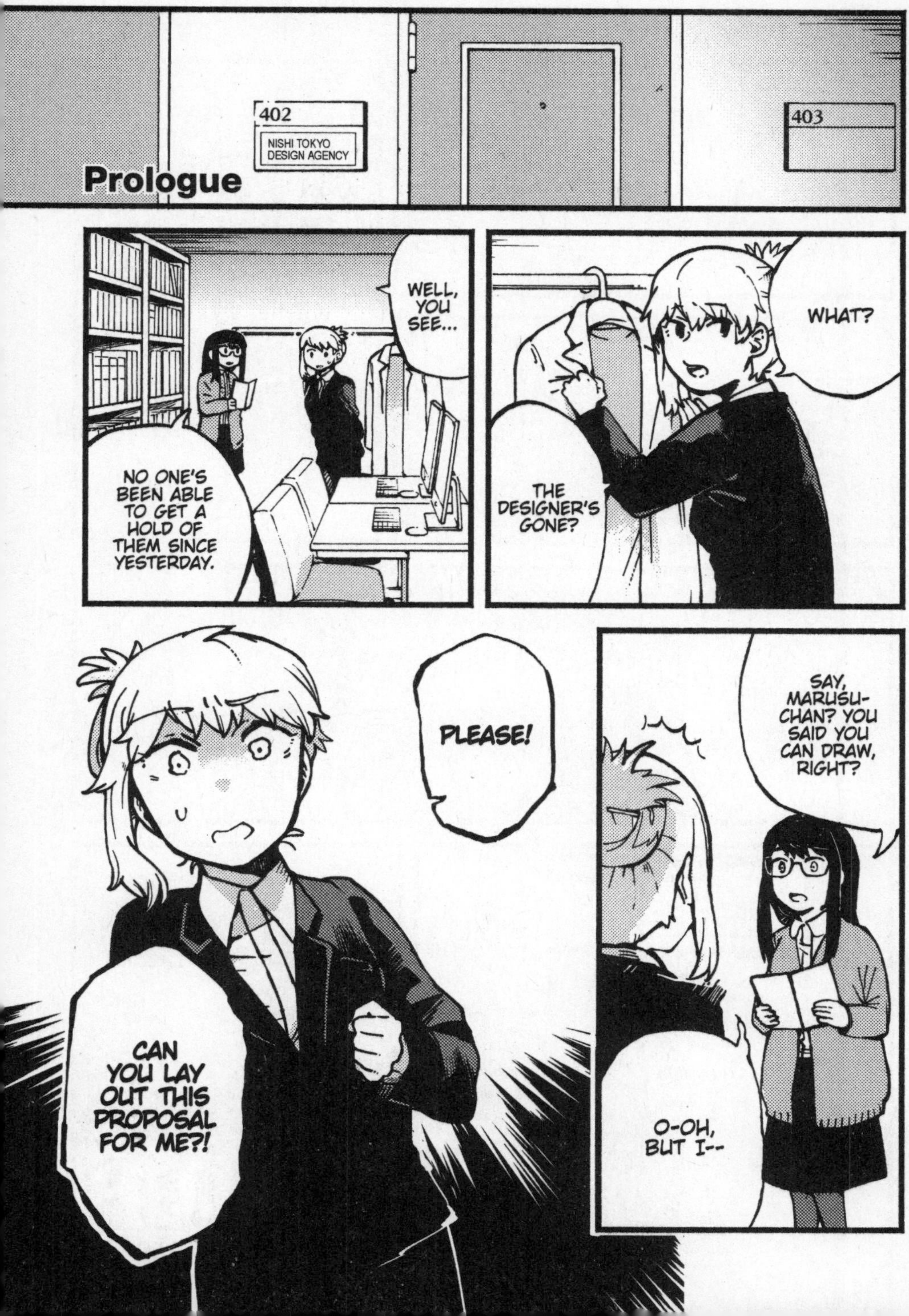
403
402
NISHI TOKYO DESIGN AGENCY
Prologue
WHAT?
THE DESIGNER'S GONE?
WELL, YOU SEE...
NO ONE'S BEEN ABLE TO GET A HOLD OF THEM SINCE YESTERDAY.
SAY, MARUSU-CHAN? YOU SAID YOU CAN DRAW, RIGHT?
O-OH, BUT I--
PLEASE!
CAN YOU LAY OUT THIS PROPOSAL FOR ME?!

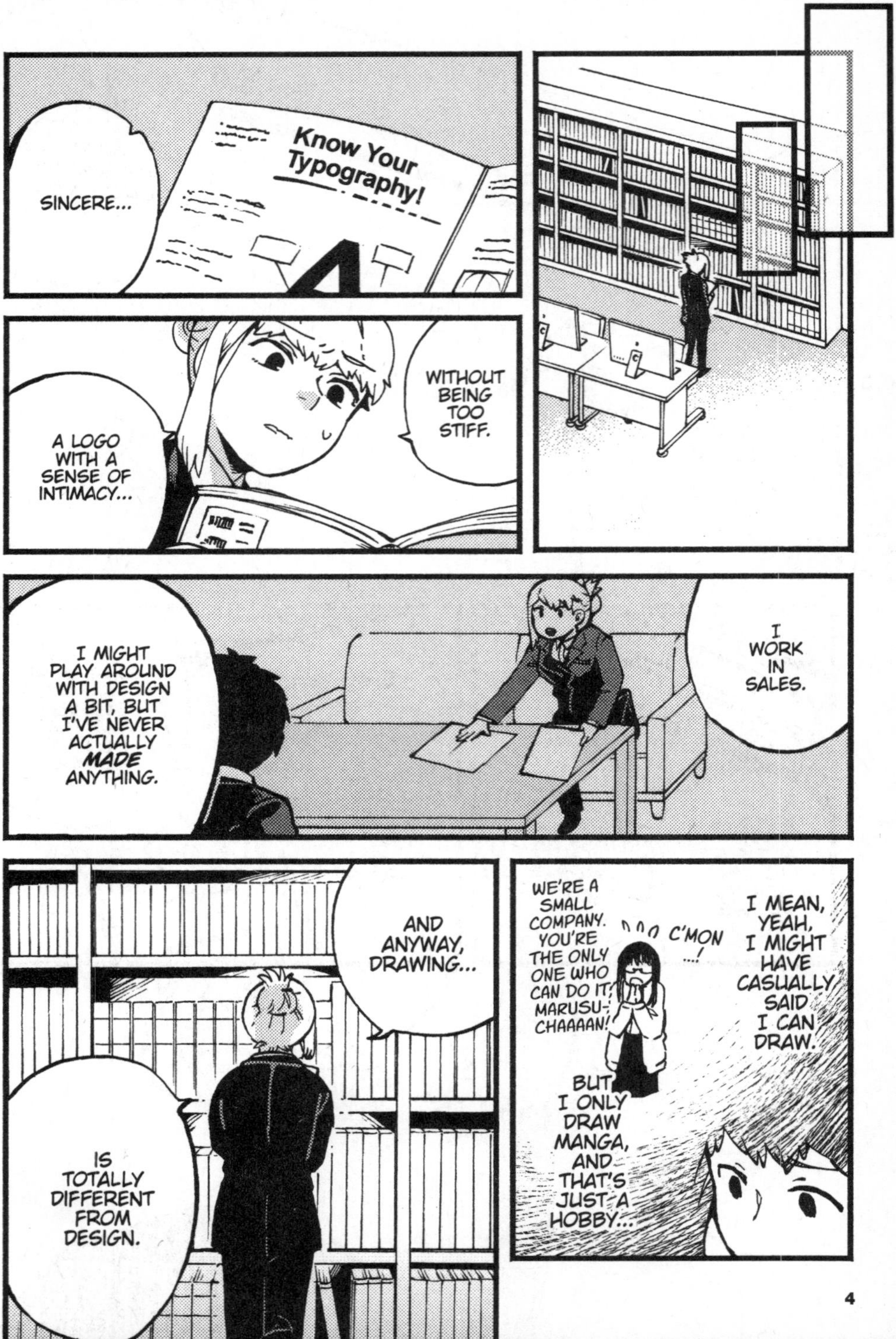
Know Your Typography!
SINCERE...
WITHOUT BEING TOO STIFF.
A LOGO WITH A SENSE OF INTIMACY...
I WORK IN SALES.
I MIGHT PLAY AROUND WITH DESIGN A BIT, BUT I'VE NEVER ACTUALLY MADE ANYTHING.
I MEAN, YEAH, I MIGHT HAVE CASUALLY SAID I CAN DRAW.
C'MON ...!
WE'RE A SMALL COMPANY. YOU'RE THE ONLY ONE WHO CAN DO IT, MARUSU-CHAAAAN!
BUT I ONLY DRAW MANGA, AND THAT'S JUST A HOBBY...
AND ANYWAY, DRAWING...
IS TOTALLY DIFFERENT FROM DESIGN.

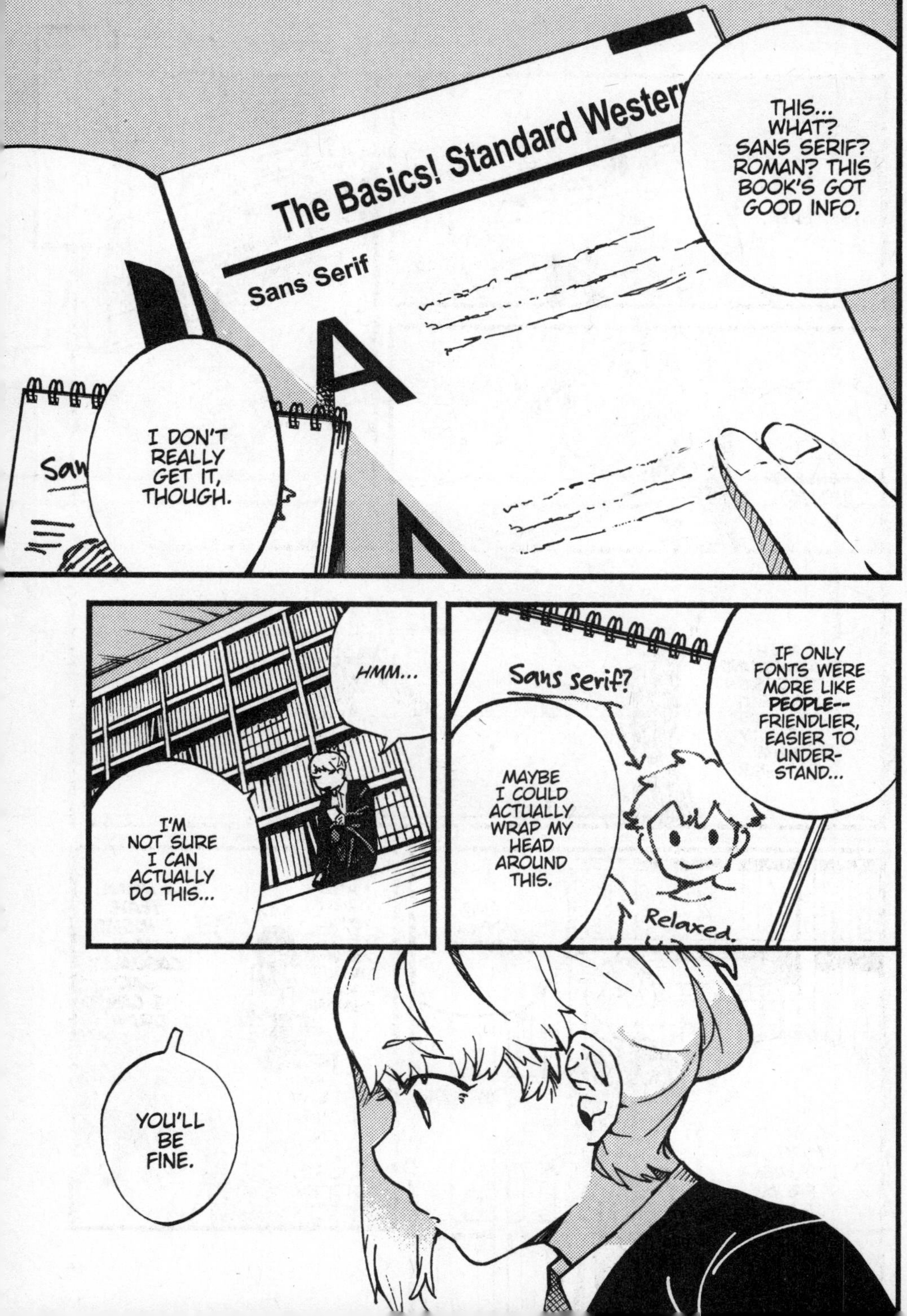
The Basics! Standard Wester
THIS... WHAT? SANS SERIF? ROMAN? THIS BOOK'S GOT GOOD INFO.
Sans Serif
I DON'T REALLY GET IT, THOUGH.
IF ONLY FONTS WERE MORE LIKE PEOPLE-- FRIENDLIER, EASIER TO UNDERSTAND...
Sans serif?
MAYBE I COULD ACTUALLY WRAP MY HEAD AROUND THIS.
Relaxed.
HMM...
I'M NOT SURE I CAN ACTUALLY DO THIS...
YOU'LL BE FINE.

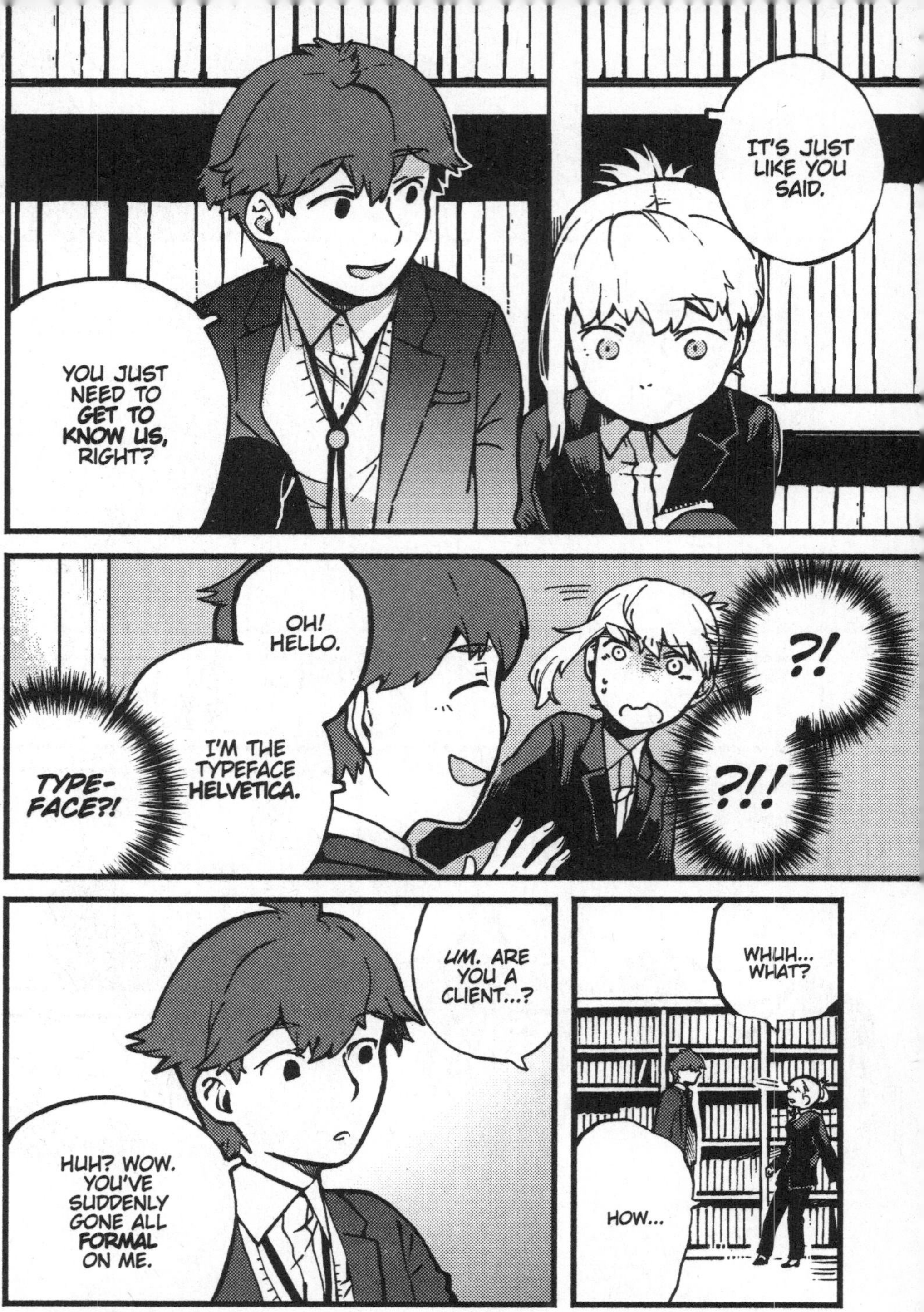
IT'S JUST LIKE YOU SAID.
YOU JUST NEED TO GET TO KNOW US, RIGHT?
?!
?!!
OH! HELLO.
I'M THE TYPEFACE HELVETICA.
TYPE-FACE?!
WHUH... WHAT?
HOW...
UM. ARE YOU A CLIENT...?
HUH? WOW. YOU'VE SUDDENLY GONE ALL FORMAL ON ME.

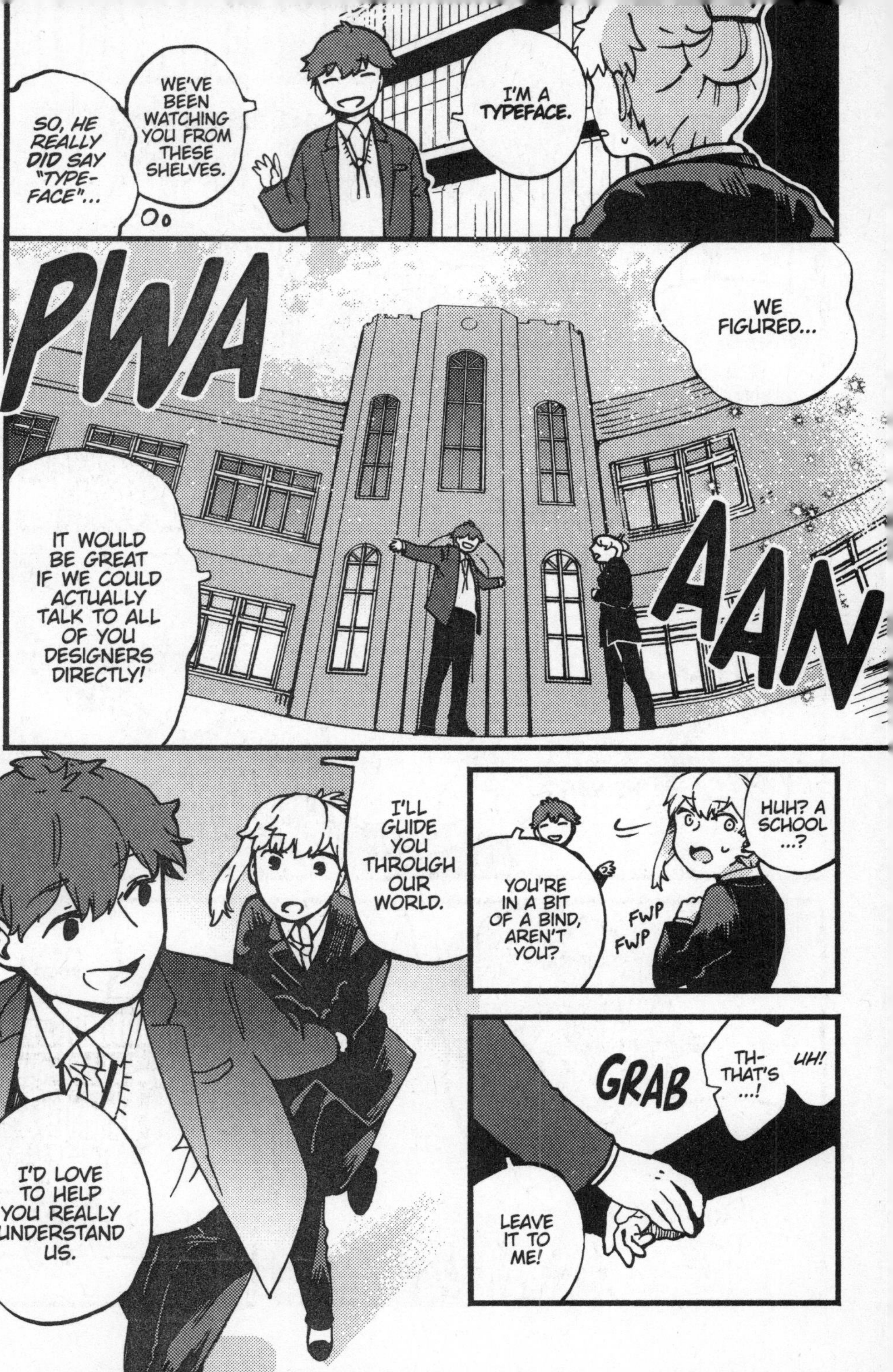
I'M A TYPEFACE.
WE'VE BEEN WATCHING YOU FROM THESE SHELVES.
SO, HE REALLY DID SAY "TYPE-FACE"...
WE FIGURED...
PWA
AAN
IT WOULD BE GREAT IF WE COULD ACTUALLY TALK TO ALL OF YOU DESIGNERS DIRECTLY!
HUH? A SCHOOL ...?
YOU'RE IN A BIT OF A BIND, AREN'T YOU?
FWP FWP
UH!
TH- THAT'S ...!
GRAB
LEAVE IT TO ME!
I'LL GUIDE YOU THROUGH OUR WORLD.
I'D LOVE TO HELP YOU REALLY UNDERSTAND US.

Table of Contents

Part 3: Other Styles - Script, Display, Blackletter

Font Q&A

Main Elements of Western Fonts

Arm
Serif
Axis
Link
Ear
Loop
Terminal
Tail
Typography
Stem
Shoulder
Bowl
Counter
Arch
Ascender line
Cap line
Ascender
Mean line
Cap height
X-height
Baseline
Descender
Descender line

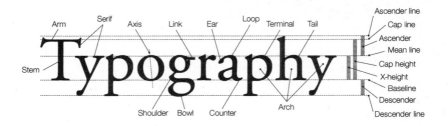

Serif	Decorative projections at the beginning or end of a stroke.
Stem	Stroke that forms the skeleton of the letterform.
Arm	Stroke that projects horizontally.
Axis	Shaft line to show the inclination of the curved area.
Ear	Short protrusion that can be seen on letterforms such as *g*.
Terminal	Fatter part that emphasizes the end of a stroke.
Shoulder	Upper curve on letterforms such as *b* and *h.*
Bowl	Closed, elliptical curve.
Arch	Open curved line.
Link	Stroke that connects one element to another.
Loop	Area closed off by a curve.
Tail	Part at the end of the letterform that extends like a tail.
Counter	Area enclosed inside a straight or curved stroke.

Ascender	Part that extends above a lowercase x-height.
Ascender line	Line marking the maximum ascender height.
Cap line	Line marking the height of uppercase letterforms.
Cap height	Height of uppercase letterforms.
X-height	Height of a lowercase *x.*
Mean line	Line to show the x-height.
Baseline	Standard line for upper- and lowercase letterforms.
Descender	Part that descends below the baseline.
Descender line ..	Line marking the maximum descender depth.

※ In this book, Western typefaces are presented in five groups: sans serif, roman, script, display, and blackletter. There are many different schools of thought on categorization. Clarendon and Rockwell, listed here as roman typefaces, can also be categorized as display types; while Trajan, a display type here, is sometimes put in the roman category, and Peignot in the sans serif group.

PART 1

Sans Serif Types

Helvetica
Futura
Gill Sans
Arial
Franklin Gothic
Impact
Frutiger
DIN
Optima
Gotham

Sans Serif Notes

Helvetica

Cheerful son of a noble family and an honors student.
Always seems busy, probably has a lot of work to do.

Futura

A bit of a space-cadet.
Her thinking's pretty logical, though.

Gill Sans

Sarcastic guy in glasses.
Not friendly, but deep down he's kind.

Arial

Puppyish kid with complicated feelings towards
Helvetica.

Franklin Gothic

The father-figure everyone turns to.
Loves to talk, has a playful side.

Impact

Young man with a rock-and-roll vibe.
Surprisingly close with Arial.

Frutiger

Gets along with anyone.
Amiable and cosmopolitan.

DIN

Serious and polite.
A building guide, together with Frutiger.

Optima

Free spirit who runs a café on the school grounds.
Very mysterious.

Gotham

His love of movies colors his every action.
The strong and silent type.

Helvetica

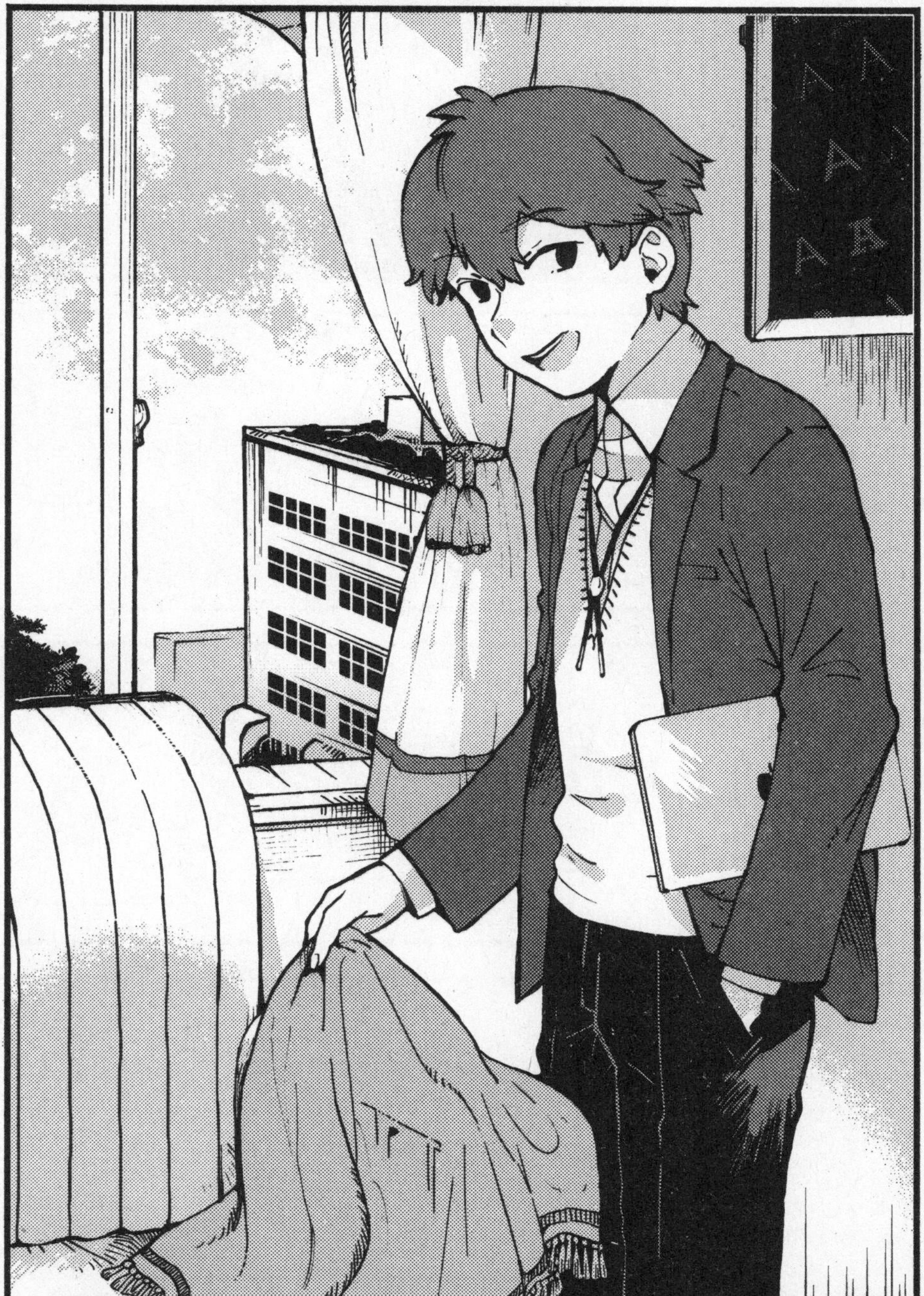

Highly versatile king of typefaces

Pleased to Meet You

HELVETICA... I SAW YOU IN THE TYPEFACE BOOK.
MM, THAT'S RIGHT.
HOW ABOUT A PROPER INTRO-DUCTION?
I'M **HELVETICA.**
SO BASICALLY, MY NAME MEANS "SWISS," AND JUST AS YOU'D EXPECT...
I WAS BORN IN SWITZERLAND, IN 1957.
NINE-TEE--
WAIT, THAT MEANS YOU'RE A **SENIOR CITIZEN...?**
GULP
OH MY, NO! IN THIS WORLD...
I'M STILL A **BABY,** REALLY.
THIS WORLD IS REALLY CONFUS-ING!!

Helvetica was created by typeface designers Max Miedinger and Eduard Hoffmann, who were commissioned by Haas Type Foundry to produce a new typeface similar to a nineteenth-century Grotesque type.

Welcome to the Typeface Research Society

AND THIS...
IS WHERE ALL THE TYPE-FACES GET TO-GETHER.
WE CALL IT THE TYPEFACE RESEARCH SOCIETY.
WHAT DO YOU DO HERE, HELVETICA-SAN?
I'M THE MEDIATOR.
HEH. WELL, I MEAN...
THEY DID ASK ME, AFTER ALL.
I GUESS PEOPLE SAY I'M PRETTY RELAXED AND TRUST-WORTHY.
HA HA! IT'S EMBAR-RASSING TO SAY THAT MYSELF.
HOW ABOUT WE GET GOING?
THIS GUY'S A BIG DEAL!
HE'S PRETTY MODEST ABOUT IT, BUT HE'S DEFINITELY A BIG DEAL!

From the 1950s to the 1960s, the Swiss Style was popular. A horizontal/vertical grid would be set on the surface for printing, allowing efficient placement of text and photos. With its simplicity and versatile, subdued personality, Helvetica is still widely used today.

What is Sans Serif?

YOU MIGHT WANT TO THINK OF THIS LIKE AN EXTRA-CURRICULAR ACTIVITY AT SCHOOL.
THAT REMINDS ME. YOU WERE WONDERING ABOUT SANS SERIF, WEREN'T YOU?
OH, RIGHT!
ROUGHLY SPEAKING, IT'S THE CLASS WE'RE PUT INTO.
Sans serif
Sans: Without
Serif: Protrusions/ Whiskers
SERIF MEANS "WHIS-KERS."
AND SANS IS FRENCH FOR "WITH-OUT."
ALL THE ROMAN TYPES HAVE THESE LITTLE DECORATIONS LIKE THORNS ON THE LETTER-FORMS.
A A
Without serif.
With serif.
WE DON'T HAVE THOSE.
THAT MAKES US "SANS SERIF."
AND THAT'S WHY... I...
I WANT TO BE CAREFUL NOT TO SAY ANYTHING THORNY.
YOU'LL TELL ME IF I DO, RIGHT?
HUH?
WAS THAT PART OF THE LESSON ...?

Typefaces like Helvetica, which are made up of straight lines with little ornamentation, fall into a category called "sans serif." These fonts have high visibility and are easily distinguished from a distance or up close, so they're useful in displays and signs, and they produce real results.

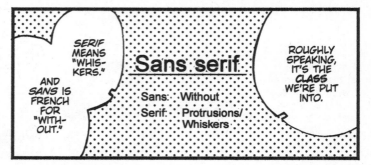

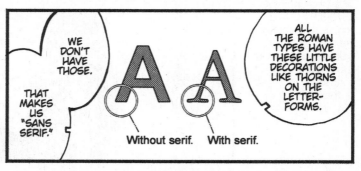

Amazing Helvetica

SO, YOU CAN SEE WORK THAT I'VE DONE ALL OVER TOWN.
MUJI
OH! IS THAT...?
STATIONERY, TRANSPORTATION...
Post-it
I'M SURE YOU'VE USED A PRODUCT I'VE REPRESENTED AT LEAST ONCE.
Lufthansa
THAT'S INCREDIBLE. YOU'RE EVERYWHERE.
OH, AND... THERE'S THIS, TOO.
?
HIS OWN...
Helvetica
MOVIE!!

Helvetica is extremely versatile, so it's become the world's most popular typeface. It's used in the logo type for Panasonic, Post-it ® notes, and many other diverse companies and products. Helvetica has even been the subject of books–and yes, a movie.

The Burden of Fame

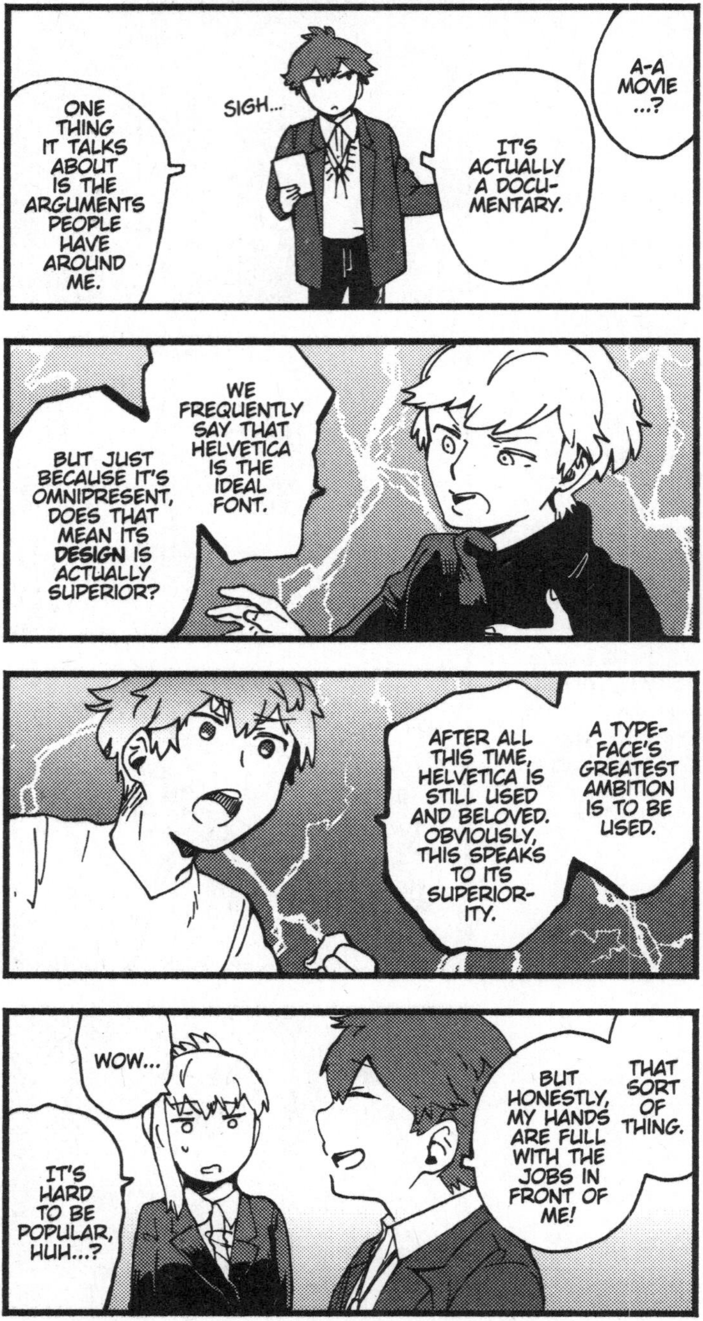
A-A MOVIE ...?
IT'S ACTUALLY A DOCU-MENTARY.
SIGH...
ONE THING IT TALKS ABOUT IS THE ARGUMENTS PEOPLE HAVE AROUND ME.
WE FREQUENTLY SAY THAT HELVETICA IS THE IDEAL FONT.
BUT JUST BECAUSE IT'S OMNIPRESENT, DOES THAT MEAN ITS **DESIGN** IS ACTUALLY SUPERIOR?
A TYPE-FACE'S GREATEST AMBITION IS TO BE USED.
AFTER ALL THIS TIME, HELVETICA IS STILL USED AND BELOVED. OBVIOUSLY, THIS SPEAKS TO ITS SUPERIOR-ITY.
THAT SORT OF THING.
BUT HONESTLY, MY HANDS ARE FULL WITH THE JOBS IN FRONT OF ME!
WOW...
IT'S HARD TO BE POPULAR, HUH...?

Helvetica frequently inspires debates because it is used so commonly..But given that it looks good no matter which way it's used, the typeface is an extremely powerful ally for designers.

Family Reunion

HEY, HELVETICA!
WHOOPS.
I'VE BEEN LOOKING FOR YOU!
FUTURA.
THE FAMILY'S COME FOR A VISIT. LOOKS LIKE A BIG GROUP.
OH, REALLY? THANKS FOR THE HEADS-UP.
OKAY, THEN. I'D BETTER GET GOING.
OKAAAY.
I'LL FINISH SHOWING THE VISITOR AROUND.
OH. THANKS... UH?
YOU'RE A TYPEFACE, TOO?
YES, THAT'S RIGHT. I'M FUTURA~!
MORE TYPEFACES...!

Individual typefaces often have variants with thicker or thinner strokes, inclined letterforms, or other changes. These groups of variants are called "families," and are based on the design policy of the original.

Helvetica

CATEGORY:	Sans serif
CLASSIFICATION:	Neo-grotesque
YEAR OF CREATION:	1957 (Neue Haas Grotesk), revised 1960
DESIGNER(S):	Max Miedinger, Eduard Hoffmann
FOUNDRY:	Haas Type Foundry (Switzerland), Stempel (Germany)

The world's standard, a beloved typeface.

Helvetica was released under the name Neue Haas Grotesk in 1957 by the Haas Type Foundry. After World War II, the nineteenth-century sans serif typeface Akzidenz Grotesk (1896) enjoyed a resurgence, primarily in Switzerland, so Eduard Hoffman (1892–1980), the typeface director at Haas, planned a new font based on this sans serif type and asked Max Miedinger (1910–1980) to carry out the design work. When it was released for sale by the German company Stempel in 1960, it was renamed "Helvetica" to reflect its Swiss origins and adapted for machine typesetting, leading to its global spread.

The main features of Helvetica are an x-height (the vertical span of the lowercase x which indicates the height of lowercase letters) greater than that of Akzidenz, a wider counter, and a horizontal cut on the tips of letters such as C and S. Additionally, the space between letters is small, so letters can be combined efficiently for setting, but the type is also ideal for expansion and use in logos. Because idiosyncrasies are kept to a minimum, like the colorless transparency of water, Helvetica is easy to use in a variety of situations. One could call it the sans serif type most representative of the twentieth century. In Japan, it is used in the logos of major corporations such as Panasonic, making it broadly familiar.

USAGE EXAMPLES

- Panasonic (electronics company)
- Post-it ® (sticky notes)
- Lufthansa (German airline company)

ABCDEFGHIJ KLMNOPQRS TUVWXYZ
abcdefghijklmn
opqrstuvwxyz
0123456789

Helvetica Regular

Futura

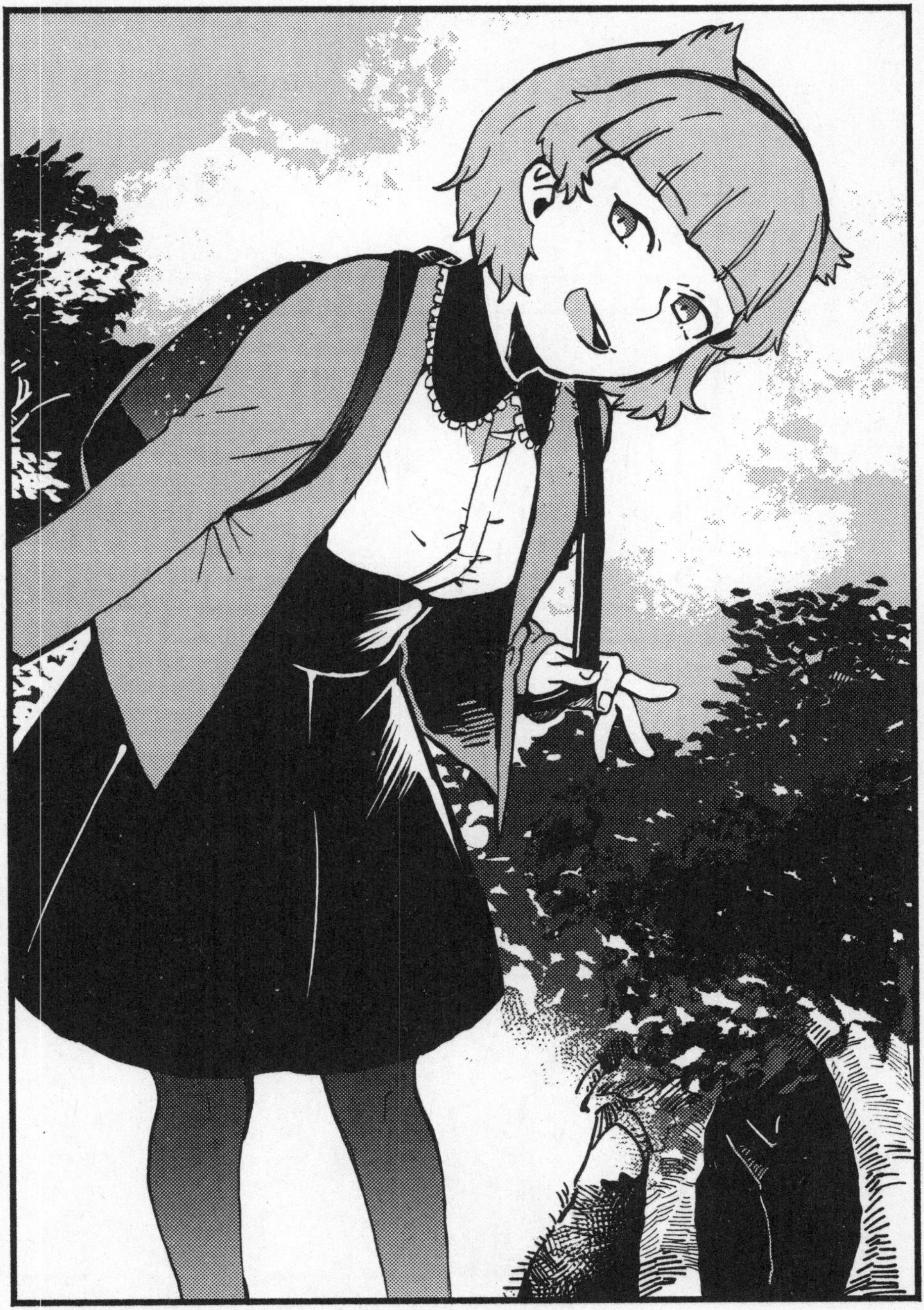

Geometrical shape in pursuit of functional beauty

One Hundred Years and Still Going Strong

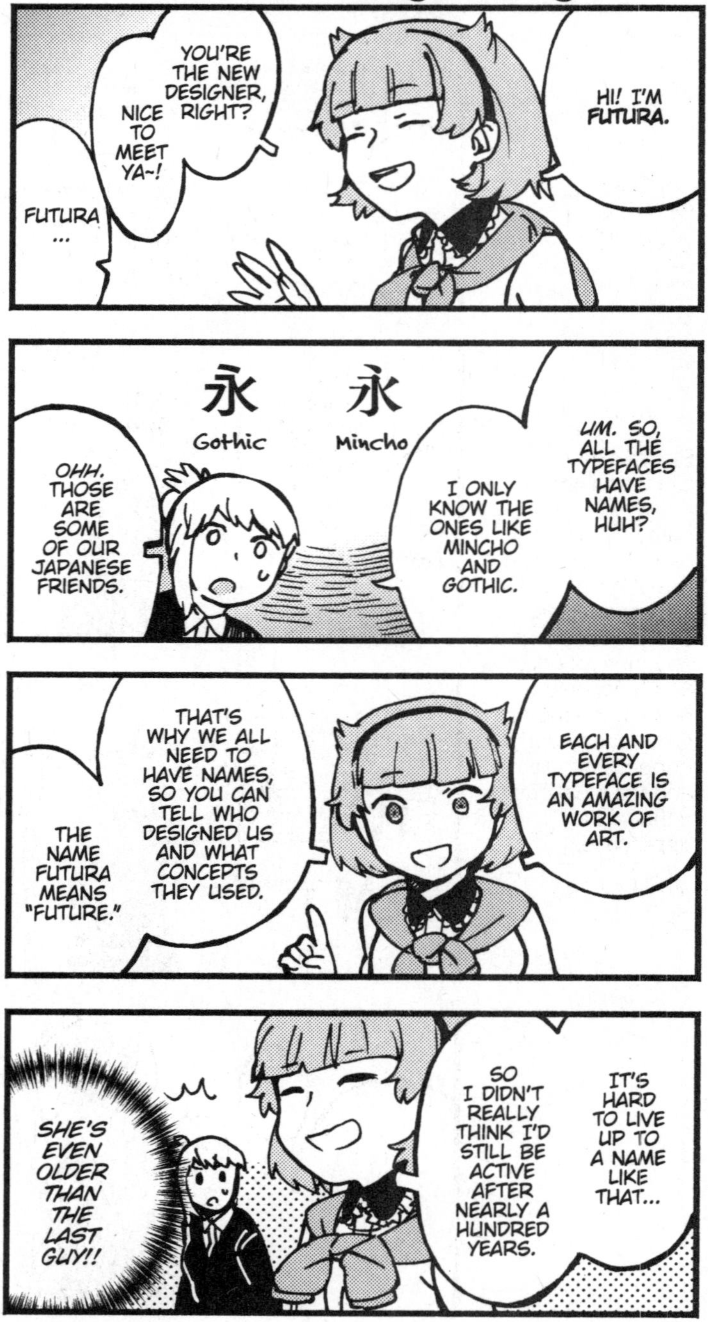
HI! I'M FUTURA.
YOU'RE THE NEW DESIGNER, RIGHT?
NICE TO MEET YA~!
FUTURA...
UM. SO, ALL THE TYPEFACES HAVE NAMES, HUH?
I ONLY KNOW THE ONES LIKE MINCHO AND GOTHIC.
永
Mincho
永
Gothic
OHH. THOSE ARE SOME OF OUR JAPANESE FRIENDS.
EACH AND EVERY TYPEFACE IS AN AMAZING WORK OF ART.
THAT'S WHY WE ALL NEED TO HAVE NAMES, SO YOU CAN TELL WHO DESIGNED US AND WHAT CONCEPTS THEY USED.
THE NAME FUTURA MEANS "FUTURE."
IT'S HARD TO LIVE UP TO A NAME LIKE THAT...
SO I DIDN'T REALLY THINK I'D STILL BE ACTIVE AFTER NEARLY A HUNDRED YEARS.
SHE'S EVEN OLDER THAN THE LAST GUY!!

Futura was designed in 1927 by Paul Renner, a teacher at the Printing Trade School in Munich. Renner used geometrical shapes to design a sensible typeface based on the zeitgeist of the times.

Geometry Girl

HELVETICA TOLD ME...
YOU'RE HAVING TROUBLE WITH A LOGO DESIGN?
I AM. IT WAS REALLY SUDDEN.
THAT'S ROUGH!
WE'RE ALWAYS GLAD TO HELP.
IF THERE'S SOMETHING YOU DON'T UNDER-STAND, JUST SAY--
HM?
THIS POSTER IS FIVE MILLIMETERS OFF.
FWP
PLAP
PLAP
HA HA HA! SORRY!
THIS KIND OF THING JUST REALLY BUGS ME.
...
I LIKE THINGS TO BE JUST SO, YOU KNOW?

Futura almost looks as if it were drawn with a compass and a ruler. This is in line with the Bauhaus educational ideal of the time, which sought a rational and functional beauty. Examples include the nearly perfectly circular *O* and the lowercase *u* that looks uppercase.

Cleanliness is Key

OH! RIGHT!
GOOD MORNING...
THAT SHIRT YOU WERE WEARING THE OTHER DAY, MARUSU, WAS MY WORK.
Supreme
WHAT?
HUNH. I DON'T REALLY GET IT.
BUT THIS MIGHT BE GOOD FOR FUTURE REFERENCE.
YOU DON'T GET TOO MANY CHANCES TO SPEAK DIRECTLY WITH TYPEFACES.
UM, FUTURA-SAN?
WHAT DO YOU THINK YOUR BEST FEATURE IS?
YOUR APPEAL.
MY BEST FEATURE ...?
LET'S SEE...
I GUESS IT'D BE MY **CLEAN LOOK.**
OH!
AND I'M PRETTY SIMPLE, SO I'M THE HARDEST TO COPY.

With its clean lines and almost graphic circles, Futura is used in the logos for fashion brands, cosmetics, and automobile companies, among other things. One striking example is the fashion brand Supreme, which references Futura.

Typeface of Spaceship Earth

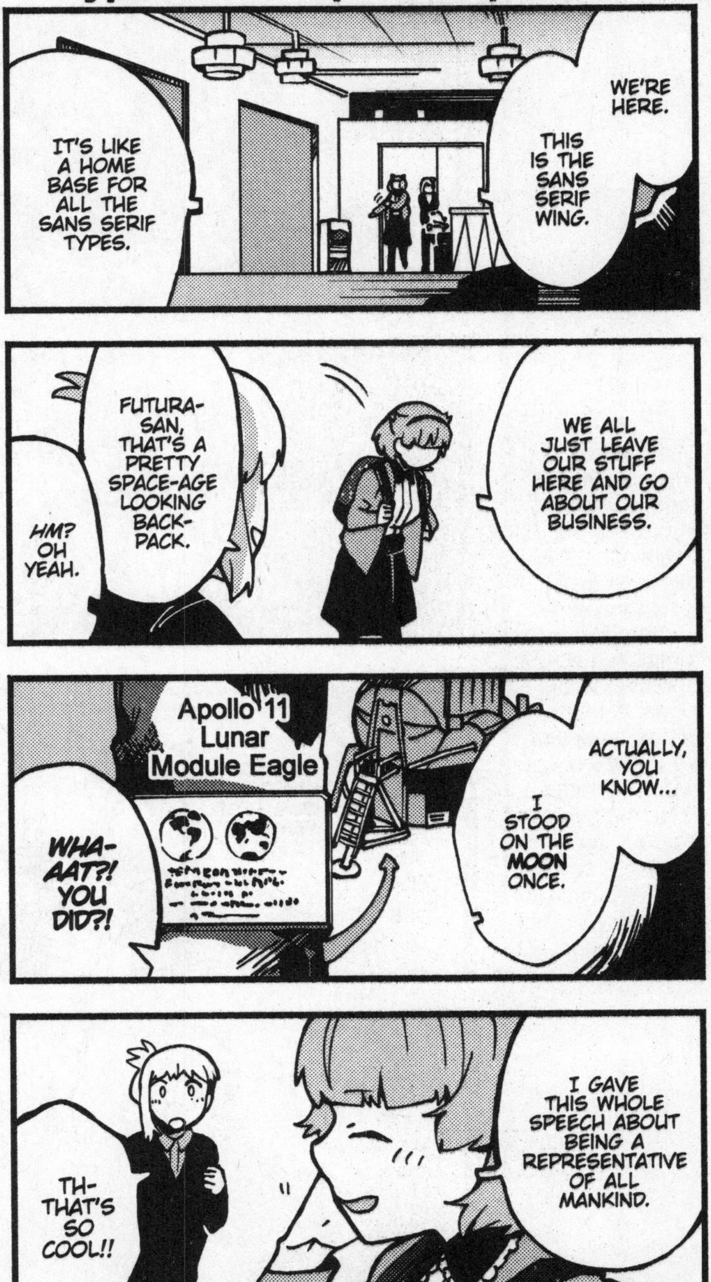
WE'RE HERE.
THIS IS THE SANS SERIF WING.
IT'S LIKE A HOME BASE FOR ALL THE SANS SERIF TYPES.
WE ALL JUST LEAVE OUR STUFF HERE AND GO ABOUT OUR BUSINESS.
FUTURA-SAN, THAT'S A PRETTY SPACE-AGE LOOKING BACK-PACK.
HM? OH YEAH.
ACTUALLY, YOU KNOW...
I STOOD ON THE MOON ONCE.
Apollo 11 Lunar Module Eagle
WHA-AAT?! YOU DID?!
I GAVE THIS WHOLE SPEECH ABOUT BEING A REPRESENTATIVE OF ALL MANKIND.
TH-THAT'S SO COOL!!

Futura is the typeface used on the plate attached to Apollo 11, the first ship in human history to land on the moon. The plate reads: "Here men from the planet Earth first set foot upon the moon July 1969, A.D."

A Wee Bit Flighty

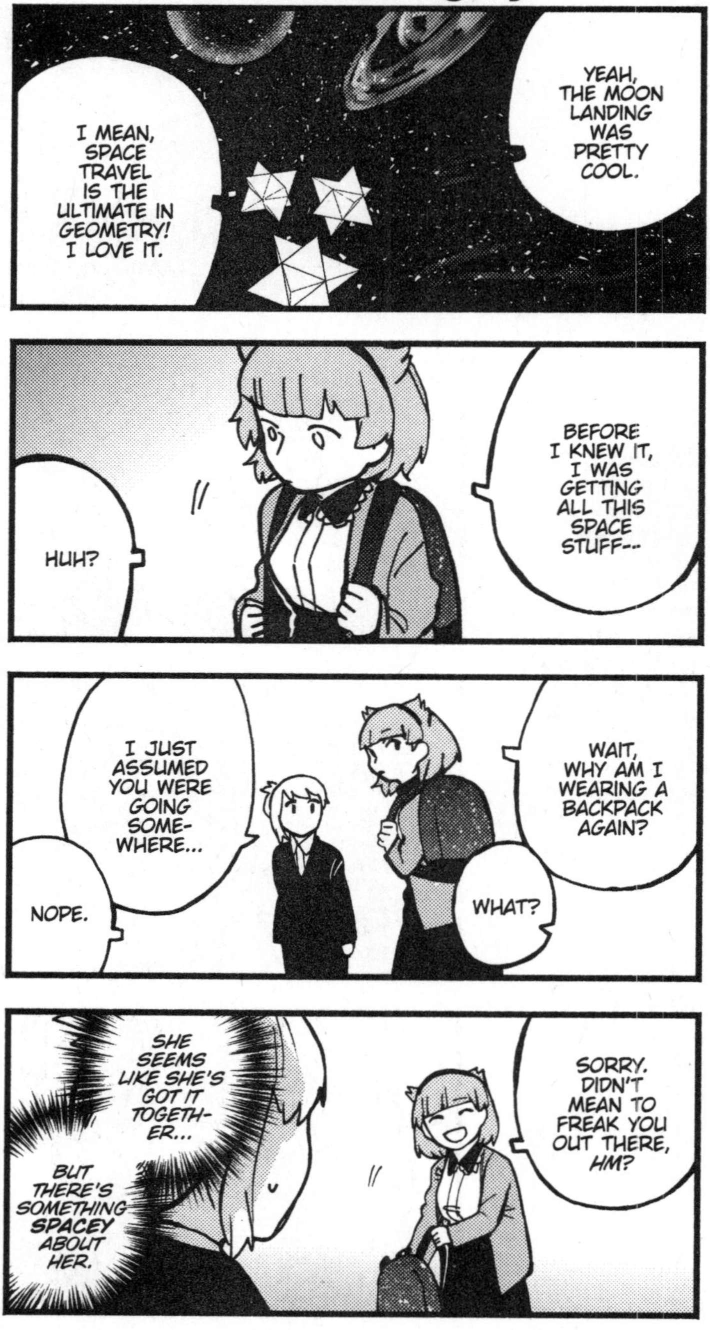
YEAH, THE MOON LANDING WAS PRETTY COOL.
I MEAN, SPACE TRAVEL IS THE ULTIMATE IN GEOMETRY! I LOVE IT.
BEFORE I KNEW IT, I WAS GETTING ALL THIS SPACE STUFF--
HUH?
WAIT, WHY AM I WEARING A BACKPACK AGAIN?
I JUST ASSUMED YOU WERE GOING SOME-WHERE...
WHAT?
NOPE.
SORRY. DIDN'T MEAN TO FREAK YOU OUT THERE, HM?
SHE SEEMS LIKE SHE'S GOT IT TOGETH-ER...
BUT THERE'S SOMETHING SPACEY ABOUT HER.

Visual effect is an important consideration in Futura, so the uppercase *O* is not a perfect circle, the sides of the letterforms are slightly thinner, and the joints of bowls (the elliptical curved area) such as in the *b* or *d*, are thinner. These adjustments make Futura's letters the easiest to read of all characters with geometrical and graphical forms.

Regional Character?

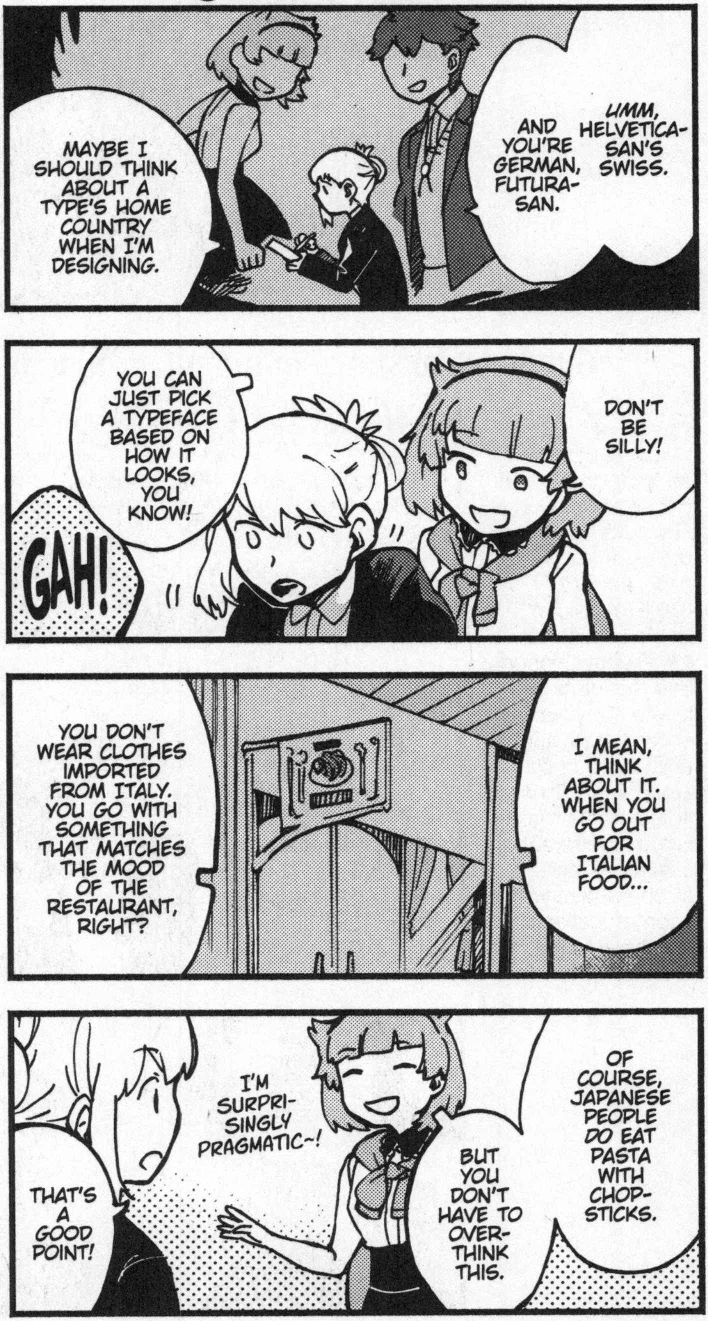
UMM, HELVETICA-SAN'S SWISS.
AND YOU'RE GERMAN, FUTURA-SAN.
MAYBE I SHOULD THINK ABOUT A TYPE'S HOME COUNTRY WHEN I'M DESIGNING.
DON'T BE SILLY!
YOU CAN JUST PICK A TYPEFACE BASED ON HOW IT LOOKS, YOU KNOW!
GAH!
I MEAN, THINK ABOUT IT. WHEN YOU GO OUT FOR ITALIAN FOOD...
YOU DON'T WEAR CLOTHES IMPORTED FROM ITALY. YOU GO WITH SOMETHING THAT MATCHES THE MOOD OF THE RESTAURANT, RIGHT?
OF COURSE, JAPANESE PEOPLE DO EAT PASTA WITH CHOP-STICKS.
BUT YOU DON'T HAVE TO OVER-THINK THIS.
I'M SURPRI-SINGLY PRAGMATIC~!
THAT'S A GOOD POINT!

Typefaces often reflect the fashions and culture of their times. But it's not true that a particular country's typeface can only be used for that country's designs. It's best to choose a typeface that's most effective for your project.

Futura

CATEGORY:	Sans serif
CLASSIFICATION:	Geometric
YEAR OF CREATION:	1927
DESIGNER(S):	Paul Renner
FOUNDRY:	Bauer Type Foundry (Germany)

Geometrical shape in pursuit of functional beauty.

Futura is a sans serif type based on the modern design that spread across Europe in the 1920s based on the establishment of the German modern design school Bauhaus. The designer, Paul Renner (1878–1956), was a painter, typeface designer, and typography theorist who also taught typography at art schools in Frankfurt and the Printing Trade School in Munich. He started work on Futura in 1924 at the request of the Bauer Type Foundry, and the type, originally created with ruler and compass, was completed as moveable type in 1927. The family later grew with the addition of italic and bold types. With the rise of the Nazi government in 1933, Renner was arrested as a communist and pushed out of teaching, after which he became a painter in Geneva.

Combining geometrical beauty with readability thanks to careful tweaks, Futura spread to countries around the world, beginning with the United States. It was seen as the "typeface of modern times" and became a global bestseller.

USAGE EXAMPLES
....
☐ Supreme (U.S. fashion brand)

ABCDEFGHIJ
KLMNOPQRS
TUVWXYZ
abcdefghijklmn
opqrstuvwxyz
0123456789

Futura Std Medium

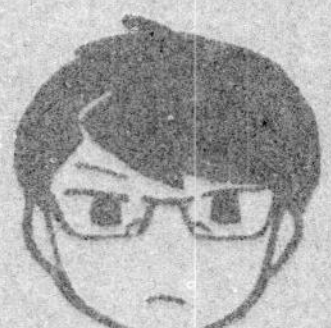

Gill Sans

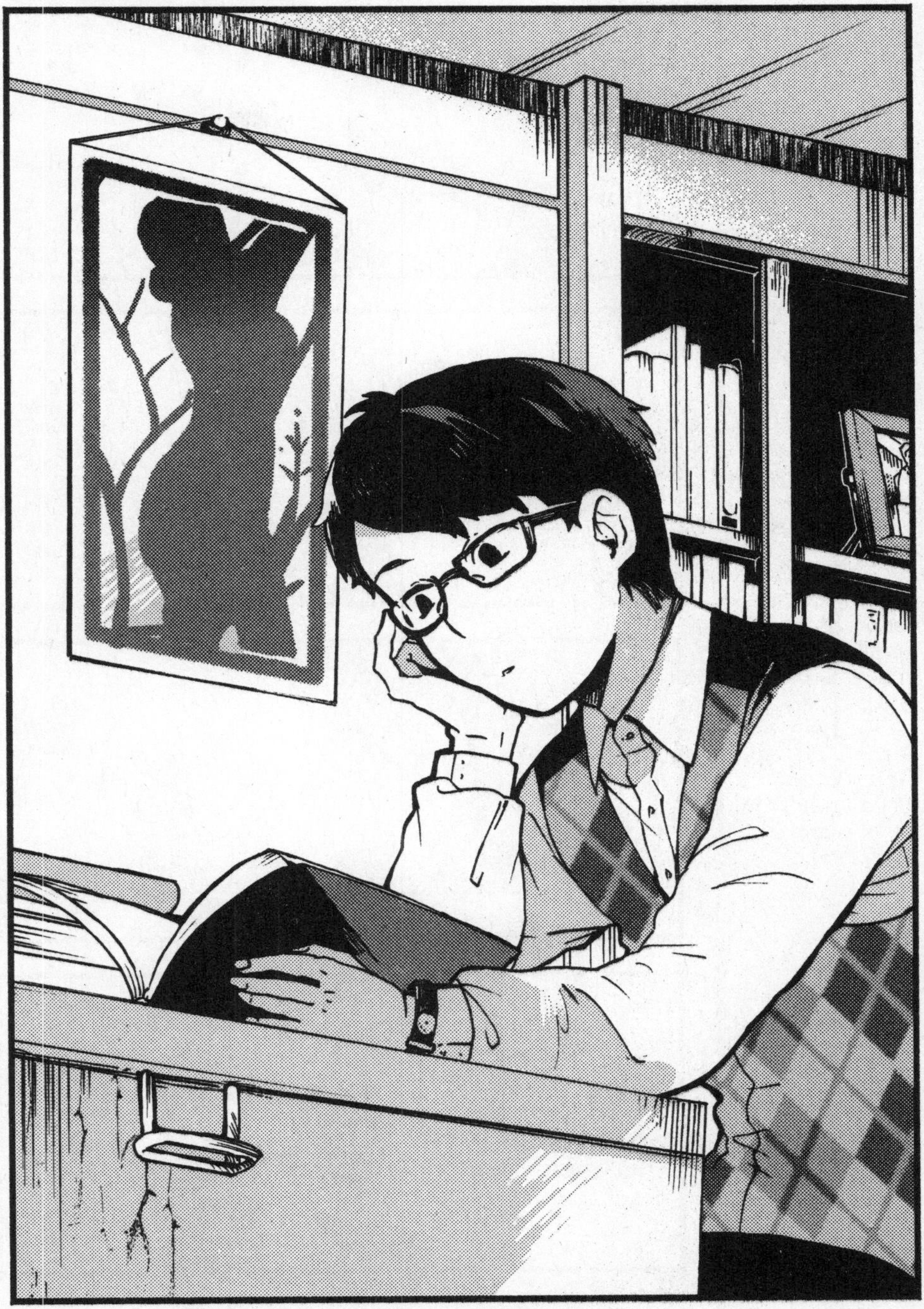

A fusion of traditional shape and modern sensibility

Grumpy Old Font

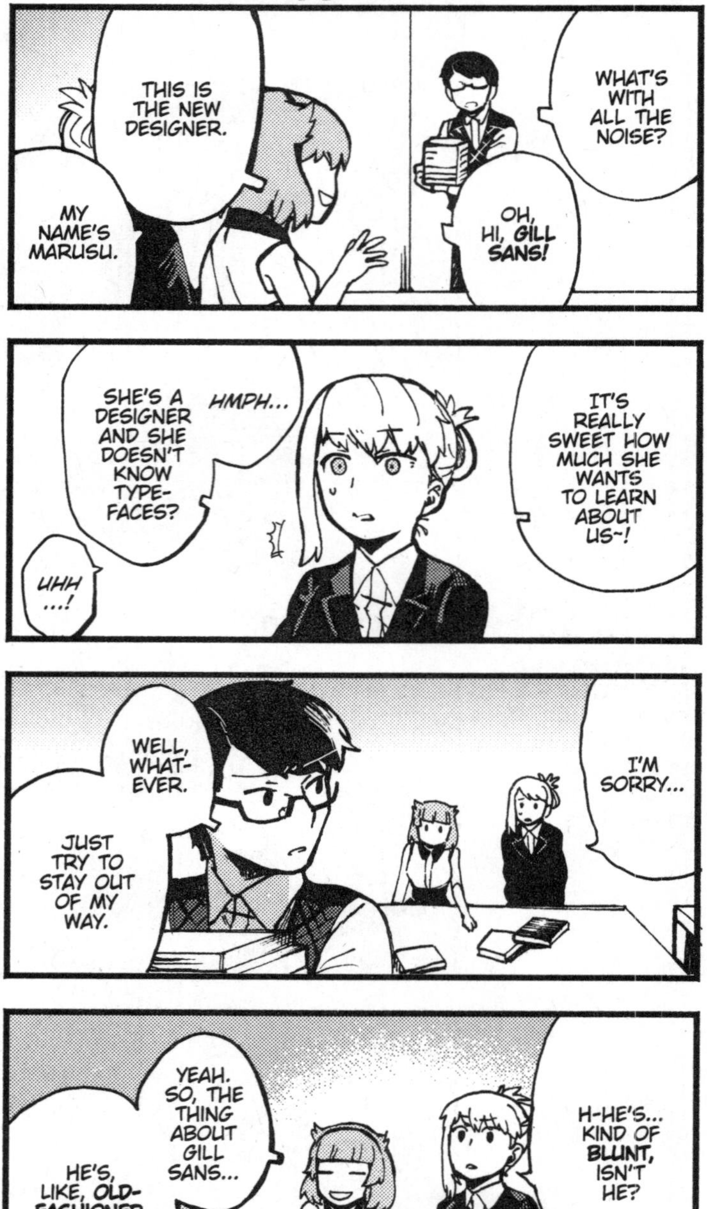
WHAT'S WITH ALL THE NOISE?
OH, HI, **GILL SANS!**
THIS IS THE NEW DESIGNER.
MY NAME'S MARUSU.
IT'S REALLY SWEET HOW MUCH SHE WANTS TO LEARN ABOUT US~!
HMPH...
SHE'S A DESIGNER AND SHE DOESN'T KNOW TYPE-FACES?
UHH ...!
I'M SORRY...
WELL, WHATEVER.
JUST TRY TO STAY OUT OF MY WAY.
H-HE'S... KIND OF **BLUNT,** ISN'T HE?
YEAH. SO, THE THING ABOUT GILL SANS...
HE'S, LIKE, **OLD-FASHIONED,** YOU KNOW?

The basic framework that became Gill Sans was created in reference to ancient Roman type, combining the uppercase letters of ancient Roman monuments and the penmanship of lowercase letters in the Middle Ages. Traces of handwritten strokes remain in its form.

Humanist?

GILL SANS MAY NOT LOOK IT, BUT HE'S A **HUMANIST.**
OH, BUT I DON'T MEAN THE DOCTRINE, THOUGH.
SANS SERIF FONTS ARE SPLIT UP INTO CATEGORIES BY SHAPE.
Grotesque
ABC
•Akzidenz Grotesk
Neo-Grotesque
ABC
•Helvetica
THE EARLY ONES WERE "GRO-TESQUES," ROUGH-HEWN AND POWER-FUL.
AND THEN THEY DEVELOPED INTO THE VERSATILE "NEO-GROTESQUES," LIKE HELVETICA.
TYPEFACES LIKE ME ARE IN THE "GEOMETRIC" GROUP-- WE'RE GEOMETRICAL AND RATIONAL.
Geometric
ABC
•Futura
Humanist
ABC
•Gill Sans
AND THEN THERE'S THE "HUMANIST" GROUP, WHICH LOOKS A BIT LIKE HAND-WRITING.
SO ANYWAY, COULD YOU GIVE GILL SANS THESE PAPERS?
THANKS SO MUCH!
WHAT?! NO WAY! HE'LL EAT ME ALIVE!!

Sans serif fonts are divided into four main groups. Gill Sans is part of the group known as "Humanist sans serif." It has a feel of human handwriting in its letterforms, elements such as the lowercase *g* on two levels, which is rare among sans serif fonts.

Raised by an English Sculptor

EXCUSE ME...
KA CHAK
FUTURA-SAN ASKED ME TO BRING YOU THESE PAPERS.
Sans serif building, private room.
WHOA!
A SCULP-TURE?
DON'T TOUCH THAT.
MY TEACHER WAS THE BRITISH SCULPTOR ERIC GILL.
THEREFORE, IT ONLY FOLLOWS THAT HIS WORK WOULD BE IN HERE.
AMAZING! SO BEAUTIFUL!
HEY. ARE YOU LISTENING TO ME?

Eric Gill, the creator of Gill Sans, was a famed British sculptor. In addition to Gill Sans, he also created roman typefaces reminiscent of ancient monuments, such as Perpetua and Joanna.

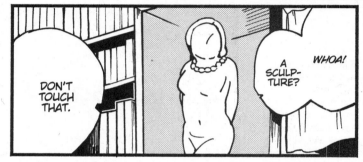

Serious Influence

FUTURA-SAN WAS TELLING ME...
HE'S VERY PROUD OF HIS ACCOMPLISHMENTS.
YOU'RE A REPRESENTATIVE OF **HUMANIST** TYPEFACES.
OH. WELL.
I CAME INTO THE WORLD IN 1927.
I'VE ACTUALLY HAD QUITE THE INFLUENCE ON THE OTHER HUMANIST FONTS.
WHAT?! THAT'S AMAZING!
AND YOU DO A LOT OF WORK, DON'T YOU, GILL SANS-SAN?!
OH. UM, WELL... YES.
BLUSH
HUH? DIDN'T EXPECT **THAT** REACTION.

Gill Sans was a pioneering typeface that combines excellent visibility with a traditional form. While it is a sans serif, in some characters, such as the lowercase *r*, the thickness of the vertical and horizontal strokes is extremely different.

British Gentleman

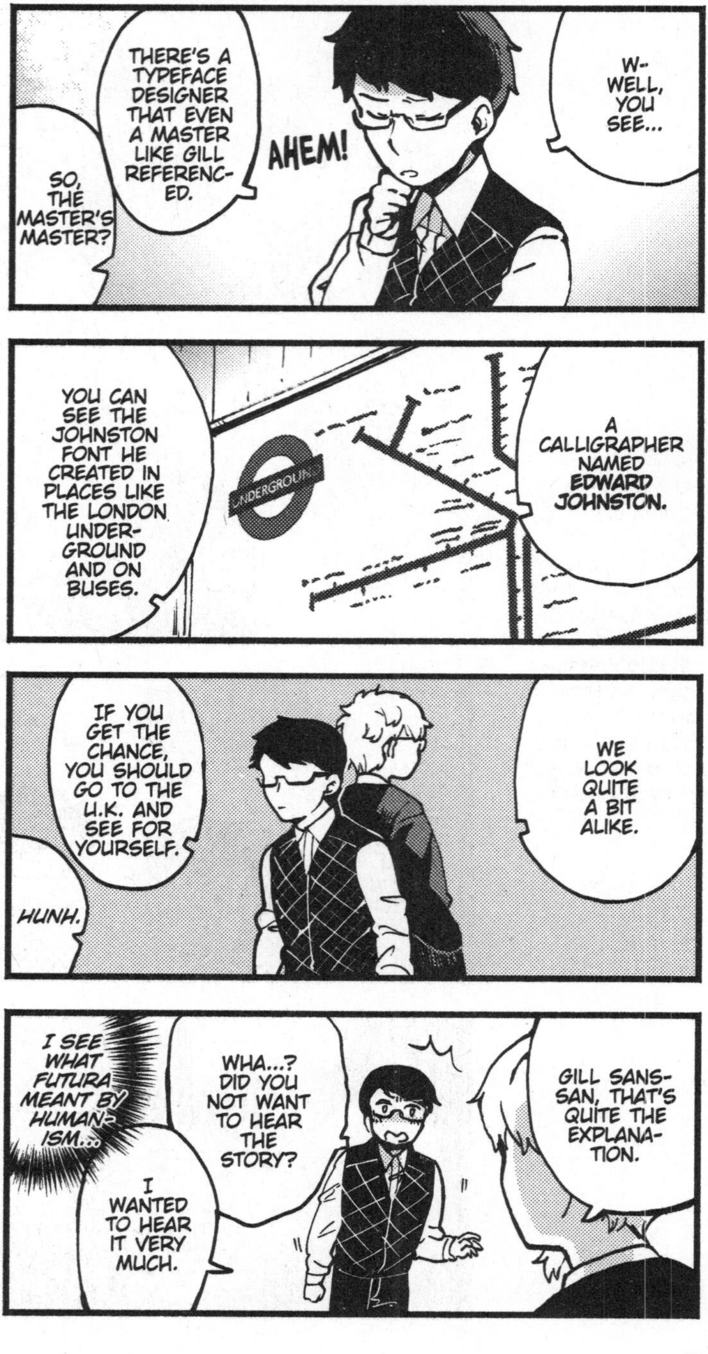
W-WELL, YOU SEE...
AHEM!
THERE'S A TYPEFACE DESIGNER THAT EVEN A MASTER LIKE GILL REFERENC-ED.
SO, THE MASTER'S MASTER?
A CALLIGRAPHER NAMED EDWARD JOHNSTON.
YOU CAN SEE THE JOHNSTON FONT HE CREATED IN PLACES LIKE THE LONDON UNDER-GROUND AND ON BUSES.
WE LOOK QUITE A BIT ALIKE.
IF YOU GET THE CHANCE, YOU SHOULD GO TO THE U.K. AND SEE FOR YOURSELF.
HUNH.
GILL SANS-SAN, THAT'S QUITE THE EXPLANA-TION.
WHA...? DID YOU NOT WANT TO HEAR THE STORY?
I SEE WHAT FUTURA MEANT BY HUMAN-ISM...
I WANTED TO HEAR IT VERY MUCH.

The Johnston typeface can be seen in transit facilities such as the London Underground. Gill Sans has been the corporate typeface for the British broadcaster BBC and is used in the logo for the fashion brand Margaret Howell. Given such conspicuous use, the typeface has taken on a British flavor.

Heart of Gold...?!

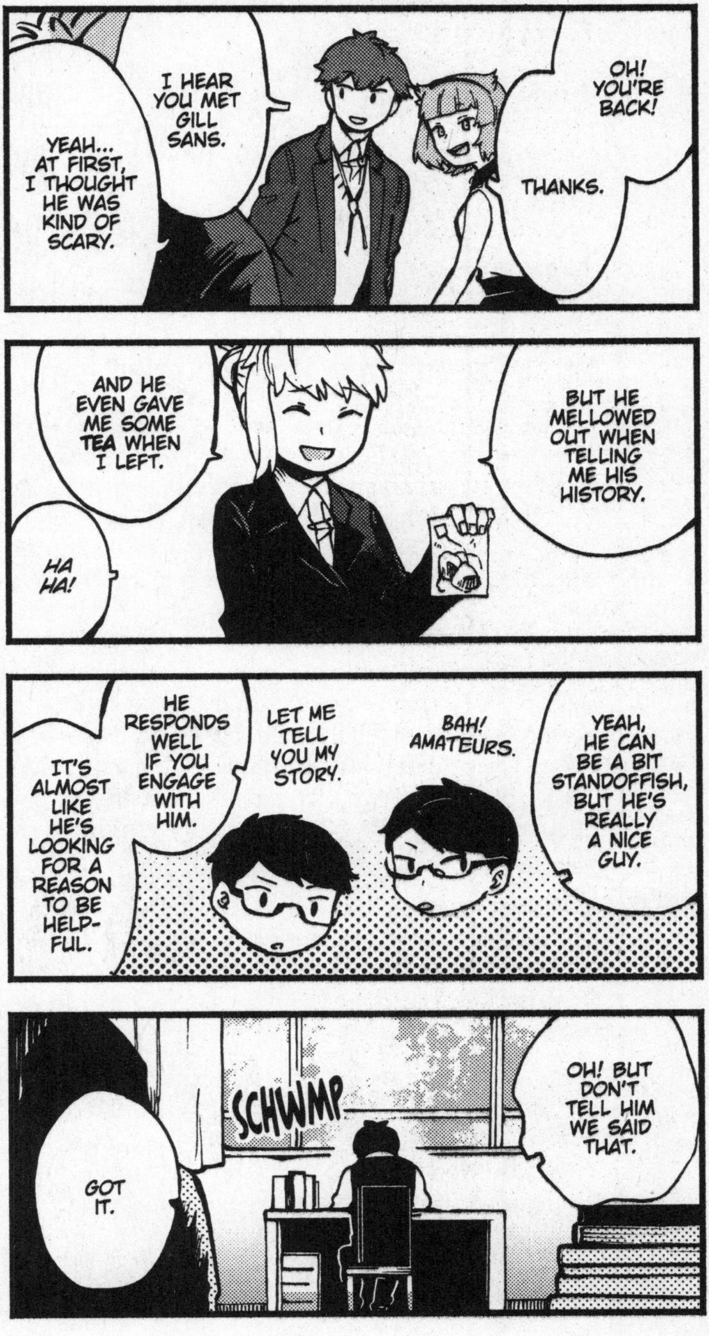
OH! YOU'RE BACK!
THANKS.
I HEAR YOU MET GILL SANS.
YEAH... AT FIRST, I THOUGHT HE WAS KIND OF SCARY.
BUT HE MELLOWED OUT WHEN TELLING ME HIS HISTORY.
AND HE EVEN GAVE ME SOME TEA WHEN I LEFT.
HA HA!
YEAH, HE CAN BE A BIT STANDOFFISH, BUT HE'S REALLY A NICE GUY.
BAH! AMATEURS.
LET ME TELL YOU MY STORY.
HE RESPONDS WELL IF YOU ENGAGE WITH HIM.
IT'S ALMOST LIKE HE'S LOOKING FOR A REASON TO BE HELP-FUL.
OH! BUT DON'T TELL HIM WE SAID THAT.
SCHWMP
GOT IT.

The logo for the Family Mart convenience store is a sans serif font called Corinthian, which was influenced by Gill Sans. The bold uppercase shape and the warmth of the lowercase letters are the reasons for its popularity.

Gill Sans

CATEGORY:	Sans serif
CLASSIFICATION:	Humanist
YEAR OF CREATION:	1928
DESIGNER(S):	Eric Gill
FOUNDRY:	Monotype (England)

Strait-laced but warm, a human font.

Gill Sans is a modern sans serif type born in 1928 in England. The designer, Eric Gill (1882–1940), was a sculptor who built a community of artists with his compatriots in Ditchling, East Sussex. After training as an architect, Gill studied calligraphy under Edward Johnston (1872–1944), the designer of the London Underground typeface and the father of modern calligraphy. Gill became especially proficient in carving inscriptions into gravestones. A Bristol bookstore sign he produced during a quiet period caught the eye of the typographer Stanley Morison (1889–1967), and Gill ended up trying his hand at type design. Gill Sans followed the teachings of Johnston and was based on the uppercase letters on the epitaph of the ancient Roman emperor Trajan, but also has a geometrical structure that gives rise to a beautiful, almost humanistic modern sans serif type.

In the 1930s, Gill Sans was used in posters, timetables, tickets, and other items as the exclusive typeface of the railway company LNER (London and North Eastern Railway), making it a forerunner in the unification of a corporate brand. The typeface has now become symbolic of England as the exclusive typeface of the BBC.

USAGE EXAMPLES

☐ BBC (British Broadcasting Company)
☐ Margaret Howell (British fashion brand)
☐ Tommy Hilfiger (American fashion brand)

ABCDEFGHIJ
KLMNOPQRS
TUVWXYZ
abcdefghijklmn
opqrstuvwxyz
0123456789

Gill Sans Std Regular

Arial

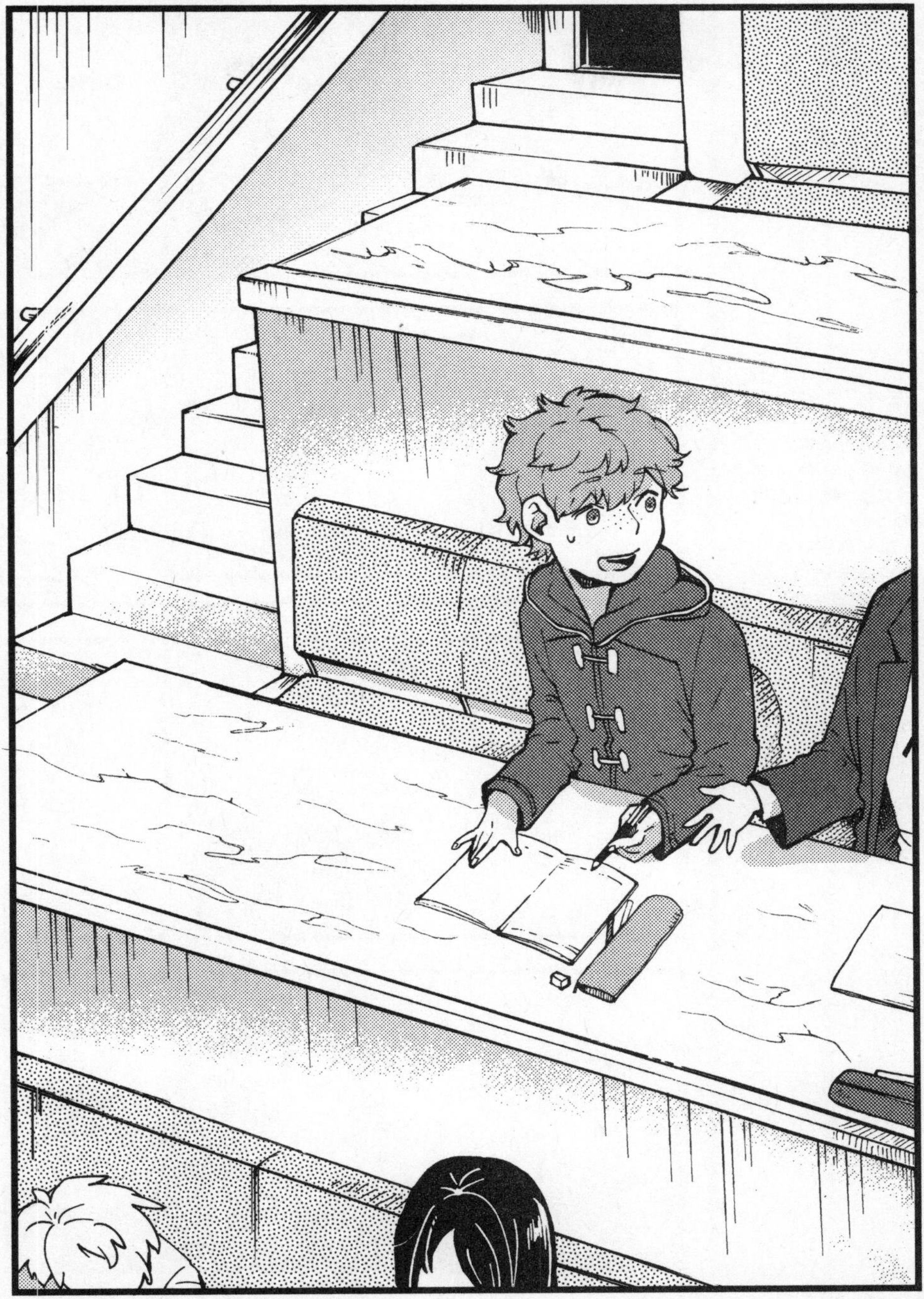

Typeface with an identity crisis

Arial Lacks Confidence

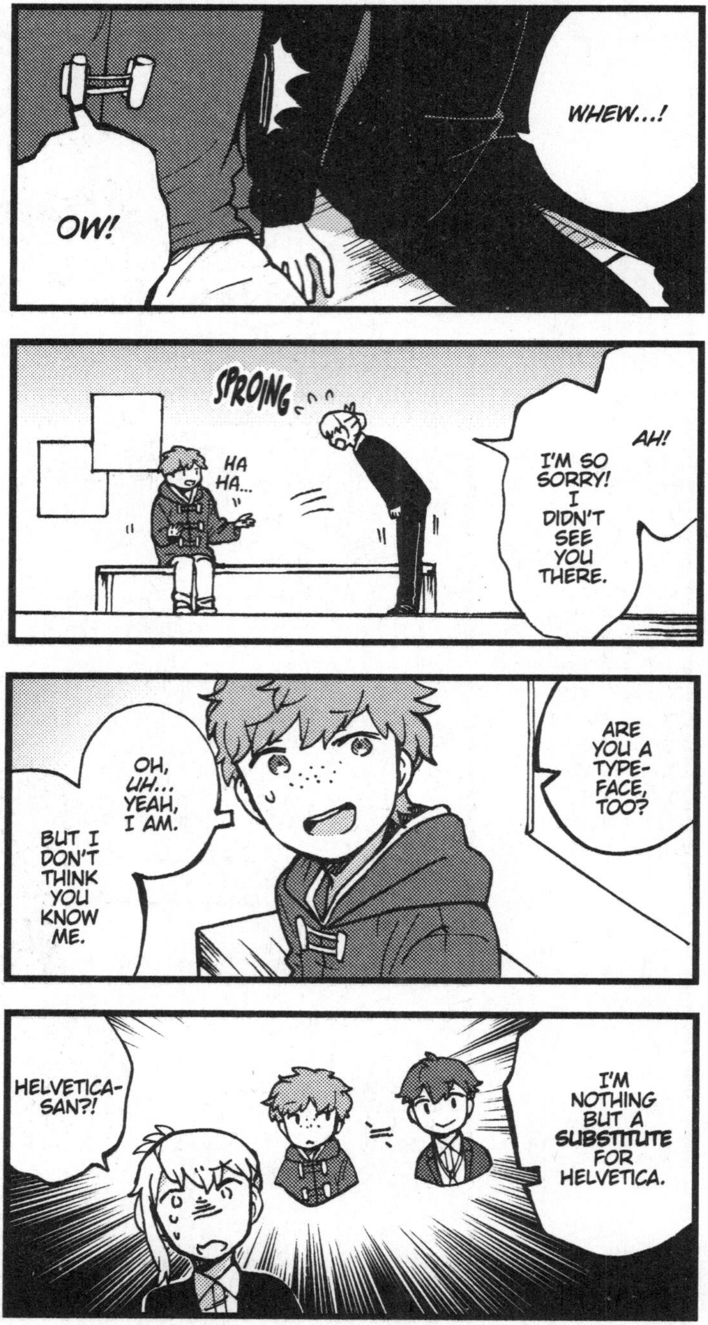
WHEW...!
OW!
AH!
I'M SO SORRY! I DIDN'T SEE YOU THERE.
SPROING
HA HA...
ARE YOU A TYPE-FACE, TOO?
OH, UH... YEAH, I AM.
BUT I DON'T THINK YOU KNOW ME.
I'M NOTHING BUT A SUBSTITUTE FOR HELVETICA.
HELVETICA-SAN?!

Arial was developed in 1982 under the designers Robin Nicholas and Patricia Saunders. It shares many features with Helvetica and engendered much discussion around the new concept of a substitute typeface.

Code Name: Sonoran

UH, UM.
SO, WHAT DO YOU THINK THIS IS CALLED?
Arial
A TYPE-FACE WITH A TYPE-FACE BOOK...
OH! ISN'T THAT ARIAL?
I KNEW IT.
SEE, THE TRUTH IS...
Zurich
Myriad
AYREAL?
AIRREAL?
ERR, NEXT IS...
AIREAL.
HERE.
NO ONE EVER KNOWS HOW TO PRO-NOUNCE MY NAME.
SO I'M FINE WITH WHAT-EVER'S EASIEST FOR YOU.
THAT'S AN INCREDIBLY HUMAN PROBLEM...

Arial was created in the 1980s for use in the IBM bitmap laser printer, and at the time of installation, it was given the name Sonoran Sans Serif. Later, in 1992, it was adopted as the core font for Windows 3.1 and became known around the world.

Ignorance is Bliss

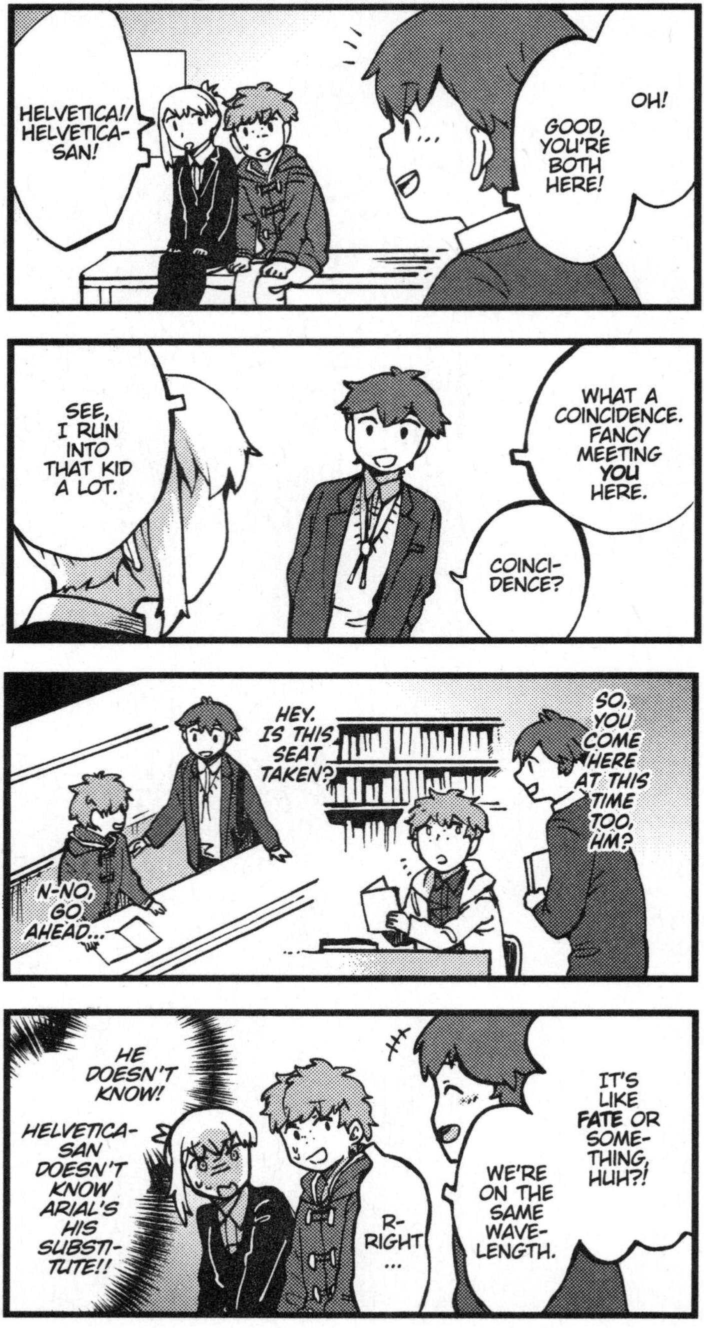
OH!
GOOD, YOU'RE BOTH HERE!
HELVETICA!! HELVETICA-SAN!
WHAT A COINCIDENCE. FANCY MEETING YOU HERE.
COINCI-DENCE?
SEE, I RUN INTO THAT KID A LOT.
SO, YOU COME HERE AT THIS TIME TOO, HM?
HEY. IS THIS SEAT TAKEN?
N-NO, GO AHEAD...
IT'S LIKE FATE OR SOMETHING, HUH?!
WE'RE ON THE SAME WAVE-LENGTH.
R-RIGHT...
HE DOESN'T KNOW!
HELVETICA-SAN DOESN'T KNOW ARIAL'S HIS SUBSTITUTE!!

A quarter of a century after Helvetica's birth, Arial was created to resemble it, designed so that the width of the letterforms is exactly the same. Other typefaces also work as substitutes for Helvetica, with letters that are basically the same width or with minor differences in size.

The Proof's on the Diagonal

HE SAYS HE'S A SUB, BUT...
YOU TWO DON'T REALLY LOOK ALIKE, DO YOU?
WELL, PEOPLE WHO USE US BOTH GET TOTALLY DIFFERENT IMPRESSIONS.
HUH? WHAT ARE YOU TALKING ABOUT?
?
OH, NOTHING...
JUST THINKING THAT THERE'S A LOT OF WAYS TO TELL SANS SERIFS APART.
WELL THEN, I THINK YOU CAN TELL IT'S ME FROM THE WAY THE BRUSH IS VERTICAL OR HORIZONTAL AT THE BEGINNING AND END OF STROKES.
t
t
I'M... THE KEY TO ME IS THAT I'M DIAGONAL THERE.
HE'S AMAZING. JUST CHATTING SO CASUALLY LIKE THAT...
AAH! THAT'S--
DON'T LET IT GET YOU DOWN!
YOU'RE TOTALLY FINE!

One way to distinguish between these two types: In contrast with the vertical or horizontal beginnings and endings of Helvetica's strokes, Arial's structure is cut almost diagonally. You can easily tell the two apart by the shape of the *R* leg or the downward extension of the *G* vertical stroke.

Finding Yourself

OHH, I'M BEING CALLED TO A MEETING.
SEE YOU LATER!
S-SURE!
I WISH I COULD FIND MY OWN STYLE...
BUT, ARIAL-SAN.
?
YOU'VE GOT **PLENTY** OF STRENGTHS.
THERE'S NO NEED TO BE SO DOWN ON YOURSELF.
...!!
UH. UM.
THANK YOU.
BLUSH
SO, LIKE, WHAT WOULD THOSE BE...?
UH!
NGH! BEING A NEWBIE DESIGNER IS **FRUSTRAT-ING!!**

Because Arial was designed under the assumption that it would be displayed or printed at low resolution, it's incredibly readable on a computer screen. The openings of lowercase letters like *a* and *c* are larger, making it easy to tell the different letters apart even when they're very small.

Where Does a Substitute Belong?

HOW DID A TYPEFACE LIKE YOU COME TO BE IN THE FIRST PLACE, ARIAL-SAN?
WOULDN'T HELVETICA-SAN BE SURPRISED IF HE FOUND OUT?
WHEN DIGITAL FONTS REALLY STARTED GOING MAIN-STREAM...
Arial
ABCDEFGHIJKLMN
abcdef···
Typeface: A group of letter-forms designed with a certain theme.
YOU NEEDED TO CREATE A **TYPEFACE PROGRAM** FOR THAT.
THERE'S NOT MUCH OF A DIFFERENCE BETWEEN DIGITIZING AN EXISTING TYPE-FACE THAT'S OWNED BY ANOTHER COMPANY...
Digitized.
Moveable type.
OOO.OTF
Font: A means of expressing a typeface.
AND CREATING A NEW ONE IN YOUR OWN COMPANY, IN TERMS OF WORK.
THAT'S HOW I WAS BORN. MY UP-BRINGING'S COMPLI-CATED...
BUT I HOPE SOMEDAY PEOPLE WILL SEE ME FOR **MYSELF.**

Until the creative and artistic merits of typefaces and the strengths and weaknesses of their ornamentation and strokes are recognized, there will be no copyright for a typeface itself, so many substitutes are created. With digital fonts for use in computers, a copyright is generated for the program itself.

※ Whether or not a copyright is recognized and whether or not a license fee is necessary for use are two separate issues.

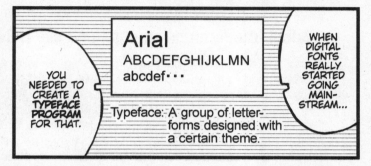

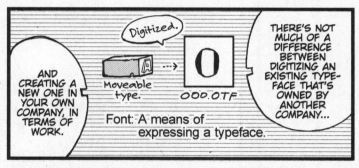

Arial

CATEGORY:	Sans serif
CLASSIFICATION:	Neo-grotesque
YEAR OF CREATION:	1982
DESIGNER(S):	Robin Nicholas, Patricia Saunders
FOUNDRY:	Monotype (England)

Substitute font designed to look like Helvetica.

Arial is a relatively new sans serif type designed by Robin Nicholas (1947–) and Patricia Saunders (1933–2019) of the Monotype Corporation. Having started work in the drawing office of Monotype at the age of eighteen, Nicholas was the head of the lettering division in 1982, the same year in which Saunders returned to the office after raising her children. Together, they produced a sans serif type, which was released under the name Sonoran as a font for IBM printers, but which was eventually renamed Arial and installed as the standard for Windows 3.1. Since then it has been adopted in all Windows machines as well as in Mac OS X to become the most widely disseminated font in the world.

With an original design based on an old Monotype sans serif called "Grotesque," Arial closely resembles Helvetica, except for the *G* without the protrusion like the spur of a bird, the *R* with its long tail, the *a* with no tail, and the *t* with its slanted start and end strokes. The width of the letterforms is basically the same in both Arial and Helvetica, so Arial took on the role of substitute font—documents created in Helvetica can be opened in Arial without the formatting changing—making it a typeface that is the subject of much fierce debate among designers.

※ *Arial is pronounced in a variety of different ways.*

USAGE EXAMPLES
....
□ Installed on the majority of computers, including Windows PCs and Macs.

ABCDEFGHIJ
KLMNOPQRS
TUVWXYZ
abcdefghijklmn
opqrstuvwxyz
0123456789

Arial Regular

Franklin Gothic • Impact

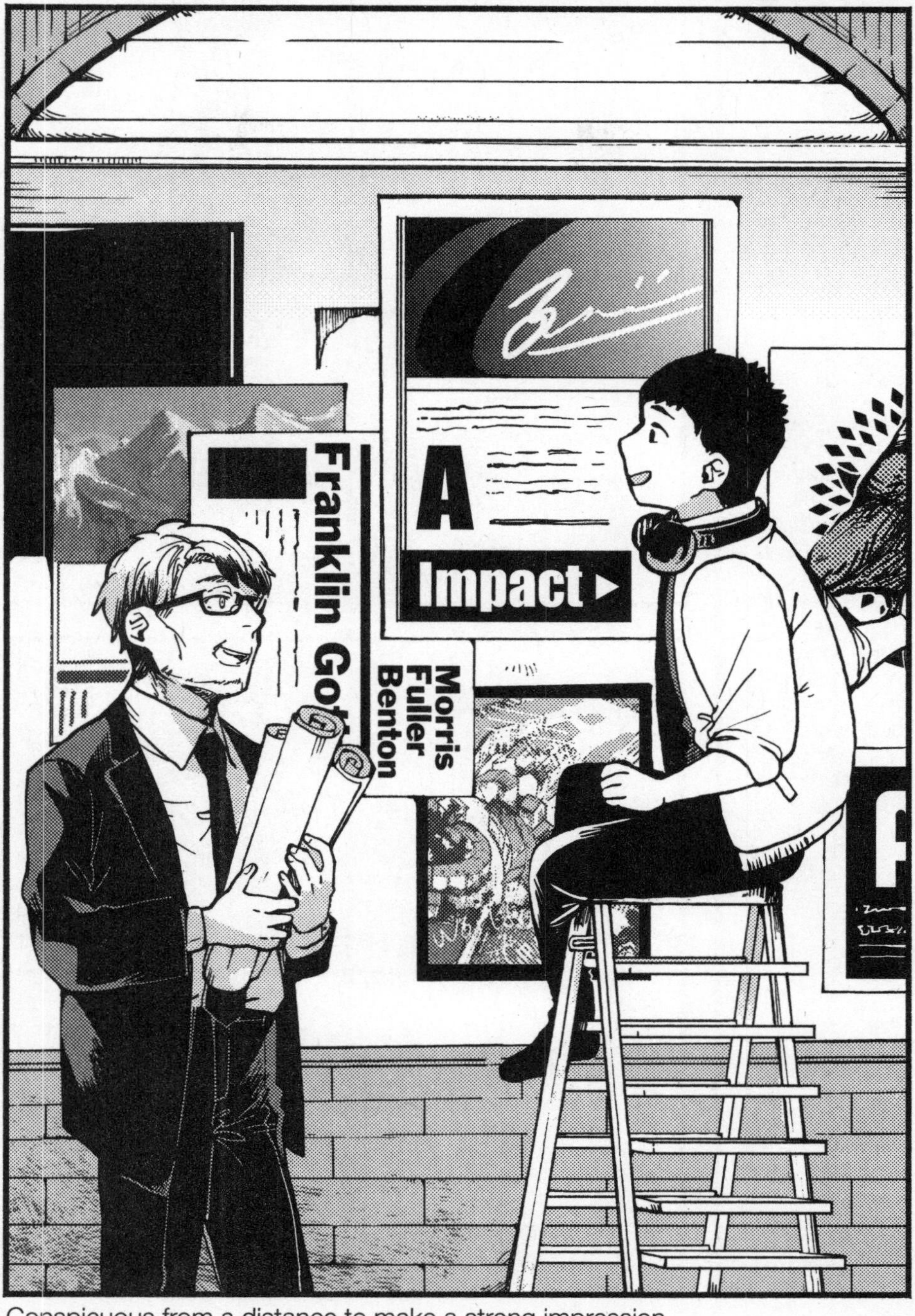
Franklin Go
A
Impact ▸
Morris
Fuller
Benton

Conspicuous from a distance to make a strong impression

Trusty Franklin Gothic

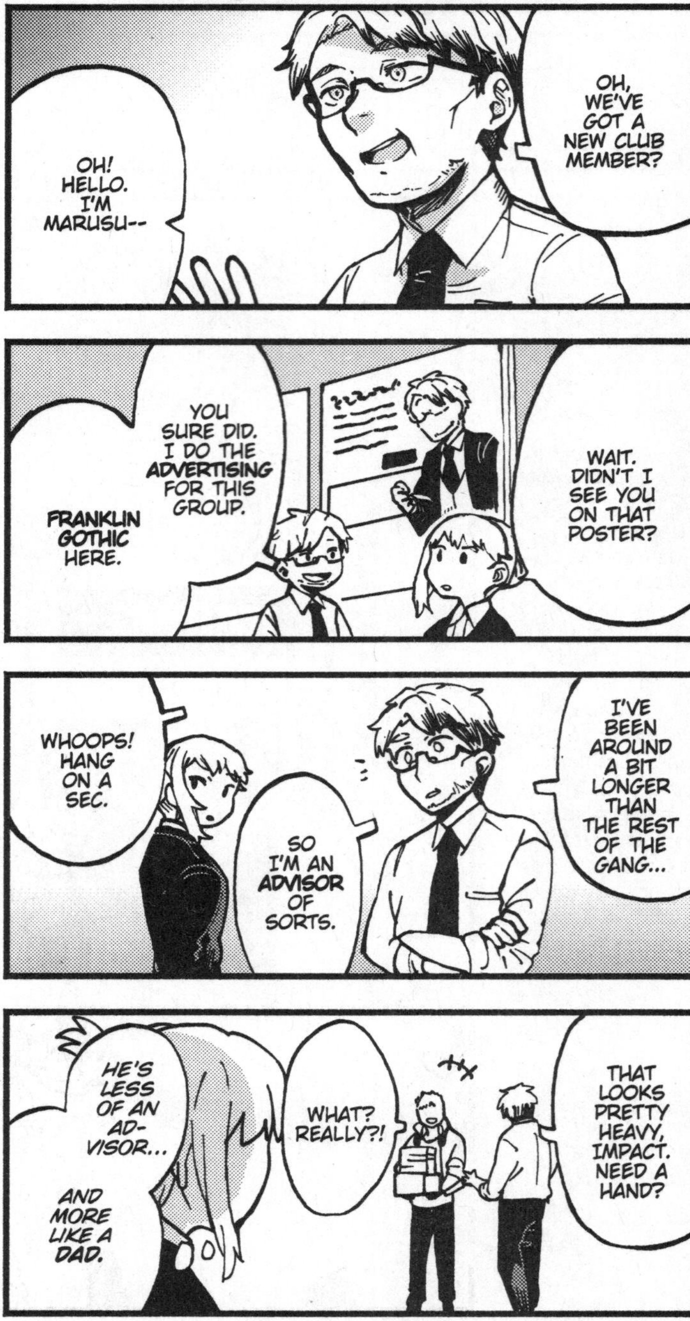
OH, WE'VE GOT A NEW CLUB MEMBER?
OH! HELLO. I'M MARUSU--
WAIT. DIDN'T I SEE YOU ON THAT POSTER?
YOU SURE DID. I DO THE ADVERTISING FOR THIS GROUP.
FRANKLIN GOTHIC HERE.
I'VE BEEN AROUND A BIT LONGER THAN THE REST OF THE GANG...
SO I'M AN ADVISOR OF SORTS.
WHOOPS! HANG ON A SEC.
THAT LOOKS PRETTY HEAVY, IMPACT. NEED A HAND?
WHAT? REALLY?!
HE'S LESS OF AN AD-VISOR...
AND MORE LIKE A DAD.

Franklin Gothic was born in the United States in the early 1900s for the purpose of captions and headlines in newspapers and magazines. It had a powerful impact on the development of later sans serif types, alongside News Gothic, which was created for body text.

Keep Fighting, Dad!

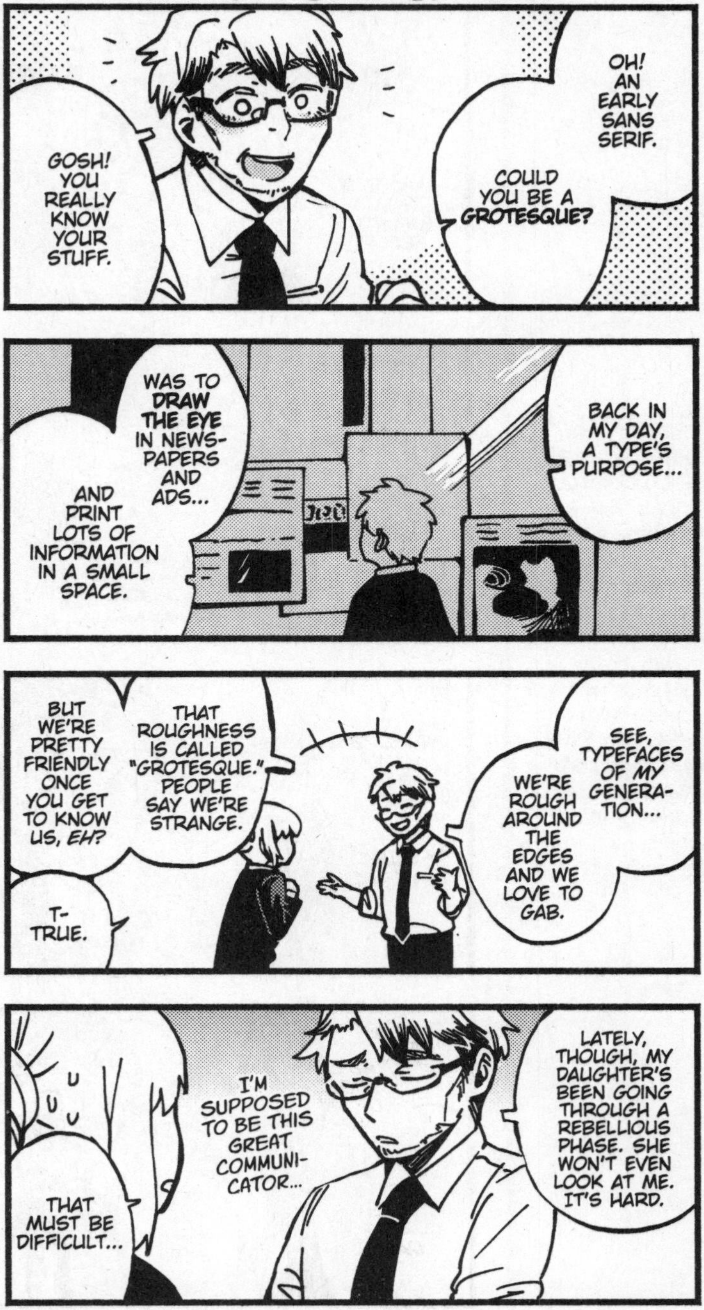
OH! AN EARLY SANS SERIF.
COULD YOU BE A GROTESQUE?
GOSH! YOU REALLY KNOW YOUR STUFF.
BACK IN MY DAY, A TYPE'S PURPOSE...
WAS TO DRAW THE EYE IN NEWS-PAPERS AND ADS...
AND PRINT LOTS OF INFORMATION IN A SMALL SPACE.
SEE, TYPEFACES OF MY GENERA-TION...
WE'RE ROUGH AROUND THE EDGES AND WE LOVE TO GAB.
THAT ROUGHNESS IS CALLED "GROTESQUE." PEOPLE SAY WE'RE STRANGE.
BUT WE'RE PRETTY FRIENDLY ONCE YOU GET TO KNOW US, EH?
T-TRUE.
LATELY, THOUGH, MY DAUGHTER'S BEEN GOING THROUGH A REBELLIOUS PHASE. SHE WON'T EVEN LOOK AT ME. IT'S HARD.
I'M SUPPOSED TO BE THIS GREAT COMMUNI-CATOR...
U U U
THAT MUST BE DIFFICULT...

The reason behind the birth of Franklin Gothic was the growing number of newspapers and magazines, and the increased demand for advertising. Its tall form was in widespread use at a time when people wanted to fit the most letters in the least space. Franklin Gothic falls into the oldest category of sans serifs, but it's still in use today.

Brace for Impact

YO, POPS!
THANKS FOR THE HELP BEFORE!
LOOM
OH! A NEW DESIGNER?
AH! IT'S IMPACT-SAN FROM BEFORE.
SO, LIKE, ME AND THE OLD MAN? WE BOTH LIKE TO ROCK OUT IN DISPLAYS AND STUFF, SO WE'RE PRETTY TIGHT.
ASIAN KUNG-FU GENERATION
MM-HMM.
I COULD'VE DONE THAT JOB WITH THE BAND.
OH! HEY, THERE.
THE NAME'S IMPACT.
YA KNOW WHAT THEY SAY ABOUT NAMES AND NATURES?
BAM
WELL, I WAS LITERALLY BORN TO MAKE A SPLASH.
SO KEEP ME IN MIND!
WOW, TYPEFACE NAMES ARE PRETTY STRAIGHTFORWARD, HUH...?

Categorized as Neo-Grotesque, Impact has a longish shape that's unique in its class, but it's similar to Franklin Gothic in that it was made for headlines. The strokes are extremely thick, and the typeface packs a visual punch.

Unsung Hero

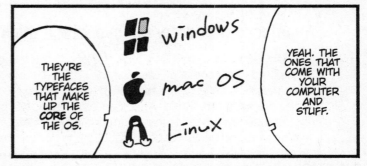

Along with Arial, Impact is one of the fonts that comes standard in Windows computers. In actual design work, Mac computers are used the majority of the time, but in terms of simple penetration rates, the trophy goes to Windows.

SO, LIKE, MARUSU?
D'YA KNOW WHAT A "CORE FONT" IS?
CORE...?
YEAH. THE ONES THAT COME WITH YOUR COMPUTER AND STUFF.
windows
mac OS
Linux
THEY'RE THE TYPEFACES THAT MAKE UP THE **CORE** OF THE OS.
SO, I'M A WINDOWS CORE FONT, AND WINDOWS MACHINES ARE LIKE NINETY PERCENT OF THE COMPUTERS IN USE NOW.
windows
WHAT? THAT'S INCRED-IBLE!
RIGHT?!
I MEAN, **NINETY PERCENT**--THAT'S PRETTY MUCH THE **WHOLE WORLD**, RIGHT?
WE'RE BUSTIN' OUR BUTTS OUT THERE.
YOU CAN REALLY COUNT ON IMPACT'S **CORE STRENGTH**, *HMM?*

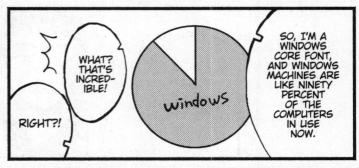

Franklin Gothic / Impact

	Franklin Gothic	Impact
CATEGORY:	Sans serif	Sans serif
CLASSIFICATION:	Grotesque	Neo-grotesque
YEAR OF CREATION:	1902	1965
DESIGNER(S):	Morris Fuller Benton	Geoffrey Lee
FOUNDRY:	American Type Founders (USA)	Stephenson Blake (UK)

Typefaces that draw the eye with a thick core.

Franklin Gothic is a sans serif type designed by the American typeface designer Morris Fuller Benton (1872–1948). At the end of the nineteenth century, the merger of twenty-three type foundries led to the establishment of American Type Founders in an America that had become a great manufacturing power. Selected as the first head of the design department, Benton sorted through the work from each individual company, and, referencing the European Grotesque moveable type, he designed a new sans serif type in 1902. Extremely thick, the type's *a* and *g* were the same as roman type, with a two-layered construction. MoMA Gothic, used in the logo for the New York Museum of Modern Art, is a famous digitization of Franklin Gothic in 2004.

Impact is a sans serif type released in 1965 by Stephenson Blake, a long-standing type founder in the British engineering city of Sheffield. Its proportions are long and tall, with a tall x-height and a short ascender and descender. The strokes are extremely thick, with high letterform density, making the typeface quite conspicuous. The designer, Geoffrey Lee (1929–2005), was employed at the time as a director at the Pembertons advertising agency, and he perfected the typeface with the aim of making an impact in displays, advertisements, and similar places.

USAGE EXAMPLES

- ☐ Popular in menus at cafés and restaurants.

ABCDEFGHIJ
KLMNOPQRS
TUVWXYZ
abcdefghijklmn
opqrstuvwxyz
0123456789

Franklin Gothic Std
No. 2 Roman

ABCDEFGHIJ
KLMNOPQRS
TUVWXYZ
abcdefghijklmn
opqrstuvwxyz
0123456789

Impact Regular

Frutiger • DIN

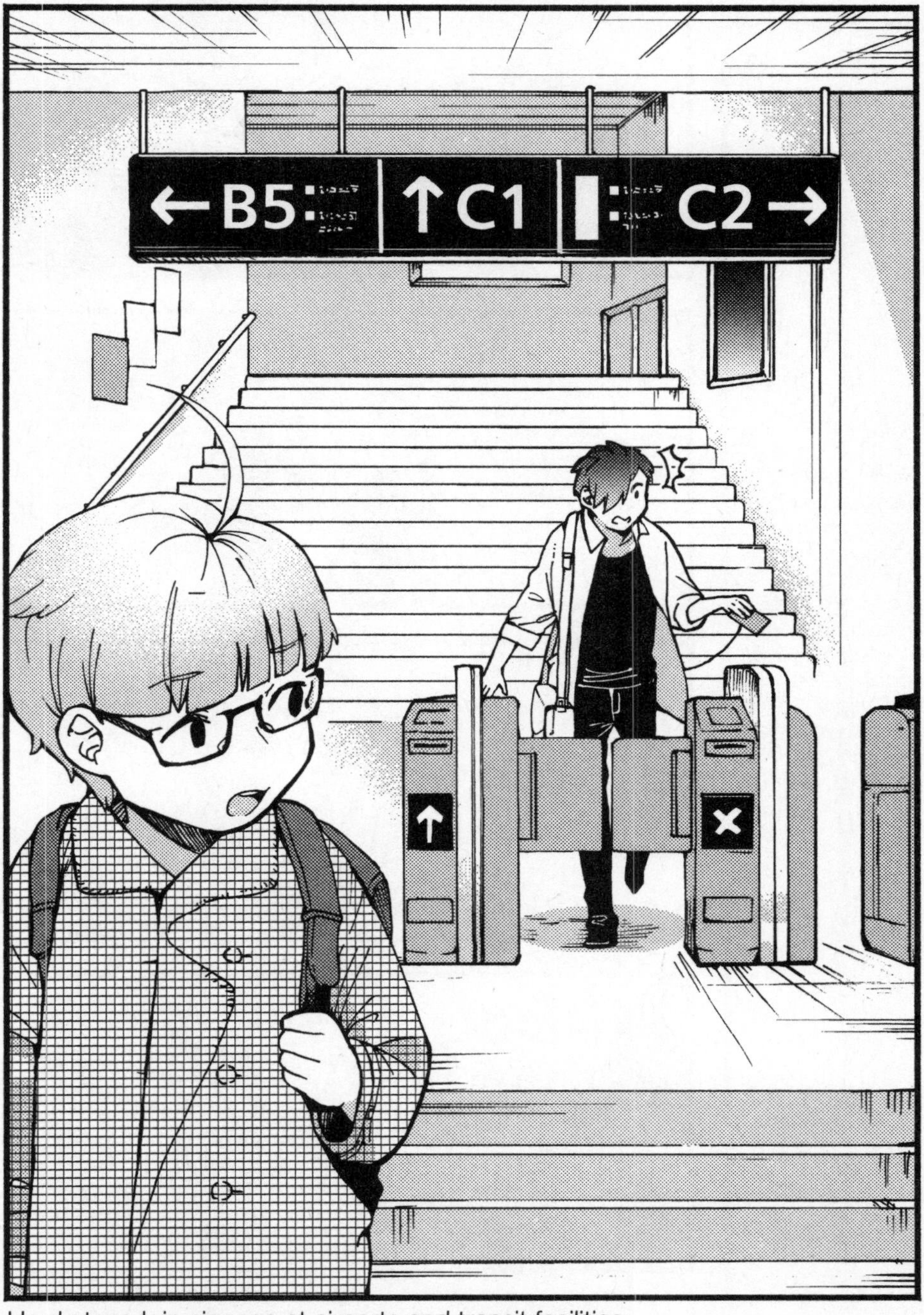
←B5
↑C1
C2→

Hard at work in signage at airports and transit facilities

Typeface Pilot

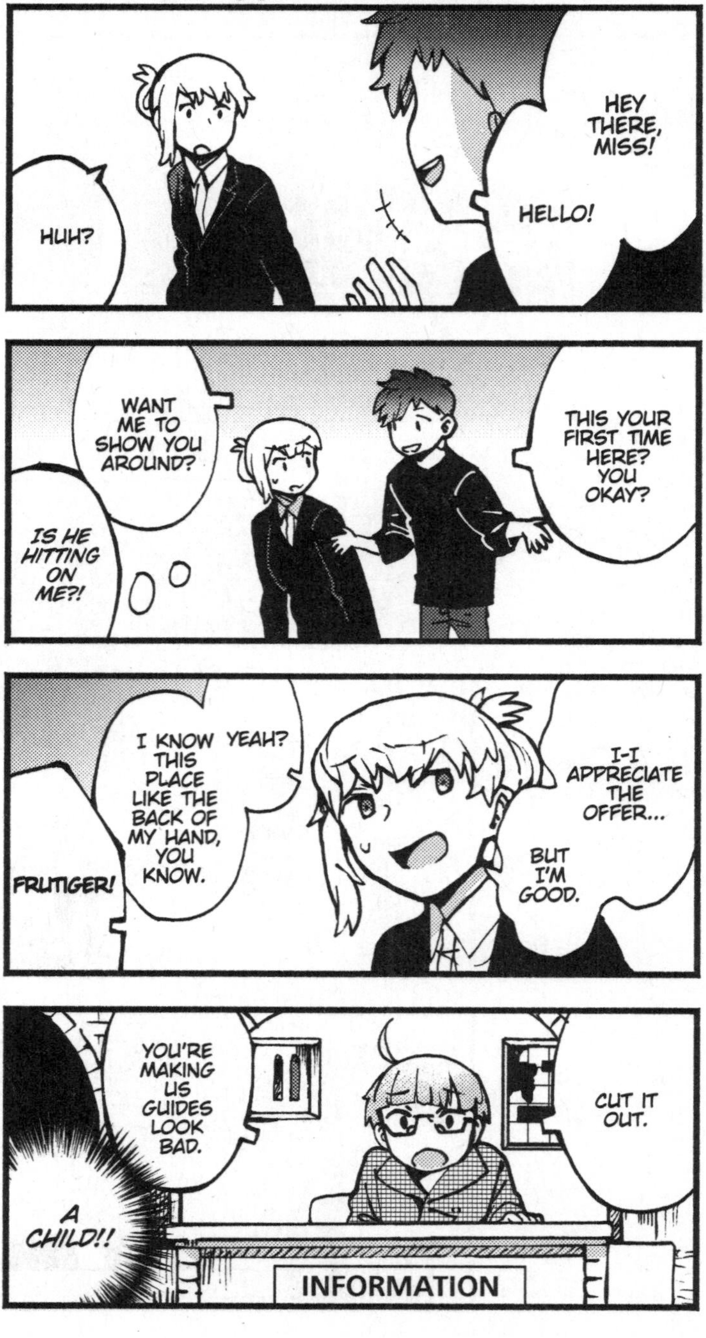
HEY THERE, MISS!
HELLO!
HUH?
THIS YOUR FIRST TIME HERE? YOU OKAY?
WANT ME TO SHOW YOU AROUND?
IS HE HITTING ON ME?!
I-I APPRECIATE THE OFFER...
BUT I'M GOOD.
YEAH?
I KNOW THIS PLACE LIKE THE BACK OF MY HAND, YOU KNOW.
FRUTIGER!
CUT IT OUT.
YOU'RE MAKING US GUIDES LOOK BAD.
A CHILD!!
INFORMATION

Frutiger and DIN are often used on road and directional signs in European transit facilities. Frutiger was designated for use in directional signs at France's Charles de Gaulle airport, while DIN was used for German roadwork standards.

Group Coordinator Frutiger

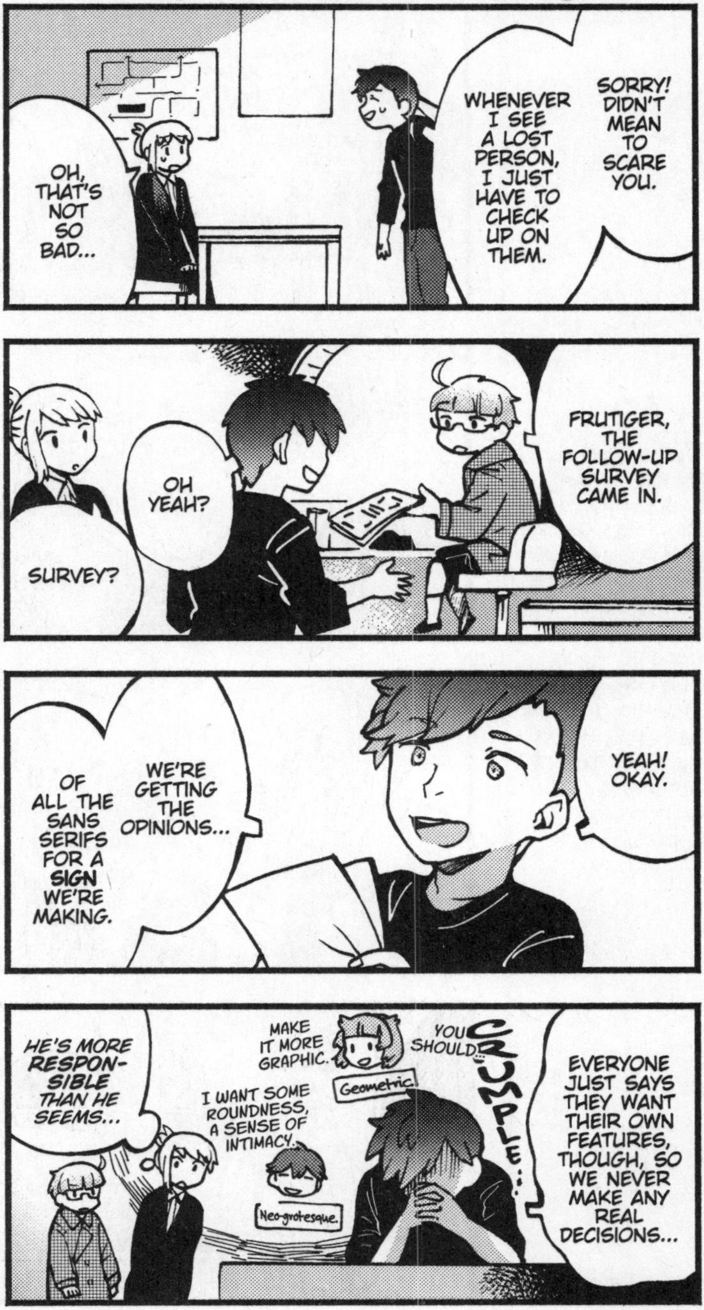
SORRY! DIDN'T MEAN TO SCARE YOU.
WHENEVER I SEE A LOST PERSON, I JUST HAVE TO CHECK UP ON THEM.
OH, THAT'S NOT SO BAD...
FRUTIGER, THE FOLLOW-UP SURVEY CAME IN.
OH YEAH?
SURVEY?
YEAH! OKAY.
WE'RE GETTING THE OPINIONS...
OF ALL THE SANS SERIFS FOR A SIGN WE'RE MAKING.
EVERYONE JUST SAYS THEY WANT THEIR OWN FEATURES, THOUGH, SO WE NEVER MAKE ANY REAL DECISIONS...
CRUMPLE...
YOU SHOULD...
MAKE IT MORE GRAPHIC.
Geometric
I WANT SOME ROUNDNESS, A SENSE OF INTIMACY.
Neo-grotesque
HE'S MORE RESPONSIBLE THAN HE SEEMS...

Frutiger is a typeface that the Swiss designer Adrian Frutiger worked on around the end of the 1960s for airport signage. It was released for public use in 1976. Frutiger is classified as a Humanist sans serif, and it increases readability.

Polite by Design

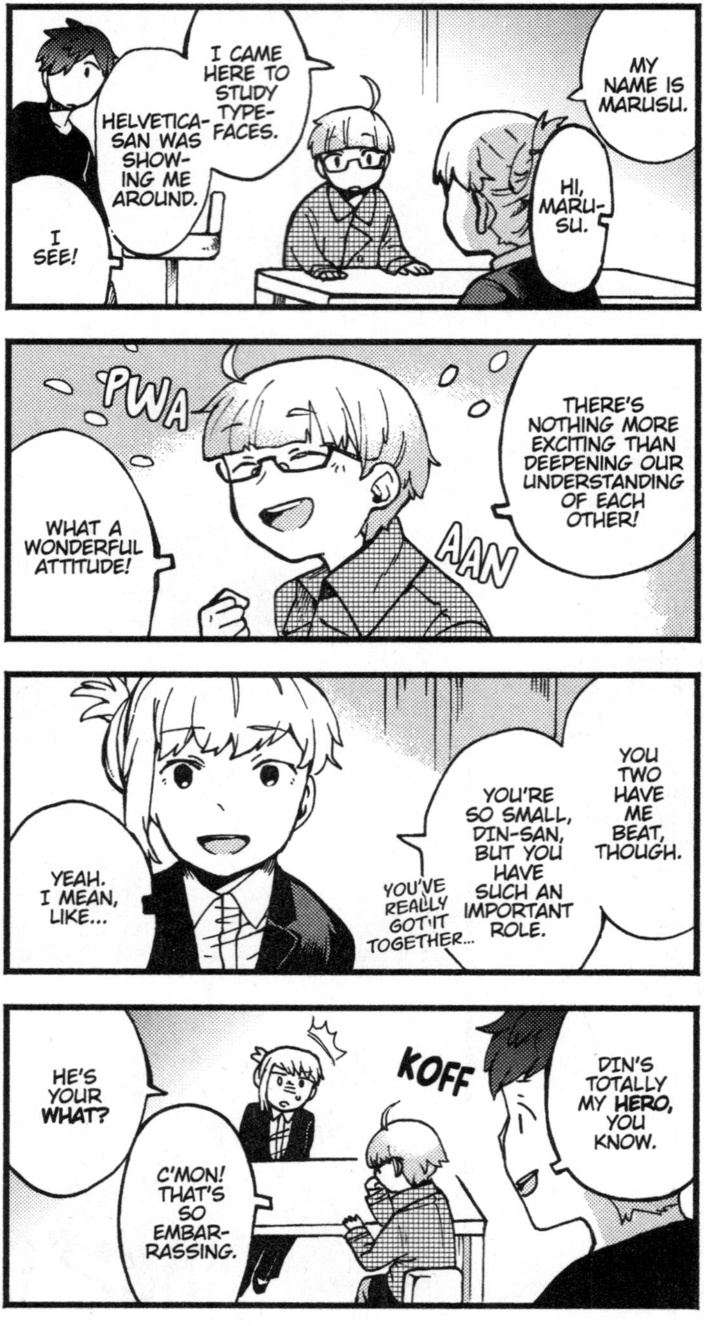
MY NAME IS MARUSU.
HI, MARUSU.
I CAME HERE TO STUDY TYPEFACES.
HELVETICA-SAN WAS SHOWING ME AROUND.
I SEE!
THERE'S NOTHING MORE EXCITING THAN DEEPENING OUR UNDERSTANDING OF EACH OTHER!
PWA
AAN
WHAT A WONDERFUL ATTITUDE!
YOU TWO HAVE ME BEAT, THOUGH.
YOU'RE SO SMALL, DIN-SAN, BUT YOU HAVE SUCH AN IMPORTANT ROLE.
YOU'VE REALLY GOT IT TOGETHER...
YEAH. I MEAN, LIKE...
DIN'S TOTALLY MY **HERO**, YOU KNOW.
KOFF
HE'S YOUR **WHAT?**
C'MON! THAT'S SO EMBARRASSING.

DIN was released by the German Institute for Standardization in 1931. Originally used in construction, it has only come to be used for design purposes relatively recently, but with its slightly longer form and lack of ornamentation, it gives a cool impression.

Powerful Ally of Street Corners

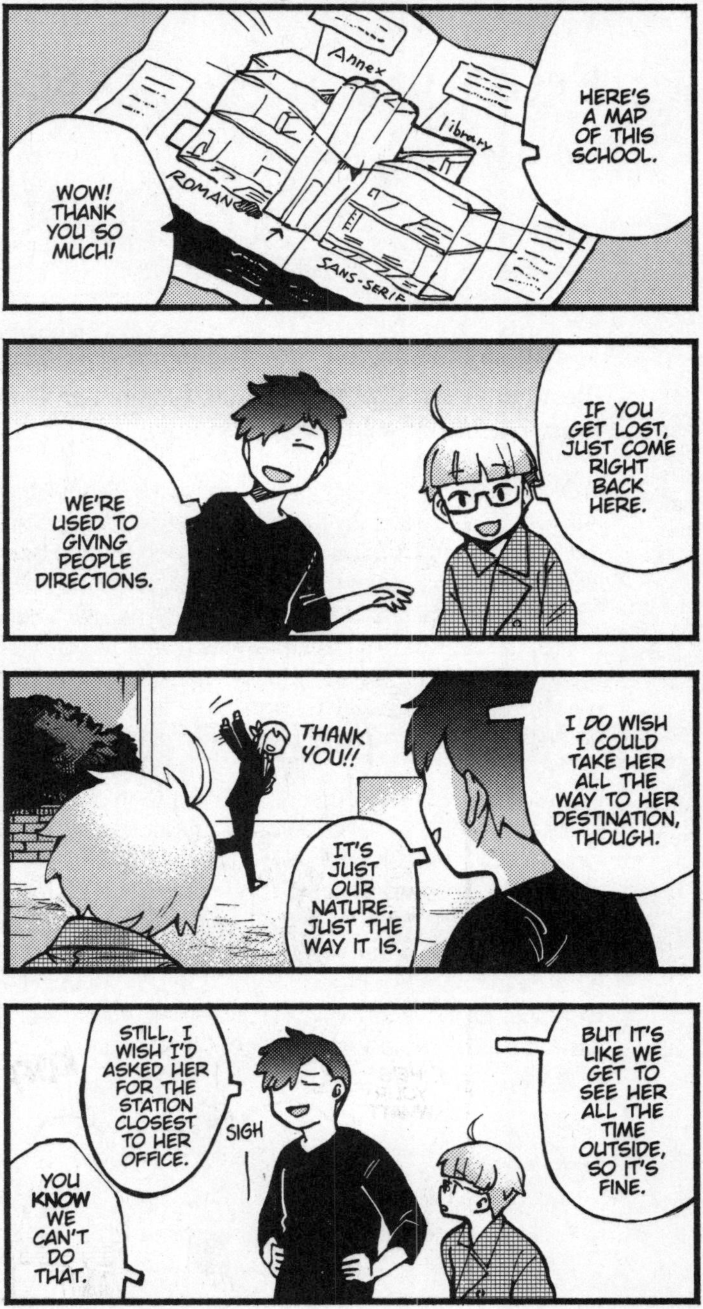
HERE'S A MAP OF THIS SCHOOL.
Annex
library
ROMAN
SANS-SERIF
WOW! THANK YOU SO MUCH!
IF YOU GET LOST, JUST COME RIGHT BACK HERE.
WE'RE USED TO GIVING PEOPLE DIRECTIONS.
I DO WISH I COULD TAKE HER ALL THE WAY TO HER DESTINATION, THOUGH.
THANK YOU!!
IT'S JUST OUR NATURE. JUST THE WAY IT IS.
BUT IT'S LIKE WE GET TO SEE HER ALL THE TIME OUTSIDE, SO IT'S FINE.
STILL, I WISH I'D ASKED HER FOR THE STATION CLOSEST TO HER OFFICE.
SIGH
YOU KNOW WE CAN'T DO THAT.

Because of its high readability, Frutiger has been adopted for Western signage in Japan as well, on JR station wayfinding signs and on the platform station name signs for Keikyu Railway and Tokyo Metro. In addition to being used for the platform station name signs on the Keisei Electric Railway, the Uniqlo logo type has a construction that closely resembles DIN.

Frutiger   DIN

CATEGORY:	Sans serif	Sans serif
CLASSIFICATION:	Humanist	Geometric
YEAR OF CREATION:	1976	1931
DESIGNER(S):	Adrian Frutiger	--
FOUNDRY:	Linotype (U.K.)	German Institute for Standardization

Excellent readability, popular typefaces that are discernable at a glance.

Frutiger was released for public use in 1976 by Adrian Frutiger (1928–2015), based on the new typeface Frutiger designed for the signs at the Charles de Gaulle airport in the Parisian suburb of Roissy in 1970. Frutiger had previously released the sans serif type masterpiece Univers, which had twenty-one families, at the end of the 1950s, but this new font was not of the same nineteenth-century Grotesque lineage. Instead, Frutiger was aiming for a new typeface that was easily recognizable as a display, easy to see at an angle or in the dark, with excellent visibility.

DIN (an acronym of Deutsches Institut für Normung or Deutsche IndustrieNorm) is a sans serif type perfected by the German Institute for Standardization with the aim of unifying construction standards. The first DIN 1451, released in 1931, was easily reproduced on graph paper with a ruler and compass, highly distinctive at a glance, and could be easily read later with automatic character recognition, so it was used in blueprints and technical texts. When it was digitized, however, a large number of families were created from it, and it enjoys great popularity in the world of modern design.

USAGE EXAMPLES
....
□ Frutiger: Charles de Gaulle airport directional signage
□ Frutiger: Keihin Railway, Toei Subway, and Tokyo Metro station signs
□ DIN: Tokyo 2020 Olympic/Paralympic emblem

ABCDEFGHIJ
KLMNOPQRS
TUVWXYZ
abcdefghijklmn
opqrstuvwxyz
0123456789

Frutiger LT Std 55 Roman

ABCDEFGHIJ
KLMNOPQRS
TUVWXYZ
abcdefghijklmn
opqrstuvwxyz
0123456789

DIN 1451 Std Mittelschrift

Optima

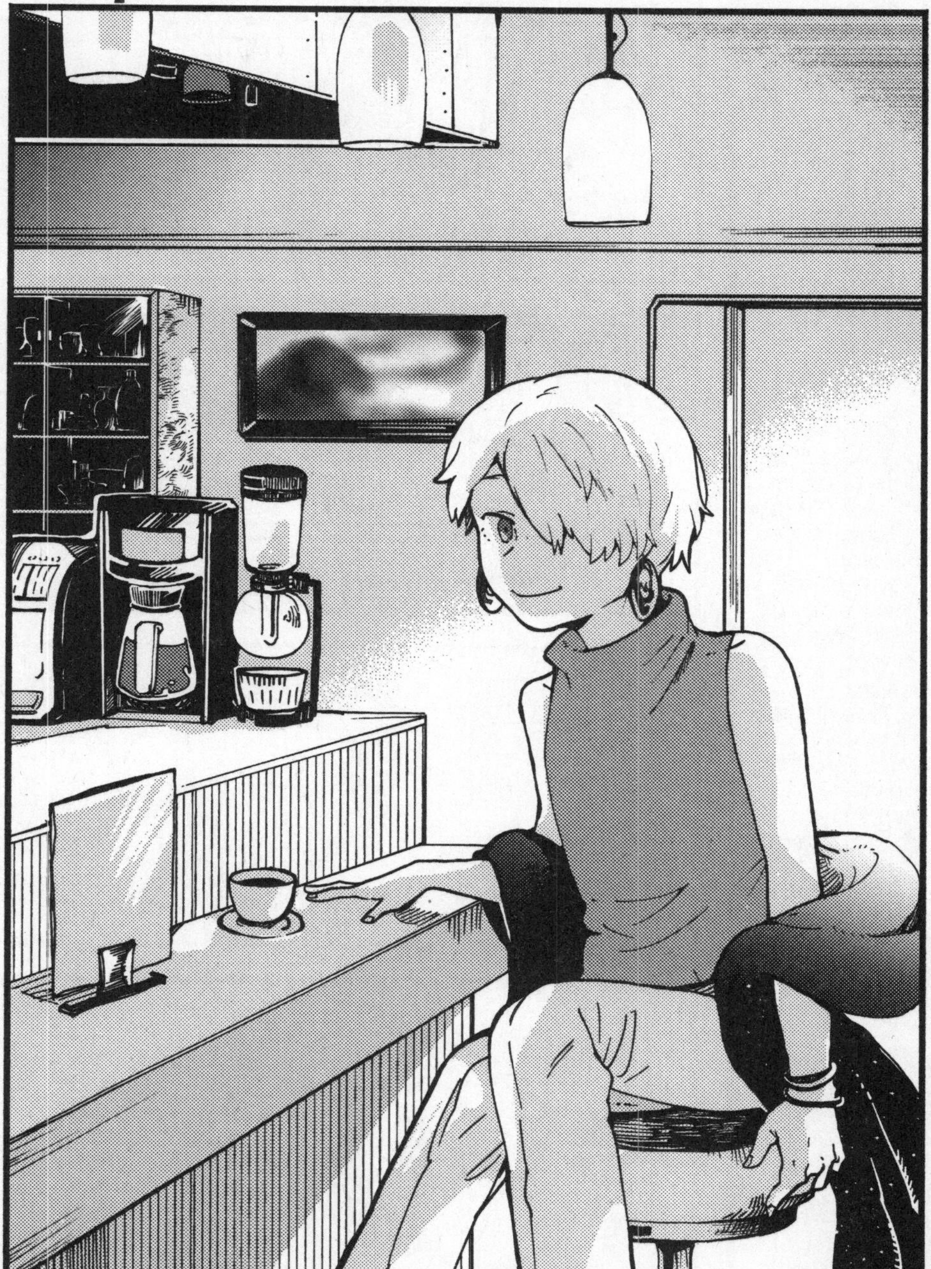

Elegant, curving beauty

Roman Type with no Serif?

A BREAK AREA...?
KLAKKA KLAK
EXCUSE M--
OH MY! WELCOME!
COME ON IN! HAVE A SEAT!
WAH! WHAT IS THIS PLACE?
WELL, YOU SEE, THE BASE OF THIS BUILDING IS THE SCHOOL.
BUT NO ONE USES THE GYM THESE DAYS.
SO I JUST DID A LITTLE... YOU KNOW.
A LITTLE?!
THE RE-MODELING SPIRIT IS STRONG IN THIS ONE!!

Optima was released in 1958 by the German typeface designer and calligrapher Hermann Zapf. Zapf was influenced by epitaphs carved into tombstones he saw in Italy, and this type has such graceful, classical proportions that it is said to be a roman type without any serifs.

Slim and Elegant

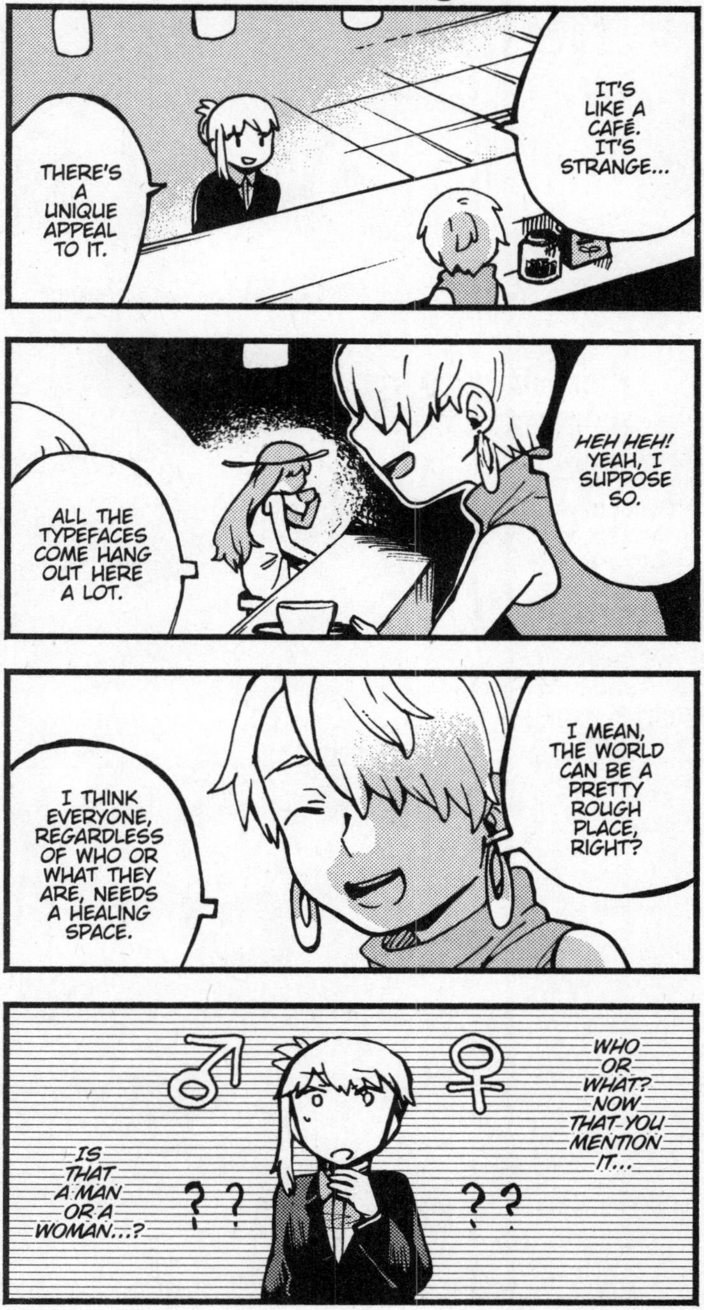
IT'S LIKE A CAFÉ. IT'S STRANGE...
THERE'S A UNIQUE APPEAL TO IT.
HEH HEH! YEAH, I SUPPOSE SO.
ALL THE TYPEFACES COME HANG OUT HERE A LOT.
I MEAN, THE WORLD CAN BE A PRETTY ROUGH PLACE, RIGHT?
I THINK EVERYONE, REGARDLESS OF WHO OR WHAT THEY ARE, NEEDS A HEALING SPACE.
WHO OR WHAT? NOW THAT YOU MENTION IT...
IS THAT A MAN OR A WOMAN...?

The horizontal and vertical strokes and thicknesses differ quite significantly in Optima, and this contrast actually brings it closer to roman types. Influenced by those classical shapes, the base of the uppercase *M* is wide, and overall, the type has a slim, feminine appearance.

Luxury

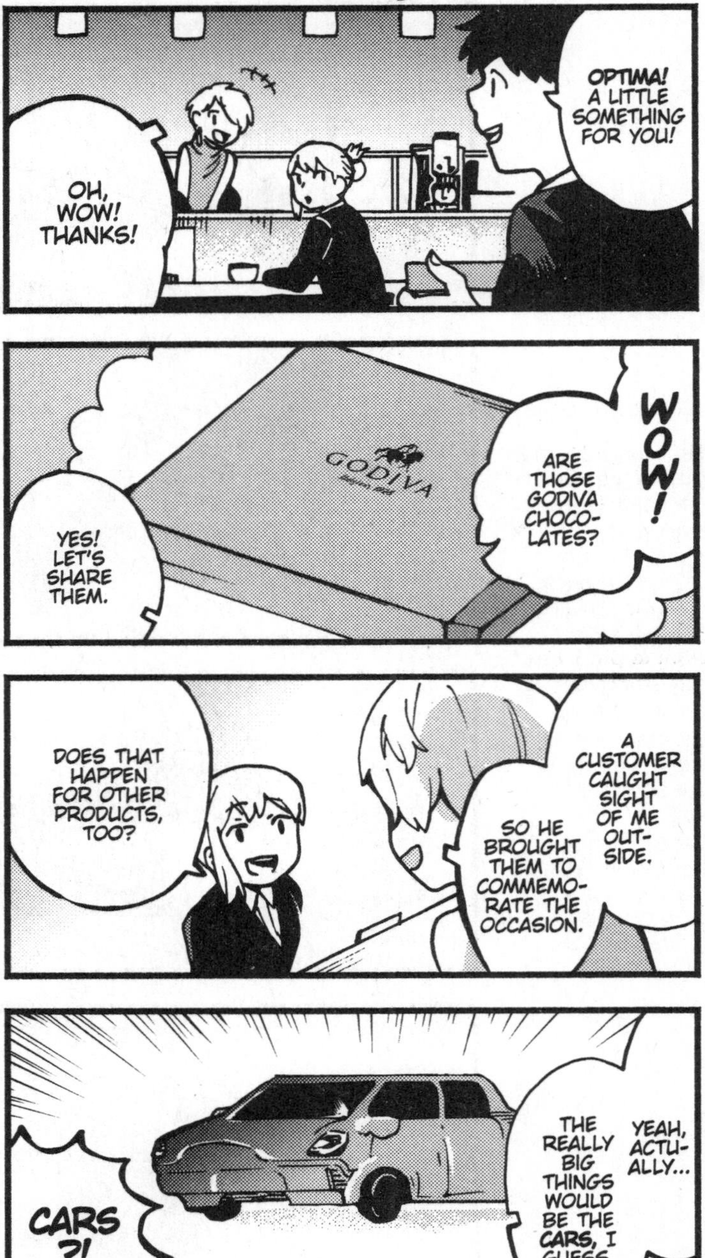
OPTIMA! A LITTLE SOMETHING FOR YOU!
OH, WOW! THANKS!
WOW!
ARE THOSE GODIVA CHOCO-LATES?
GODIVA
YES! LET'S SHARE THEM.
A CUSTOMER CAUGHT SIGHT OF ME OUT-SIDE.
SO HE BROUGHT THEM TO COMMEMO-RATE THE OCCASION.
DOES THAT HAPPEN FOR OTHER PRODUCTS, TOO?
YEAH, ACTU-ALLY...
THE REALLY BIG THINGS WOULD BE THE **CARS**, I GUESS.
CARS ?!

Optima exudes an air of elegance and luxury, and the logo for Godiva chocolates was based on this typeface. The logo for the British luxury car manufacturer Aston Martin also uses Optima.

Blending Seamlessly into Daily Life

OKAY, HERE'S THE THING.
I GET MORE THAN MY FAIR SHARE OF SIGHTING REPORTS.
YOU DO?
I THINK I HAVE MORE EASILY RECOGNIZABLE CHARACTERS THAN OTHER SANS SERIFS.
M O f
Wide base.
Roman type style.
Slightly narrower parts.
「M」 「O」 「f」
OHHH.
NOW THAT YOU MENTION IT, MY POUCH IS...
MARY QUANT
WELL, I'M JUST HONORED THAT MY WORK HAS BECOME A PART OF PEOPLE'S LIVES.
IF YOU SEE ME, MARUSU, LET ME KNOW, OKAY?
IT REALLY MAKES ME HAPPY.
OF COURSE!

The word "optima" means "optimal." In Japan, the logo for Lumine, a chain of shopping centers, uses this typeface. It's a powerful ally when you want to produce something simple but also beautiful and feminine.

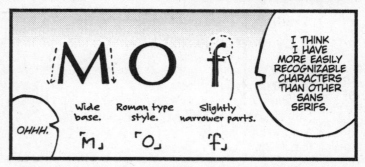

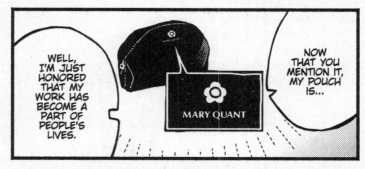

Optima

CATEGORY: Sans serif

CLASSIFICATION: Humanist

YEAR OF CREATION: 1958

DESIGNER(S): Hermann Zapf

FOUNDRY: Linotype (Germany)

A refined, versatile typeface for use in body or display text.

Optima has such beautiful classical proportions that it is referred to as a roman type without serifs and put into the category of a warm Humanist sans serif. The ends of the inflected strokes spread out gently in a beautiful way, suggestive of the presence of a serif, and the type can be very versatile, useable in both body text and headlines.

After training as a lithographer in his youth, creator Hermann Zapf (1918–2015) studied calligraphy independently, influenced by Rudolf Koch (1876–1934) and Edward Johnston (1872–1944). In 1947, he became a director at Stempel in Frankfurt, where he released Palatino in 1950 and Melior in 1952. He then completed Optima in 1958 after six years of work using all of his calligraphy skills, after being inspired by the epitaphs on tombstones from around 1530 at the Basilica di Santa Croce in Florence. Currently, it is used in the logos for Godiva chocolates and the shopping center Lumine, and is a permanent presence around us.

USAGE EXAMPLES
....
- ☐ Aston Martin (automotive company)
- ☐ Godiva (Belgian chocolate company)
- ☐ Lumine (train station shopping center)

ABCDEFGHIJ
KLMNOPQRS
TUVWXYZ
abcdefghijklmn
opqrstuvwxyz
0123456789

Optima Regular

Gotham

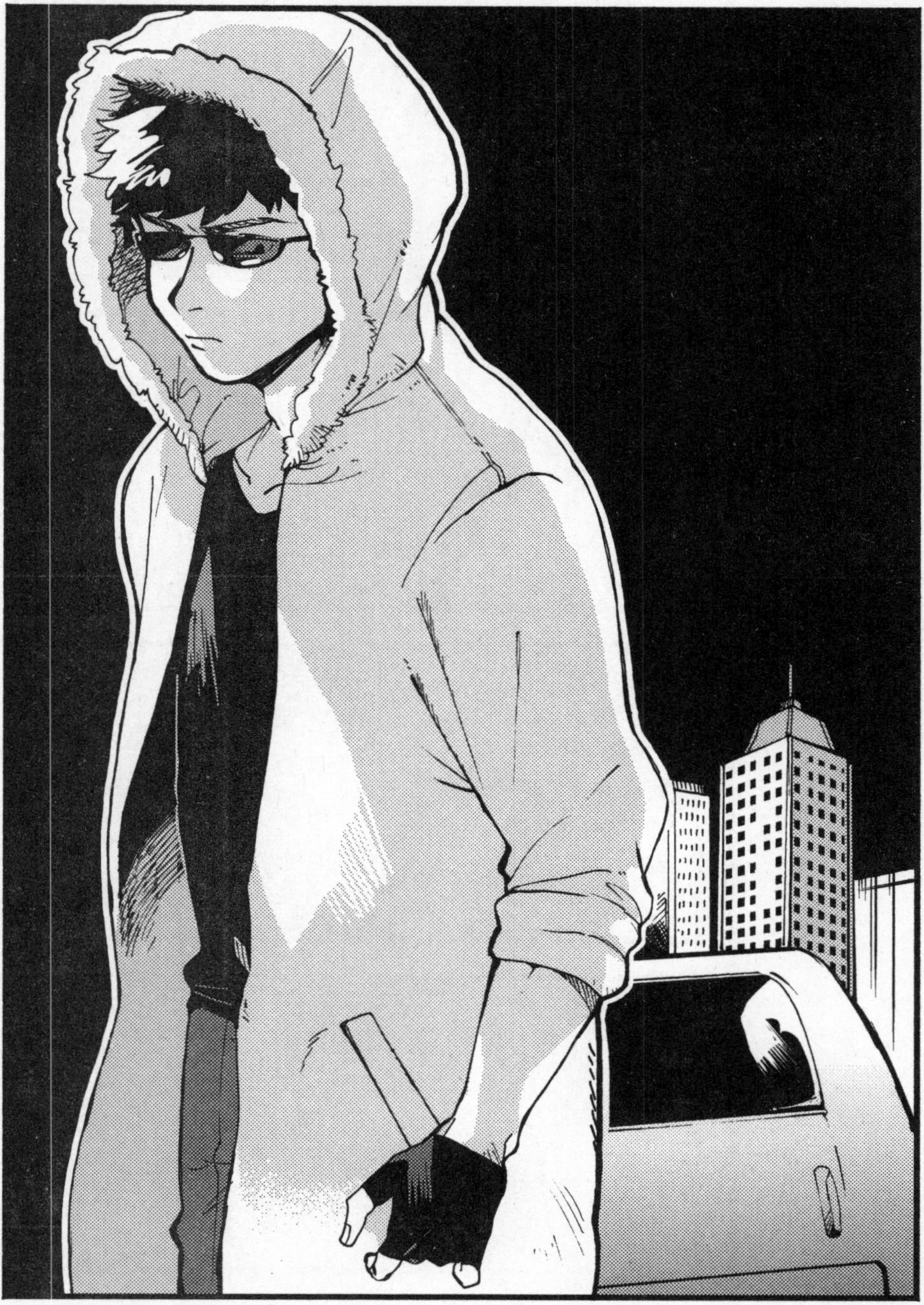

Strong and reliable

We'll Meet in our Dreams

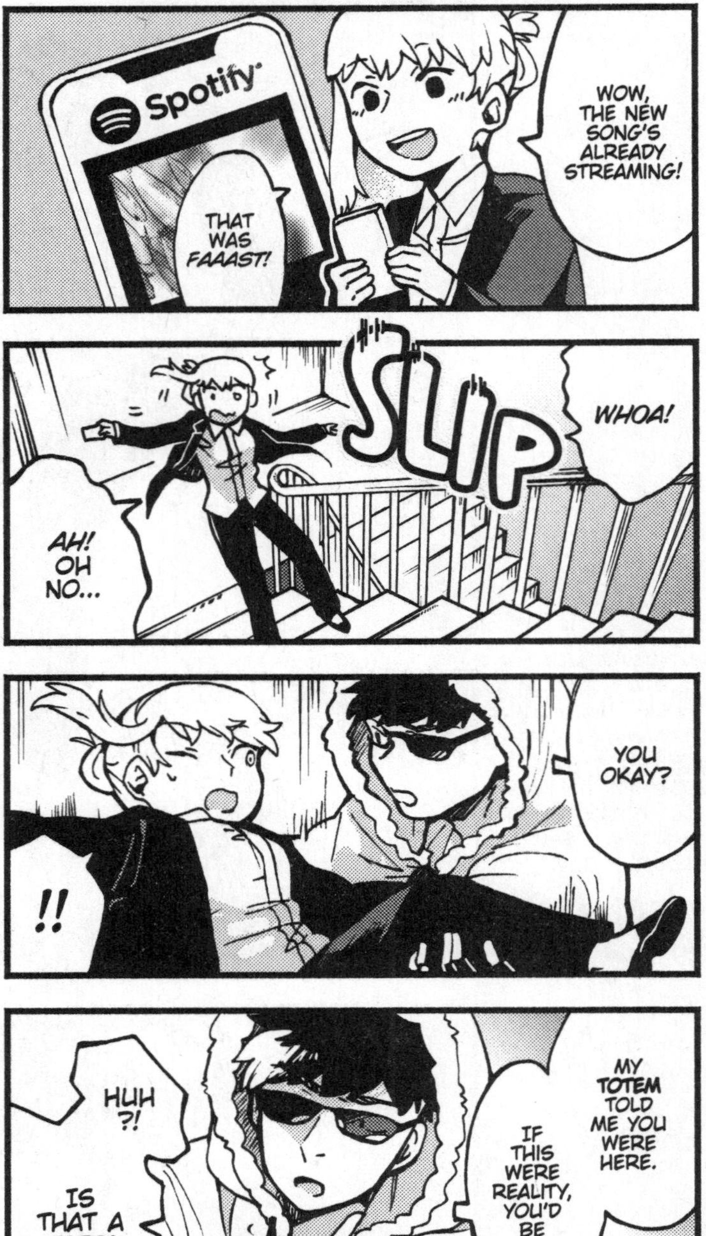
Spotify
WOW, THE NEW SONG'S ALREADY STREAMING!
THAT WAS FAAAST!
WHOA!
SLIP
AH! OH NO...
YOU OKAY?
!!
MY TOTEM TOLD ME YOU WERE HERE.
IF THIS WERE REALITY, YOU'D BE DEAD.
HUH ?!
IS THAT A TOP?!

Gotham was produced in 2000, and while it is a new type, it's used in the logos of many companies and films. You can catch sight of it in the music-streaming service Spotify, and the films *Inception* and *Gran Torino*.

Tough Guy Gotham

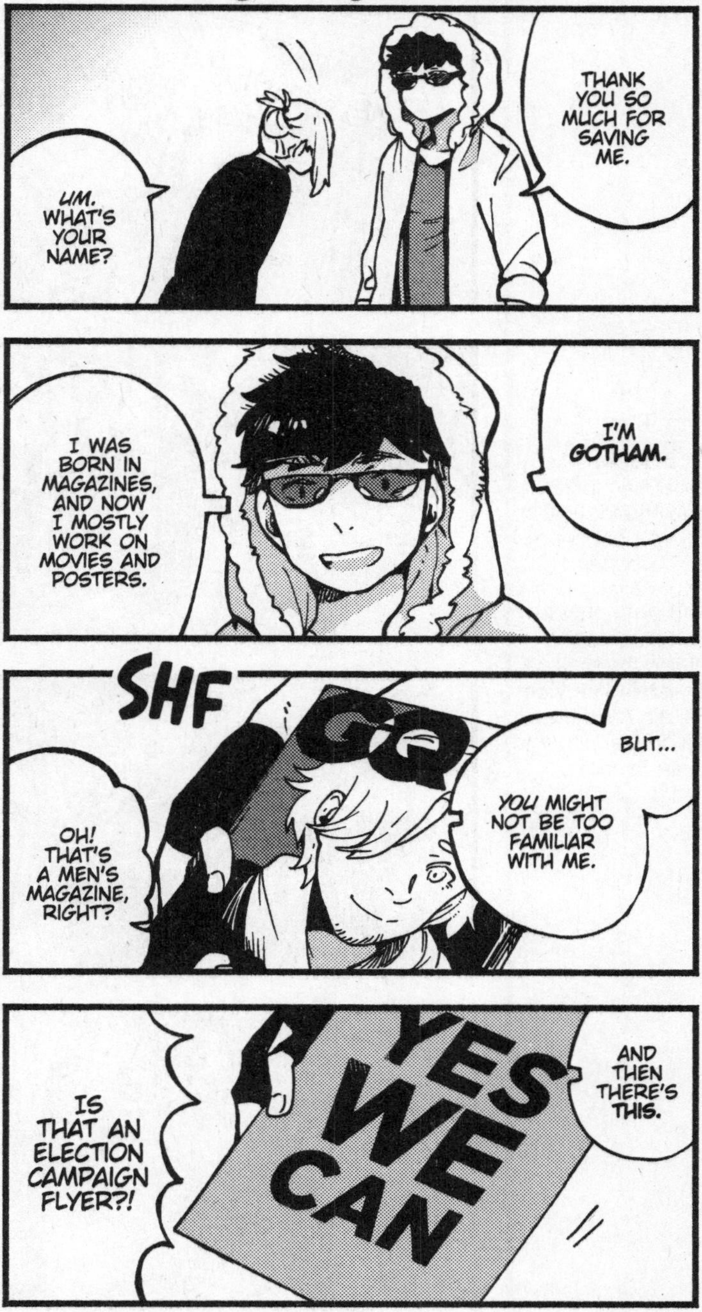
THANK YOU SO MUCH FOR SAVING ME.
UM. WHAT'S YOUR NAME?
I'M GOTHAM.
I WAS BORN IN MAGAZINES, AND NOW I MOSTLY WORK ON MOVIES AND POSTERS.
SHF
GQ
BUT...
YOU MIGHT NOT BE TOO FAMILIAR WITH ME.
OH! THAT'S A MEN'S MAGAZINE, RIGHT?
AND THEN THERE'S THIS.
YES WE CAN
IS THAT AN ELECTION CAMPAIGN FLYER?!

Created by the American typeface designer Tobias Frere-Jones, Gotham was originally set aside for the exclusive use of the men's fashion magazine *GQ* and leaped to fame when Barack Obama used it in his campaign posters in the 2008 American presidential election.

Hero from the Big Apple

THAT MAGAZINE AND THAT FLYER...
IT SEEMS LIKE YOU'RE FROM THE U.S.
YEAH, ORIGINALLY.
SEE THAT? IT'S WHERE I GREW UP. IT'S A PRETTY BIG DEAL.
I DO A LOT MORE WORK OVERSEAS NOW...
BUT I'VE GOT PRETTY STRONG ROOTS IN THAT PLACE.
OHH.
SO THAT'S WHY YOU HAVE...
I MEAN, GUN CULTURE IS BIG OVER THERE, RIGHT?
OH, I TRADED IT FOR THIS WHEN I CAME TO JAPAN.
TOO RISKY...
BANG
H-HOW CONSIDER-ATE.

Gotham was inspired by the lettering on signs in New York City. With an abundant family and a form that offers a powerful and direct impression, it's a modernistic, stout, geometric sans serif.

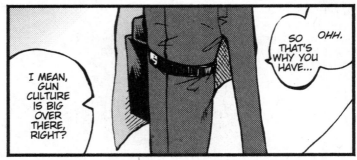

The Sans Serif We Deserve

SANS SERIF ITSELF IS ACTUALLY A PRETTY RECENT TYPEFACE STYLE.
TYPEFACE FAMILY TREE
1100~
1400~
1600~
1800~
BLACKLETTER
ROMAN
SANS SERIF
SCRIPT
BUT I'M A NEWBIE EVEN AMONG THEM.
I HOPE YOU'LL BE KIND IF YOU RUN INTO ME SOME-WHERE ELSE ONE DAY.
YES, OF COURSE!
AH!
HUH ...?
DID I FALL ASLEEP?

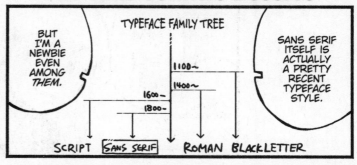

As you can tell from looking at Gotham, a relatively new typeface, recent sans serifs tend to emphasize readability and visibility. You can observe how the form of typefaces changes in response to people's needs.

Gotham

CATEGORY:	Sans serif
CLASSIFICATION:	Geometric sans serif
YEAR OF CREATION:	2000
DESIGNER(S):	Tobias Frere-Jones
FOUNDRY:	Hoefler & Frere-Jones Type (USA)

Vigorous and confident, an American presence.

Gotham is a new sans serif type released in 2000 by the American typeface design agency Hoefler & Frere-Jones Type on a commission from the men's fashion magazine GQ. Tobias Frere-Jones (1970–), the designer, gathered reference material from the city of New York, collecting simple lettering from the signs, bronze plates, and stone inscriptions that filled the streets. He took particular inspiration from the typeface on the sign for the Port Authority Bus Terminal, the entrance to the city for long-distance buses. Thus, unlike the Swiss-made Helvetica, the German-made Grotesk, and the Art Deco style that arrived via France, Gotham is an American sans serif type filled with vigor and confidence.

The construction is geometrical enough for an engineer to compose with a ruler and compass, and the type is classified as a geometric sans serif, but the combination of letters is clear-cut and easy to read. It was used in President Obama's 2008 election campaign and is famous for communicating his slogan to voters in a straightforward manner.

USAGE EXAMPLES

□ GQ (men's fashion magazine established in the USA)
□ Spotify (music streaming service out of Sweden)
□ Inception (title logo for the 2010 film)
□ Gran Torino (title logo for the 2008 film)
□ Change (Barack Obama's 2008 presidential campaign logo)

ABCDEFGHIJ
KLMNOPQRS
TUVWXYZ
abcdefghijklmn
opqrstuvwxyz
0123456789

Gotham Medium

Sans Serif Type Notes

Sans serif refers to typefaces with no serifs (extensions or “whiskers”) at the tips of the letterforms. The majority of these types have uniform strokes and much greater visibility than the serifed roman types, so they are more appropriate for headlines and diagrams. They are also used when emphasis on the letterform is desired, but readability drops when it’s used in longer texts.

The history of sans serif type is surprisingly short, with the style making its first appearance in the nineteenth century. These types are currently classed into four main groups.

GROTESQUE

The first sans serifs. They give a powerful, rough-hewn impression.
Ex. Akzidenz Grotesk, Franklin Gothic

ABC123

Franklin Gothic

HUMANIST

Sans serif with a hint of serif. Offers a sense of softness and humanity.
Ex. Gill Sans, Frutiger

ABC123

Gill Sans

NEO-GROTESQUE

Developed from Grotesque. Extremely versatile, gives a modern impression.
Ex. Helvetica, Univers

ABC123

Helvetica

GEOMETRIC

Sans serif with a geometrical frame. Rational, refined structure.
Ex. Futura, Gotham

ABC123

Futura

SANS SERIF AND ROMAN TYPES COMPARED

Helvetica

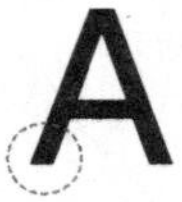

Sans serif type, no serif. Visible from a distance. Good for displays.

Times New Roman

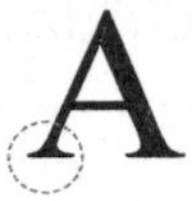

Roman type with serif. Easy to distinguish even when letters are small. Good for body text.

Helvetica

Panasonic

Electronics manufacturer logo
Credit: Panasonic Corporation

Optima

GODIVA
Belgium 1926

Belgian chocolate company logo
Credit: Godiva Chocolatier

Optima

LUMINE

Station building shopping center logo
Credit: Lumine Co., Ltd.

Frutiger

よこはま
KK 37
横 浜
Yokohama 横浜 요코하마
神奈川
Kanagawa
（そごう・ポルタ前）
38
戸部
Tobe

Keihin Railway Yokohama platform station name signs
Frutiger typeface is used for “Yokohama” and “KK37”

What the Font?!

A Manga Guide to Western Typeface

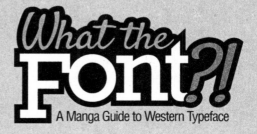

PART 2

Roman Types

Roman Type Bios

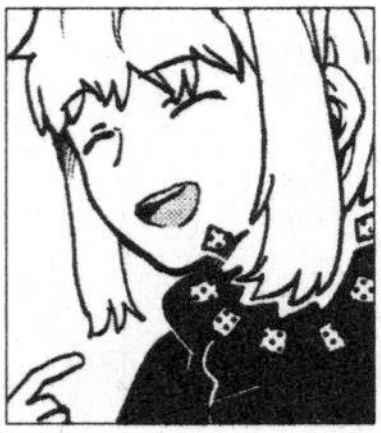

Caslon

Everybody's reliable big sister.
A little flighty sometimes, but you can count on her.

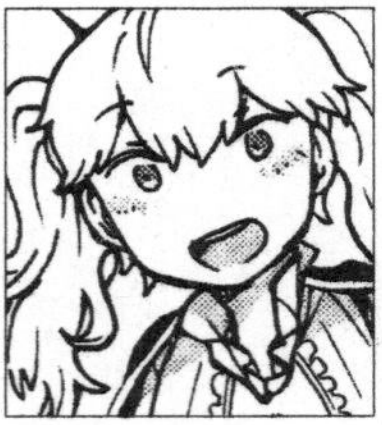

Garamond

Little rich French girl.
Her friendship with Caslon transcends time and national borders.

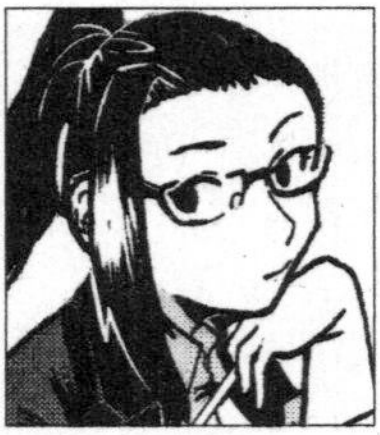

Times New Roman

Strict, but looks out for people.
Maybe a little like Gill Sans?

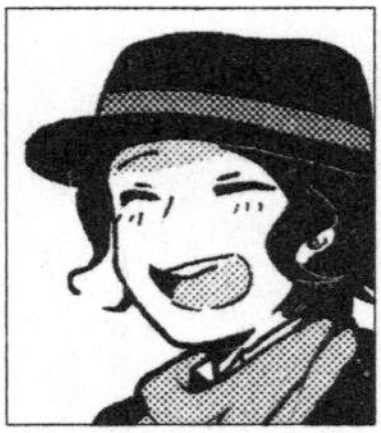

Bodoni

Stylish leader who's up for anything.
A strong core shines through.

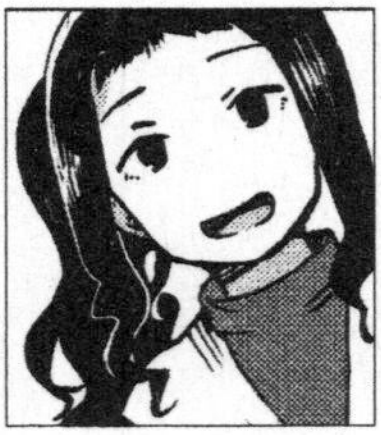

Didot

Bodoni's friend, slender and elegant.
Tends to be mistaken for family.

Clarendon

This girl does everything to perfection.
Loves to have fun with the gang.

Rockwell

Clarendon's *protégé*.
Very kind, beloved by children.

Centaur

Jenson's older twin.
Mysterious, loves galleries.

Jenson

Centaur's younger twin.
Sure-footed, loves museums.

Caslon

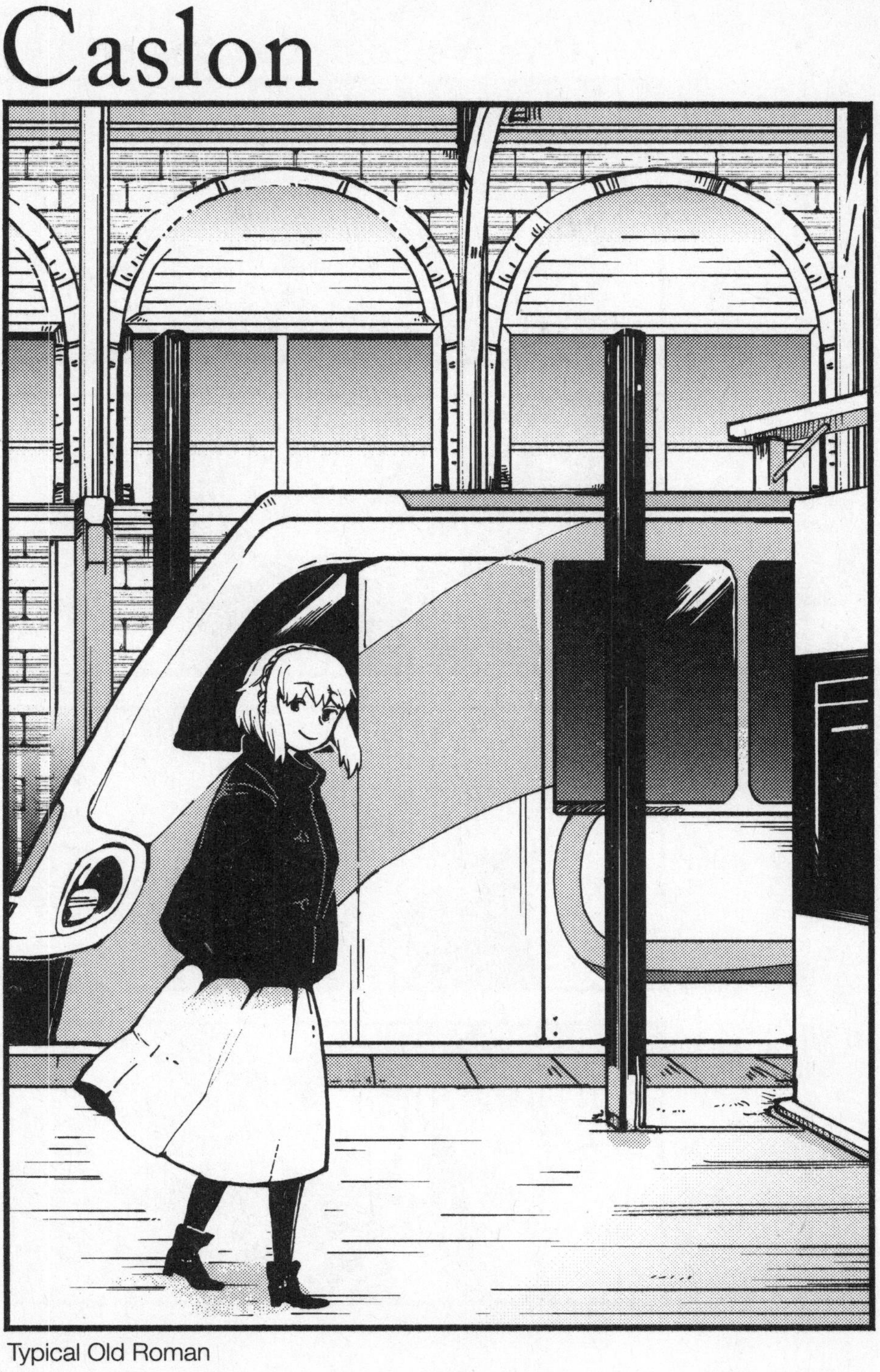

Typical Old Roman

If You're Lost, Call Caslon

I...I LEFT EVERYONE BEHIND...
WHIRL WHIRL...
AND NOW IT LOOKS LIKE I'M LOST AGAIN.
THE ROMAN WING?
BUMP
OW!
OH! I'M SO SORRY!
ARE YOU OKAY? YOU'RE NOT HURT, ARE YOU?
HERE. A HAND-KERCHIEF AND A BANDAGE.
WHOA...

Beloved for centuries, Caslon is a highly versatile body text typeface. It's so reliable that in the days of moveable type, people used to say that if you were stuck for a design, you should just put your book together with Caslon.

Reliable Big Sister

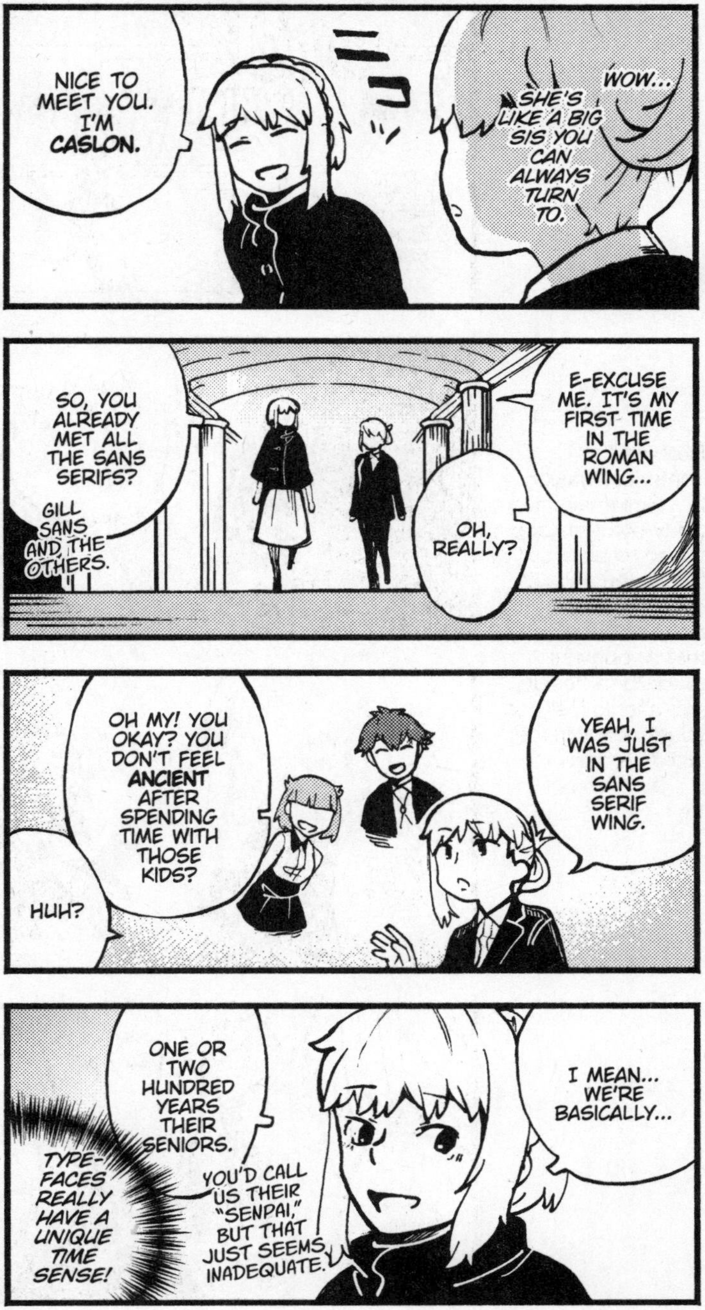
WOW... SHE'S LIKE A BIG SIS YOU CAN ALWAYS TURN TO.
NICE TO MEET YOU. I'M **CASLON.**
E-EXCUSE ME. IT'S MY FIRST TIME IN THE ROMAN WING...
OH, REALLY?
SO, YOU ALREADY MET ALL THE SANS SERIFS?
GILL SANS AND THE OTHERS.
YEAH, I WAS JUST IN THE SANS SERIF WING.
OH MY! YOU OKAY? YOU DON'T FEEL **ANCIENT** AFTER SPENDING TIME WITH THOSE KIDS?
HUH?
I MEAN... WE'RE BASICALLY...
ONE OR TWO HUNDRED YEARS THEIR SENIORS.
YOU'D CALL US THEIR "SENPAI," BUT THAT JUST SEEMS INADEQUATE.
TYPE-FACES REALLY HAVE A UNIQUE TIME SENSE!

Caslon was produced in 1725 by William Caslon I of England. It was designed to incorporate a handwritten flavor into the mechanical technology of printing, and it's classified as Old Roman.

Right-handed Letters

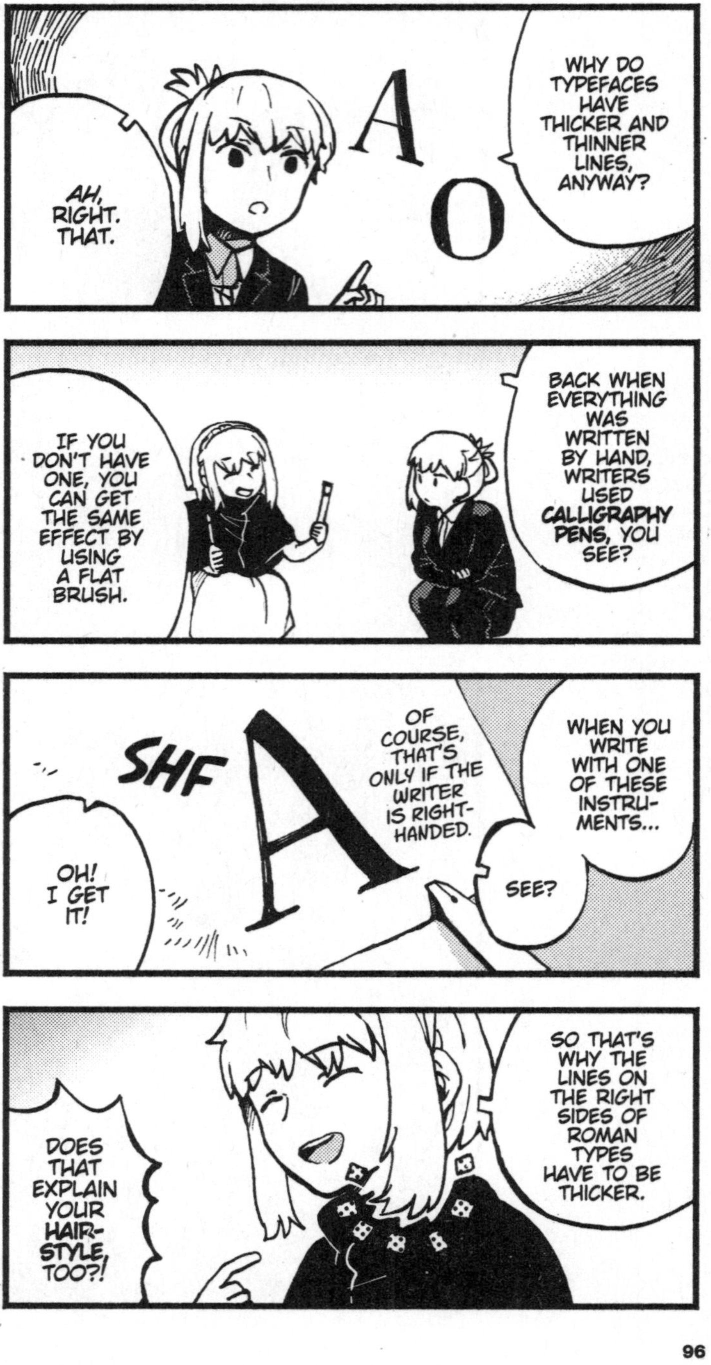
WHY DO TYPEFACES HAVE THICKER AND THINNER LINES, ANYWAY?
A
O
AH, RIGHT. THAT.
BACK WHEN EVERYTHING WAS WRITTEN BY HAND, WRITERS USED **CALLIGRAPHY PENS,** YOU SEE?
IF YOU DON'T HAVE ONE, YOU CAN GET THE SAME EFFECT BY USING A FLAT BRUSH.
WHEN YOU WRITE WITH ONE OF THESE INSTRU-MENTS...
SEE?
OF COURSE, THAT'S ONLY IF THE WRITER IS RIGHT-HANDED.
A
SHF
OH! I GET IT!
SO THAT'S WHY THE LINES ON THE RIGHT SIDES OF ROMAN TYPES HAVE TO BE THICKER.
DOES THAT EXPLAIN YOUR **HAIR-STYLE,** TOO?!

Classified as Old Roman, Caslon includes traces of handwritten character shapes. The serifs of the uppercase *A, T,* and *Z,* among others, open outward as if reproducing calligraphy strokes, a defining characteristic of the type.

Incredible Journey

YOU'RE SO STYLISH, CASLON-SAN.
DO YOU LIKE GOING OUT AND DOING STUFF?
HM?
WELL, ACTUALLY...
?
I'M REALLY MORE THE INDOOR TYPE.
I WAS SHIPPED ALL THE WAY ACROSS THE ATLANTIC DURING THE COLONIAL AGE, AND I HATED IT.
?!
I DID GET TO HELP THE AMERICANS WIN THEIR INDEPENDENCE, BUT STILL.
SO ROUGH AND STORMY...
WAIT. THAT'S AMAZING, BUT YOU MAKE IT SOUND HORRIBLE.

In the era of colonization, Caslon came to America from Britain. This typeface was later used in the United States Declaration of Independence in 1776.

Relaxed Impression

TO BE HONEST...
I LIKE TO SPEND MY TIME QUIETLY SURROUNDED BY BOOKS.
THIS IS... A LIBRARY, RIGHT?
THE CENTER OF THE BUILDING'S A **BOOK STORAGE** SPACE.
IT HOLDS MATERIALS RELATED TO OUR WORK.
SO YOU CAN JUST PICK ONE UP...
AND REMEMBER: "OH, THAT'S RIGHT. I DID THIS."
THAT'S WHY I REMEMBERED THAT DECLARATION OF INDEPEN-DENCE.
When in the Course
WHOA! THAT'S ACTUALLY KIND OF CREEPY!

Caslon was influenced by Dutch type and gives an impression of relaxed refinement. Also, because the contrast between the thickness of the strokes is relatively small, even among roman types, it's usually not chosen for longer texts.

Lots of Friends

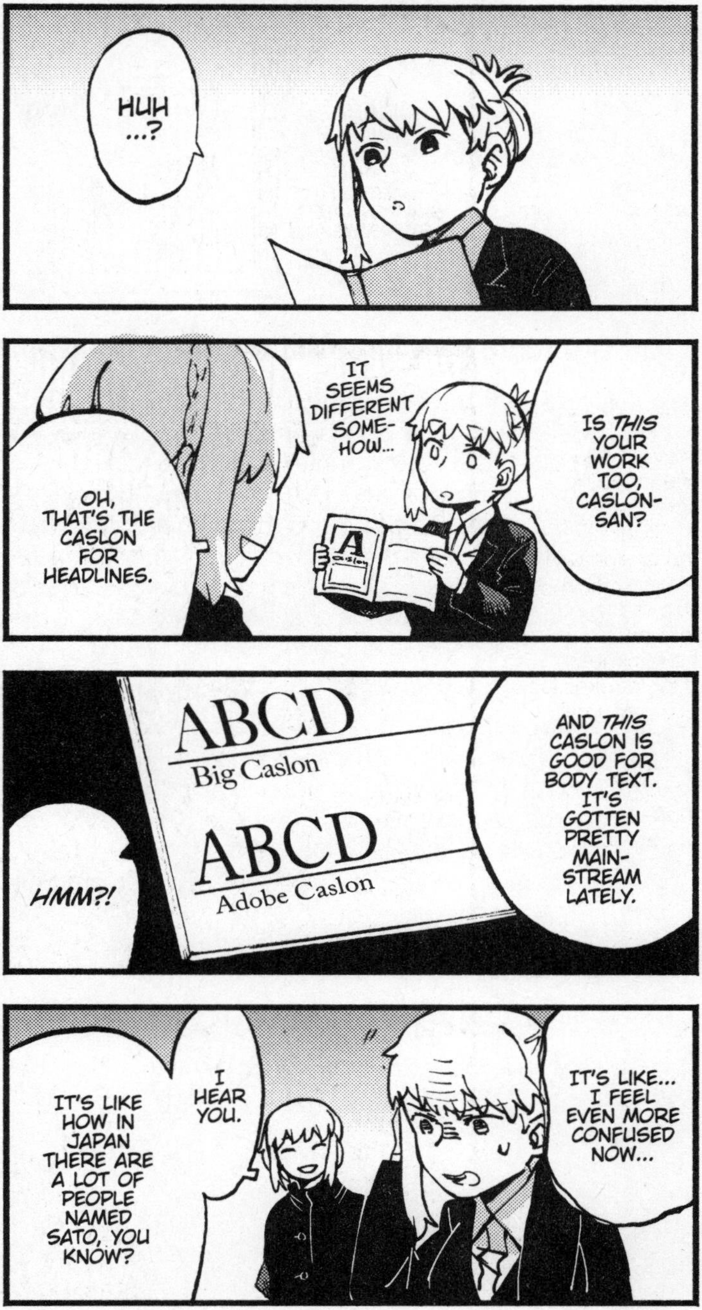

HUH ...?
IS *THIS* YOUR WORK TOO, CASLON-SAN?
IT SEEMS DIFFERENT SOMEHOW...
OH, THAT'S THE CASLON FOR HEADLINES.
AND *THIS* CASLON IS GOOD FOR BODY TEXT. IT'S GOTTEN PRETTY MAINSTREAM LATELY.
ABCD
Big Caslon
ABCD
Adobe Caslon
HMM?!
IT'S LIKE... I FEEL EVEN MORE CONFUSED NOW...
I HEAR YOU.
IT'S LIKE HOW IN JAPAN THERE ARE A LOT OF PEOPLE NAMED SATO, YOU KNOW?

When a typeface has a history as long as Caslon's, a variety of companies re-release variants as digital fonts for design work. There is Big Caslon, appropriate for headlines with its wide form, and ITC Founder's Caslon, which faithfully reproduces the original letterpress print, among others.

Caslon

CATEGORY:	Roman
CLASSIFICATION:	Old Style
YEAR OF CREATION:	1725
DESIGNER(S):	William Caslon I
FOUNDRY:	England

Old style that is both beautiful and practical.

Caslon was the first pure roman type created in England, by the British type founder and typeface designer William Caslon I (1692–1766). After going to apprentice at a metal workshop in London at the age of thirteen, Caslon did ornamental designs on rifles and other items, in addition to casting silver objects, before he established a type foundry in 1720. At first, he tried his hand at Arabic characters, but he went on to complete this old-style roman type under the influence of the excellent roman types of the Dutch type engraving master Christoffel Van Dijck (1601–1669).

In the American colonies, Benjamin Franklin is said to have preferred Caslon, and it was used for the first printing of the United States Declaration of Independence in 1776. This beautiful and practical typeface was reproduced by Chiswick Press, which launched a movement in England in 1840 producing private editions in pursuit of the ideal of the beautiful book. Caslon was also beloved by Irish playwright George Bernard Shaw.

USAGE EXAMPLES
....

□ United States Declaration of Independence (1776, used in body text)
□ *The New Yorker* (American magazine, used in body text)

ABCDEFGHIJ
KLMNOPQRS
TUVWXYZ
abcdefghijklmn
opqrstuvwxyz
0123456789

Adobe Caslon Pro Regular

Garamond

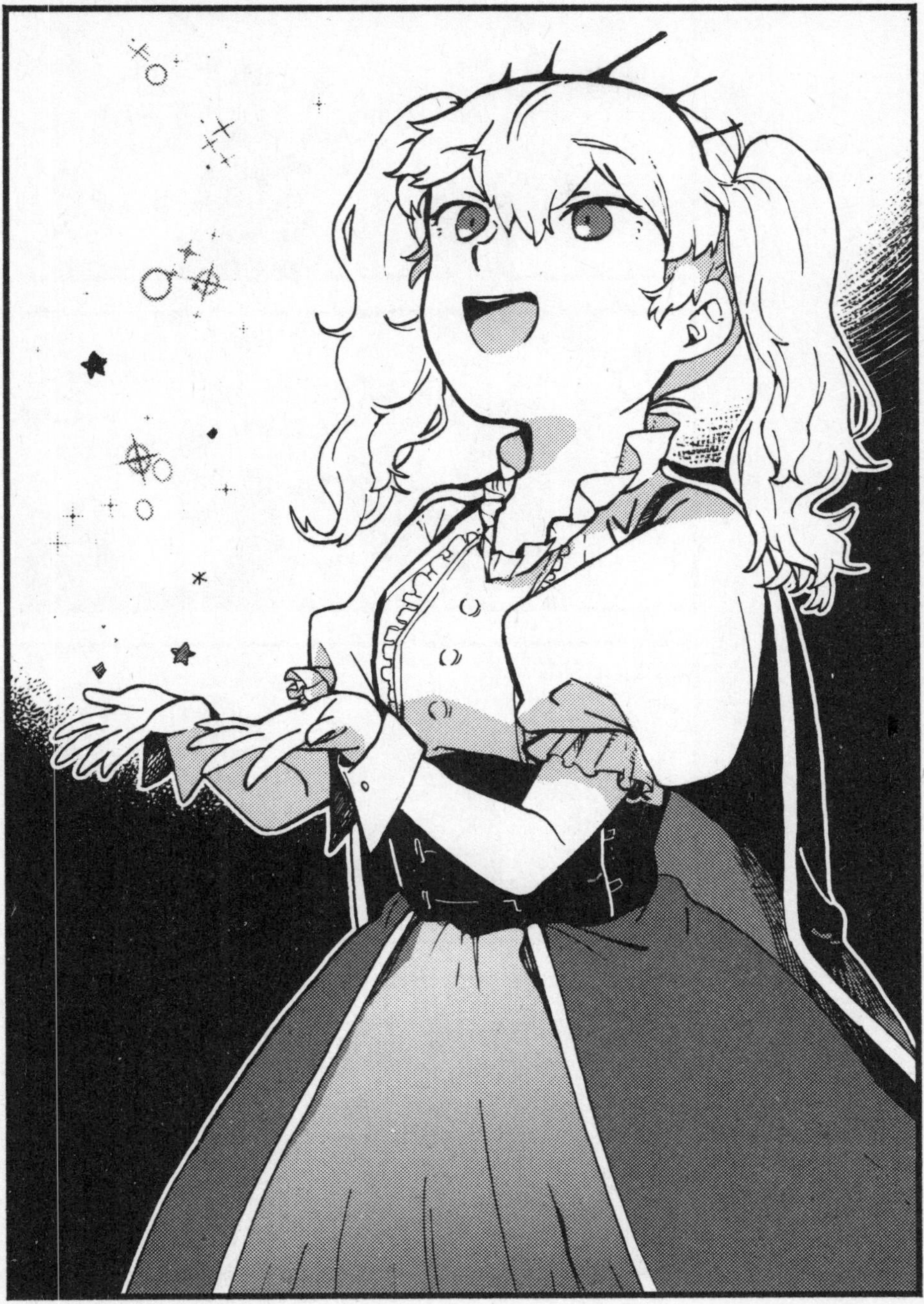

Elegant Old Roman

Famous to Those in the Know

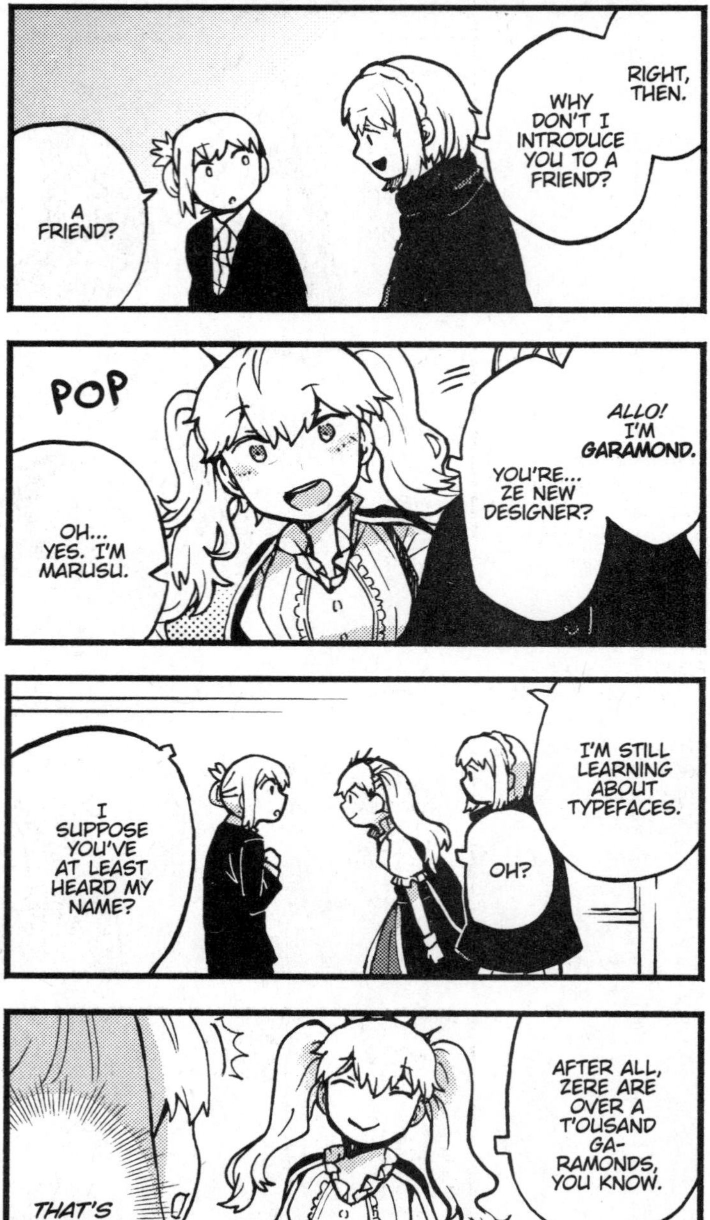
RIGHT, THEN.
WHY DON'T I INTRODUCE YOU TO A FRIEND?
A FRIEND?
ALLO! I'M GARAMOND.
YOU'RE... ZE NEW DESIGNER?
POP
OH... YES. I'M MARUSU.
I'M STILL LEARNING ABOUT TYPEFACES.
OH?
I SUPPOSE YOU'VE AT LEAST HEARD MY NAME?
AFTER ALL, ZERE ARE OVER A T'OUSAND GA-RAMONDS, YOU KNOW.
THAT'S HUGE.

Garamond is a typical Old Roman type. In the seventeenth century, it became the official typeface of the French royal printing office. It saw a revival in the twentieth century, and now foundries all over have produced typefaces bearing the Garamond name.

Beloved for Five Hundred Years

SO, WE ROMAN TYPES?
MOST OF US GO BACK TO THE **MOVEABLE TYPE** DAYS.
WE'VE GOT ZAT KIND OF HISTORY.
YOU DO HAVE A KIND OF...
ALMOST MIDDLE AGES LOOK TO YOU...
HEE HEE! YOU 'AVE EET!
ZIS IS **NORMAL** FOR ME.
BUT TO YOU...
EET'S A **COSTUME** FROM THE AGE OF FAIRY TALES, OUI?
ZAT MEANS PEOPLE 'AVE LOVED ME FOR SO LONG...
THAT THE VERY **FLOW OF TIME** HAS CHANGED, OUI?!
SHAKE
I'M SO HAPPY!!
SHAKE
SO POSI-TIVE!
THAT'S SOMEONE WITH UN-SHAKEABLE FAITH IN HER-SELF!!

Garamond is a typeface created by the French punch engraver Claude Garamond. It first appeared in texts printed in 1530. Because it was influenced by Italian Renaissance style, it makes a classical, noble, and elegant impression.

Complicated Family

SO... WHAT DID YOU MEAN...
WHEN YOU SAID THERE WERE MORE THAN A **THOUSAND** GARA-MONDS?
WHY, I'M SIMPLY SO POPULAR THAT **EVERYONE** TOOK ON ZE NAME.
Garamond
a
Garamond
a
Garamond
a
ZE GARAMOND BRAND.
AND THEN ZIS TYPEFACE DESIGNED BY SOME-ONE ELSE WAY BACK WHEN...
Adobe Garamond
→ Garamond line
ITC Garamond
→ Jannon line
Granjon
→ Garamond line
(typeface with a different name)
WHY, EVERYONE THOUGHT EET WAS **ME.**
IT'S LIKE IF THE SATO CLAN SPLIT INTO BRANCH FAMILIES AND OTHER TRIBES.
IT GETS REAL MIXED UP, HUH, GARA-MOND?
NOD NOD
EET EES COMPLI-CATED...

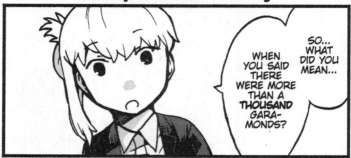

After Claude Garamond's death, a typeface designed by Jean Jannon was used in France's first typeface specimen book, and it was generally mistaken for Garamond's type. Because of this, there are two lines of Garamonds: one that follows the original typeface, and the Jannon line that follows Jean Jannon's typeface.

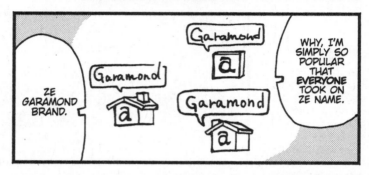

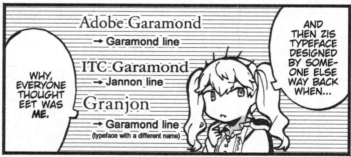

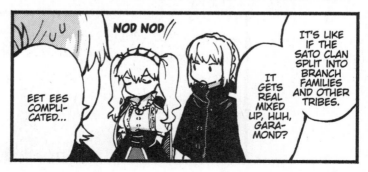

Italics?

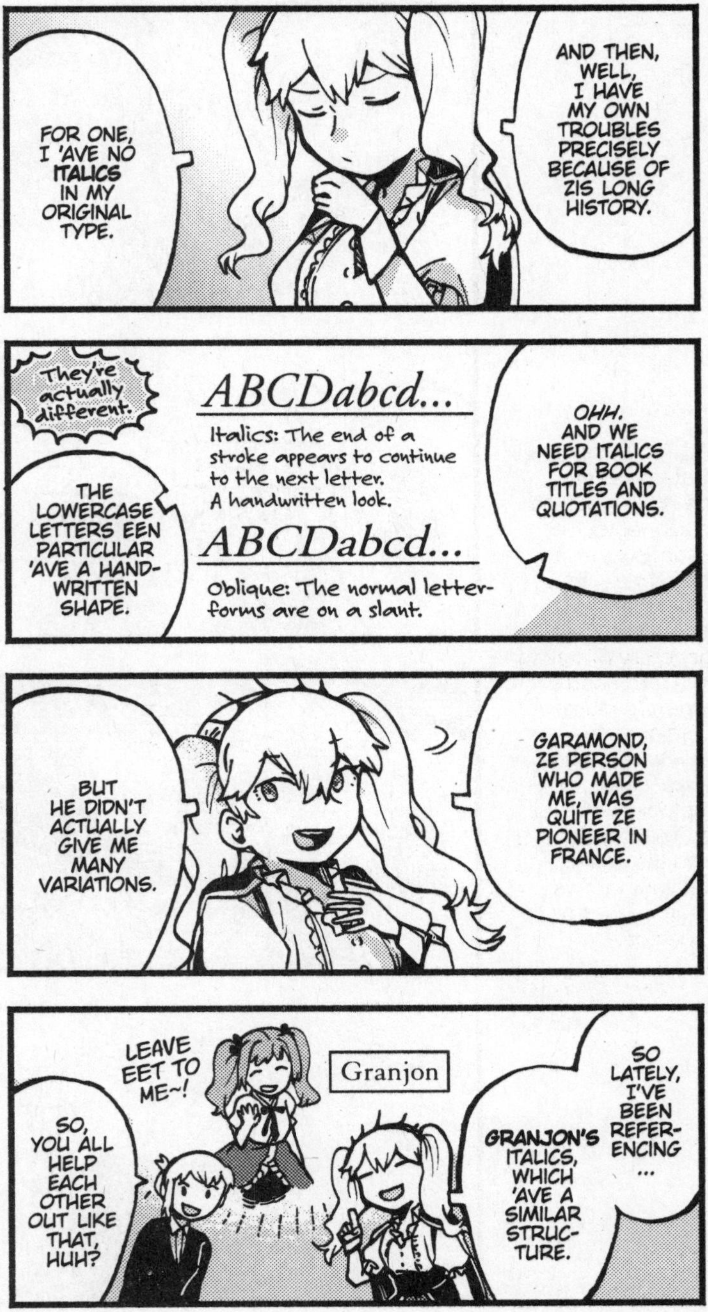
AND THEN, WELL, I HAVE MY OWN TROUBLES PRECISELY BECAUSE OF ZIS LONG HISTORY.
FOR ONE, I 'AVE NO ITALICS IN MY ORIGINAL TYPE.
OHH. AND WE NEED ITALICS FOR BOOK TITLES AND QUOTATIONS.
ABCDabcd...
Italics: The end of a stroke appears to continue to the next letter. A handwritten look.
They're actually different.
ABCDabcd...
Oblique: The normal letterforms are on a slant.
THE LOWERCASE LETTERS EEN PARTICULAR 'AVE A HANDWRITTEN SHAPE.
GARAMOND, ZE PERSON WHO MADE ME, WAS QUITE ZE PIONEER IN FRANCE.
BUT HE DIDN'T ACTUALLY GIVE ME MANY VARIATIONS.
SO LATELY, I'VE BEEN REFERENCING ...
GRANJON'S ITALICS, WHICH 'AVE A SIMILAR STRUCTURE.
Granjon
LEAVE EET TO ME~!
SO, YOU ALL HELP EACH OTHER OUT LIKE THAT, HUH?

Italic type was first used at the beginning of the sixteenth century to print a booklet of ancient Roman poetry. Because Garamond didn't have italics at the time, the assistant Robert Granjon's typeface became the base for Garamond italics.

Change Your Thinking

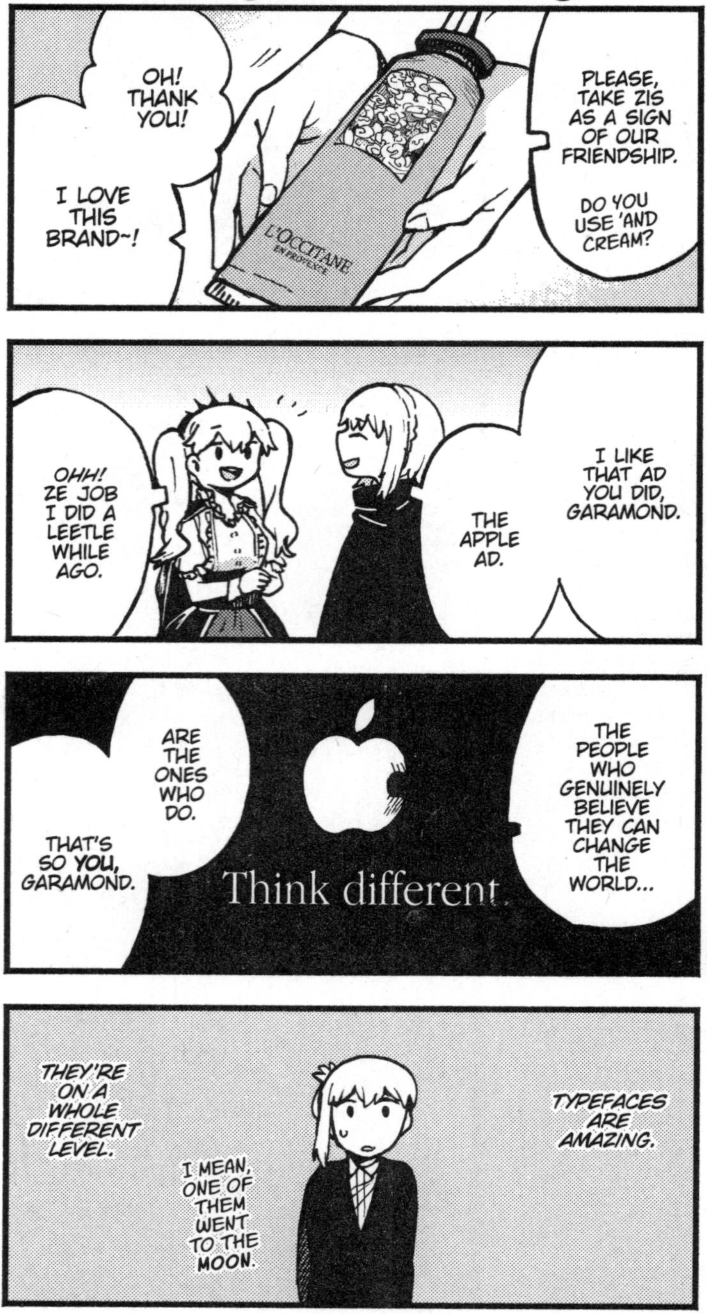
PLEASE, TAKE ZIS AS A SIGN OF OUR FRIENDSHIP.
DO YOU USE 'AND CREAM?
OH! THANK YOU!
I LOVE THIS BRAND~!
L'OCCITANE
EN PROVENCE
I LIKE THAT AD YOU DID, GARAMOND.
THE APPLE AD.
OHH! ZE JOB I DID A LEETLE WHILE AGO.
THE PEOPLE WHO GENUINELY BELIEVE THEY CAN CHANGE THE WORLD...
Think different.
ARE THE ONES WHO DO.
THAT'S SO YOU, GARAMOND.
TYPEFACES ARE AMAZING.
I MEAN, ONE OF THEM WENT TO THE MOON.
THEY'RE ON A WHOLE DIFFERENT LEVEL.

Garamond is used in the logo type for cosmetics company L'Occitane, the fashion brand Cecil McBee, and others. Additionally, in 1984, Apple introduced Apple Garamond and used it in their corporate typeface as well as in their widely known 1997 "Think Different" slogan.

History Runs On

SO, BOTH OF YOU...
ARE CLASSIFIED AS OLD ROMAN, RIGHT?
OUI, ZAT'S RIGHT.
THE SHAPE THAT WOULD BECOME THE BASE FOR ROMAN TYPES WAS CREATED IN ITALY.
AND IT CAME TO MY COUNTRY, ENGLAND...
THROUGH FRANCE AND HOLLAND.
AND THEN ZE SO-CALLED TRANSITIONAL ROMAN...
Garamond
O Q W
Baskerville
O Q W
CONNECTS US WITH ZE NEXT GENERATION OF TYPE-FACES.
THAT REMINDS ME. TIMES NEW ROMAN'S LECTURE IS TODAY, RIGHT?
MM-HMM. SHE'S AN EXAMPLE OF A TRANSI-TIONAL.
L-LECTURE?!

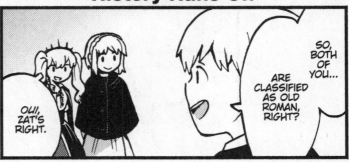

Garamond is also an Old Roman type. Distinctive features include the old-style numbers that protrude through the baseline, the peak of the 4 being closed, and the section where the uppercase *W* crosses in the center.

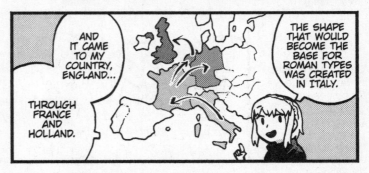

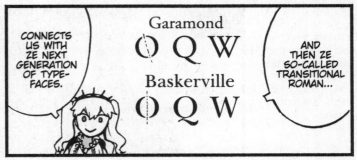

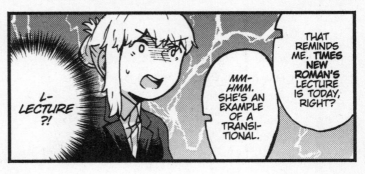

Garamond

CATEGORY:	Roman
CLASSIFICATION:	Old Style
YEAR OF CREATION:	1531
DESIGNER(S):	Claude Garamond
FOUNDRY:	France

Familiar and beloved, with many variations.

Garamond is a roman type created in connection with Claude Garamond (1480–1561), a sixteenth-century French type founder. Garamond began to study type foundry around 1510 and had exchanges with Geoffrey Tory (ca. 1480–ca. 1533), a Renaissance humanist and prominent engraver, as he studied typeface design. He became independent around 1530 and launched his own type foundry, working not only on Latin but also Greek and Hebrew typefaces. Then, taking as his examples the roman typeface masterpiece by Griffo, a punch cutter with Venetian printer Aldus, and the style of calligrapher Arrighi, he brought the uppercase, lowercase, and italics into harmony to produce a beautiful and easy-to-read type. The influence of this typeface is said to have been the start of the eradication of blackletter from Western Europe, excluding Germany.

Garamond died in extreme poverty and misfortune, but the punches and matrices he left behind were inherited by the large Antwerp printer Plantin, and the type has since been reproduced by many type and font companies. Apple used its own unique Garamond (Apple Garamond) up until 2010.

USAGE EXAMPLES

- L'Occitane (French cosmetics company)
- Abercrombie & Fitch (American fashion brand)

ABCDEFGHIJ
KLMNOPQRS
TUVWXYZ
abcdefghijklmn
opqrstuvwxyz
0123456789

Adobe Garamond Pro Regular

Times New Roman

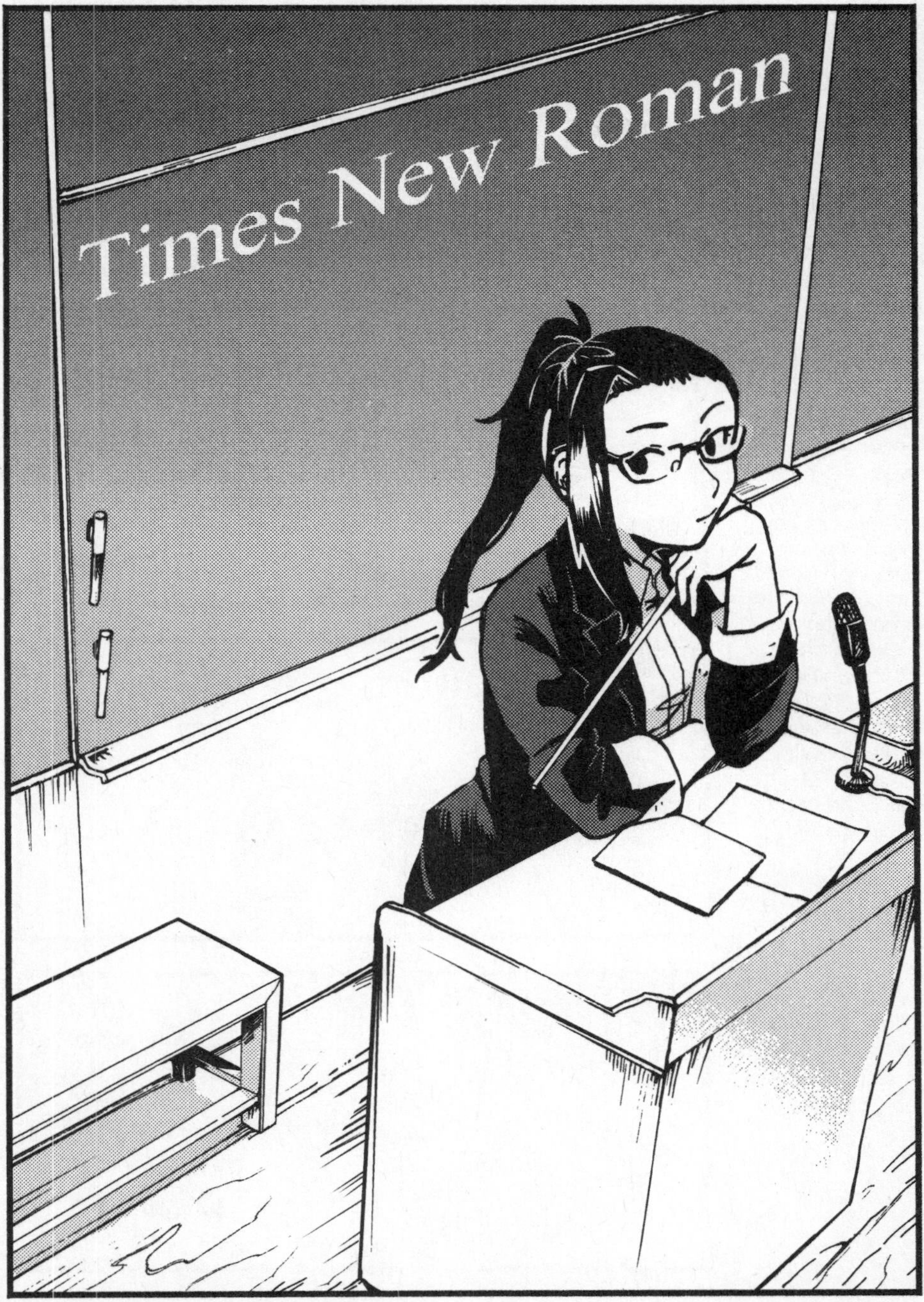
Times New Roman

Extremely readable body type

Created for the Newspaper

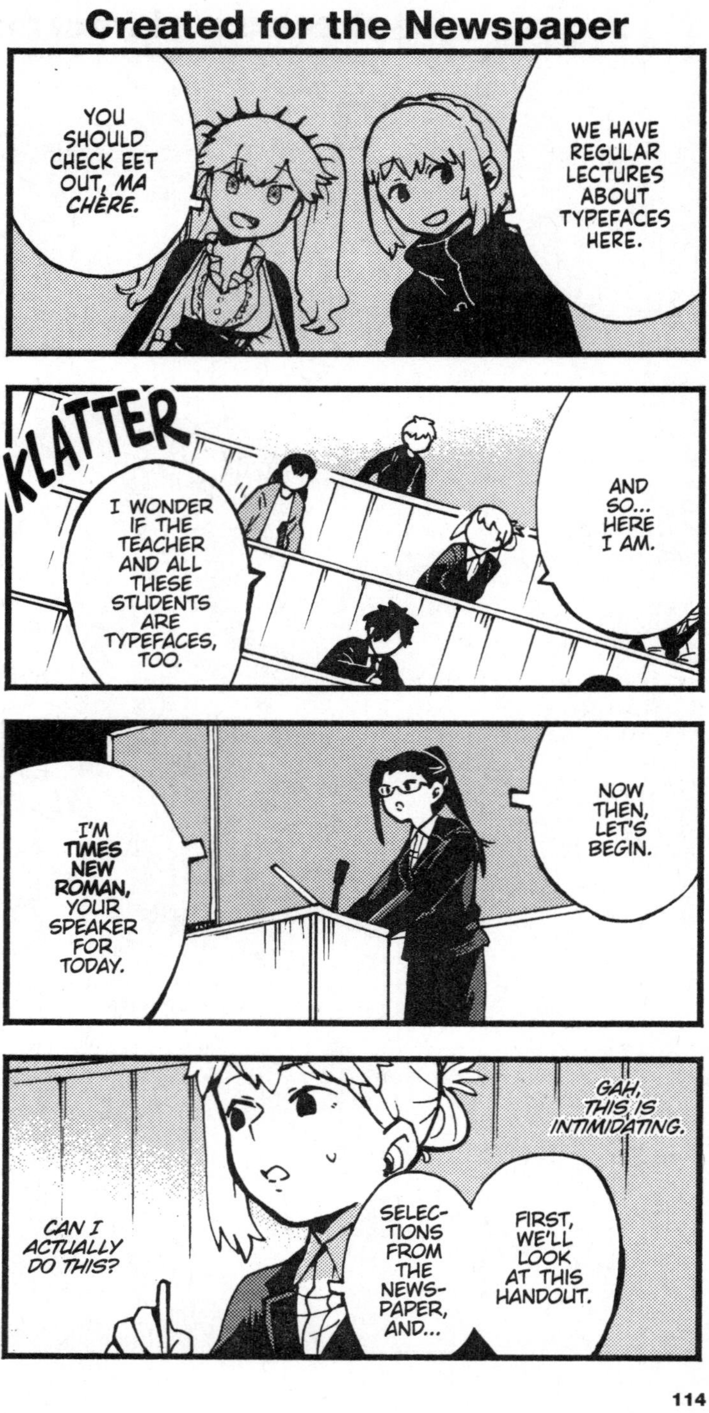
WE HAVE REGULAR LECTURES ABOUT TYPEFACES HERE.
YOU SHOULD CHECK EET OUT, *MA CHÈRE.*
AND SO... HERE I AM.
KLATTER
I WONDER IF THE TEACHER AND ALL THESE STUDENTS ARE TYPEFACES, TOO.
NOW THEN, LET'S BEGIN.
I'M **TIMES NEW ROMAN,** YOUR SPEAKER FOR TODAY.
GAH, THIS IS INTIMIDATING.
FIRST, WE'LL LOOK AT THIS HANDOUT.
SELEC-TIONS FROM THE NEWS-PAPER, AND...
CAN I ACTUALLY DO THIS?

Times New Roman was developed in 1932 by the typeface designer Stanley Morison with assistance from Victor Lardent. Commissioned for use as body text for the British newspaper *The Times,* it is often used to this day as the body text of books and other printed matter.

Freedom of Information

HM? SO, WE MEET AGAIN, NEWBIE.
GILL SANS-SAN!
WHAT ARE YOU DOING HERE?
THIS IS A PLACE FOR US TYPEFACES TO EXCHANGE INFORMATION.
IT'S BEST TO HEAR ABOUT ROMAN TYPES FROM ROMAN TYPES THEM-SELVES.
MAKES SENSE...
ACTUALLY, THAT'S THE REASON I'M HERE-- I WAS TOLD THE SAME THING.
SHE GIVES CAREFUL CONSIDERATION TO HER AUDIENCE WHEN SHE LECTURES.
YOU'D DO WELL TO TAKE ADVANTAGE OF THIS CHANCE AND LISTEN CLOSELY.

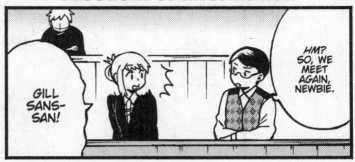

The *Times* commissioned Times New Roman with the objective of readability and typographical reform. The models for its form are considered to be Frank Hinman Pierpoint's Plantin and Eric Gill's Perpetua.

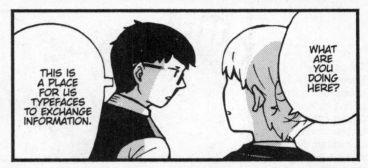

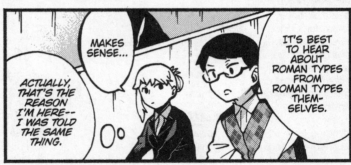

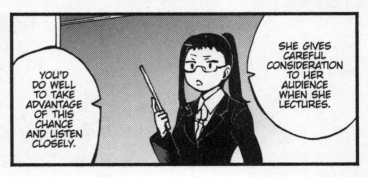

High Readability

I'D LIKE TO TALK ABOUT THE TRANSITIONS IN ROMAN TYPE.
AFTER THE LECTURE, PLEASE SUMMARIZE THE DETAILS...
AND SUBMIT THEM TO ME IN A PAPER.
I GUESS IT'S LIKE WRITING ESSAYS IN COLLEGE.
UMM, SO THEN...
HUH?
I ACTUALLY UNDER-STAND THIS.
IT'S LIKE THE DETAILS ARE POURING INTO MY HEAD...?!

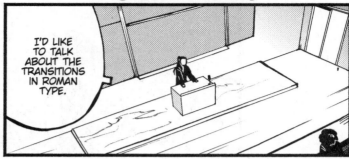

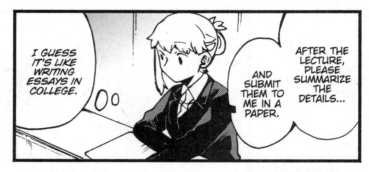

Times New Roman has fine, restrained serifs, and is tall with a high x-height, making it excellent for visibility and readability in longer texts. The strokes were designed to be thicker to compensate for high-speed printing on poor quality newspaper, and the type was basically created with the person reading it in mind.

※X-height: The height of a lowercase *x*. The baseline for the height of lowercase letters.

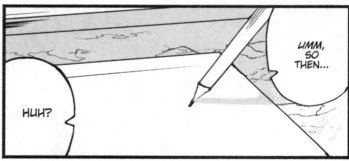

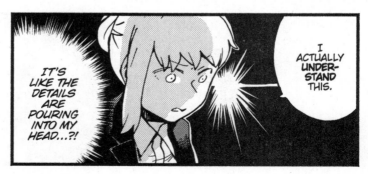

Outstanding Utility

EXCUSE ME.
I'D LIKE TO SUBMIT MY REPORT.
OH!
YOUR TALK WAS VERY EASY TO UNDER-STAND.
MM-HMM, MM-HMM.
I'M GLAD TO HEAR IT.
OF THE THREE THOUSAND OR SO LANGUAGES IN THE WORLD, ONLY ABOUT A **HUNDRED** HAVE THEIR OWN CHARACTERS.
A HUNDRED ...?!
WHICH MEANS IT'S OUR DUTY TO MAIN-TAIN THOSE CHARAC-TERS FOR POSTERITY.
WOW...
OKAY, HERE.
YOU DID A GOOD JOB.
TYPE-FACES ARE SO COOL!!

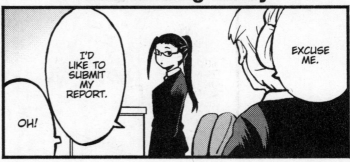

One reason that Times New Roman is widely used as a body text typeface is that it has many character and symbols. This includes not only Latin letters, but also a full complement of Cyrillic characters and symbols, giving it a convenience and utility not seen in other type groups.

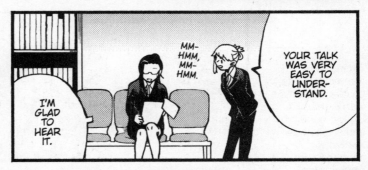

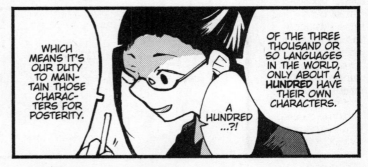

Lots of Lookalikes

HI! LET'S HANG OUT!
OH! HELLO, TIMES!
HM? ANOTHER TIMES NEW ROMAN-SAN?
SHE'S A RELATIVE.
MY NAME'S TIMES.
DO WE REALLY LOOK THAT MUCH ALIKE?
I THINK WE'RE ACTUALLY PRETTY DIFFERENT, THOUGH.
Monotype
Times New Roman
Linotype
Times
(Times Roman)
OHH. BUT REMEMBER, HELVETICA GOT US CONFUSED THAT TIME AS WELL.
AH, EXCUSE ME. SORRY.
HELVETICA-SAN, TOO?!

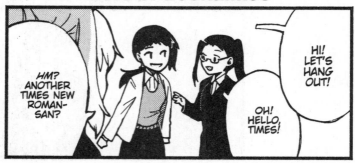

Times New Roman, developed by Monotype, was licensed to Linotype, famous for its automatic linecasting machine, who produced it as Times. Ever since, Times has been used widely for printing newspapers, magazines, and other texts.

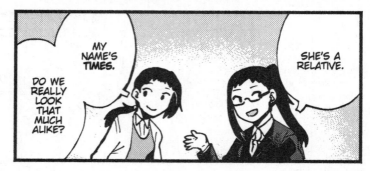

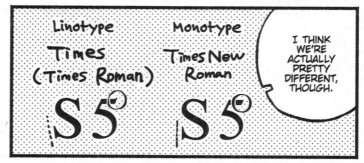

A Wee Bit Shy

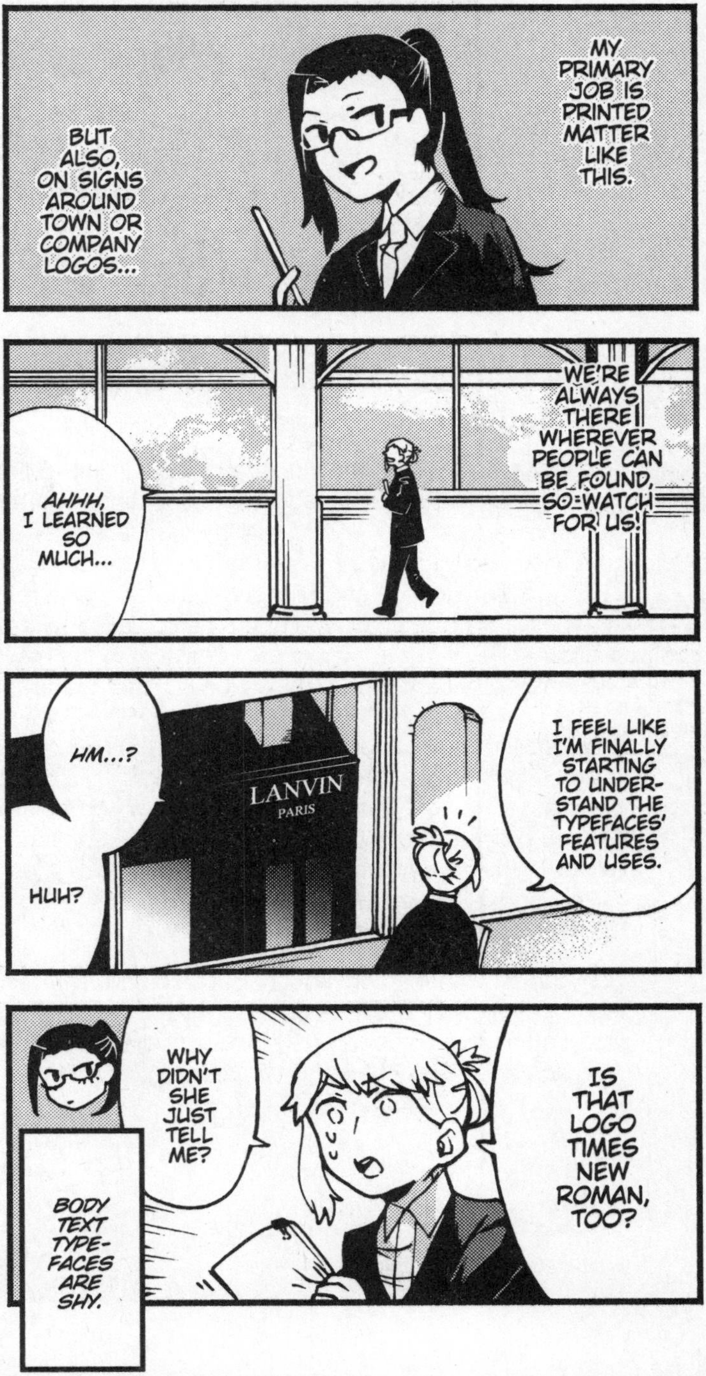

MY PRIMARY JOB IS PRINTED MATTER LIKE THIS.
BUT ALSO, ON SIGNS AROUND TOWN OR COMPANY LOGOS...
WE'RE ALWAYS THERE WHEREVER PEOPLE CAN BE FOUND, SO WATCH FOR US!
AHHH, I LEARNED SO MUCH...
I FEEL LIKE I'M FINALLY STARTING TO UNDERSTAND THE TYPEFACES' FEATURES AND USES.
LANVIN
PARIS
HM...?
HUH?
IS THAT LOGO TIMES NEW ROMAN, TOO?
WHY DIDN'T SHE JUST TELL ME?
BODY TEXT TYPEFACES ARE SHY.

Reliable and with no conspicuous quirks, this typeface is found not only in the body text of newspapers and books but also in corporate logos that want to project an impression of history and honesty, such as HSBC Holdings* and Lanvin.

** HSBC changed to a new logo in April 2018.*

Times New Roman

CATEGORY: Roman

CLASSIFICATION: Transitional

YEAR OF CREATION: 1931 (used in 1932)

DESIGNER(S): Stanley Morison, Victor Lardent

FOUNDRY: Monotype (England)

Very practical, familiar from its use as a computer font.

On October 3, 1932, the oldest and most influential newspaper in England, *The Times*, changed their printing format and letterpress type. They eliminated the old blackletter used for the titles and introduced a new roman type for the body text. Typography historian and Monotype advisor Stanley Morison (1889–1967) worked on the type's design along with Victor Lardent (1905–1968), who was a designer in the newspaper's advertising department. Morison judged the newspaper's printing to be poor quality and its typesetting behind the times, so he considered newspaper type readability while referencing cutting-edge psychological studies. After investigating a number of existing typefaces, he set Plantin, a roman type by Robert Granjon of the Antwerp printer, as the departure point. The completed type was made with enough thickness for easy readability even at small sizes, and equipped with a functional beauty that could fit many letters in a small space.

In contrast with the conventional Old Roman, *The Times* named the type "New Roman," and before long it was available for general sale, after which it became a standard typeface, to the point where it is equipped now in nearly every computer.

USAGE EXAMPLES
....

☐ *The Times* (British newspaper. Used for body text from 1932 to 1982.)

☐ Lanvin (French fashion brand)

ABCDEFGHIJ
KLMNOPQRS
TUVWXYZ
abcdefghijklmn
opqrstuvwxyz
0123456789

Times New Roman Regular

Bodoni • Didot

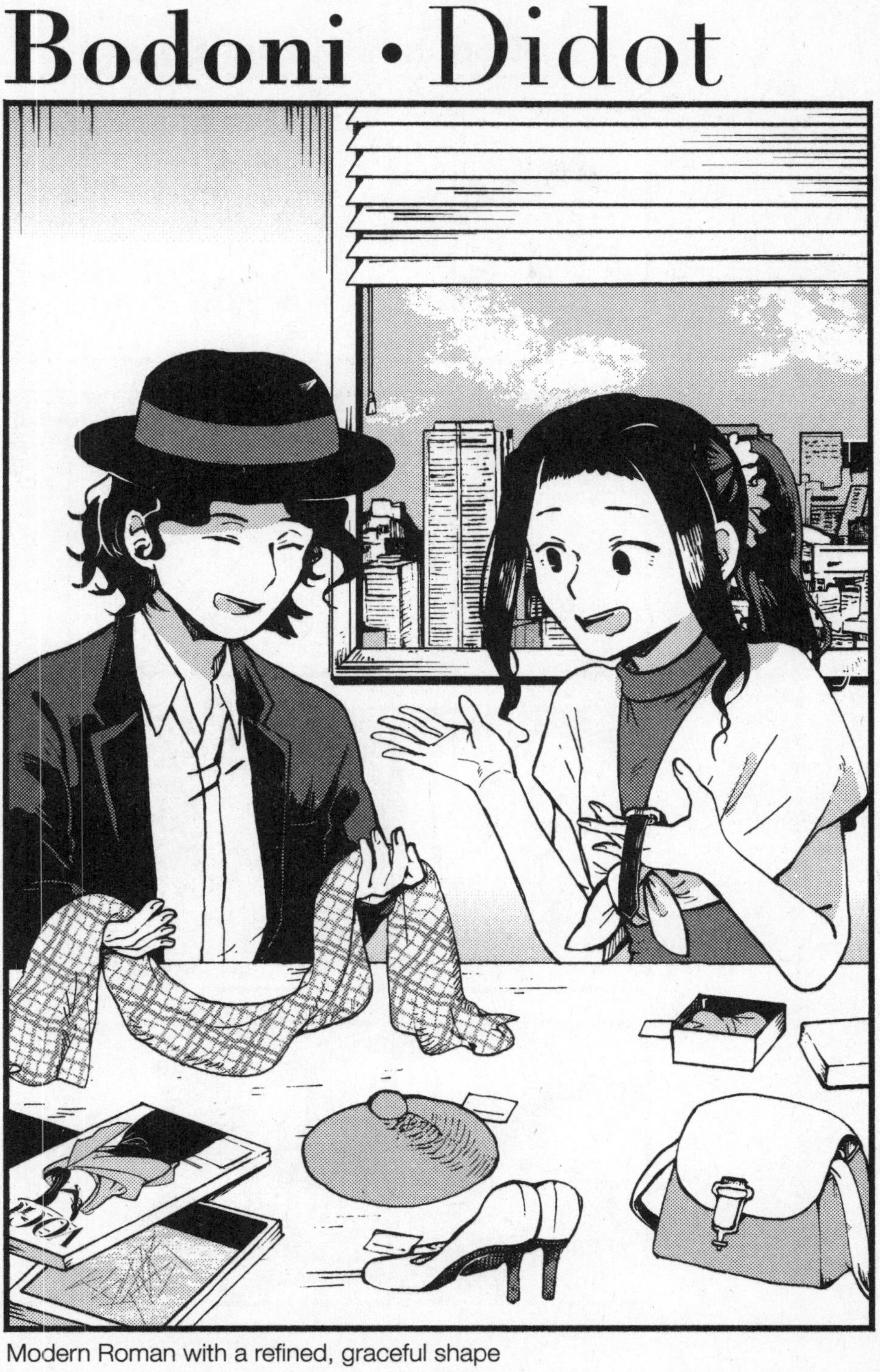

Modern Roman with a refined, graceful shape

Bodoni's Strong Core

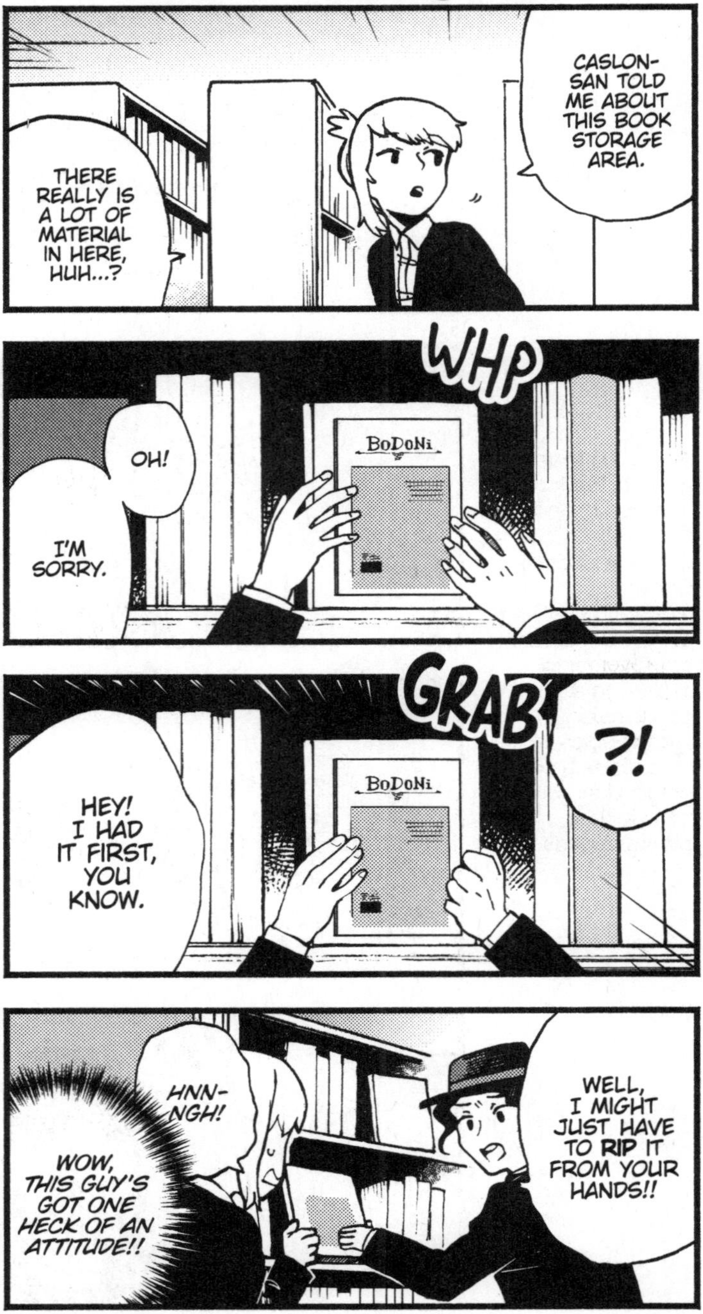

CASLON-SAN TOLD ME ABOUT THIS BOOK STORAGE AREA.
THERE REALLY IS A LOT OF MATERIAL IN HERE, HUH...?
WHP
BoDoNi
OH!
I'M SORRY.
GRAB
?!
BoDoNi
HEY! I HAD IT FIRST, YOU KNOW.
WELL, I MIGHT JUST HAVE TO RIP IT FROM YOUR HANDS!!
HNN-NGH!
WOW, THIS GUY'S GOT ONE HECK OF AN ATTITUDE!!

Bodoni has extremely fine, straight-line serifs (hairline serif), and the thickness of the vertical and horizontal strokes differs significantly. While it is refined with a modern sensibility, it's a typeface that makes you feel its core strength.

Sad Story

HA HA HA!
TUNK
SORRY ABOUT BEFORE.
THAT BOOK YOU PICKED UP THERE...
IT'S ABOUT MY MASTER, GIAMBATTISTA BODONI.
IS THAT WHERE YOU GOT YOUR NAME, BODONI-SAN?
HE WAS BORN IN 1740 IN NORTHERN ITALY TO A POOR PRINTING FAMILY.
Roma
Saluzzo
BECAUSE HE KEPT PRINTING DURING THE CHAOS OF THE FRENCH REVOLUTION...
HE EVEN DEDICATED HIS OWN WRITING TO THE NAPOLEON.
SOB SOB
THIS STORY... I CAN'T TELL IT WITHOUT CRYING...
IT'S A REAL ROLLER-COASTER...

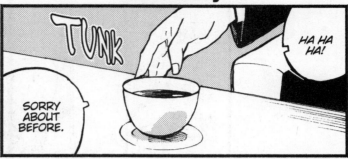

A typical Modern Roman, Bodoni was completed in 1790 by Giambattista Bodoni, who managed the Duke of Parma's press. Improvements in printing and papermaking technologies of the time made types like Bodoni, with thin serifs and high contrast, possible.

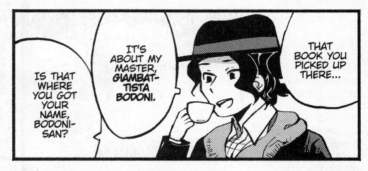

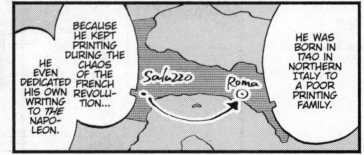

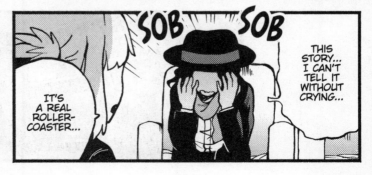

Attention-seeker

SO HE ENDED UP BEING CALLED THE "KING OF PRINTING," HM?
HE DIIIIID.
IT WAS A LONG JOURNEY.
IT'S REALLY AN HONOR TO STILL BE SUCH A PART OF THE PRINTING WORLD.
SHF
OH! THAT'S A CD JACKET!
LOGOS ARE ACTUALLY QUITE GLORIOUS, AREN'T THEY?
IT'S NICE TO DO WORK THAT LETS YOU STAND OUT!
OH! I FEEL LIKE I'VE HEARD THAT BEFORE.
DING!
HM?
WHAT IS IT?
MARUSU IS COMING TO UNDER-STAND THE NATURE OF HEAD-LINE TYPE-FACES.

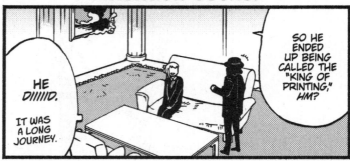

Although generally used in body text, Bodoni is also suitable for places that use large characters, such as displays and logos. It's used in fashion magazines, cosmetics, and the like.

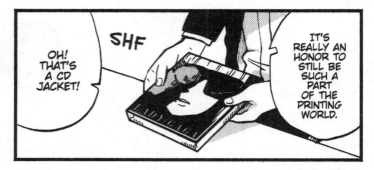

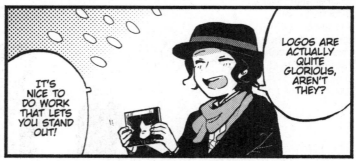

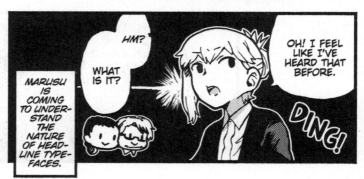

(Not) Family Resemblance

BODONI! HELLO!
HERE'S THE WORK YOU ASKED FOR.
OH! THANKS!
OKAY, I'LL LEAVE THE REST TO YOU~!
YOU REALLY LOOK ALIKE.
IS THAT A MEMBER OF YOUR FAMILY?
OHH, THAT'S DIDOT.
SHE'S FROM A DIFFERENT COUNTRY AND HAD A DIFFERENT UPBRING-ING.
?!

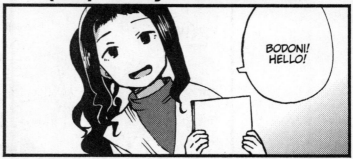

Didot can be seen alongside Bodoni on luxury brands and in fashion magazines. They look very much alike at first glance, but Bodoni has a thicker stem. Also, in contrast with Bodoni's Italian roots, Didot is by the French printer Firmin Didot.

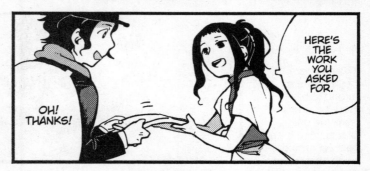

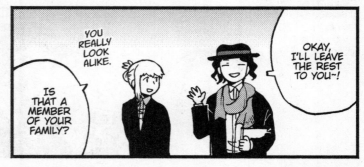

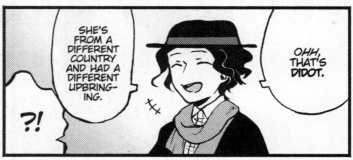

Tokens of Gratitude

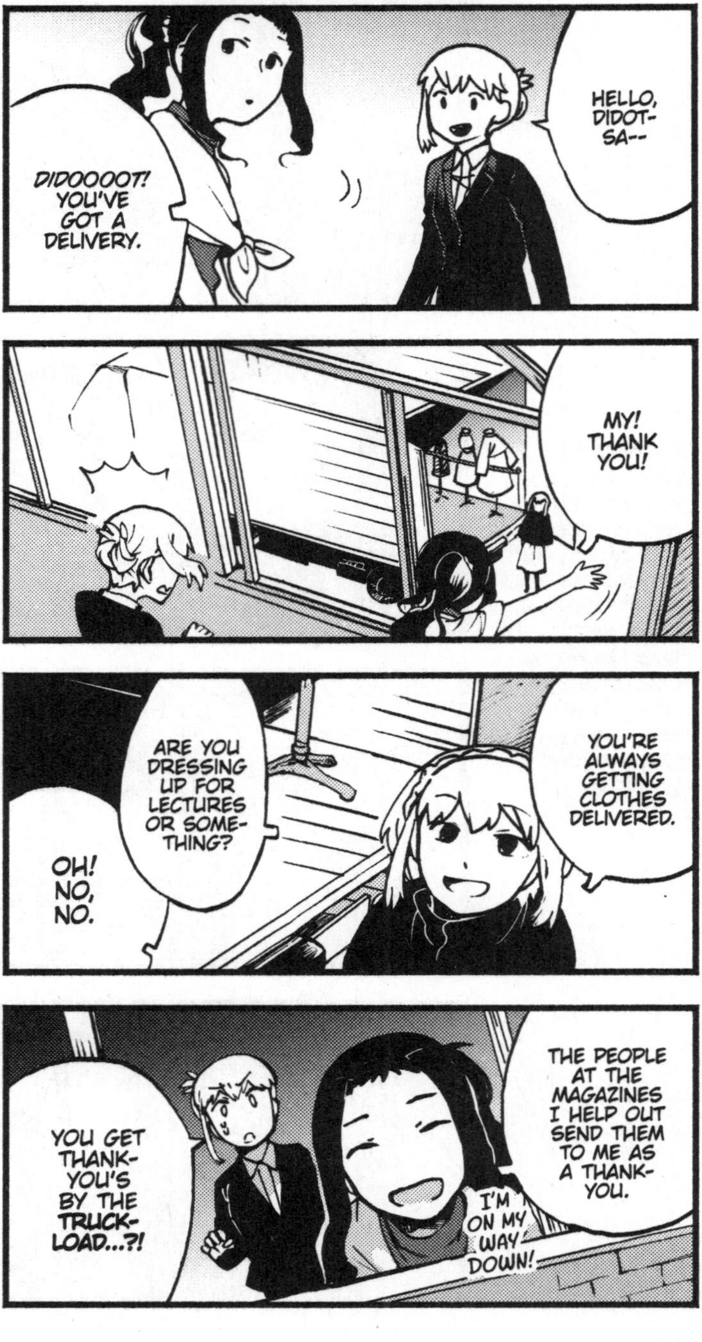
HELLO, DIDOT-SA--
DIDOOOOT! YOU'VE GOT A DELIVERY.
MY! THANK YOU!
YOU'RE ALWAYS GETTING CLOTHES DELIVERED.
ARE YOU DRESSING UP FOR LECTURES OR SOME-THING?
OH! NO, NO.
THE PEOPLE AT THE MAGAZINES I HELP OUT SEND THEM TO ME AS A THANK-YOU.
I'M ON MY WAY DOWN!
YOU GET THANK-YOU'S BY THE TRUCK-LOAD...?!

The characteristics of Didot are a strong stroke contrast and a feminine grace. The fashion brand Giorgio Armani and the fashion magazine *Vogue* use modified versions of Didot.

Cutting-edge Fashion

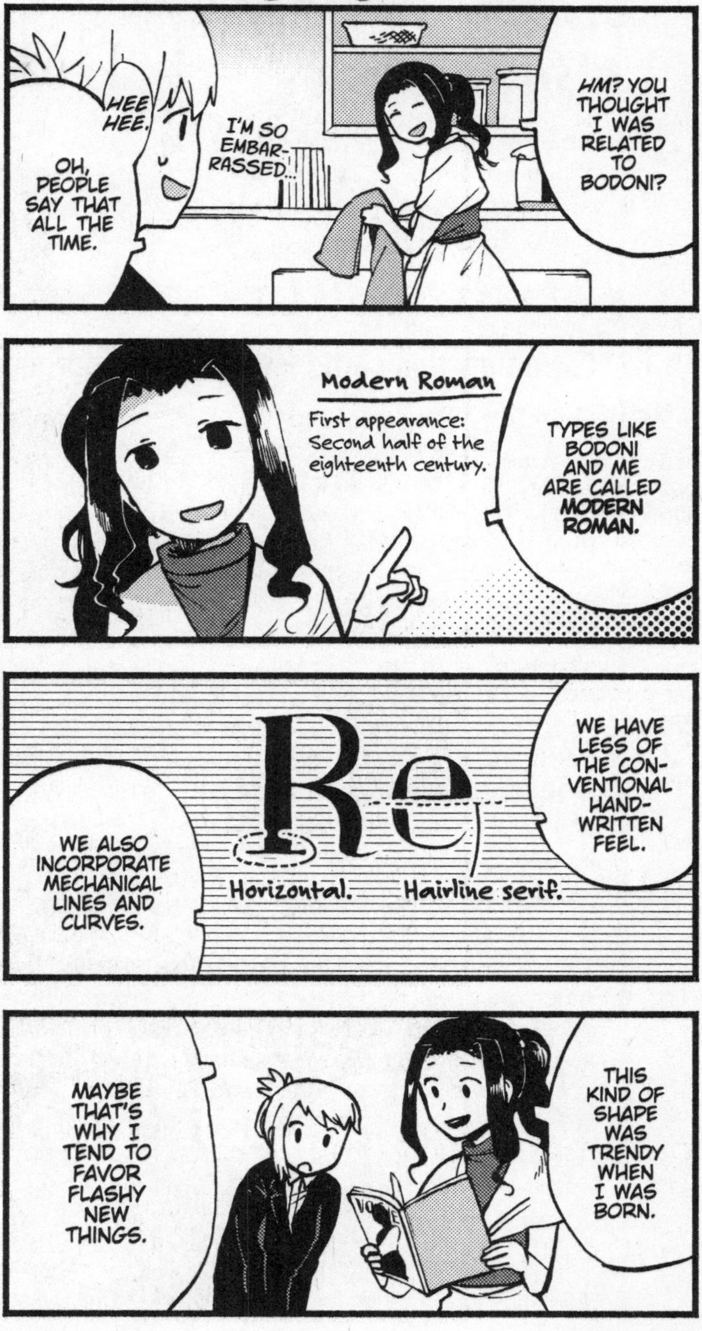
HM? YOU THOUGHT I WAS RELATED TO BODONI?
I'M SO EMBARRASSED...
HEE HEE.
OH, PEOPLE SAY THAT ALL THE TIME.
TYPES LIKE BODONI AND ME ARE CALLED MODERN ROMAN.
Modern Roman
First appearance: Second half of the eighteenth century.
WE HAVE LESS OF THE CONVENTIONAL HANDWRITTEN FEEL.
Re
Hairline serif.
Horizontal.
WE ALSO INCORPORATE MECHANICAL LINES AND CURVES.
THIS KIND OF SHAPE WAS TRENDY WHEN I WAS BORN.
MAYBE THAT'S WHY I TEND TO FAVOR FLASHY NEW THINGS.

Bodoni and Didot have geometrical forms that eliminate handwritten elements, such as the horizontal bar of the lowercase e. Unlike Old Roman which gives a feeling of tradition, these types make a modern impression.

Bodoni   Didot

CATEGORY:	Roman	Roman
CLASSIFICATION:	Modern style	Modern style
YEAR OF CREATION:	1790	1790
DESIGNER(S):	Giambattista Bodoni	Firmin Didot
FOUNDRY:	Italy	France

Extremely thin serifs for a modern, gorgeous impression.

Giambattista Bodoni (1740–1813) was one of the type founders who devised the Modern Roman style at the end of the eighteenth century. In 1768, he was appointed to head the Duke of Parma's royal press; initially, he used the French Fournier typeface, but when the type foundry was given permission, he began working on his own typeface. Then, around 1790, Bodoni was completed as a commission from the Vatican. With an emphasis on regularity, the maximally thick stems and the smooth curves form a geometrical structure, while the maximally thin hairline serifs create a clear contrast in the strokes. It is said that every time Bodoni printed something, if there was a letterform he didn't like, he would remake the matrix. In his book *Manuale typografico*, published posthumously in 1818, 665 specimens of typeface are listed, and the four criteria of regularity, clarity, refinement, and elegance are given as requirements for a beautiful typeface.

Didot, another typical Modern Roman, was completed by the Didot family. After establishing himself in publishing and sales in 1713, François started printing as well. A generation later, François Ambroise developed a point system to express type size, and a generation after that, Firmin Didot (1764–1836) released roman types from 1784 to 1811. Due to its sharp hairlines, the contrast in Didot is even more extreme than in Bodoni, and the type symbolizes the severity of neoclassicism. It is said that Old Roman style typefaces disappeared from printed matter for a time around 1840.

USAGE EXAMPLES

☐ Bodoni: Lady Gaga (used on *The Fame* jacket, official website)
☐ Didot: *Vogue* (fashion magazine launched in the U.S.)

ABCDEFGHIJ
KLMNOPQRS
TUVWXYZ
abcdefghijklmn
opqrstuvwxyz
0123456789 Bodoni LT Std Regular

ABCDEFGHIJ
KLMNOPQRS
TUVWXYZ
abcdefghijklmn
opqrstuvwxyz
0123456789 Didot Regular

Clarendon

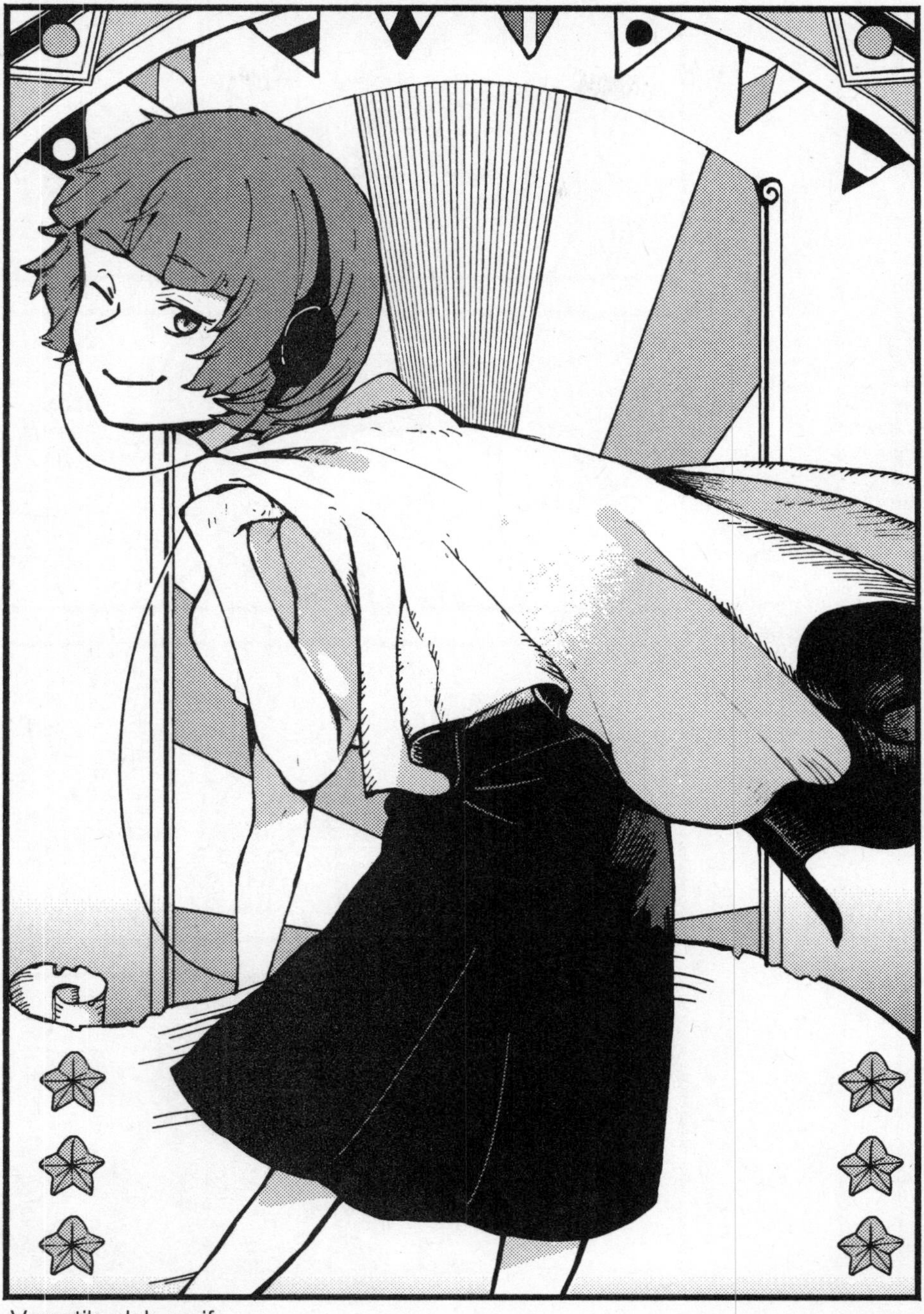

Versatile slab serif

Photo Shoot

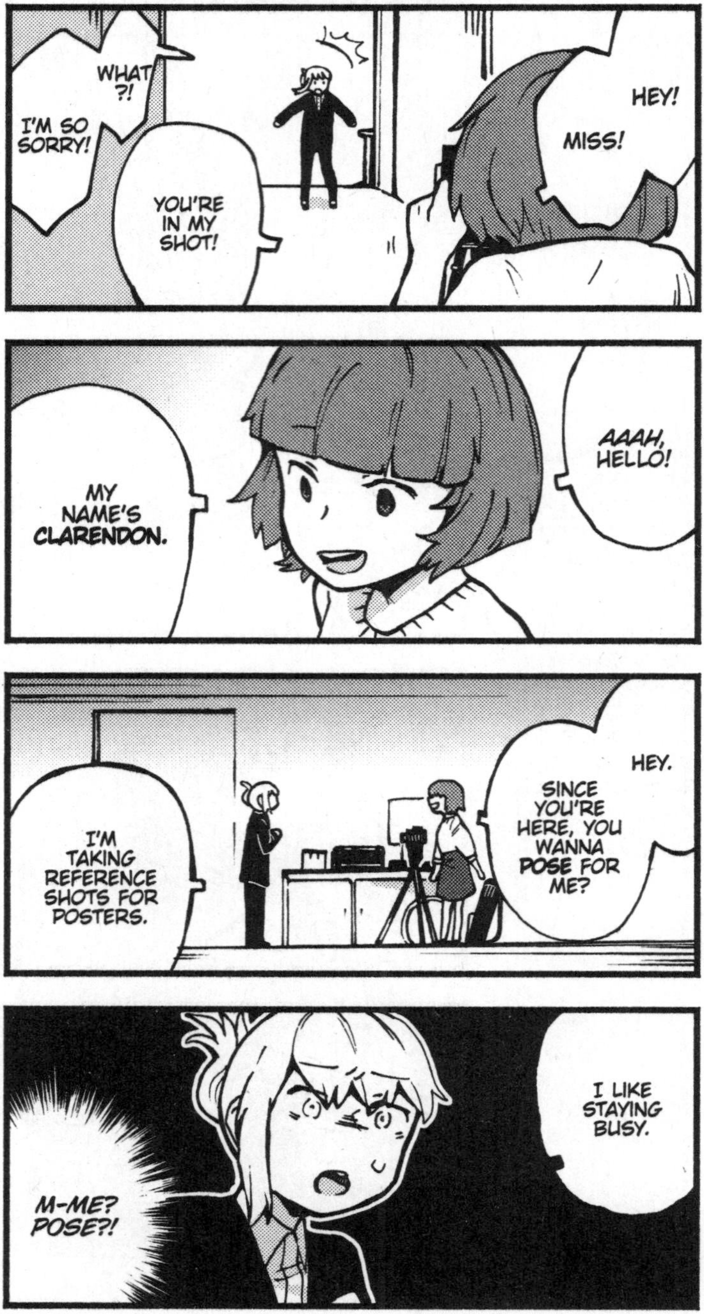
HEY!
MISS!
YOU'RE IN MY SHOT!
WHAT ?!
I'M SO SORRY!
AAAH, HELLO!
MY NAME'S **CLARENDON.**
HEY.
SINCE YOU'RE HERE, YOU WANNA **POSE** FOR ME?
I'M TAKING REFERENCE SHOTS FOR POSTERS.
I LIKE STAYING BUSY.
M-ME? POSE?!

Clarendon was created in 1845 by British typeface designer Robert Besley. In England at the beginning of the nineteenth century, thick typefaces cropped up that would be visible in posters and advertisements. After that, this style developed rapidly.

Multipurpose Clarendon

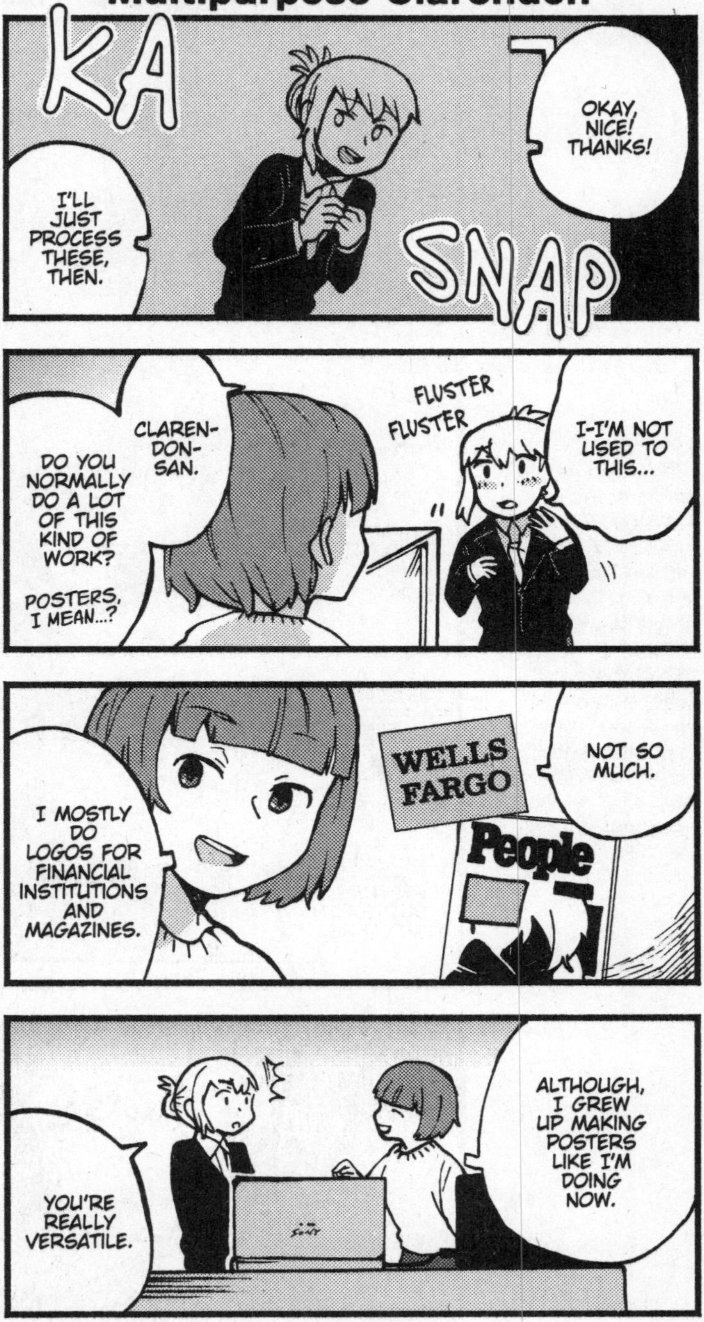
KA
OKAY, NICE! THANKS!
I'LL JUST PROCESS THESE, THEN.
SNAP
I-I'M NOT USED TO THIS...
FLUSTER FLUSTER
CLAREN-DON-SAN.
DO YOU NORMALLY DO A LOT OF THIS KIND OF WORK?
POSTERS, I MEAN...?
NOT SO MUCH.
WELLS FARGO
People
I MOSTLY DO LOGOS FOR FINANCIAL INSTITUTIONS AND MAGAZINES.
ALTHOUGH, I GREW UP MAKING POSTERS LIKE I'M DOING NOW.
YOU'RE REALLY VERSATILE.

Because it has slab serifs, Clarendon's form is close to roman type, but it also has a modern look, similar to the sans serif types. It's easy to match and use in a lot of places. One example is the logo of the American financial institution Wells Fargo.

Jack of All Trades

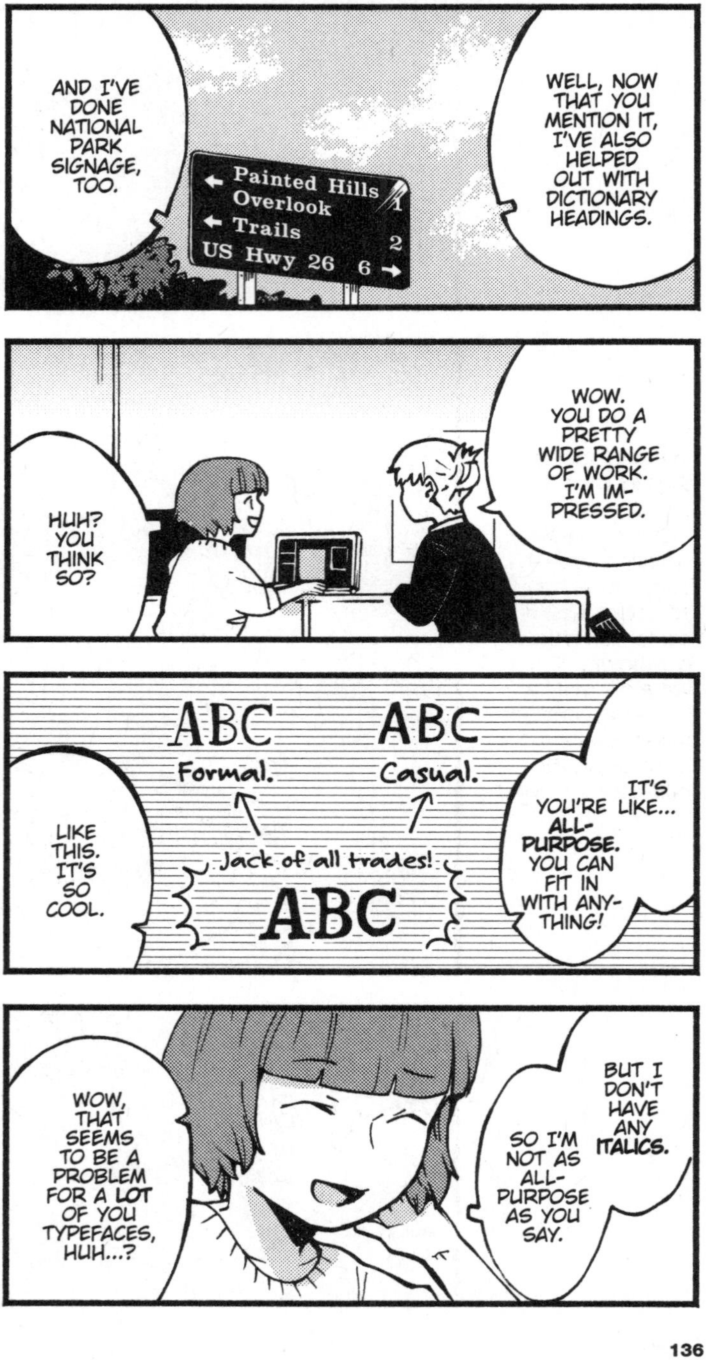
WELL, NOW THAT YOU MENTION IT, I'VE ALSO HELPED OUT WITH DICTIONARY HEADINGS.
Painted Hills Overlook 1
Trails 2
US Hwy 26 6
AND I'VE DONE NATIONAL PARK SIGNAGE, TOO.
WOW. YOU DO A PRETTY WIDE RANGE OF WORK. I'M IM-PRESSED.
HUH? YOU THINK SO?
IT'S YOU'RE LIKE... **ALL-PURPOSE.** YOU CAN FIT IN WITH ANY-THING!
ABC
Casual.
ABC
Formal.
Jack of all trades!
ABC
LIKE THIS. IT'S SO COOL.
BUT I DON'T HAVE ANY **ITALICS.**
SO I'M NOT AS ALL-PURPOSE AS YOU SAY.
WOW, THAT SEEMS TO BE A PROBLEM FOR A **LOT** OF YOU TYPEFACES, HUH...?

The characteristic features of Clarendon are the number 2 with its almost handwritten strokes, the way the end strokes of the legs slip up, and the large bowl-shaped terminal. The typeface didn't originally have italics, so several substitute types were created to compensate.

French Clarendon

CIRCUS
ALL DONE!
THANKS FOR YOUR HELP!
SO, THE POSTER'S FOR A CIRCUS, THEN?
YES, EXACTLY. IT BELONGS TO A RELATIVE.
HUNH...
THIS PHOTO IS REALLY DYNAMIC.
HA HA HA! YEAH, YA GOT ME.
I LIKE PIZAZZ. SOMETIMES I GET CARRIED AWAY...
IT'S YOUR PERSONALITY SHINING THROUGH~!

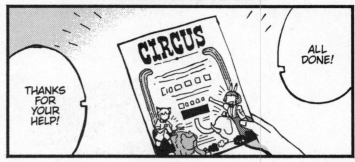

In the middle of the nineteenth century, the French Clarendon variation appeared. With a long body and emphasized serifs, its vertical characters were optimal for headlines, and the thicker serifs are symbolic of the mid-century mood.

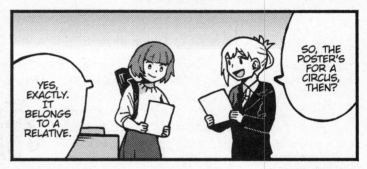

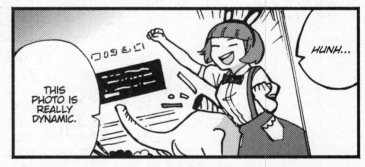

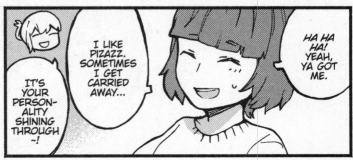

Clarendon

CATEGORY:	Roman
CLASSIFICATION:	Slab serif
YEAR OF CREATION:	1845
DESIGNER(S):	Robert Besley, Benjamin Fox
FOUNDRY:	Fann Street (England)

All-purpose style for use in formal or casual settings.

Clarendon was designed in 1845 by Robert Besley (1794–1876) and punch engraver Benjamin Fox (?–1877) of the type foundry Fann Street, which produced and sold advertising type for flyers and posters at the beginning of the nineteenth century. Because it has a tall x-height, thick strokes, and smooth joints between the serifs called "brackets" that resemble a frog's webbed feet, it had more intimacy and readability than the Egyptian type currently on the scene. Along with the Modern Romans, it was used in headlines or for emphasis (proper nouns, etc.) in a text, so it is said to have also exterminated the italic types that had been used for emphasis up to that point.

The first typeface to receive a three-year copyright protection, Clarendon spread throughout the world after that period ended. Through the 1950s and 1960s, it had a revival in the West and was used in advertisements for globalizing companies and products, where it gained popularity. The Sony corporate logo flattened the original proportions and turned them into a brand, a famous example of emulating the Clarendon style from the '60s.

USAGE EXAMPLES

□ Wells Fargo (American financial institution)

□ *People* (American magazine)

ABCDEFGHIJ KLMNOPQRS TUVWXYZ

abcdefghijklmn opqrstuvwxyz

0123456789

Clarendon LT Std Roman

Rockwell

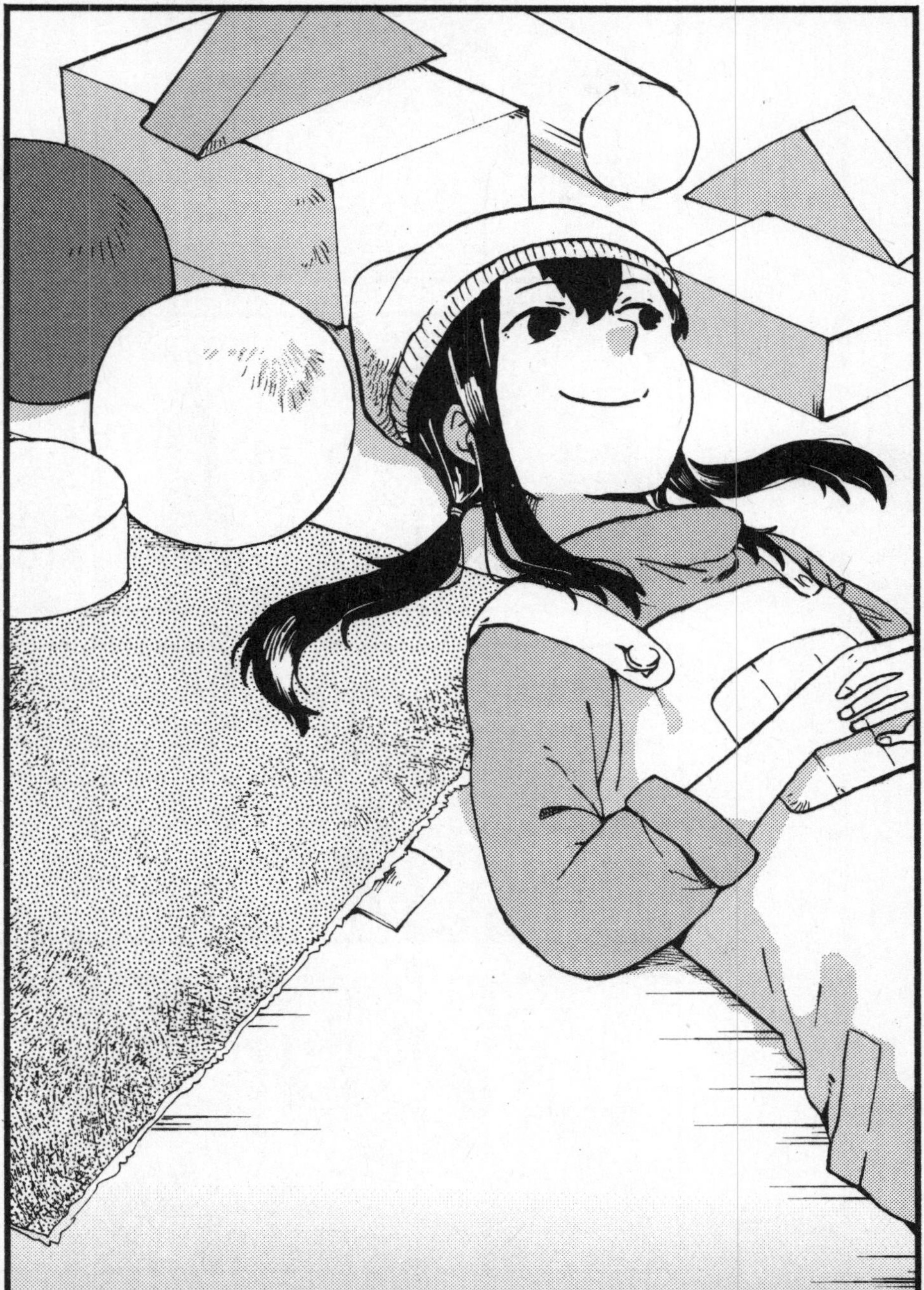

Stable slab serif

Kid-friendly

HM?
I HAVEN'T SEEN THAT BUILDING YET.
TAK
TAK TAK
ROCK-WEEEELL!
SO, THERE ARE KIDS HERE, TOO...
READ US A BOOK!
H-HELP...
CHATTER
CHATTER
YIKES!
THEY'RE MOBBING HER!!

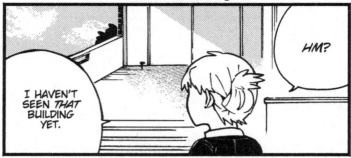

Rockwell was released by Monotype in 1934. Because it has a friendly, intimate feel, it is often used in books and other materials for children.

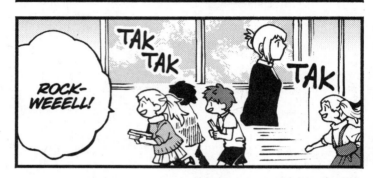

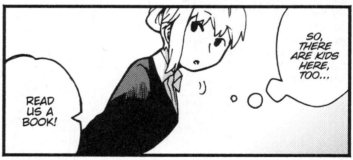

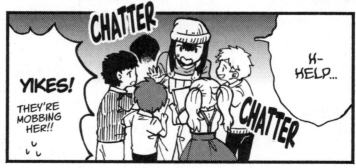

Hard to be a Slab Serif?

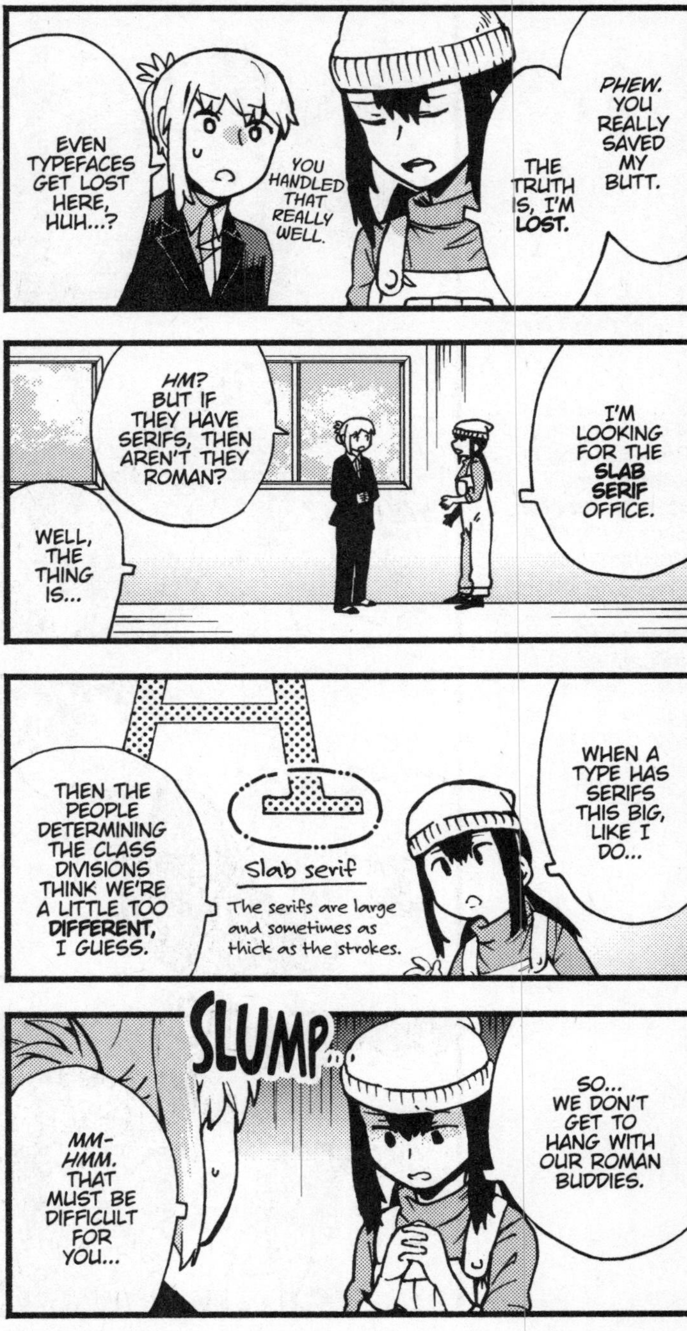
PHEW. YOU REALLY SAVED MY BUTT.
THE TRUTH IS, I'M LOST.
YOU HANDLED THAT REALLY WELL.
EVEN TYPEFACES GET LOST HERE, HUH...?
I'M LOOKING FOR THE SLAB SERIF OFFICE.
HM? BUT IF THEY HAVE SERIFS, THEN AREN'T THEY ROMAN?
WELL, THE THING IS...
WHEN A TYPE HAS SERIFS THIS BIG, LIKE I DO...
Slab serif
The serifs are large and sometimes as thick as the strokes.
THEN THE PEOPLE DETERMINING THE CLASS DIVISIONS THINK WE'RE A LITTLE TOO DIFFERENT, I GUESS.
SLUMP
SO... WE DON'T GET TO HANG WITH OUR ROMAN BUDDIES.
MM-HMM. THAT MUST BE DIFFICULT FOR YOU...

Rockwell falls into the category of "slab serif," or typefaces with square serifs. Because the thickness of the stroke and the serif are basically the same, they are sometimes treated as a separate, independent category from roman type.

Different Isn't Bad

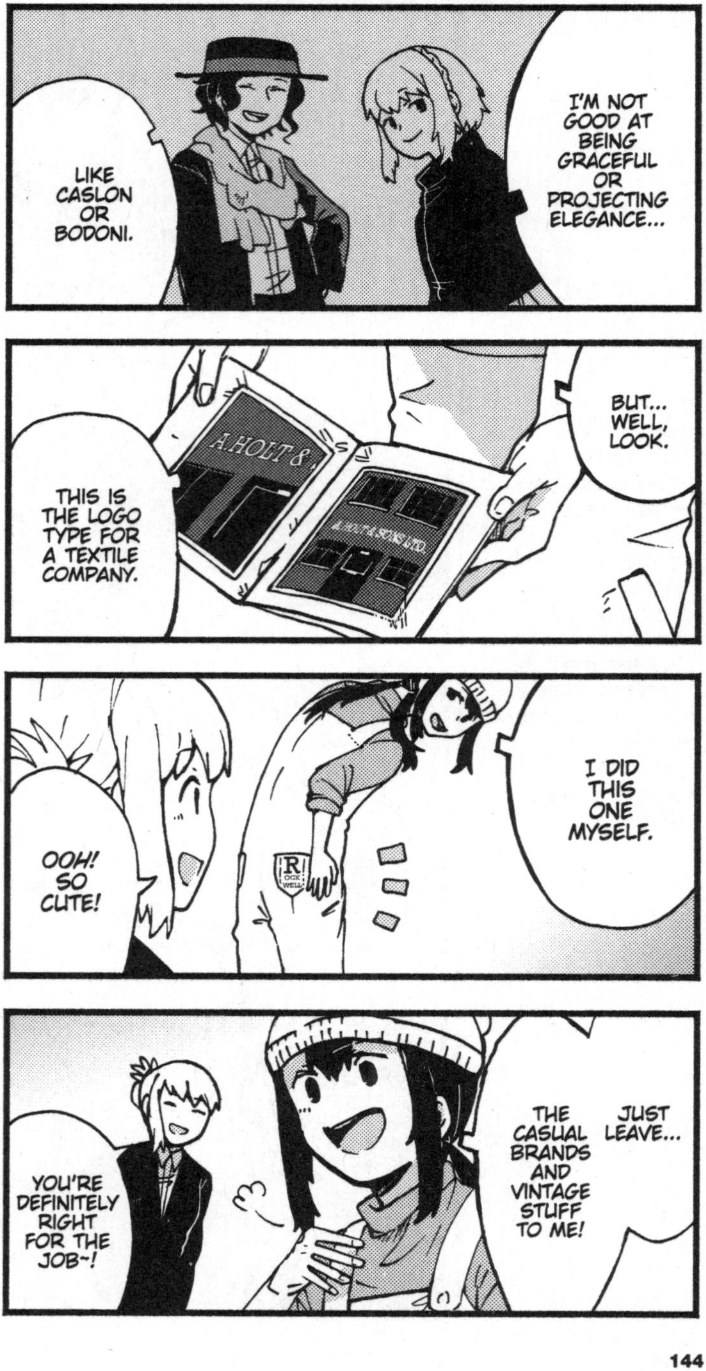
I'M NOT GOOD AT BEING GRACEFUL OR PROJECTING ELEGANCE...
LIKE CASLON OR BODONI.
BUT... WELL, LOOK.
THIS IS THE LOGO TYPE FOR A TEXTILE COMPANY.
A.HOLT &
A.HOLT & SONS LTD.
I DID THIS ONE MYSELF.
OOH! SO CUTE!
JUST LEAVE...
THE CASUAL BRANDS AND VINTAGE STUFF TO ME!
YOU'RE DEFINITELY RIGHT FOR THE JOB~!

The "slab" in slab serifs means a thick, rectangular plank. With its solid sense of stability combined with serifs, it projects an unusually casual image and is popular in vintage-style designs.

Sans Serif Hero

OOH...
SHE LOOKS JUST AS AWESOME AS EVER...
HM?
FUTURA-SAN?
YEAH.
SHE'S MY HERO.
RED | VENTURES
IF I HAD TO CHOOSE ...
I'D SAY I HAVE A LOT IN COMMON WITH THE SANS SERIFS.
ESPECIALLY SINCE ONE OF MY GOALS IS **HIGH VISIBILITY**, TOO.
Y'KNOW... I GUESS THAT'S WHY...
THE KIDS ALWAYS MANAGE TO TRACK ME DOWN, NO MATTER WHERE I GO!
FOR BETTER OR WORSE, SHE SURE MAKES AN IMPACT!!

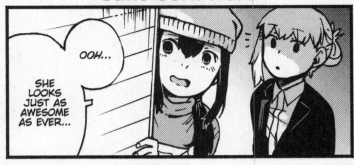

As can be seen in the uppercase *O* and *Q*, Rockwell's structure is geometrical. This is a typeface with high visibility, suited to headlines just like many sans serifs such as Futura and Franklin Gothic.

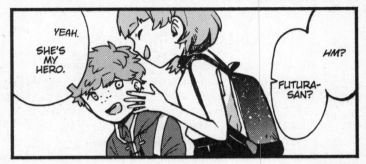

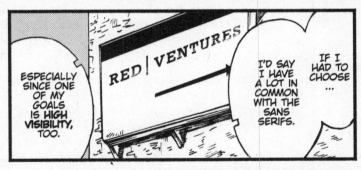

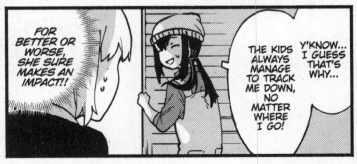

Rockwell

CATEGORY:	Roman
CLASSIFICATION:	Slab serif
YEAR OF CREATION:	1934
DESIGNER(S):	Frank Hinman Pierpoint
FOUNDRY:	Monotype (England)

Stable, projects a friendly feel.

Due to Napoleon's campaign in Egypt, attempts to "rediscover" ancient Egypt were popular at the end of the eighteenth century. This also applied to print type, leading to the appearance of "slab serifs," or square serifs that resembled stone slabs—typefaces with these serifs were called "Egyptian." Through the nineteenth century and the development of advertising, Egyptian type came to be widely used on flyers, advertisements, and theatrical posters. After World War I, Egyptian type saw renewed popularity in Europe where a movement to modernize design reached its peak around 1930. New typefaces such as Memphis, City, Beton, and Stymie were released one after the other.

The latecomer Rockwell is a perfected Egyptian type designed in 1934 by Frank Hinman Pierpoint (1860–1937) of the British Monotype Corporation. Like the sans serifs of the time, it has a geometrical structure, and all the strokes are of a uniform thickness. This allowed it to gain popularity for displays projecting a modern, exotic image. A characteristic feature is the serif on the apex of the uppercase *A*.

USAGE EXAMPLES
....
□ A. Holt & Sons (London fabric production and sales company)

ABCDEFGHIJ
KLMNOPQRS
TUVWXYZ
abcdefghijklmn
opqrstuvwxyz
0123456789

Rockwell Std Regular

Centaur • Jenson

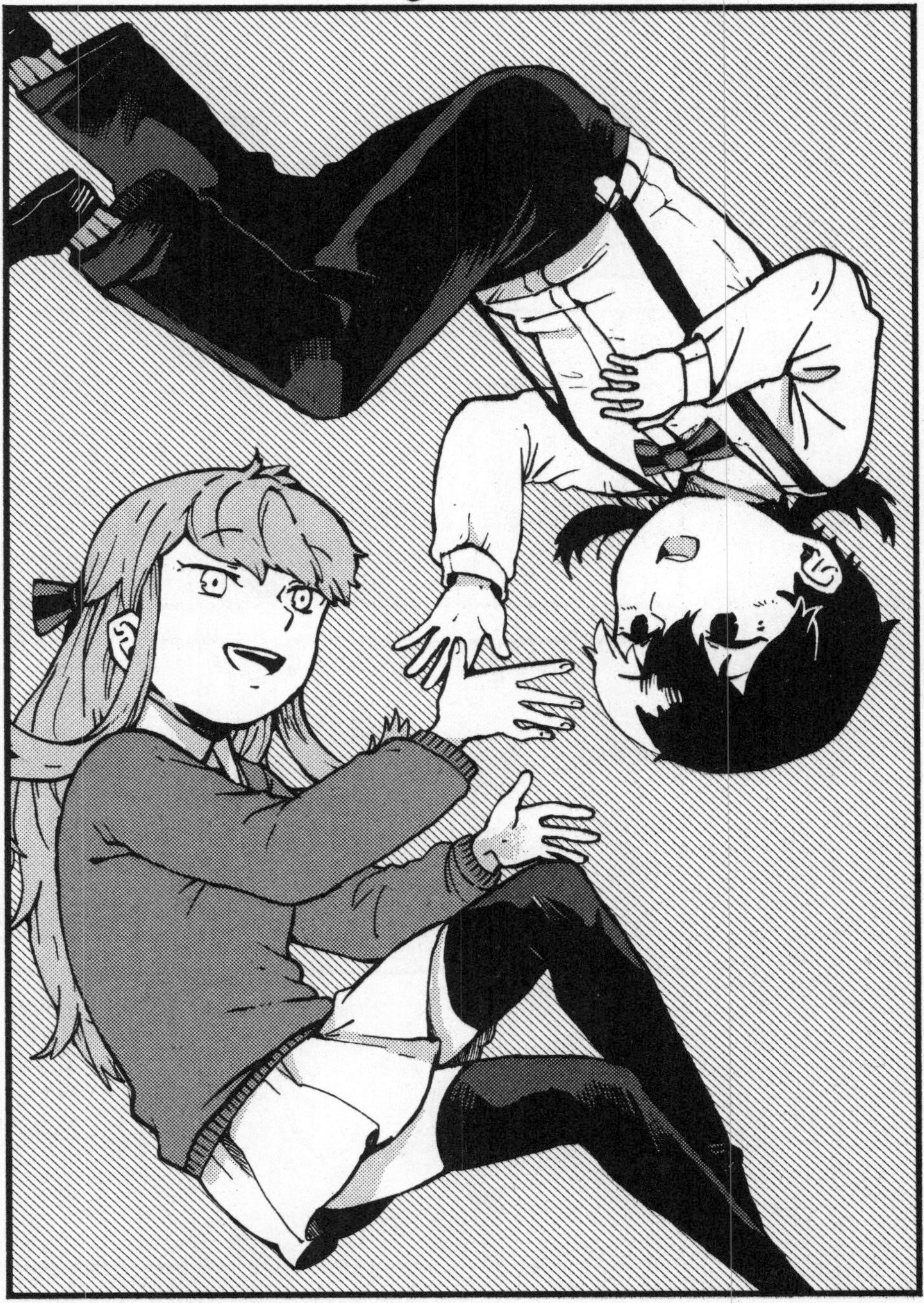

Traditional handwritten Venetian Roman

Art-loving Centaur

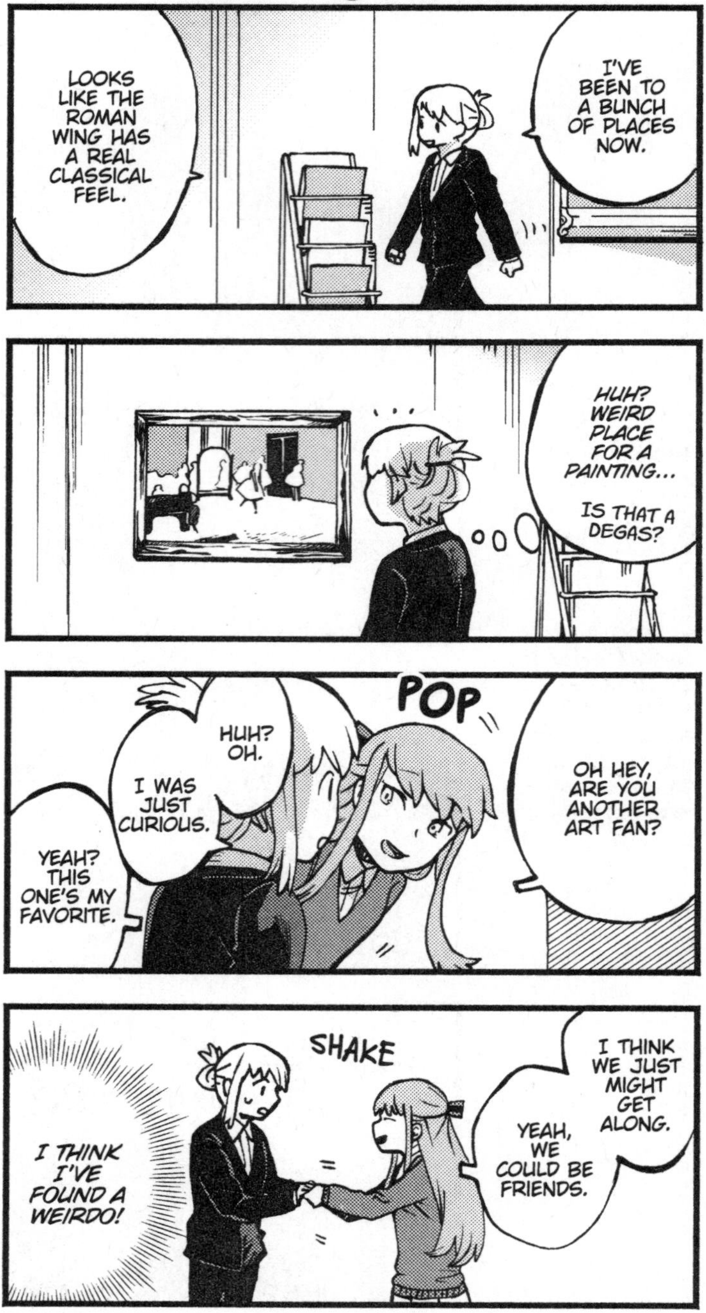
I'VE BEEN TO A BUNCH OF PLACES NOW.
LOOKS LIKE THE ROMAN WING HAS A REAL CLASSICAL FEEL.
HUH? WEIRD PLACE FOR A PAINTING...
IS THAT A DEGAS?
POP
OH HEY, ARE YOU ANOTHER ART FAN?
HUH? OH.
I WAS JUST CURIOUS.
YEAH? THIS ONE'S MY FAVORITE.
I THINK WE JUST MIGHT GET ALONG.
SHAKE
YEAH, WE COULD BE FRIENDS.
I THINK I'VE FOUND A WEIRDO!

Centaur is based on a typeface by Nicolas Jenson, who operated a press in Venice, from around 1470. Produced in 1914 by American book designer Bruce Rogers, it was revived for use at the Metropolitan Museum of Art in New York City.

Traces of a Bygone Era

AND YOU ARE...?
ME? I'M CENTAUR.
AND YOU... YOU'RE NOT A TYPEFACE, ARE YOU?
NO. I'M NOT.
I GUESS I'M A NEW DESIGNER?
HEE HEE!
SO, YOU DON'T KNOW ABOUT ME, THEN?
I SUPPOSE IT'S BEEN QUITE A LONG TIME, AFTER ALL...
SINCE HAND-WRITTEN AND PRINTED CHARACTERS LIVED SIDE-BY-SIDE.
MOST OF THE TYPEFACES AROUND HERE ARE MY *PROTÉGÉS*, SO PLEASE BE NICE TO THEM.
WHO IS SHE?! WHO IS THIS PERSON?
I'M GETTING THE IMPRESSION SHE'S A BIG DEAL!!

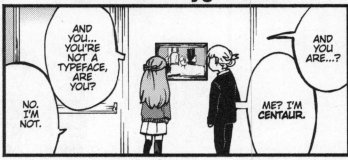

The contrast in strokes in Centaur is weak, and a strong air of handwriting remains in it. Features of this typeface are the slanted bar on the lowercase *e*, and sharp serifs with a diagonal incline, reminiscent of the time when the letters were written by hand.

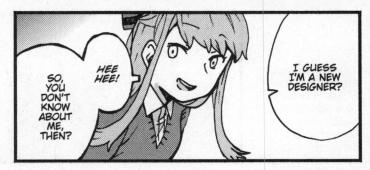

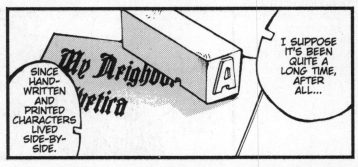

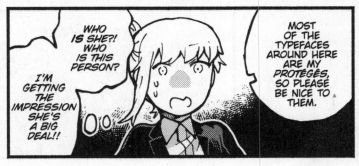

Long History

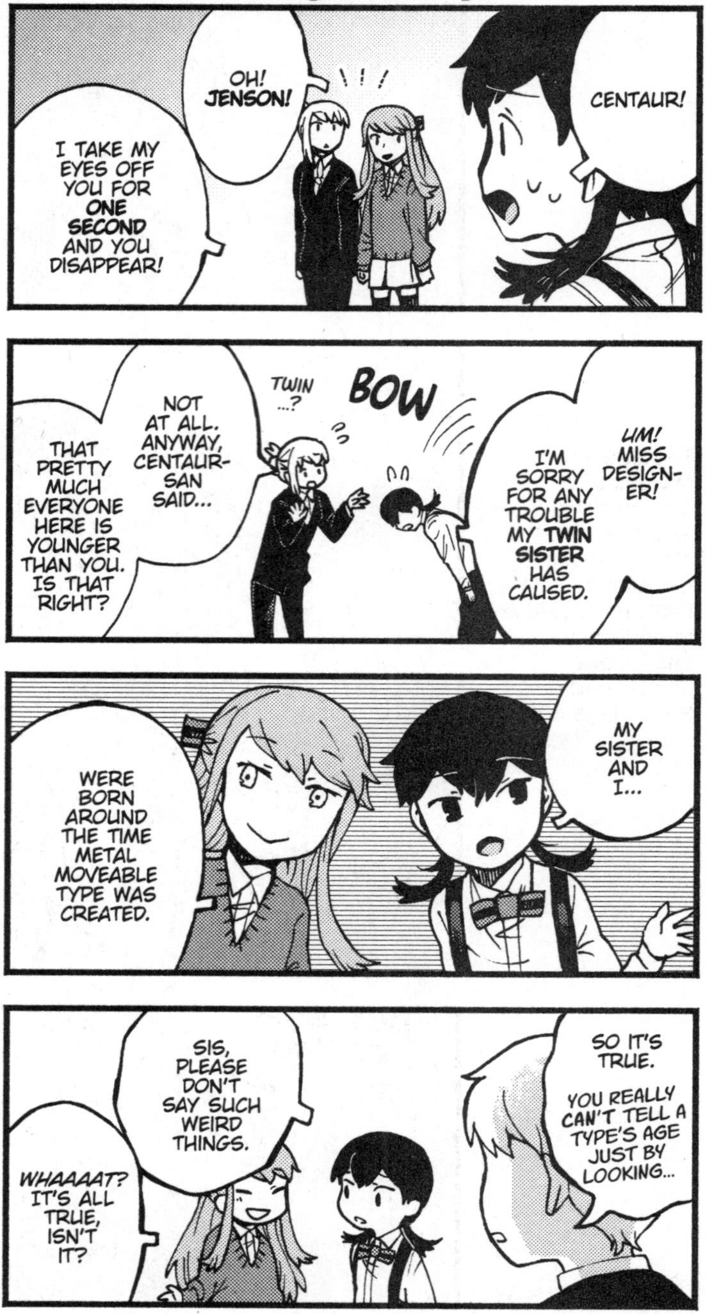
CENTAUR!
OH! JENSON!
I TAKE MY EYES OFF YOU FOR ONE SECOND AND YOU DISAPPEAR!
UM! MISS DESIGNER!
I'M SORRY FOR ANY TROUBLE MY TWIN SISTER HAS CAUSED.
BOW
TWIN ...?
NOT AT ALL. ANYWAY, CENTAUR-SAN SAID...
THAT PRETTY MUCH EVERYONE HERE IS YOUNGER THAN YOU. IS THAT RIGHT?
MY SISTER AND I...
WERE BORN AROUND THE TIME METAL MOVEABLE TYPE WAS CREATED.
SO IT'S TRUE.
YOU REALLY CAN'T TELL A TYPE'S AGE JUST BY LOOKING...
SIS, PLEASE DON'T SAY SUCH WEIRD THINGS.
WHAAAAT? IT'S ALL TRUE, ISN'T IT?

Jenson is a type revived from the typeface created by Nicolas Jenson, like Centaur. These two are categorized as Venetian Roman, which formed the basis for many roman types.

Jenson's Got it Together

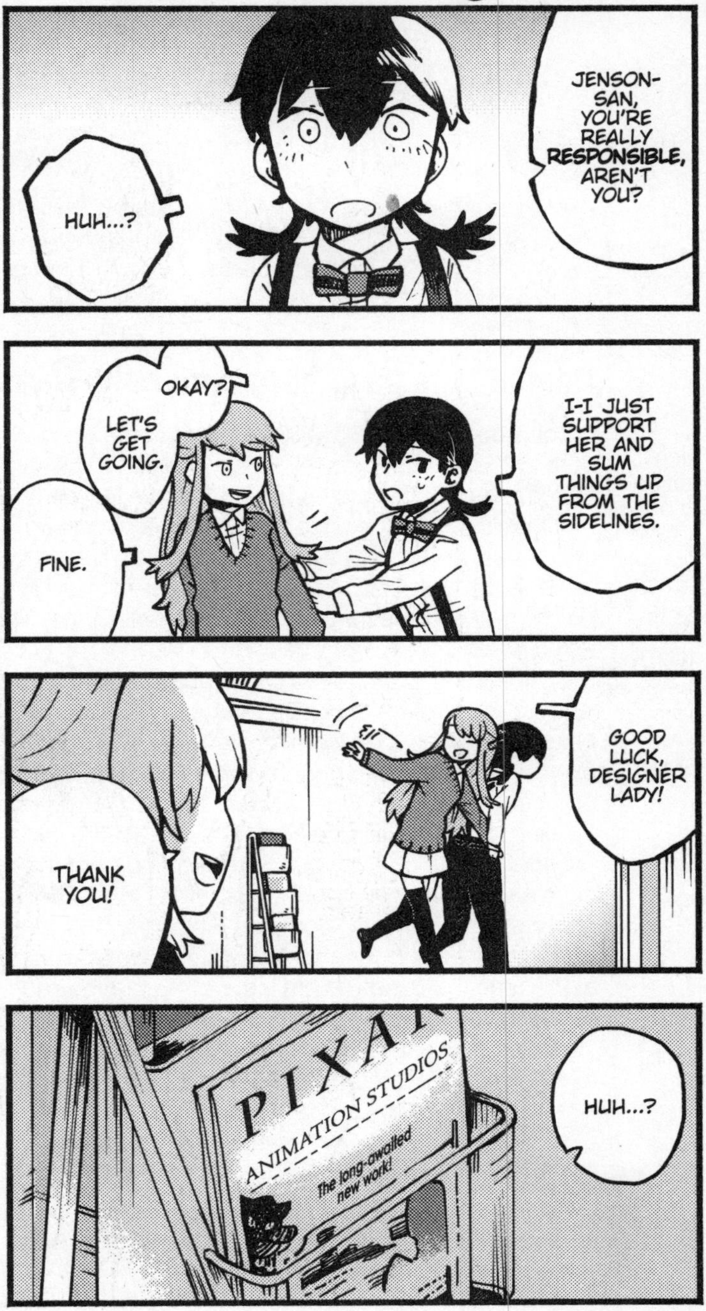
JENSON-SAN, YOU'RE REALLY RESPONSIBLE, AREN'T YOU?
HUH...?
I-I JUST SUPPORT HER AND SUM THINGS UP FROM THE SIDELINES.
OKAY?
LET'S GET GOING.
FINE.
GOOD LUCK, DESIGNER LADY!
THANK YOU!
HUH...?
PIXA
ANIMATION STUDIOS
The long-awaited new work!

The letterforms of Centaur and Jenson closely resemble each other. Jenson has a thicker frame that's more suited to body text, and it's also used in part of Pixar's logo.

Centaur   Jenson

CATEGORY:	Roman	Roman
CLASSIFICATION:	Venetian	Venetian
YEAR OF CREATION:	1915 (1470)	1996 (1470)
DESIGNER(S):	Bruce Rogers (Nicolas Jenson)	Robert Slimbach (Nicolas Jenson)
FOUNDRY:	Monotype (England)	Adobe (USA)

Roman type base born during the Renaissance.

Nicolas Jenson (1420–1480), Master of the Royal French Mint, was sent to Mainz, Germany by King Charles VII in the middle of the fifteenth century where he is said to have learned the new printing technique using moveable metal type. It's unclear as to whether or not he learned directly from Gutenberg, but he brought this skill to Venice and in 1470 he completed the roman type deemed to be the greatest masterpiece of the Renaissance. The lowercase letters were copied from the written form of the Humanists, while the uppercase letters were constructed with graceful proportions, lending the type an exquisite readability compared with the earlier blackletter types. Jenson's typeface was named Venetian, and over the following five hundred years, it became the exemplar of a beautiful roman type, revived by many successors. One of those successors, Bruce Rogers (1870–1957), was a brilliant twentieth-century American typeface and book designer. In his days as a young newspaper illustrator, Rogers was influenced by the designs of William Morris and incorporated them into his book designs. Rejecting the modernism that was fashionable in Europe at the time, he used the old letterforms of types such as Caslon and devoted himself to the creation of traditional printed matter. In 1901, he devised the Montaigne type, modeled after Jenson, and further refined it to complete Centaur in 1915.

USAGE EXAMPLES
....

□ Centaur: Oxford Lectern Bible (1935, used for body text. Bruce Rogers worked on the book design, and it is deemed one of the twentieth century's most beautiful bibles.)

□ Jenson: Pixar Animation Studios (used in part of the logo)

ABCDEFGHIJ
KLMNOPQRS
TUVWXYZ
abcdefghijklmn
opqrstuvwxyz
0123456789 Centaur MT Std Regular

ABCDEFGHIJ
KLMNOPQRS
TUVWXYZ
abcdefghijklmn
opqrstuvwxyz
0123456789 Adobe Jenson Pro Regular

Roman Type Commentary

"Roman" refers to typefaces with serifs at the ends of letters. Because the thickness of the strokes and the serifs is different, roman typefaces have a strong contrast, making them suitable for body texts and easy to read even in longer texts. They are also used in headlines, but since the thickness of the strokes is not uniform, visibility drops when they are seen from a distance.

VENETIAN
Earliest roman type. Traditional with traces of handwritten form.
Ex. Centaur, Jenson

ABC123
Centaur

OLD STYLE
Developed from Venetian.
Gives an elegant, formal impression.
Ex. Garamond, Caslon

ABC123
Garamond

TRANSITIONAL
Positioned in between old and modern styles.
Ex. Baskerville, Times New Roman

ABC123
Times New Roman

MODERN STYLE
Roman types with extreme difference in thickness of vertical and horizontal strokes. Refined form.
Ex. Bodoni, Didot

ABC123
Bodoni

SLAB SERIF
Roman types with slab serifs.
Casual feel.
Ex. Rockwell, Clarendon

ABC123
Rockwell

SERIF TYPES

Garamond

H

Bodoni

H

Rockwell

H

BRACKET SERIF
Smooth connection between serif and stem. Seen in many traditional typefaces.

HAIRLINE SERIF
Extremely thin serif lines. Seen in many modern typefaces.

SLAB SERIF
Serif thicknesses are the same as the character lines. Excellent visibility.

Caslon

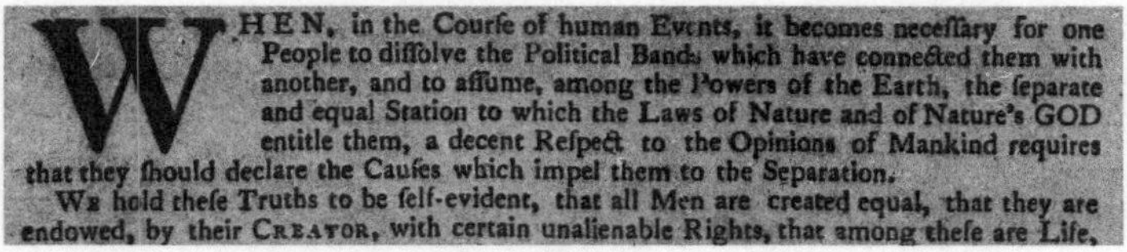

W HEN, in the Courſe of human Events, it becomes neceſſary for one People to diſſolve the Political Bands which have connected them with another, and to aſſume, among the Powers of the Earth, the ſeparate and equal Station to which the Laws of Nature and of Nature's GOD entitle them, a decent Reſpect to the Opinions of Mankind requires that they ſhould declare the Cauſes which impel them to the Separation.

We hold theſe Truths to be ſelf-evident, that all Men are created equal, that they are endowed, by their CREATOR, with certain unalienable Rights, that among theſe are Life,

U.S. Declaration of Independence (1776)
Source: Library of Congress

Clarendon

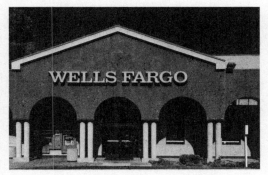

Exterior of a Wells Fargo bank in California, USA

Q What's the difference between a font and a typeface?

A Broadly speaking, both fonts and typefaces describe characters, but they each mean something slightly different. A typeface is a particular style of characters that follow fixed design rules, while a font is the complete set of characters in that design, including those used digitally and adjusted for size, weight, and other considerations, with a full complement of characters such as Japanese text, Western text, symbols, and numbers.

Additionally, there is the term "typography," a printing/design term which means the arrangement of characters (type). Typography refers to the technique of selecting the typeface that best meets the objective of the text, then expressing and combining the characters to be printed. The term arose with the invention of printing techniques in the fifteenth century. Currently, it also means typeface design and production, and design through printing methods.

What the Font?!
A Manga Guide to Western Typeface

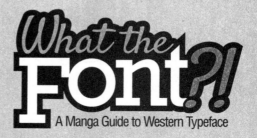

PART 3

Other Types–Script, Display, Blackletter

SCRIPT:

Zapfino

Mistral

Comic Sans

DISPLAY:

Trajan

Peignot

BLACKLETTER:

Fette Fraktur

Other Type Notes

Script Type

Zapfino

Mysterious girl.
Elegant, like the fluttering of the wind.

Mistral

Very likeable.
Cooks for Optima's café.

Comic Sans

Easygoing kid.
Good with computers and manga.

Display Type

TRAJAN

Upstanding, elegant beauty.
Speaks archaically and is proud of her long legs.

PEIGNOT

A real lone wolf.
His artistic sense is bar none.

Blackletter Type

Fette Fraktur

A fantastical dresser.
Renovating a room into a refuge.

Zapfino • Mistral

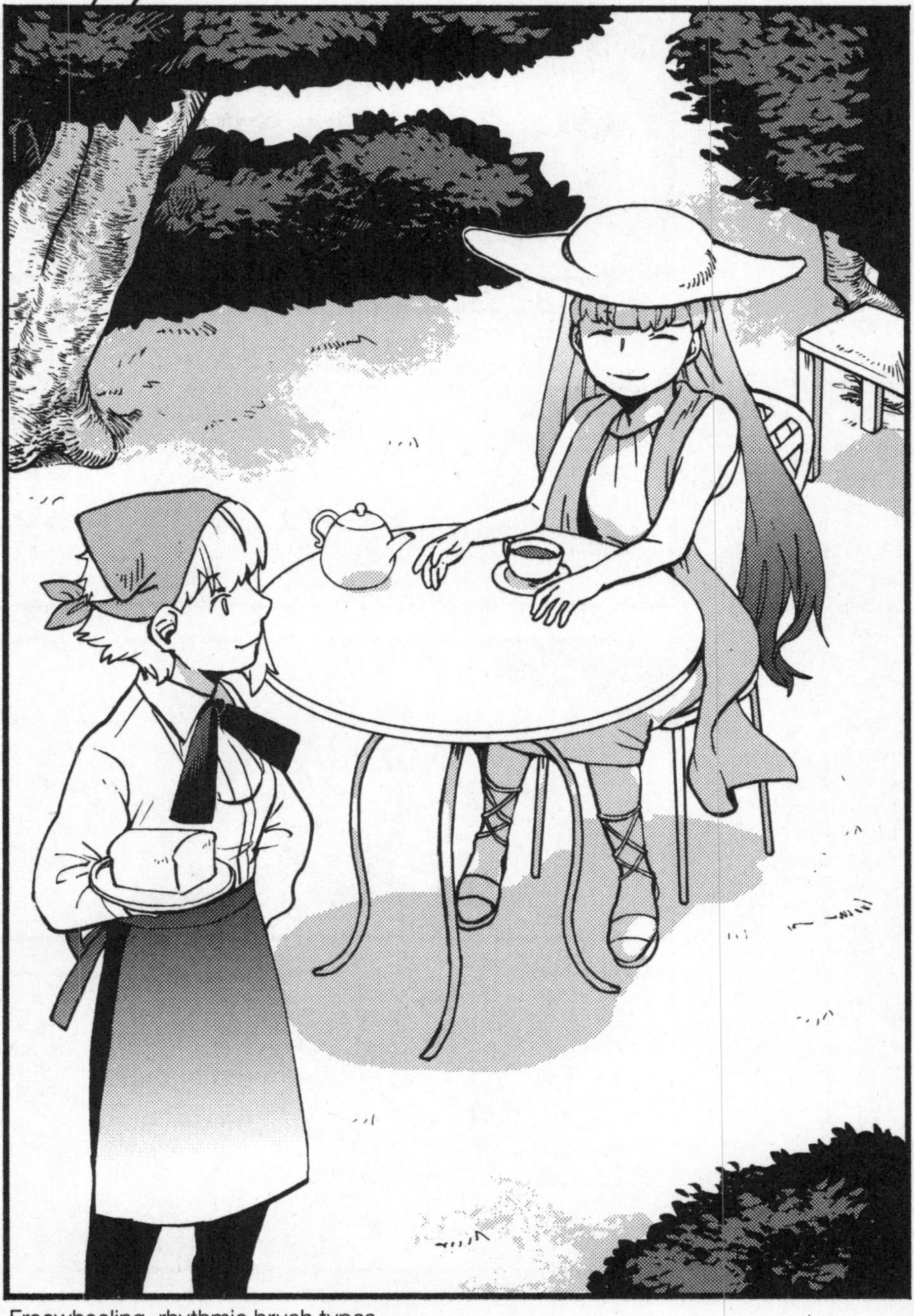

Freewheeling, rhythmic brush types

Free Spirit

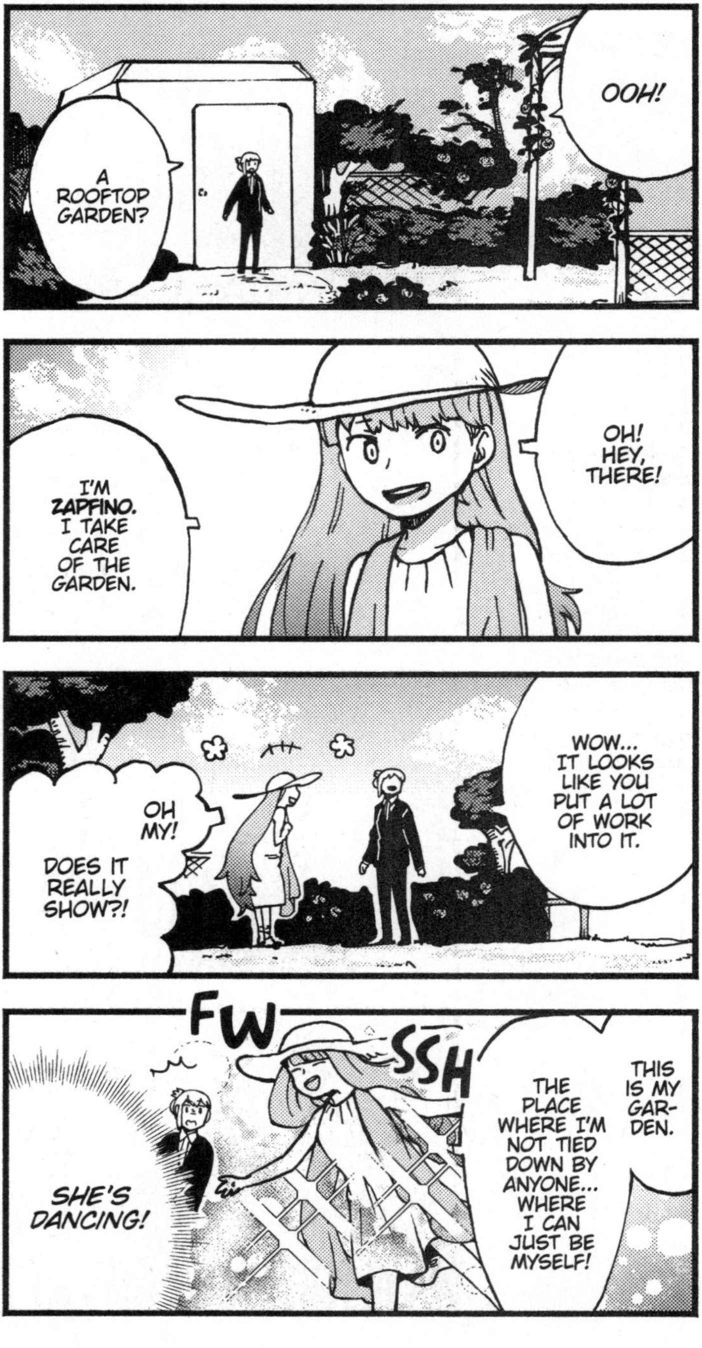
OOH!
A ROOFTOP GARDEN?
OH! HEY, THERE!
I'M ZAPFINO. I TAKE CARE OF THE GARDEN.
WOW... IT LOOKS LIKE YOU PUT A LOT OF WORK INTO IT.
OH MY!
DOES IT REALLY SHOW?!
THIS IS MY GARDEN.
FWSSH
THE PLACE WHERE I'M NOT TIED DOWN BY ANYONE... WHERE I CAN JUST BE MYSELF!
SHE'S DANCING!

Zapfino was released in 1998. The typeface environment had shifted from letterpresses using molds to phototypesetting and then to digital fonts, and the new lack of restrictions on the size and width of characters made possible a freeform look that was closer to handwriting than ever before.

What's a Script Type?

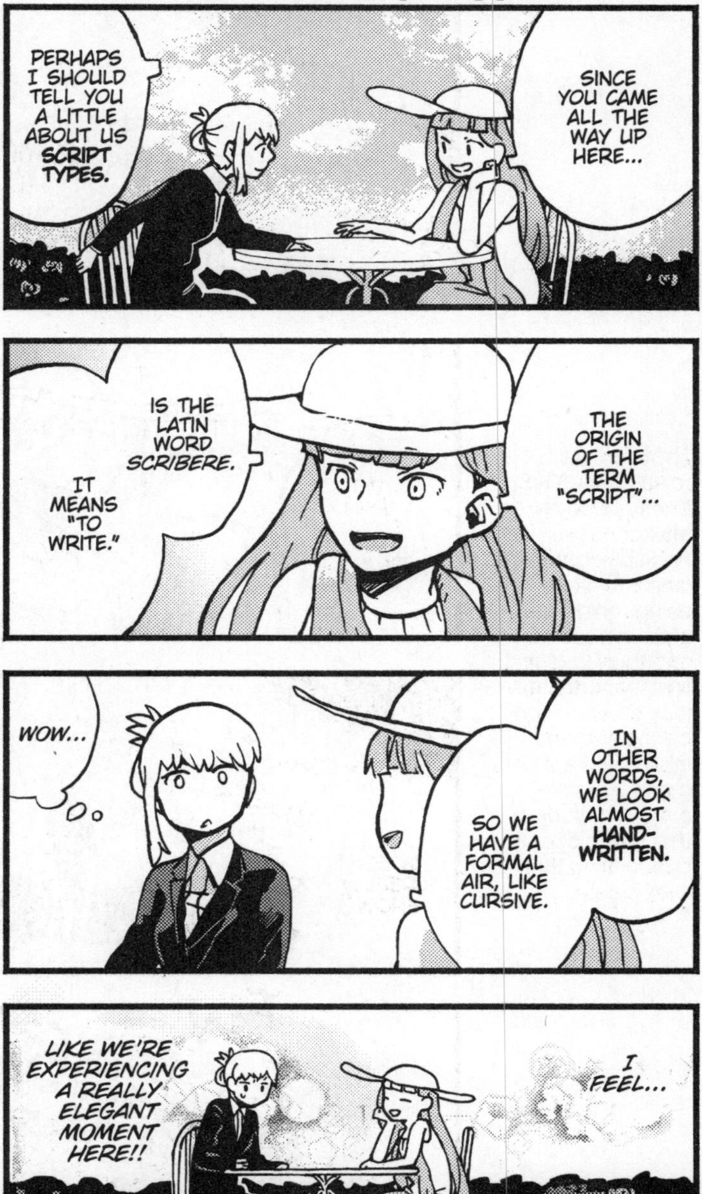
SINCE YOU CAME ALL THE WAY UP HERE...
PERHAPS I SHOULD TELL YOU A LITTLE ABOUT US **SCRIPT TYPES.**
THE ORIGIN OF THE TERM "SCRIPT"...
IS THE LATIN WORD *SCRIBERE.*
IT MEANS "TO WRITE."
IN OTHER WORDS, WE LOOK ALMOST **HAND-WRITTEN.**
SO WE HAVE A FORMAL AIR, LIKE CURSIVE.
WOW...
I FEEL...
LIKE WE'RE EXPERIENCING A REALLY ELEGANT MOMENT HERE!!

Typefaces with a form using handwritten brush strokes are put into a category called script types. Zapfino makes an elegant impression and bears the name of German calligrapher and typeface designer Hermann Zapf.

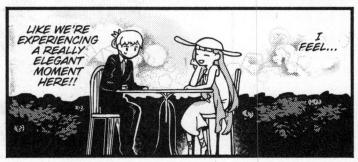

Breaking Bread Together

OH, HEY! HI THERE!
HOW ABOUT SOME FRESHLY BAKED BREAD?
OH MY! MISTRAL!
MY FRIEND HERE...
SHE'S A SCRIPT TYPE TOO, LIKE ME.
LIKE YOU...?
MMM, THAT'S RIGHT.
EVERYONE'S HAND-WRITING IS TOTALLY DIFFERENT, YES?
WE'RE LIKE THAT, TOO. WE EACH HAVE OUR OWN SPECIAL FEATURES.
Senpai
Good morning.
Marusu
Good morning.
OH, I GET IT NOW.
OUR PERSON-ALITIES ARE TOTALLY DIFFERENT, BUT WE GET ALONG OKAY.
WHAT WAS THAT SAYING...? "THOSE WHO EAT BREAD FROM THE SAME OVEN"?
COM-PANY!

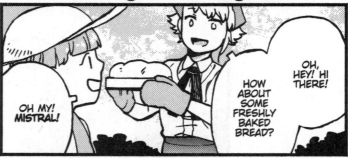

There are a variety of script typeface forms. Because Mistral—developed in 1953—has a casual look, it is often used in places like the menus of cafés and restaurants.

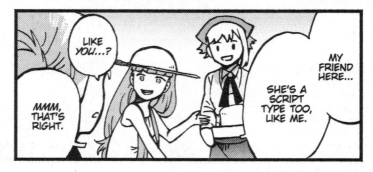

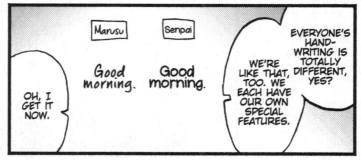

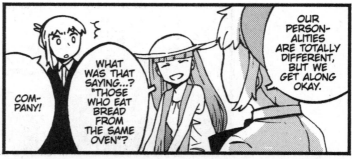

※The origin of the word "company" is thought to be "people who eat bread together."

Comfortable Together

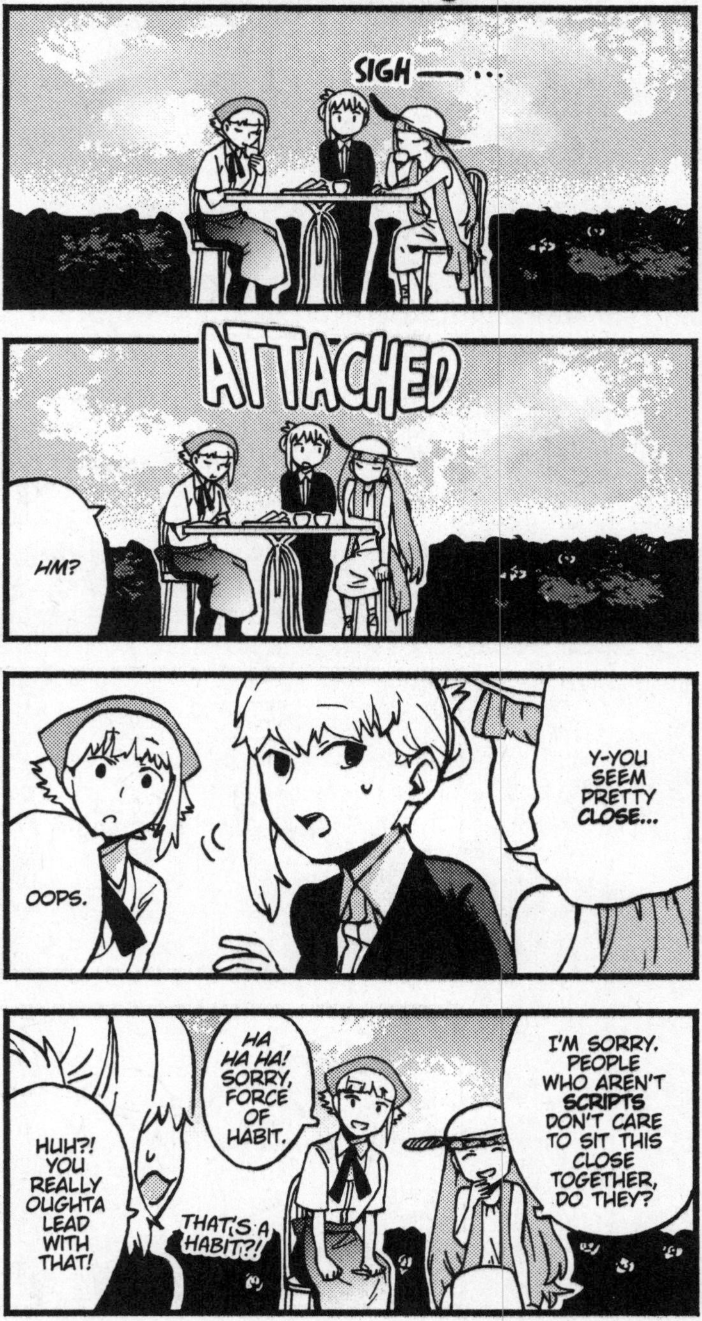
SIGH—...
ATTACHED
HM?
Y-YOU SEEM PRETTY CLOSE...
OOPS.
I'M SORRY. PEOPLE WHO AREN'T SCRIPTS DON'T CARE TO SIT THIS CLOSE TOGETHER, DO THEY?
HA HA HA! SORRY, FORCE OF HABIT.
THAT'S A HABIT?!
HUH?! YOU REALLY OUGHTA LEAD WITH THAT!

Because there are noticeable traces of the handwritten form in script types, each letter connects to the one before and behind it where the brush comes in and drops out. In order to get a smooth brushstroke with metal type, a ligature was necessary, but digital OpenType fonts can connect neighboring letters in a natural fashion.

Zapfino   *Mistral*

CATEGORY:	Script	Script
YEAR OF CREATION:	1998	1953
DESIGNER(S):	Hermann Zapf	Roger Excoffon
FOUNDRY:	Linotype (Germany)	Fonderie Olive (France)

Almost handwritten, as though jotted down with a pen or brush.

Zapfino was produced by modern German calligrapher and typeface designer Hermann Zapf (1918–2015). When he was younger, Zapf studied independently using texts by Rudolph Koch and Edward Johnston, and learned about engraving and printing techniques. He devised a script type based on sketches he drew during World War II for map creation, but it was not made a reality for quite some time. He developed the type along with the Linotype Company and released it in 1998 as a script type in line with the digital age. Composed of a three-level alphabet and a variety of ligatures, along with decorative characters and symbols, this font makes free use of OpenType technology for a dynamic, calligraphic look.

Mistral was completed in 1953 by Roger Excoffon (1910–1983), the graphic designer and typeface designer representative of twentieth-century France, for the Fonderie Olive. After studying law at university, Excoffon moved to Paris and apprenticed at a print shop. Later, he launched a design company and became the director of Fonderie Olive where he designed display typefaces that became emblematic of the mid-century style. Mistral takes the shape of the easily flowing ink from an energetic pen or brush. This sense of fluidity is its main feature.

USAGE EXAMPLES
....
□ Popular in menus at cafés and restaurants.

ABCDEFGHI
JKLMNOPQR
STUVWXYZ
abcdefghijklmn
opqrstuvwxyz
0123456789

Zapfino Regular

ABCDEFGHI
JKLMNOPQR
STUVWXYZ
abcdefghijklmn
opqrstuvwxyz
0123456789

Mistral Roman

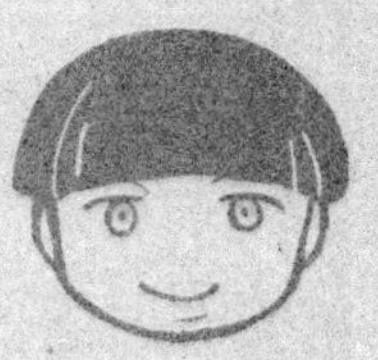

Comic Sans

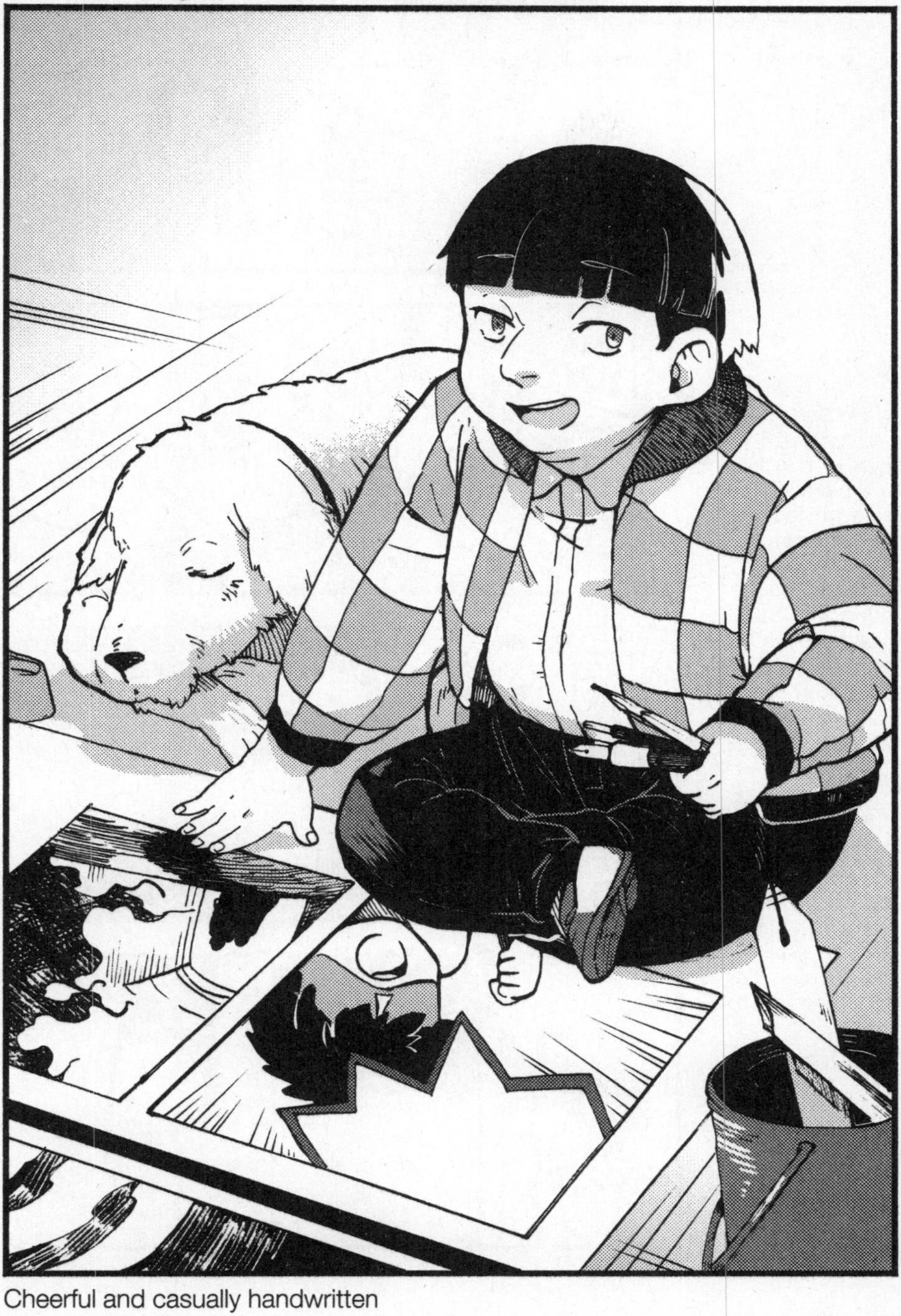

Cheerful and casually handwritten

Jump Scare

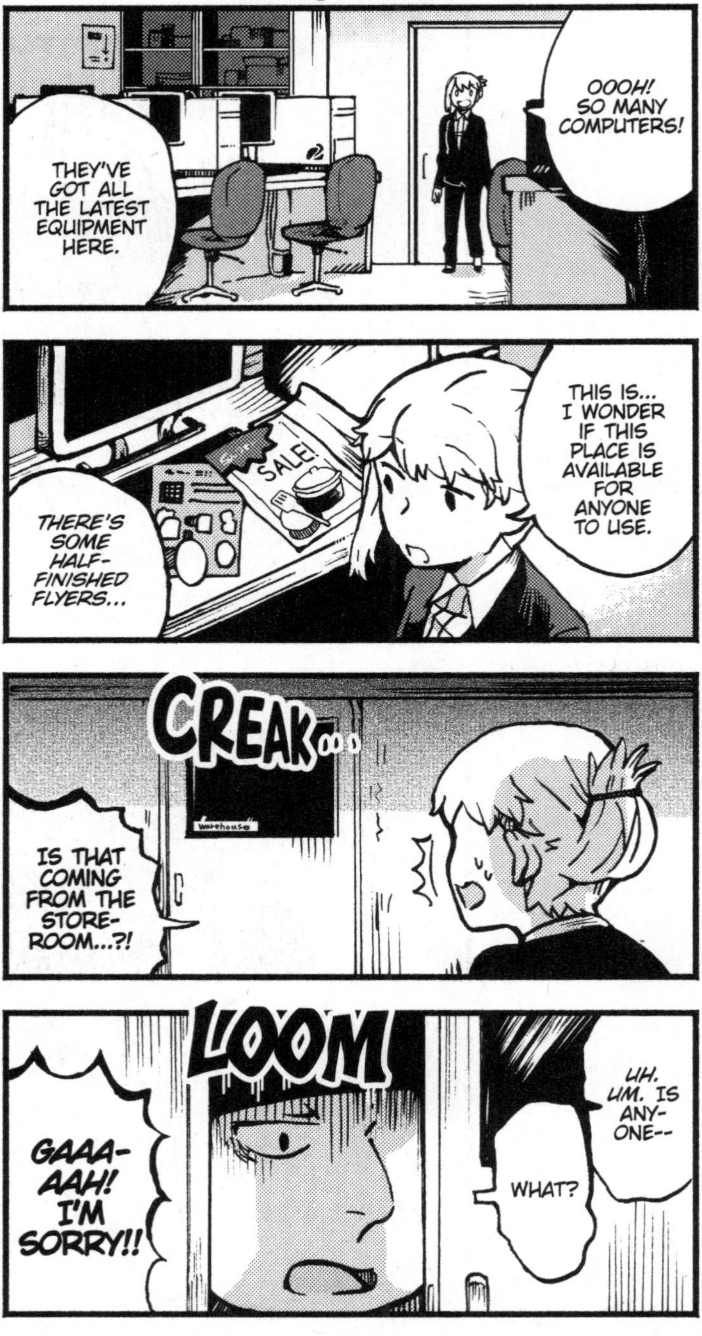
OOOH! SO MANY COMPUTERS!
THEY'VE GOT ALL THE LATEST EQUIPMENT HERE.
THIS IS... I WONDER IF THIS PLACE IS AVAILABLE FOR ANYONE TO USE.
SALE!
THERE'S SOME HALF-FINISHED FLYERS...
CREAK...
warehouse
IS THAT COMING FROM THE STORE-ROOM...?!
LOOM
UH. UM. IS ANY-ONE--
WHAT?
GAAA-AAH! I'M SORRY!!

Comic Sans is a typeface developed in 1995 for Windows95. Its playful form is often spotted in projects where a designer or specialist is not involved, such as in hospitals, schools, or on supermarket flyers.

Heartwarming

I ALWAYS HANG OUT THERE WHEN I'M STUCK FOR IDEAS...
WHAT WERE YOU DOING?
I WAS DRAWING COMICS. FOR FUN.
THAT'S ALSO WHERE I CAME FROM, SO, YA KNOW.
WOW...
SO, IS THIS ALL REFERENCE MATERIAL?
LOT OF SUPER-HERO STUFF...
HERE'S THE BOOK I'M WORKING ON NOW.
The Famous Dog
By Comic Sans
SO CUTE!

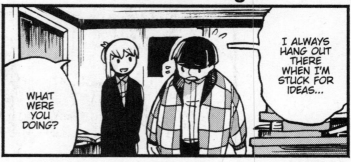

Comic Sans was created in 1994 by Vincent Connare, then a designer at Microsoft. It referenced the letterforms in the word balloons of comic books such as those from Marvel and DC.

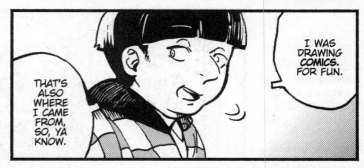

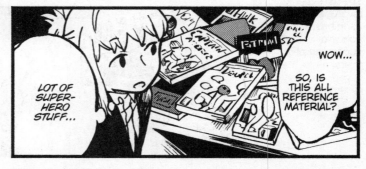

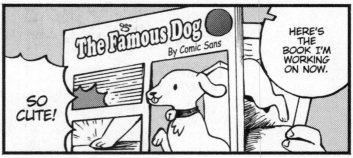

A Tiny Problem

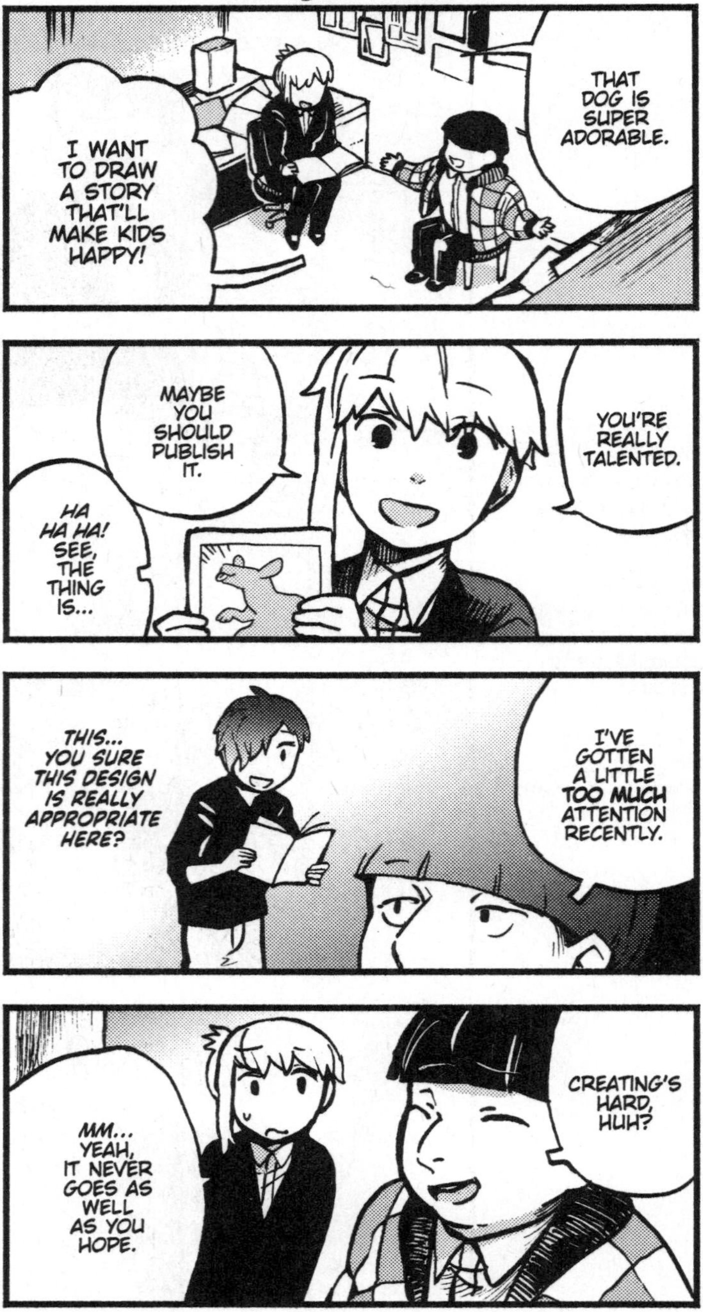
THAT DOG IS SUPER ADORABLE.
I WANT TO DRAW A STORY THAT'LL MAKE KIDS HAPPY!
YOU'RE REALLY TALENTED.
MAYBE YOU SHOULD PUBLISH IT.
HA HA HA! SEE, THE THING IS...
I'VE GOTTEN A LITTLE TOO MUCH ATTENTION RECENTLY.
THIS... YOU SURE THIS DESIGN IS REALLY APPROPRIATE HERE?
CREATING'S HARD, HUH?
MM... YEAH, IT NEVER GOES AS WELL AS YOU HOPE.

At the time of its release, there weren't many casual typefaces that could be used on computers, and Comic Sans wound up filling that role. But because so many people could use it so freely, it got used in places that weren't really appropriate for its lighthearted feel, making it the target of criticism.

Singular Sensation

BUT...
COMICS HAVE HELPED ME UNDERSTAND SOMETHING.
?
IT GOES FOR WORK AND EVERYTHING ELSE, TOO.
BEING NUMBER ONE IS GREAT.
BUT IT'S MORE IMPORTANT TO BE THE *ONLY* ONE.
COMIC SANS-SAN...
YOU'RE RIGHT! I'LL STUDY HARD AND LEARN ALL ABOUT TYPEFACES!!
KLATTER
YEAH! THAT'S THE SPIRIT!!
OH... BUT I...
AH!
I HAVE TO DO THIS WHETHER I LIKE IT OR NOT.

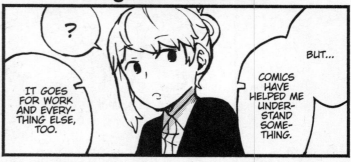

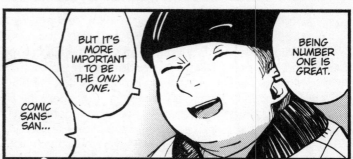

While Comic Sans is simple, the shape of each letter is different and thus easily identifiable, making this type highly visible. The British Dyslexia Association assessed Comic Sans as one of the most readable typefaces available to the general population.

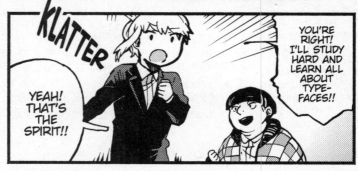

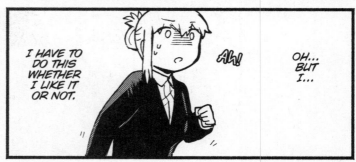

Comic Sans

CATEGORY:	Script
YEAR OF CREATION:	1995
DESIGNER(S):	Vincent Connare
FOUNDRY:	Microsoft (USA)

Whimsical structure inspired by comic-book lettering.

Comic Sans was designed by Vincent Connare (1960–) of Microsoft. Right from the start it was created not as a typeface designed for print, but rather as a font specifically for use in the interface of the children's computer program Microsoft Bob. To recreate the feel of the word balloons in comic books, Connare referenced DC and Marvel comics, specifically the Batman series *The Dark Knight Returns*, and brought together handwritten letters of various shapes. Only uppercase letter are used in comic-book word balloons, but he added lowercase letters to complete the font and later added in Greek and Cyrillic characters before it became a standard Windows font in 1995.

While some designers discouraged the use of Comic Sans due to its casual handwritten appearance, it was acknowledged as being highly identifiable because of the differences in the shapes of the letters, such as the addition of serifs to distinguish between the uppercase *I* and the lowercase *L*. In fact, the British Dyslexia Association has praised Comic Sans for its exceptional readability.

USAGE EXAMPLES
....
☐ Equipped in Microsoft computers

ABCDEFGHIJ KLMNOPQRS TUVWXYZ

abcdefghijklmn opqrstuvwxyz

0123456789

Comic Sans MS Regular

Trajan

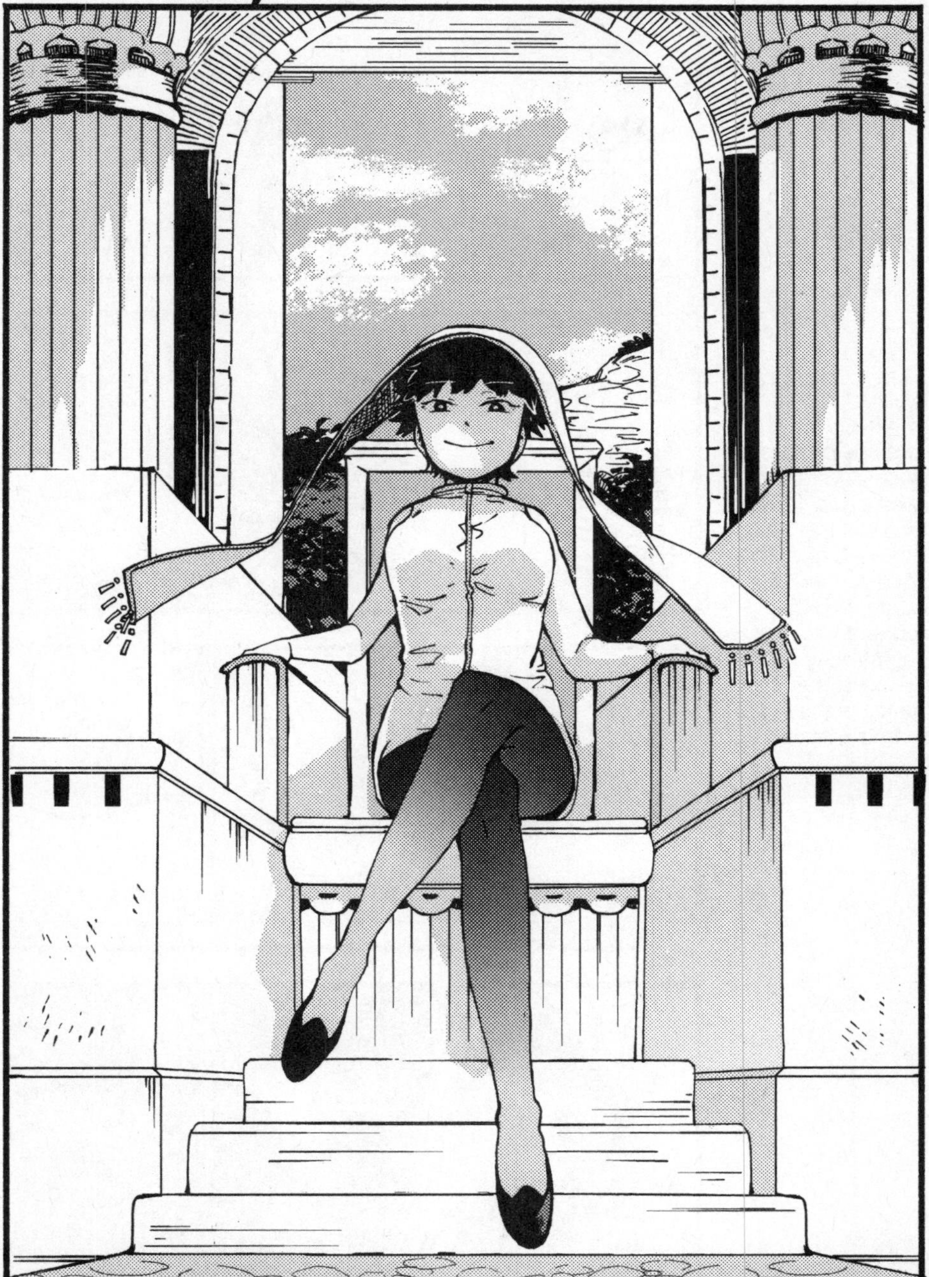

The origin of elegance

Stylish

SO, I'VE BASICALLY...
DONE THE FULL TOUR OF THIS BUILDING, TOO.
IT'S BEEN ONE HECK OF A RIDE.
I THOUGHT ALL TYPEFACES WERE BASICALLY THE SAME.
BUT THE IMPRESSIONS THEY MAKE AND THEIR FIELDS OF EXPERTISE ARE TOTALLY DIFFERENT.
CLENCH...
NO, IT'S MY WAY OF SEEING TH--
HM?
WHOA-AAAA.
...?
WHAT INCREDIBLE LEGS!!

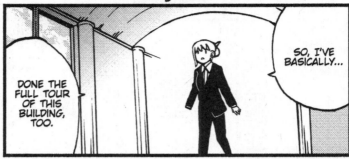

Trajan is a typeface produced by designer Carol Twombly in 1989. Its popularity has remained high since its release due to its proud appearance. The long strokes on the leg of the *R* or the tail of the *Q* are characteristic.

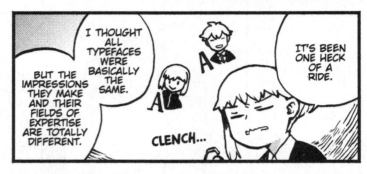

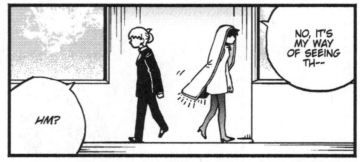

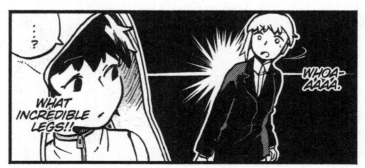

Extreme Generation Gap

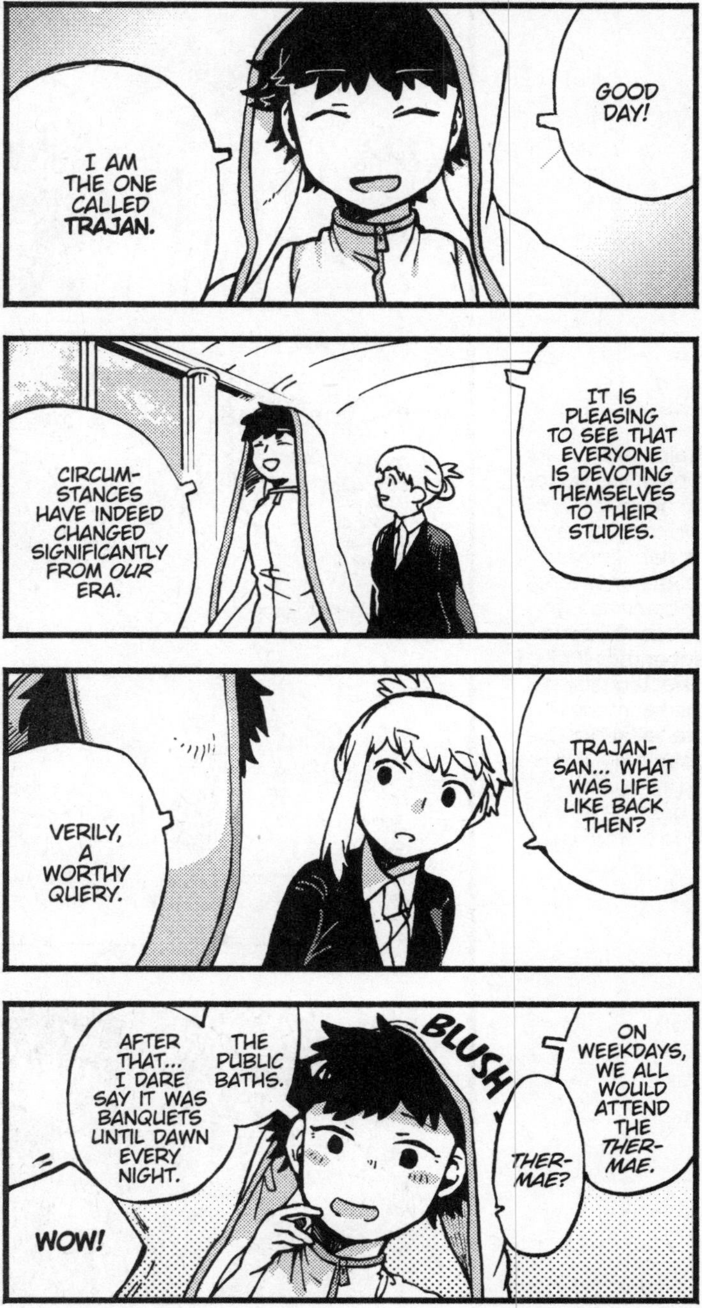
GOOD DAY!
I AM THE ONE CALLED TRAJAN.
IT IS PLEASING TO SEE THAT EVERYONE IS DEVOTING THEMSELVES TO THEIR STUDIES.
CIRCUM-STANCES HAVE INDEED CHANGED SIGNIFICANTLY FROM *OUR* ERA.
TRAJAN-SAN... WHAT WAS LIFE LIKE BACK THEN?
VERILY, A WORTHY QUERY.
ON WEEKDAYS, WE ALL WOULD ATTEND THE *THER-MAE.*
THER-MAE?
BLUSH
THE PUBLIC BATHS.
AFTER THAT... I DARE SAY IT WAS BANQUETS UNTIL DAWN EVERY NIGHT.
WOW!

Trajan was based on characters from the monument of the ancient Roman emperor Trajan produced around two thousand years ago. Additionally, as a vestige of the era when lowercase letters did not exist, this typeface was designed with only uppercase letters.

Eternal History

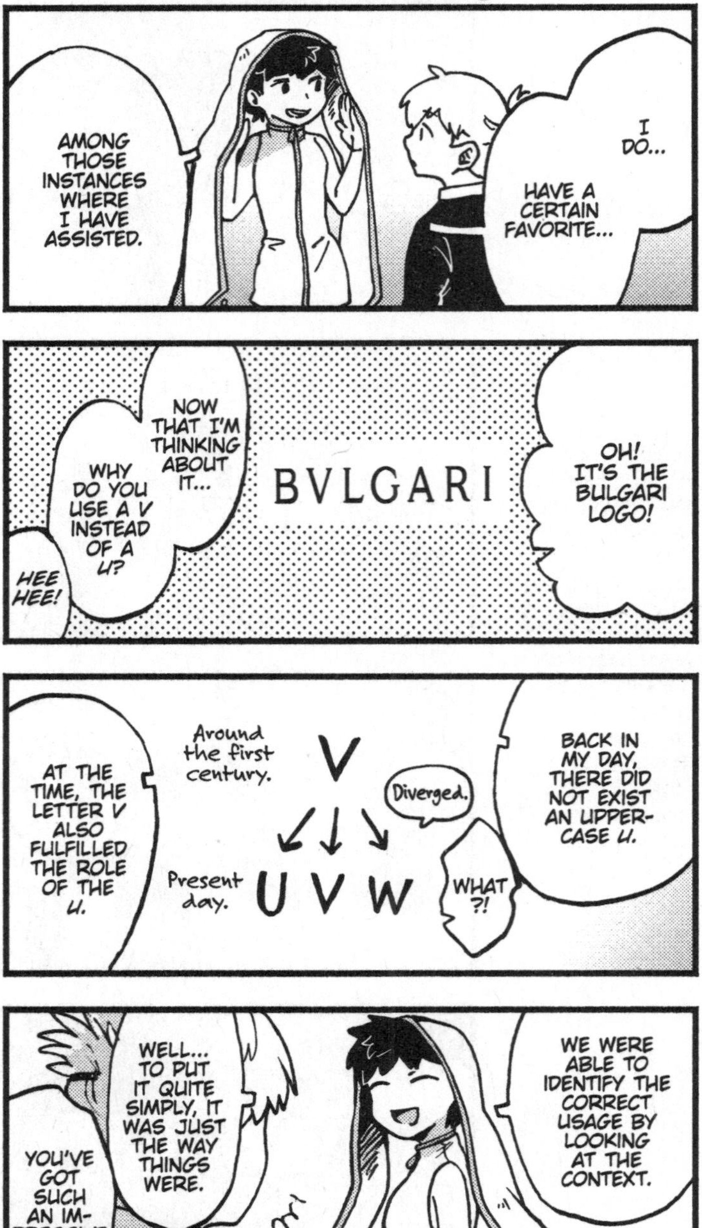
I DO...
HAVE A CERTAIN FAVORITE...
AMONG THOSE INSTANCES WHERE I HAVE ASSISTED.
OH! IT'S THE BULGARI LOGO!
BVLGARI
NOW THAT I'M THINKING ABOUT IT...
WHY DO YOU USE A V INSTEAD OF A U?
HEE HEE!
BACK IN MY DAY, THERE DID NOT EXIST AN UPPER-CASE U.
WHAT?!
Around the first century.
V
Diverged.
Present day.
U V W
AT THE TIME, THE LETTER V ALSO FULFILLED THE ROLE OF THE U.
WE WERE ABLE TO IDENTIFY THE CORRECT USAGE BY LOOKING AT THE CONTEXT.
WELL... TO PUT IT QUITE SIMPLY, IT WAS JUST THE WAY THINGS WERE.
YOU'VE GOT SUCH AN IMPRESSIVE LINEAGE!

Trajan references a typeface from an ancient era in which the Roman alphabet had only twenty-three characters. By using a logo with a typeface that reflects that era, as the fashion brand Bulgari does, one can give an impression of a product with a long history.

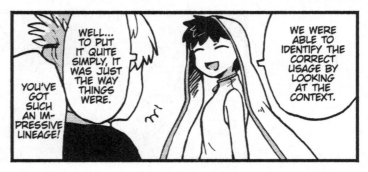

A Typeface to Remember

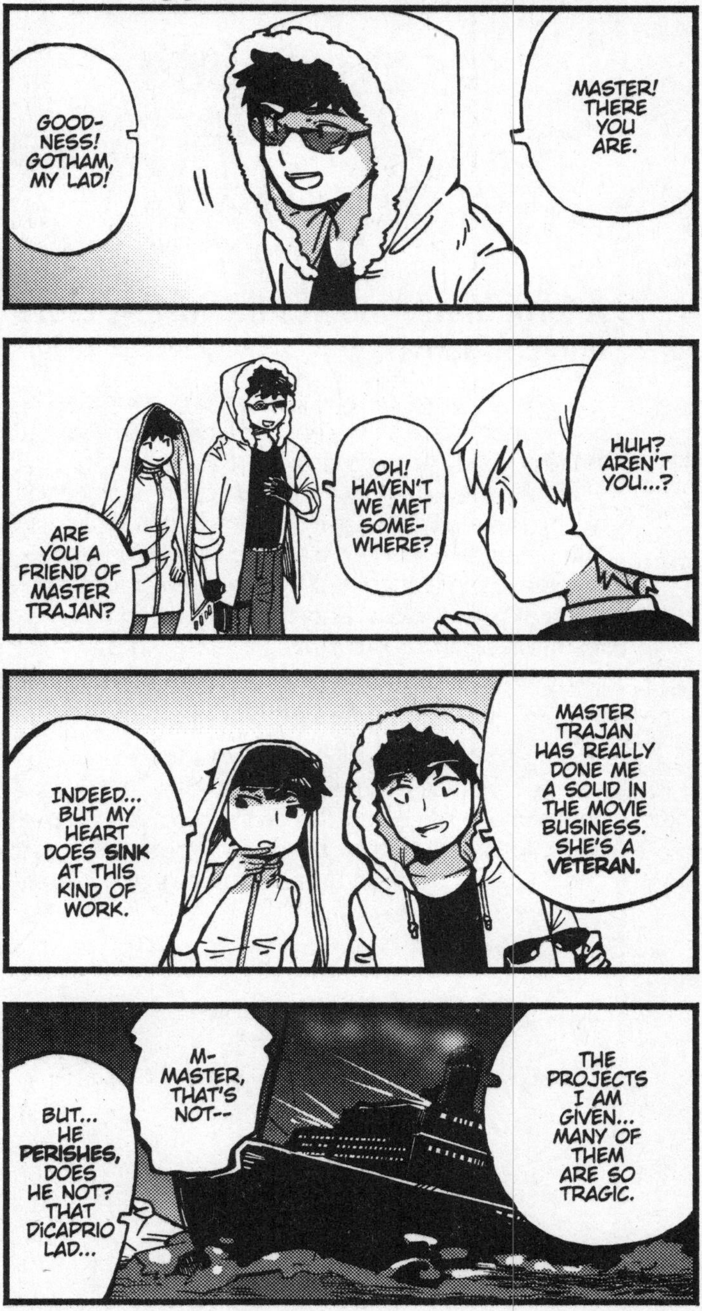
MASTER! THERE YOU ARE.
GOOD-NESS! GOTHAM, MY LAD!
HUH? AREN'T YOU...?
OH! HAVEN'T WE MET SOME-WHERE?
ARE YOU A FRIEND OF MASTER TRAJAN?
MASTER TRAJAN HAS REALLY DONE ME A SOLID IN THE MOVIE BUSINESS. SHE'S A **VETERAN.**
INDEED... BUT MY HEART DOES **SINK** AT THIS KIND OF WORK.
THE PROJECTS I AM GIVEN... MANY OF THEM ARE SO TRAGIC.
M-MASTER, THAT'S NOT--
BUT... HE **PERISHES,** DOES HE NOT? THAT DiCAPRIO LAD...

In addition to having a good balance amongst individual characters, Trajan has a stern, traditional feel, so it is used in the title logos of a variety of films. *Titanic* and *I Am Legend* are examples of this.

TRAJAN

CATEGORY:	Display/Roman
YEAR OF CREATION:	1989 (104)
DESIGNER(S):	Carol Twombly
FOUNDRY:	Adobe (USA)

A form that combines the history and style of ancient Rome.

Trajan was designed by Adobe's Carol Twombly (1959–) based on the monument of the ancient Roman emperor Trajan. Built in the year 113 to commemorate Trajan's victory in the Dacian wars, the monument is a massive pillar reaching forty meters high. In its marble base, three meters across and 1.3 meters high, 165 uppercase letters are carved in Latin across six lines, and of the existing alphabet of twenty-three characters of the time, nineteen are visible. A photograph is found in the well-known textbook *Writing & Illuminating & Lettering* by the father of modern calligraphy, Edward Johnston, who called it the eternal source from which all typefaces sprang.

Trajan had been revived by a number of typeface designers, but the font that Twombly completed in 1989 for the digital environment can be said to be the most refined of them all. With its majestic form, it is often used in the logos of companies and films, and it has become familiar to us through the titles of films such as *The Lord of the Rings* and *Titanic.*

USAGE EXAMPLES
....
□ *Titanic* (title logo for the 1997 film)
□ *The Lord of the Rings* (title logo for the 2001 film)

ABCDEFGHIJ
KLMNOPQRS
TUVWXYZ
ABCDEFGHIJ
KLMNOPQRS
TUVWXYZ
0123456789

Trajan Pro Regular

Peignot

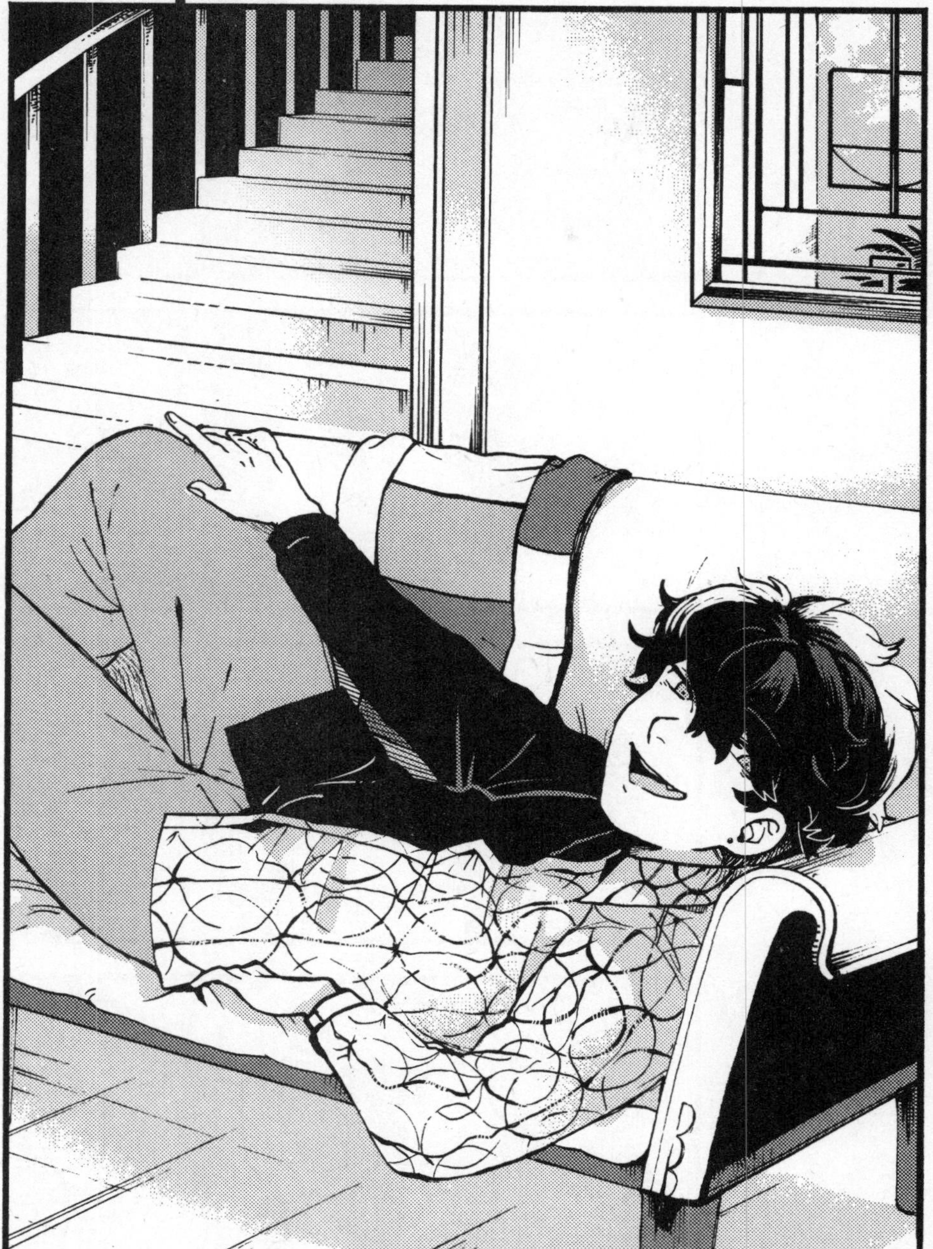

Art Deco symbol

Artistic Aspirations

SHK
PSSSH
IS THAT SPRAY PAINT?
H-HE'S PAINTING ON THE WALL!!
HM?
A VISITOR?
IT'S OKAY, DON'T WORRY.
I'M NOT PAINTING DIRECTLY ON THE WALL, AFTER ALL.
BUT WON'T YOU GET IN TROUBLE FOR DOING THAT HERE--
HUNH... SO COOL...
OH!
IT LOOKS LIKE YOU'VE GOT AN EYE FOR ART, THEN.

Peignot was produced in 1937 by the Art Deco painter and graphic designer A. M. Cassandre. The geometrical uppercase letters and the lowercase letters, which share their form while also being easy to read, produce a typeface that makes its playfulness felt.

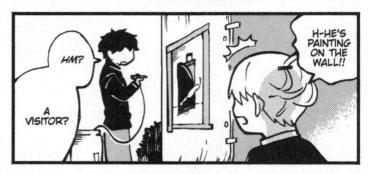

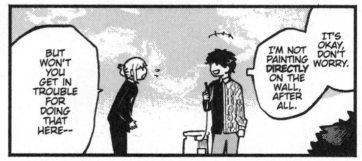

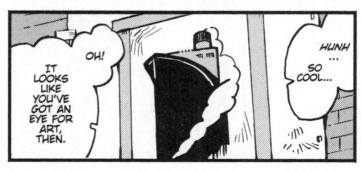

Remnant

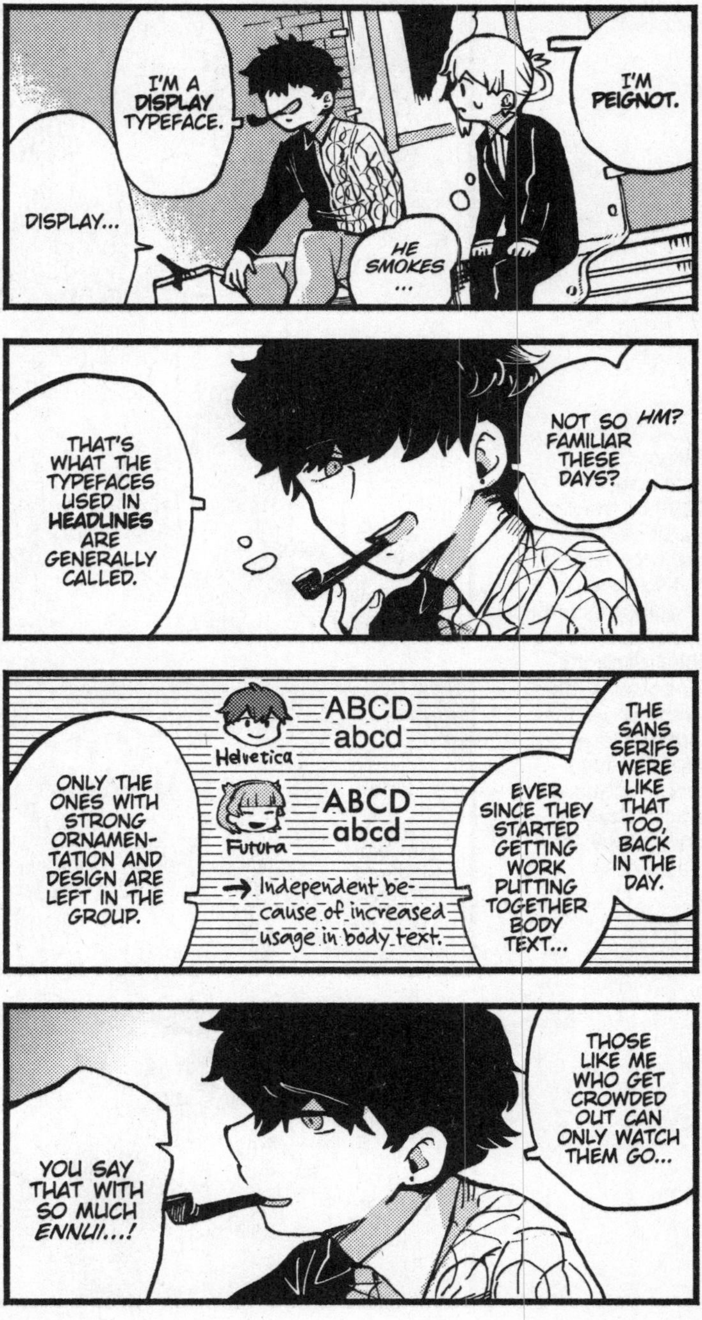
I'M PEIGNOT.
I'M A DISPLAY TYPEFACE.
HE SMOKES ...
DISPLAY...
HM?
NOT SO FAMILIAR THESE DAYS?
THAT'S WHAT THE TYPEFACES USED IN HEADLINES ARE GENERALLY CALLED.
THE SANS SERIFS WERE LIKE THAT TOO, BACK IN THE DAY.
EVER SINCE THEY STARTED GETTING WORK PUTTING TOGETHER BODY TEXT...
ABCD abcd
Helvetica
ABCD abcd
Futura
→ Independent because of increased usage in body text.
ONLY THE ONES WITH STRONG ORNAMENTATION AND DESIGN ARE LEFT IN THE GROUP.
THOSE LIKE ME WHO GET CROWDED OUT CAN ONLY WATCH THEM GO...
YOU SAY THAT WITH SO MUCH ENNUI...!

Peignot belongs to a category called "display typefaces." They're used for headlines (displays) and made to stand out in short text on posters and signs. This was also originally the main role of sans serif types, as well.

Seriously Unserious

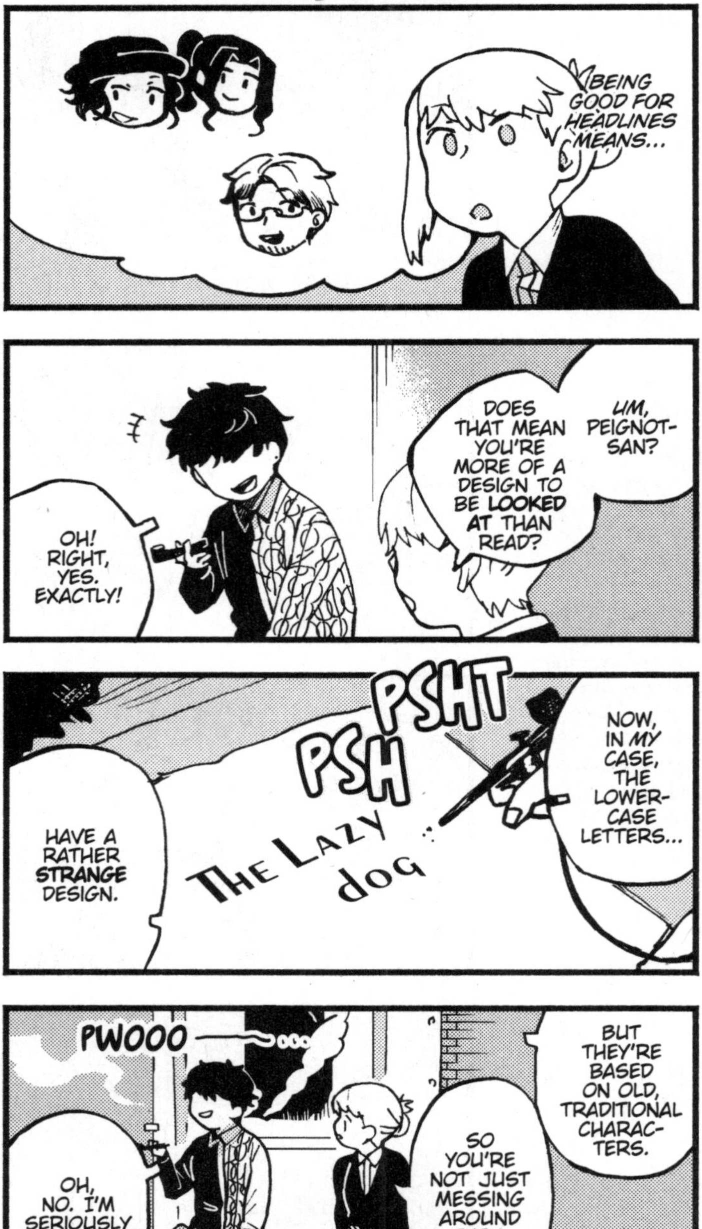
BEING GOOD FOR HEADLINES MEANS...
UM, PEIGNOT-SAN?
DOES THAT MEAN YOU'RE MORE OF A DESIGN TO BE **LOOKED AT** THAN READ?
OH! RIGHT, YES. EXACTLY!
NOW, IN *MY* CASE, THE LOWER-CASE LETTERS...
PSHT
PSH
THE LAZY dog
HAVE A RATHER **STRANGE** DESIGN.
BUT THEY'RE BASED ON OLD, TRADITIONAL CHARACTERS.
PWOOO
SO YOU'RE NOT JUST MESSING AROUND THEN, HUH...?
OH, NO. I'M SERIOUSLY UNSERIOUS.

Peignot's lowercase letters have an avant-garde shape, but they were modeled after uncial script, which appeared around the fifth century. Uppercase and lowercase letters were mixed together to create a typeface with unique characteristics.

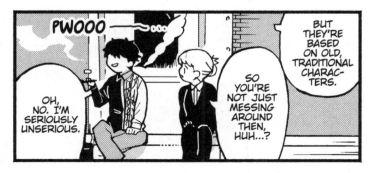

Modes of Self-expression

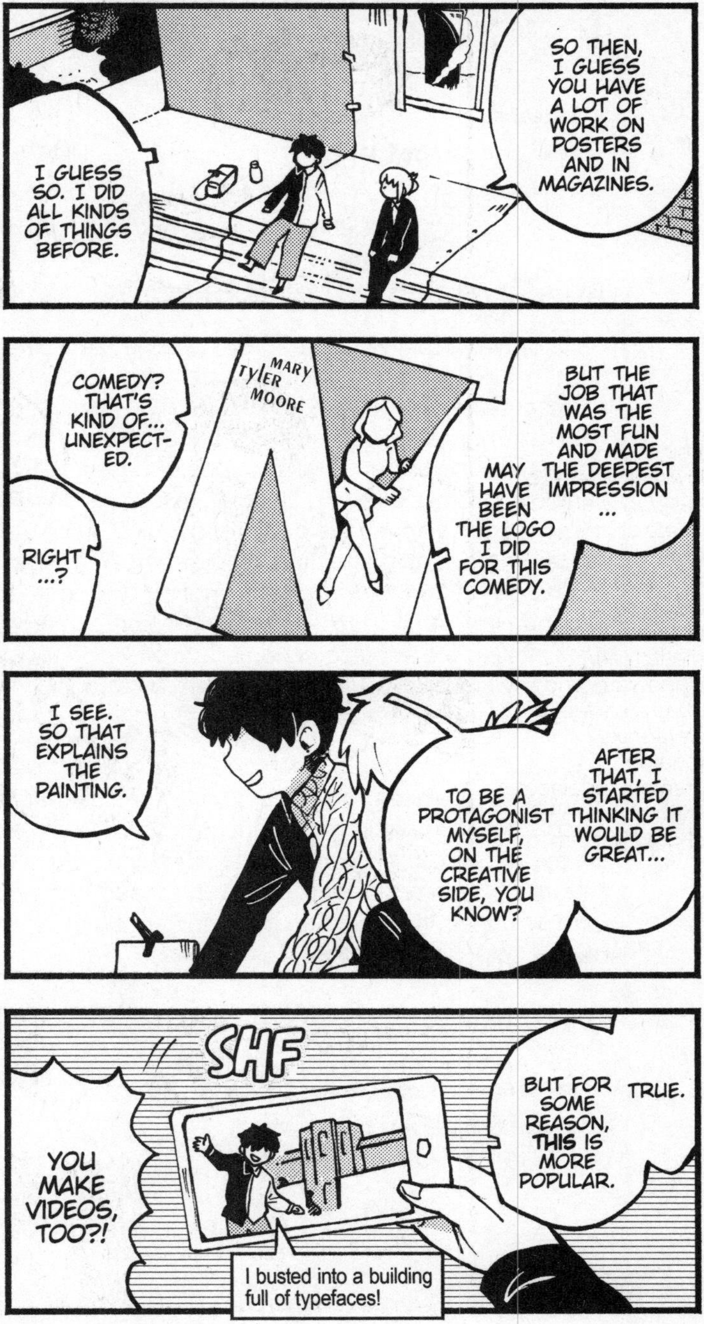
SO THEN, I GUESS YOU HAVE A LOT OF WORK ON POSTERS AND IN MAGAZINES.
I GUESS SO. I DID ALL KINDS OF THINGS BEFORE.
BUT THE JOB THAT WAS THE MOST FUN AND MADE THE DEEPEST IMPRESSION ...
MAY HAVE BEEN THE LOGO I DID FOR THIS COMEDY.
MARY Tyler MOORE
COMEDY? THAT'S KIND OF... UNEXPECTED.
RIGHT ...?
AFTER THAT, I STARTED THINKING IT WOULD BE GREAT...
TO BE A PROTAGONIST MYSELF, ON THE CREATIVE SIDE, YOU KNOW?
I SEE. SO THAT EXPLAINS THE PAINTING.
SHF
TRUE.
BUT FOR SOME REASON, **THIS** IS MORE POPULAR.
YOU MAKE VIDEOS, TOO?!
I busted into a building full of typefaces!

From the time Peignot was released until the late 1940s, it was used in printed matter like posters and advertisements. It was also used in the opening titles of the American sitcom *The Mary Tyler Moore Show*, which started airing in 1970.

PEIGNOT

CATEGORY:	Display
YEAR OF CREATION:	1937
DESIGNER(S):	A. M. Cassandre
FOUNDRY:	Deberny & Peignot (France)

Artistic design symbolic of Art Deco.

Peignot was designed in 1937 by Adolphe Mouron Cassandre (1901–1968), a French painter, poster artist, and performing artist representative of the twentieth century. Cassandre was involved with commercial advertisement production from an early stage, and he was particularly skilled at poster design reflecting the symbolic expression of Art Deco—illustrations on geometrical compositions with unique depth and daring use of color that incorporated simple and clear typography. At the Paris World's Fair held in 1925 (International Exhibition of Modern Decorative and Industrial Arts), Cassandre took first prize in typography, and after making the acquaintance of Charles Peignot of the French company Deberny & Peignot, he went on to design a new typeface named for that company.

In producing the type, Cassandre argued against the practice of dividing typefaces into upper and lowercase that had been in place since the Carolingian minuscule, the dynasty established by Emperor Charles at the end of the eighth century, and created a beautiful, modern typeface with both cases having nearly the same form. In Japan, the type can be seen frequently as the logo for the bakery café Vie de France.

USAGE EXAMPLES
....

☐ Vie de France (Japanese bakery café)

☐ LeSportsac (New York bag brand)

ABCDEFGHIJ
KLMNOPQRS
TUVWXYZ
abcdefghijklmn
opqrstuvwxyz
0123456789

Peignot LT Std Demi

Fette Fraktur

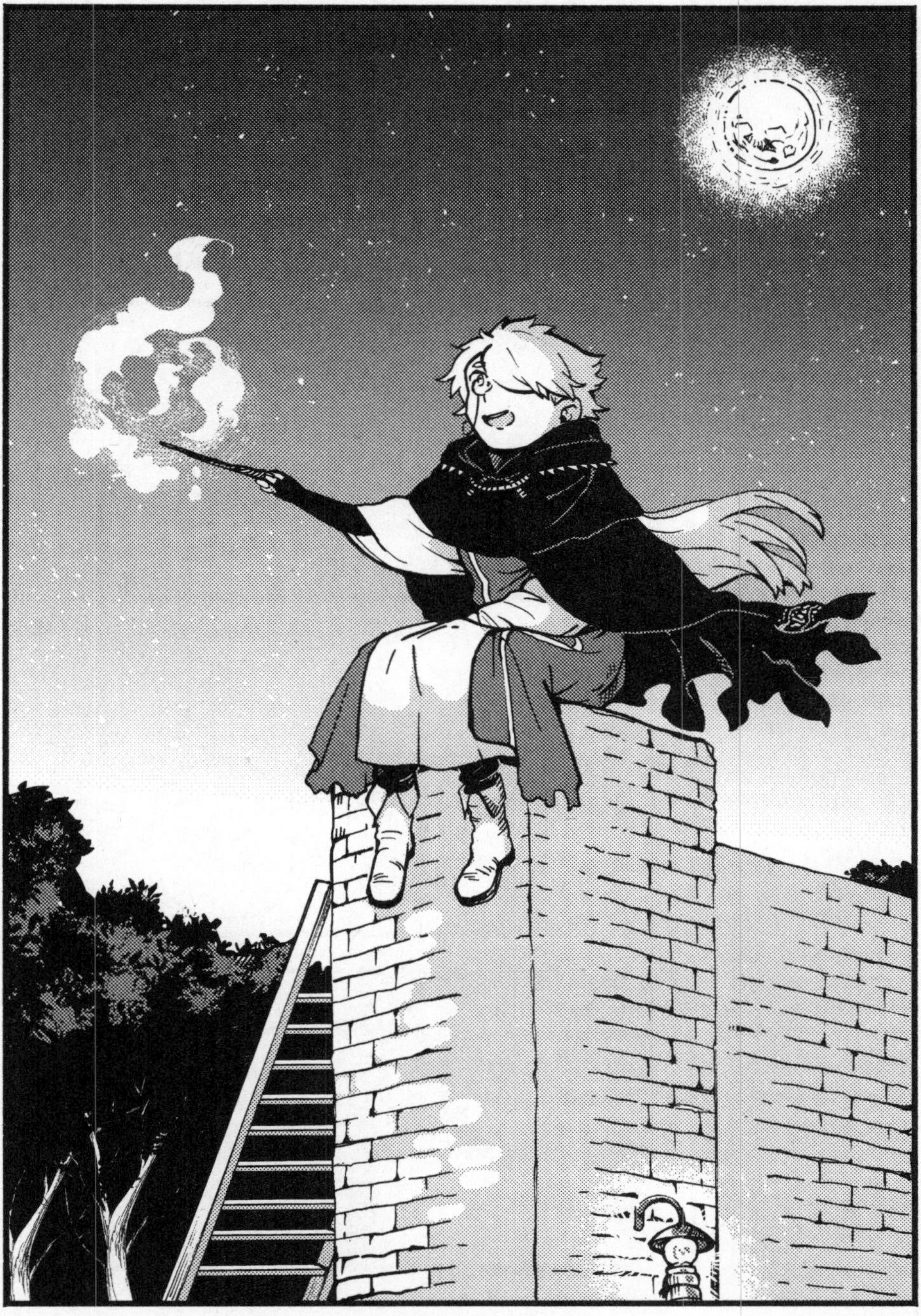

Traditional German characters in the modern day

Gothic Society

OH, FETTE FRAKTUR!
INK DELIVERY.
DANKE.
SORRY FOR HAVINK YOU COME SO OFTEN.
I'M AFRAID I DO USE A LOT OF INK.
WELL, THAT'S JUST HOW IT IS WITH BLACK-LETTER, I SUPPOSE.
HA HA!
THANKS AGAIN.
GOTHIC SOCIETY Just up the stairs!!
!!
GOTHIC ...?
BLACK-LETTER?!
SCARY ...!!
HMM? IS SOMEONE DOWN THERE?

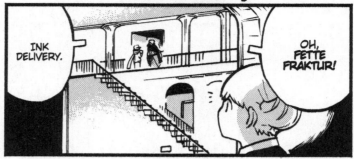

Fette Fraktur is a typeface in the blackletter group. Created in reference to calligraphy letters, these types make the page look black, which is where the name comes from. Additionally, if people in some parts of Europe refer to "gothic type" they are talking about blackletter.

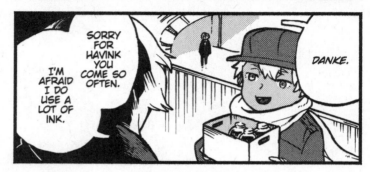

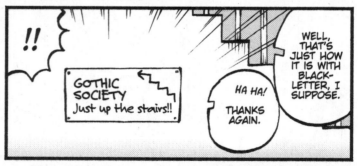

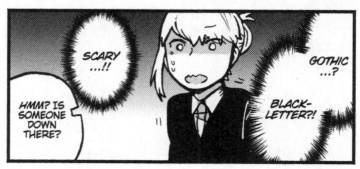

Challenging Name

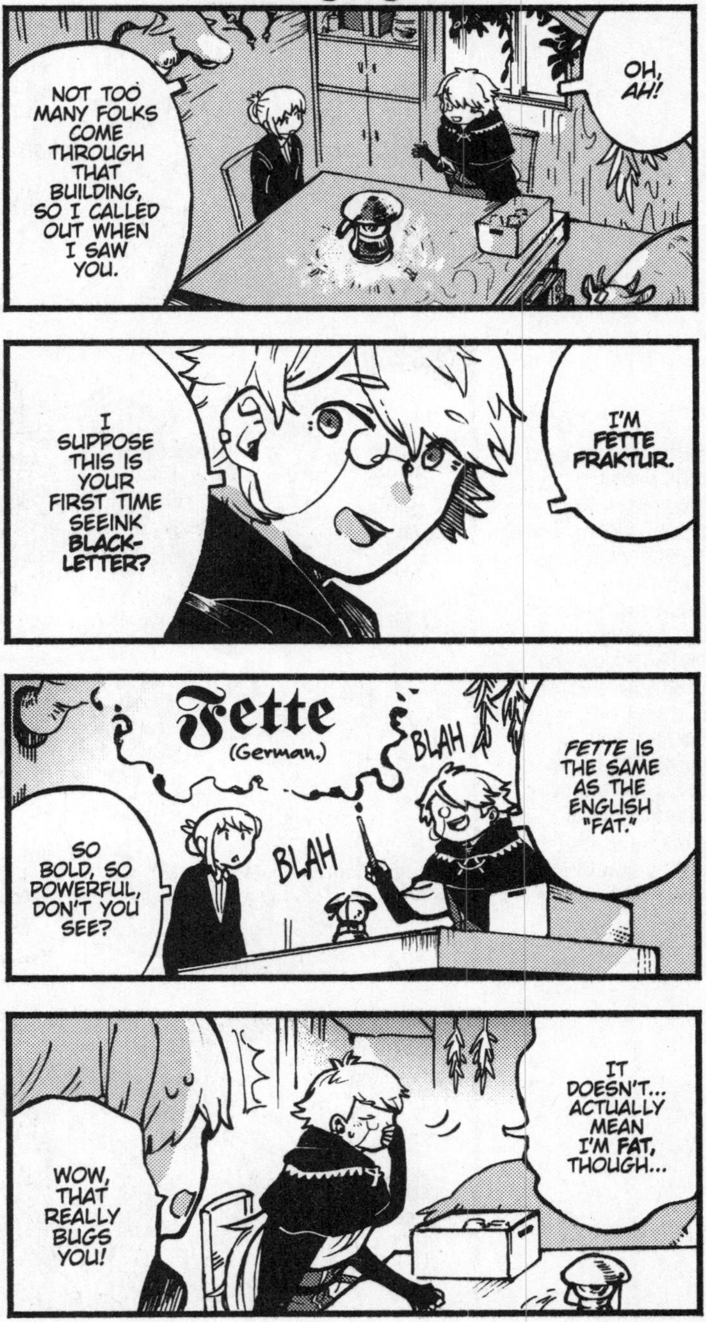
OH, AH!
NOT TOO MANY FOLKS COME THROUGH THAT BUILDING, SO I CALLED OUT WHEN I SAW YOU.
I'M FETTE FRAKTUR.
I SUPPOSE THIS IS YOUR FIRST TIME SEEINK BLACK-LETTER?
FETTE IS THE SAME AS THE ENGLISH "FAT."
Fette (German.)
BLAH
BLAH
SO BOLD, SO POWERFUL, DON'T YOU SEE?
IT DOESN'T... ACTUALLY MEAN I'M FAT, THOUGH...
WOW, THAT REALLY BUGS YOU!

Fette Fraktur was produced in 1850 by the German typeface designer Johann Christian Bauer. "Fraktur" means "broken," and this name can also refer to all blackletter types.

Hot with the Kids

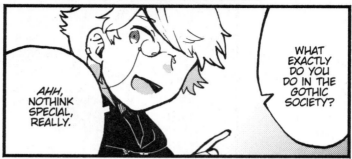

WHAT EXACTLY DO YOU DO IN THE GOTHIC SOCIETY?
AHH, NOTHINK SPECIAL, REALLY.
I JUST HEARD THAT VE HAFF **BIG FANS** IN THE OUTSIDE WORLD.
Fraktur mon Amour
SO I MADE THAT **CATCHY SIGN** AS A SORT OF SYMBOL.
A collection of blackletter types
I HAFF BEEN INTERVIEWED MANY TIMES MYSELF.
GRAAAAANG
...?
THAT SOUND...
OH! I LEFT THE MUSIC ON.
IS THAT *METAL* ?!
KACHK
NOT A FAN?
I HAFF SOME **HIP HOP,** TOO...

Blackletter type was initially often used for body text, but in recent years, Fette Fraktur can also be seen in advertisements and displays. Its main characteristic is the strong decorative elements of the uppercase letters, and it's highly popular in the publishing industry and music fields such as heavy metal.

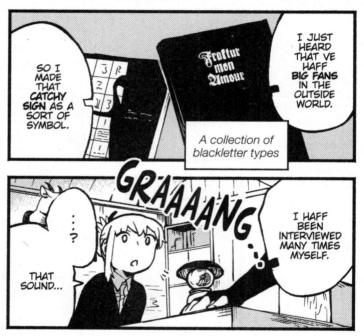

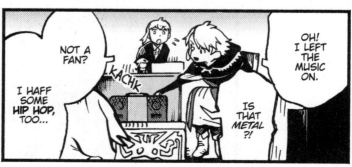

Closely Tied to Place

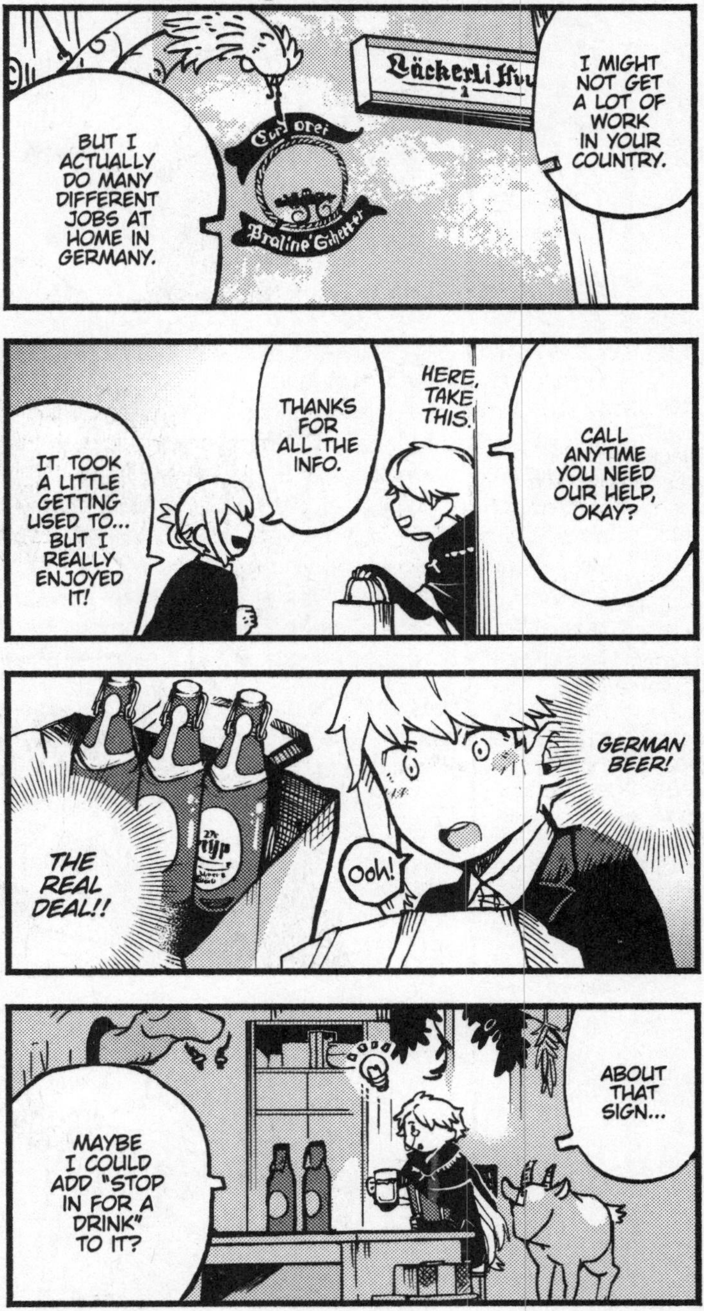
I MIGHT NOT GET A LOT OF WORK IN YOUR COUNTRY.
BUT I ACTUALLY DO MANY DIFFERENT JOBS AT HOME IN GERMANY.
CALL ANYTIME YOU NEED OUR HELP, OKAY?
HERE, TAKE THIS.
THANKS FOR ALL THE INFO.
IT TOOK A LITTLE GETTING USED TO... BUT I REALLY ENJOYED IT!
GERMAN BEER!
Ooh!
THE REAL DEAL!!
ABOUT THAT SIGN...
MAYBE I COULD ADD "STOP IN FOR A DRINK" TO IT?

Up until the middle of the twentieth century, Fette Fraktur was widely used in Germany. This sort of type was even called "German letters" and beloved. Even now, you can catch sight of it at German beer companies and on street signage.

𝕱𝖊𝖙𝖙𝖊 𝕱𝖗𝖆𝖐𝖙𝖚𝖗

CATEGORY:	Blackletter
YEAR OF CREATION:	1850
DESIGNER(S):	Johann Christian Bauer
FOUNDRY:	Bauer Type Foundry (Germany)

Stately fraktur letters have an air of mystery.

Fette Fraktur is a blackletter type designed in 1850 by the German type founder Johann Christian Bauer (1802–1867). Fraktur is based on the transcription typeface used in monasteries and similar institutions in medieval Europe, and in German-speaking Europe it was used as a stately body-text type in the Gothic period. In the 1930s, the Nazi government made Fraktur its official typeface, but then abolished it in 1941 because its use was impractical for political policies in countries outside of Germany. After the war, Fraktur disappeared from printed matter due to its association with the Nazi government, but it gradually found a new purpose in displays and advertisements.

Fette means "fat," and the black ornamentation of the fraktur characters lends the type an air of drama. Currently, it is used not only in traditional arts and culture, such as classical music, but also in advertisements and on packages that convey a sense of German culture such as sausages and beer. The famous package for the traditional Swiss candy Läckerli Huus also uses Fette Fraktur.

USAGE EXAMPLES
....

☐ Läckerli Huus (traditional Swiss candy maker)

ABCDEFGHIJ
KLMNOPQRS
TUVWXYZ
abcdefghijklmn
opqrstuvwxyz
0123456789

Fette Fraktur LT Std Regular

Other Typeface Notes

Script Type

Script types are patterned after handwriting with a pen or a brush. There are traditional "formal scripts" which were written with quills or metal pens and then reproduced as copperplate during the seventeenth and eighteenth centuries, and the more modern "casual scripts" that take advantage of the free forms of flowing ink due to the development of twentieth-century phototypesetting.

The types are also divided into "connecting," in which the letters are joined, and "non-connecting," in which they are not, but both have the feel of handwriting's flow.

Display Type

Display types were developed for use mainly in displays and titles in newspapers, magazines, and books, so they are also called "ornamental typefaces." In the early nineteenth century, with the development of printing technology and the advertising industry in the Industrial Revolution, display types were used to draw the eye in advertisements such as flyers and posters.

With very large extreme types, types with thick strokes, those bordered with silhouettes and shadows, and others with added ornamentation, the variety of creative expression grew by leaps and bounds, and it is hard to categorize these types by shape. They strongly reflect the trends of the times.

Blackletter Type

Blackletter types were used in handwritten matter in northern Europe in the Middle Ages (around the twelfth century). Because many letters could be written on the page, this typeface was used in and spread through the creation of prayer books and texts of worship in churches and monasteries. The name is said to come from the fact that the tall, whiskered strokes overlapped like the rows of pillars in a Gothic church. Blackletter types are categorized by form into Textualis, Rotunda, Schwabacher, and Fraktur.

Peignot

VIE DE FRANCE

Display type • Vie de France (Japanese bakery café) logo
Credit: Vie de France

Fette Fraktur

Läckerli Huus
BASLER ORIGINAL

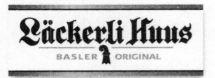

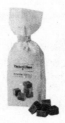

Blackletter type • Läckerli Huus (traditional Swiss candy maker) logo
Credit: Charmant Gourmand Aoyama

Q When did Western fonts originate?

A The ancient Roman emperor Trajan's monument could be said to be the origin of Roman type, and the oldest font in which letters were carved. The protrusions (serifs) that can be seen on the end of strokes, the defining feature of serif typefaces, are thought to come from the traces of letterforms carved into rocks with a chisel. For fonts in printed matter, we have the blackletter typeface used by Gutenberg and his printing press technology to print the Bible in 1450. This typeface had a form close to handwriting, following the German practice at the time of copying the Bible with a pen. Around 1470, Jenson appeared in Venice, Italy, a typeface with a Venetian form closest to the modern roman types. After that, the typeface groups Old Roman, Transitional, and Modern Roman were created between the sixteenth and nineteenth centuries.

Meanwhile, the origin of typefaces without serifs, or sans serif types, is considered to be the typeface specimen books of England's William Caslon IV at the beginning of the nineteenth century. These were initially for display usage, but in the second half of the nineteenth century, it became possible to create small, easy-to-read type for body text. Moving into the twentieth century, a variety of sans serif typeface styles appeared, such as Geometric, Humanist, and Neo-grotesque, emphasizing the trend of visible culture at the time. For details, please see the chart.

A chronological list of
typeface appearances.

Types at a Glance

Many types have multiple theories about the year of their appearance.
Revived typefaces such as Jenson, Caslon, and DIN are placed in the year
the original was produced, as a general rule.

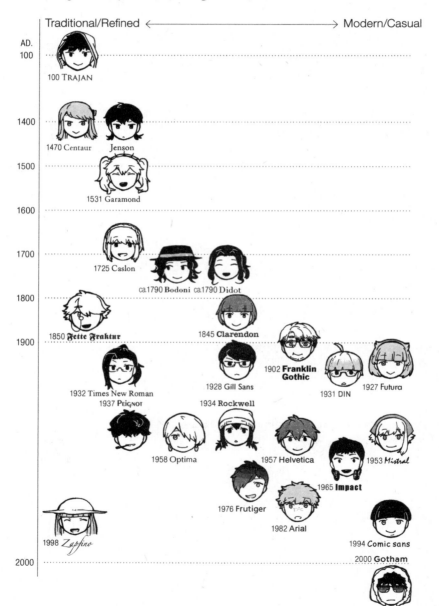

Traditional/Refined ⟵—————————————————⟶ Modern/Casual

AD.
100

100 TRAJAN

1400

1470 Centaur   Jenson

1500

1531 Garamond

1600

1700

1725 Caslon

ca.1790 Bodoni   ca.1790 Didot

1800

1850 Fette Fraktur   1845 Clarendon

1900

1902 **Franklin Gothic**

1932 Times New Roman   1928 Gill Sans   1931 DIN   1927 Futura
1937 Peignot   1934 Rockwell

1958 Optima   1957 Helvetica   1953 *Mistral*

1965 **Impact**

1976 Frutiger

1982 Arial

1998 *Zapfino*   1994 *Comic sans*

2000 **Gotham**

2000

1st Century	**Era of Sculpture and Monuments** Hand-carved letters without any conception of typefaces. At the time, lowercase letters did not yet exist.
12th Century	**Dissemination of Blackletter** Handwritten blackletter type with its ornamentation appeared. It was widely used in bibles and other religious materials.
15th Century	**Early Roman Type** Early roman type, with lingering traces of handwriting, was born. It became popular with a movement to free people and letters from traditional religion.
16th Century	**Birth of Old Roman** The printing press was invented, and typefaces more suitable for printed matter were developed. One such type, Caslon, became fashionable throughout Europe.
18th Century	**Appearance of Transitional Roman** Stroke contrast grew stronger. The British typeface Baskerville was not well-received in its home country, but other countries were inspired and adopted it.
19th Century	**Era of Modern Roman** With the technology of the Industrial Revolution, it became possible to print extremely fine lines. The roman type form was essentially perfected.
20th Century	**Development of Sans Serif Types** The sans serif types were born, influenced by modernism and emphasizing function and practicality. Helvetica in particular gained global popularity, becoming a beloved typeface.
21st Century	**Introduction of Pop Typefaces** Digital typefaces could now be mass produced, and a number of typefaces appeared one after another, computerized and applicable for many uses.

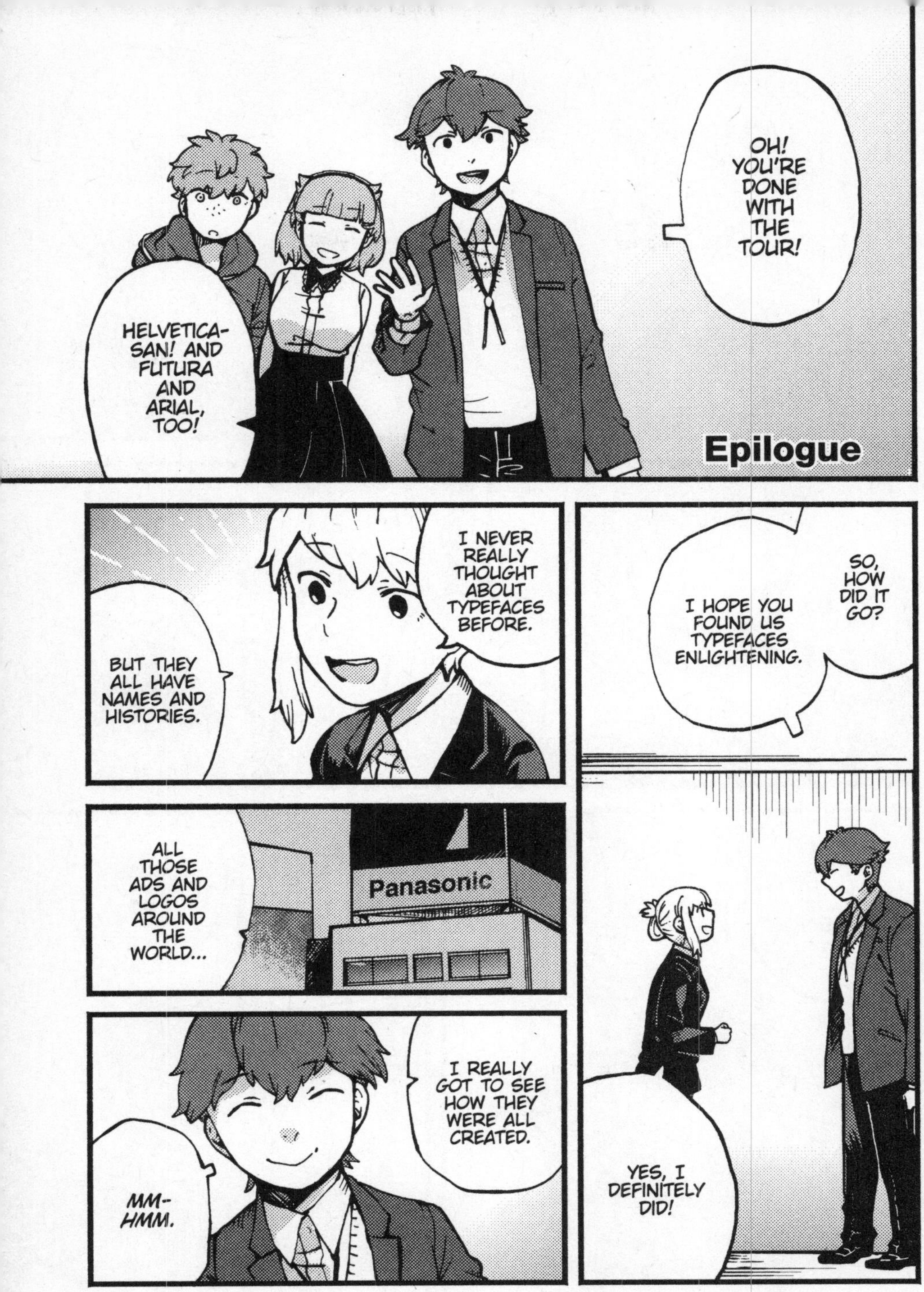
OH! YOU'RE DONE WITH THE TOUR!
HELVETICA-SAN! AND FUTURA AND ARIAL, TOO!
Epilogue
SO, HOW DID IT GO?
I HOPE YOU FOUND US TYPEFACES ENLIGHTENING.
YES, I DEFINITELY DID!
I NEVER REALLY THOUGHT ABOUT TYPEFACES BEFORE.
BUT THEY ALL HAVE NAMES AND HISTORIES.
Panasonic
ALL THOSE ADS AND LOGOS AROUND THE WORLD...
I REALLY GOT TO SEE HOW THEY WERE ALL CREATED.
MM-HMM.

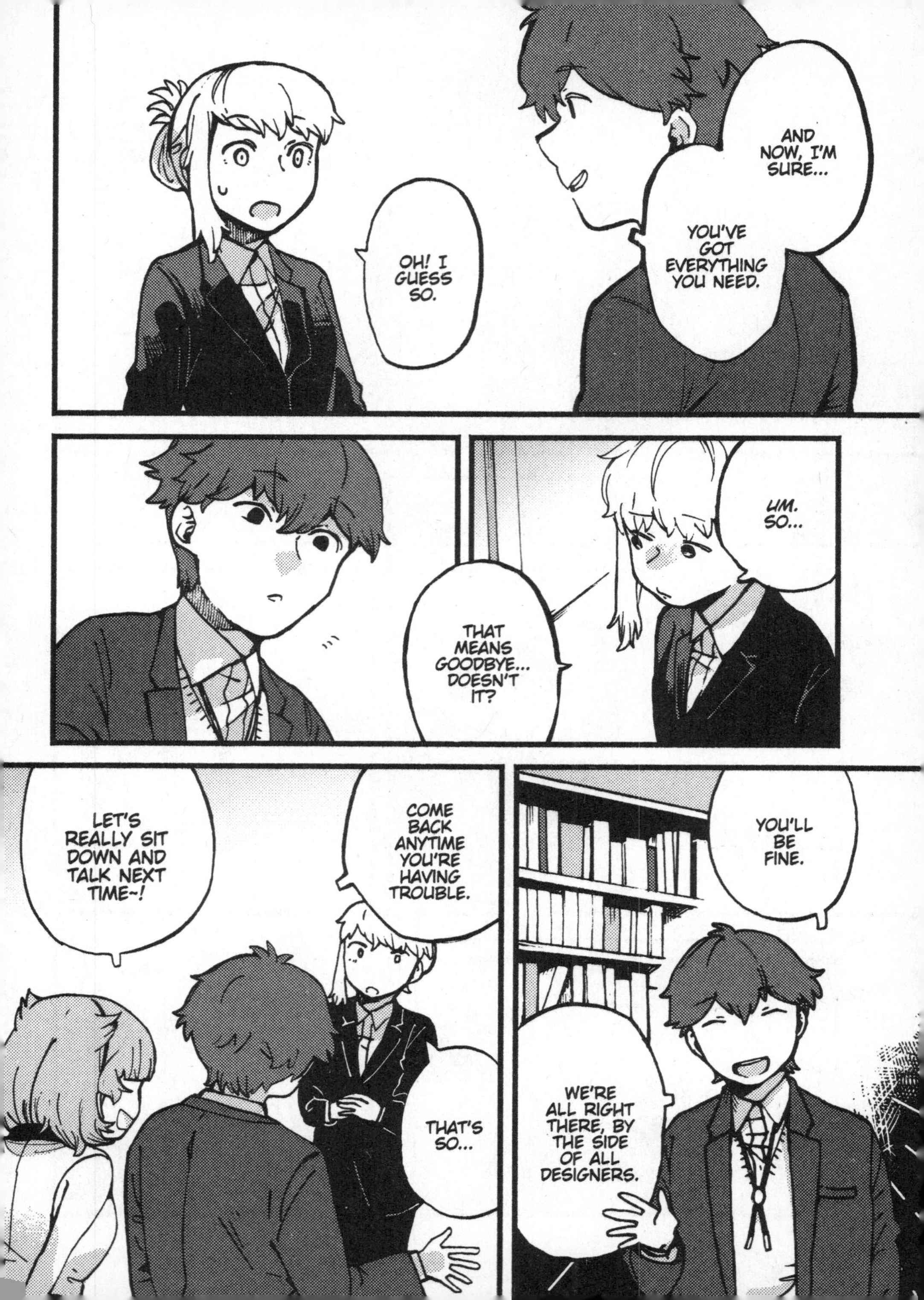
AND NOW, I'M SURE...
YOU'VE GOT EVERYTHING YOU NEED.
OH! I GUESS SO.
UM. SO...
THAT MEANS GOODBYE... DOESN'T IT?
YOU'LL BE FINE.
WE'RE ALL RIGHT THERE, BY THE SIDE OF ALL DESIGNERS.
COME BACK ANYTIME YOU'RE HAVING TROUBLE.
LET'S REALLY SIT DOWN AND TALK NEXT TIME~!
THAT'S SO...

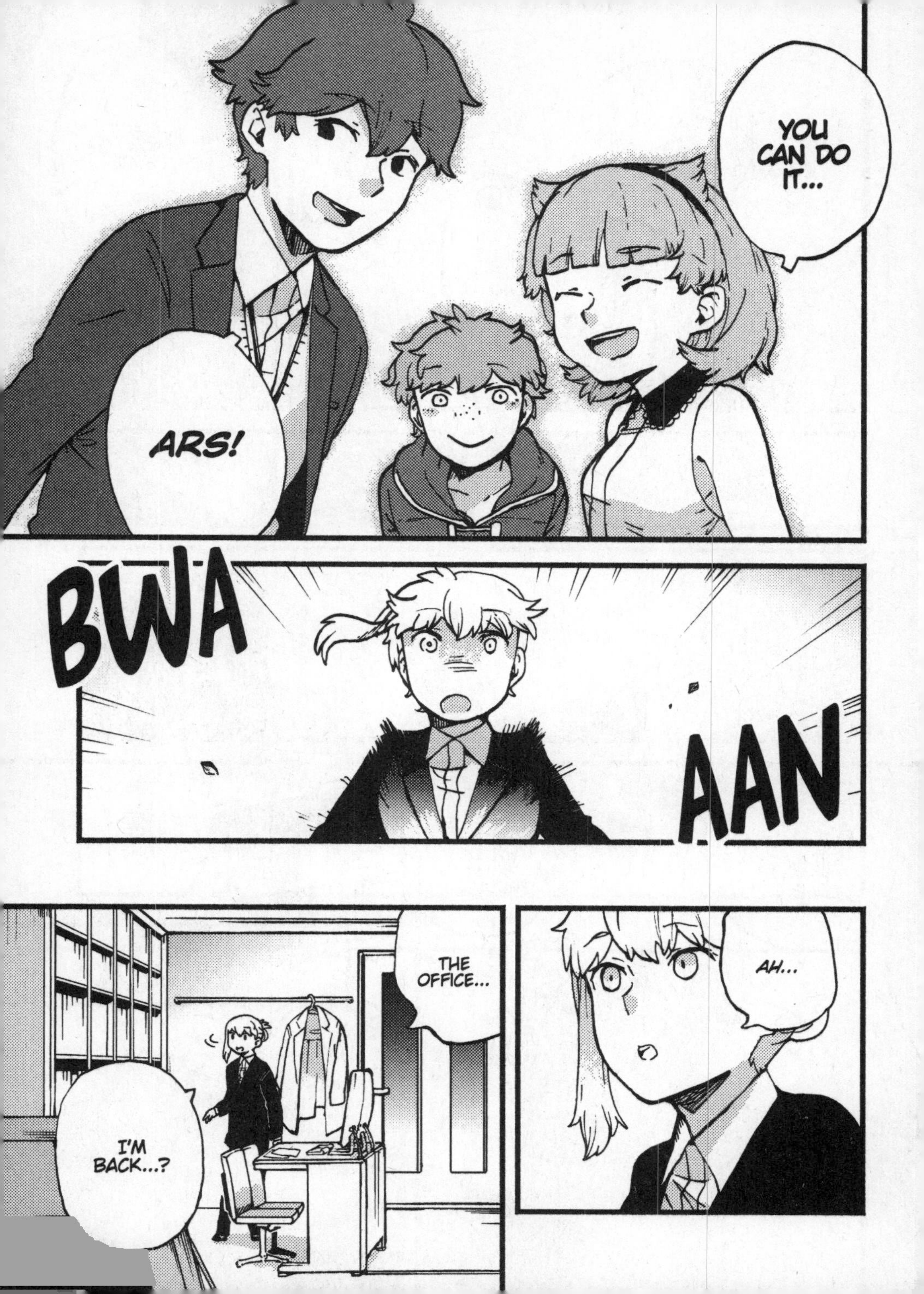
YOU CAN DO IT...
ARS!
BWA
AAN
AH...
THE OFFICE...
I'M BACK...?

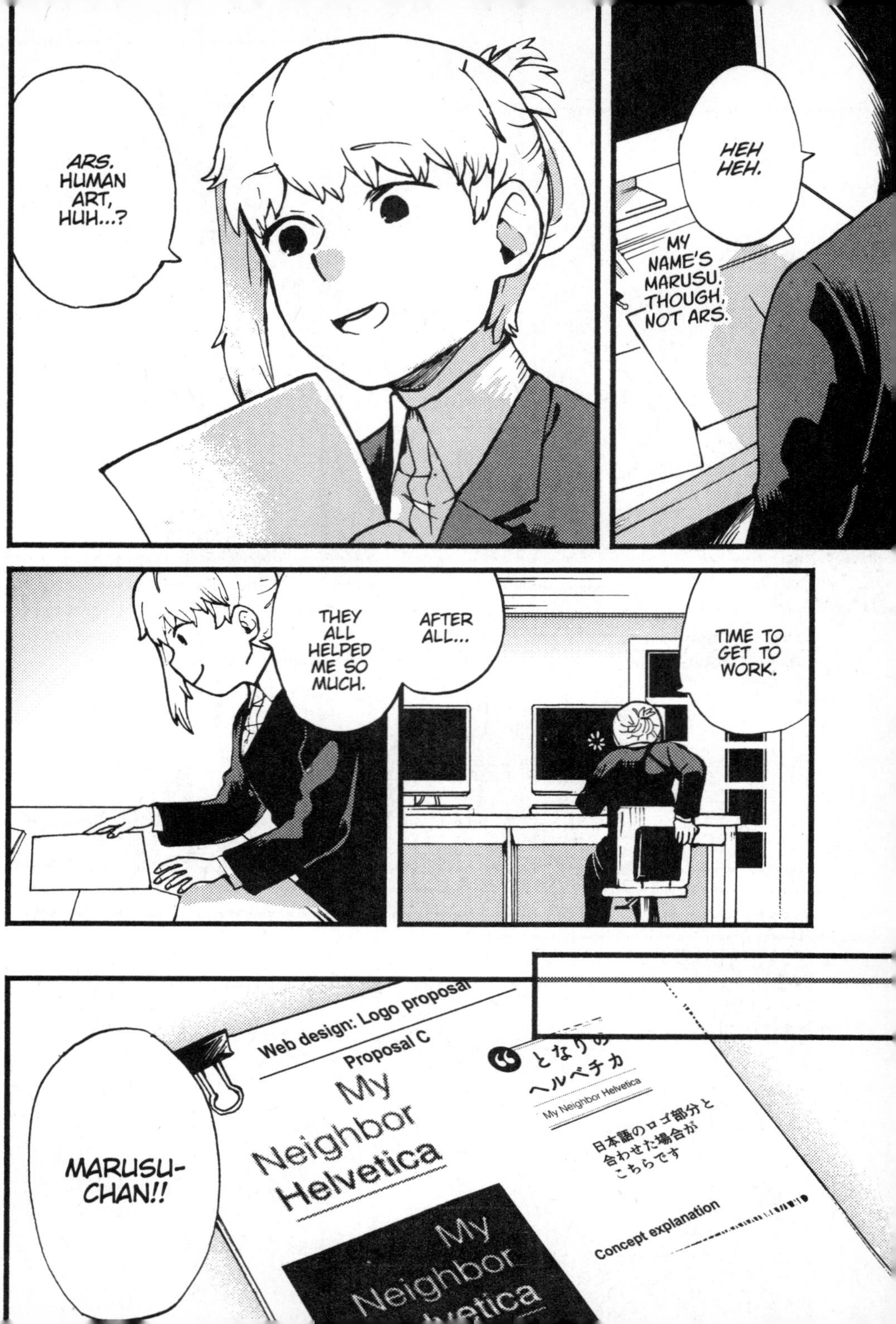
HEH HEH.
MY NAME'S MARUSU. THOUGH, NOT ARS.
ARS. HUMAN ART, HUH...?
TIME TO GET TO WORK.
AFTER ALL...
THEY ALL HELPED ME SO MUCH.
Web design: Logo proposal
Proposal C
My Neighbor Helvetica
となりのヘルベチカ
My Neighbor Helvetica
日本語のロゴ部分と合わせた場合がこちらです
Concept explanation
My Neighbor
MARUSU-CHAN!!

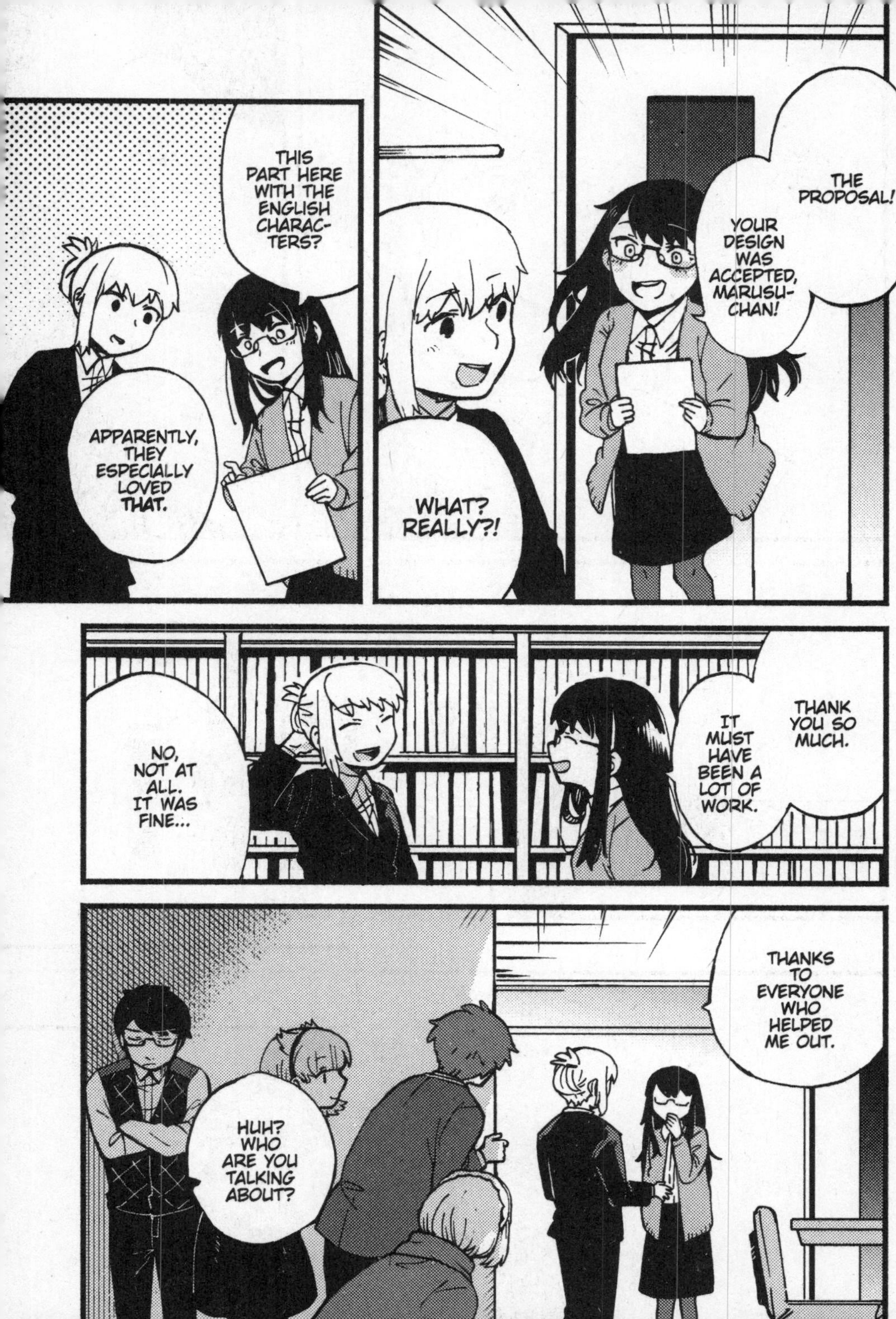
THE PROPOSAL!
YOUR DESIGN WAS ACCEPTED, MARUSU-CHAN!
WHAT? REALLY?!
THIS PART HERE WITH THE ENGLISH CHARAC-TERS?
APPARENTLY, THEY ESPECIALLY LOVED THAT.
THANK YOU SO MUCH.
IT MUST HAVE BEEN A LOT OF WORK.
NO, NOT AT ALL. IT WAS FINE...
THANKS TO EVERYONE WHO HELPED ME OUT.
HUH? WHO ARE YOU TALKING ABOUT?

What the Font?!

A Manga Guide to Western Typeface

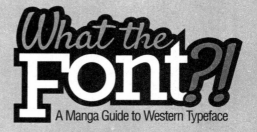

Author's Afterword

This manga sprang from the idea that it would be fun if typefaces all had their own personalities just like people do.

So, some things that happened during production: Because Helvetica and Arial are used in almost totally different places although their letters look alike, we had the two of them as really different characters from the very first planning stages. DIN has found a niche in recent years in advertisements and logos, far removed from its original use in industrial standards, so he ended up as a boy who looked like the polar opposite of how adult he acted—wise beyond his years. Throughout the book, the display typefaces are much flashier than the body text types. We brought in bits and pieces like this, incorporating the historical background of each character and opinions from people on the ground using the typefaces.

Typefaces are all around you in everyday life, helping people communicate. It would be a sincere delight if this book led to you turning your eyes to the typefaces living beside you.

—Ashiya Kuniichi

SPECIAL THANKS
Editor: Yamada Tomoko-san
Supervisor: Yamamoto Masayuki-san
Designer: Tozuka Yasuo-san
Assistant: Tanaka-san

References & Credits

Books

Inoue Kazui, *Romaji Insatsu Kenkyu* (Roman Alphabet Printing Research), Dai Nippon Printing Co., Ltd.; ICC headquarters, 2000.

Otani Hideaki, *The Helvetica Book*. MdN Corporation, 2005.

Kobayashi Akira, *Oubun Shotai—Sono Haikei to Tsukaikata* (Western Type: Background and Usage). Bijutsu Shuppan-sha Co., Ltd., 2005.

Kobayashi Akira, *Oubun Shotai 2—Teiban Shotai to Enshutsuho* (Western Type: Standard Types and Expressions). Bijutsu Shuppan-sha Co., Ltd., 2008.

Kobayashi Akira. *Font no Fushigi—Brand no Logo wa Naze Takaso ni Mieru noka* (Mysterious Fonts: Why Do Brand Logos Look Expensive?), Bijutsu Shuppan-sha Co., Ltd., 2011.

Takaoka Juzo, *Oubun Katsuji* (Western Moveable Type). Insatsu Gakkai Shuppanbu, 2004.

Tanaka Masaaki, *Bodoni Monogatari—Bodoni to Modern Romantai wo Megutte* (The Story of Bodoni—On Bodoni and Modern Roman Type). Insatsu Gakkai Shuppanbu, 1998.

Wada Kyoko (trans.), *Utsukushii Oubun Font no Kyokasho* (Beautiful Western Font Textbook) *(Design Museum Edition)*. X-Knowledge, 2013.

Yajima Shuichi, *Typography no Hensen to Design* (Typography Changes and Designs). Graphic-sha Publishing Co., Ltd. 2008.

D.B. Updike, Kawamura Mitsuo (trans.). *Oubun Katsuji Rekishi to Shotai—Ikinokori no Kenkyu* (Printing Types—Their History, Forms, And Use). Rakudasha, 2008.

Georges Jean (writer), Yajima Fumio (supervisor), *Moji no Rekishi* (The History of Letters). Sogensha Inc., 1990.

Peter Dawson, Teshima Yumiko (trans.), *Machi de Deatta Oubun Shotai Jitsureishuu* (The Field Guide to Typography). BNN, Inc., 2015.

Stan Knight, Takamiya Toshiyuki (supervisor), *Seiyo Katsuji no Rekishi—Guttenberg kara William Morris he* (Historical Types from Gutenberg to William Morris). Keio University Press, 2001.

Websites

http://tosche.net/2012/09/arial_j.html
https://themorningnews.org/article/is-gotham-the-new-interstate
https://www.youtube.com/watch?v=SaX_PwxSh5M
https://www.youtube.com/watch?v=Ow6ajKO0XsM
https://www.youtube.com/watch?v=KdlB3ooT7g4

References for Typeface Commentary/Analysis

W.P. Jaspert, W.T. Berry, A.F. Johnson, *Encyclopaedia of Type Faces,* 4th ed., Blandford, 1970

Ruari McLean, *The Thames and Hudson Manual of Typography,* Thames and Hudson, 1980

Walter Tracy, *Letters of Credit: A View of Type Design,* David R. Godine, 1990

Sebastian Carter, *Twentieth Century Type Designers,* Trefoil, 1987

Alexander Lawson, *Anatomy of a Typeface,* David R. Godine, 1990

R. Eason, S. Rookledge, *Rookledge's International Handbook of Type Designers.* Sarema Press, 1991

M. Klein, Y. Schwemer-Scheddin, E. Spiekerman, *Type & Typographers,* Architecture Design and Technology Press, 1991

Karen Cheng, *Designing Type*, Laurence King, 2005

Neil Macmillan, *An A-Z of Type Designers*, Laurence King, 2006

Fonts Utilized in *What the Font?!*

CCWildWords (dialogue), Komika Slim (asides), Arnold 2.0 (SFXs), Brushcut (SFXs), Felt Tip (SFXs), Chanl (copyright), Satisfy (logo), Rockwell Std (logo) and featuring Helvetica, Optima, Rockwell, Gill Sans, Futura, Gotham, Centaur, Arial, Caslon, Jenson, Franklin Gothic, Times New Roman, Garamond, Zapfino, Impact, Bodoni, Mistral, Frutiger, Didot, Trajan, Comic Sans, DIN, Clarendon, Peignot, and Fette Fraktur.

Author: Kuniichi Ashiya

Manga artist. Born in 1994 in Hiroshima prefecture, he has worked on many manga involving personification, such as *Tengokucho Zetsumetsuka Yoseigakari,* released in 2018 in Tokuma Shoten's *Comic Zenon.*

Supervisor: Masayuki Yamamoto

Associate Professor at Gifu University. Born in 1967 in Aichi prefecture. His area of specialization is visual design and typography. He is the author of *Shikaku Bunka to Design* (collaboration, Suiseisha 2019) among others. For this volume, he was in charge of writing the typeface commentary as well as supervising the project.

※ The personifications of the typefaces were based on the imagination of the author. The typeface production companies and copyright holders have no connection to these images.

※ This volume is presented for the first time here as a new manga based on the doujinshi *Shotai Kenkyu Circle* issued in 2016, drawn and written by Kuniichi Ashiya.

SEVEN SEAS ENTERTAINMENT PRESENTS

What the Font?!
A Manga Guide to Western Typeface

written and illustrated by KUNIICHI ASHIYA
editorial supervision: MASAYUKI YAMAMOTO

TRANSLATION
Jocelyne Allen

LETTERING AND RETOUCH
Karis Page

INTERIOR DESIGN
Clay Gardner

COVER DESIGN
Nicky Lim
(LOGO) **George Panella**

EDITOR
Shanti Whitesides

PREPRESS TECHNICIAN
Rhiannon Rasmussen-Silverstein

PRODUCTION MANAGER
Lissa Pattillo

MANAGING EDITOR
Julie Davis

ASSOCIATE PUBLISHER
Adam Arnold

PUBLISHER
Jason DeAngelis

WHAT THE FONT?! - A MANGA GUIDE TO WESTERN TYPEFACE
© 2019 Kuniichi Ashiya, Masayuki Yamamoto
Tonari no Helvetica - Manga de wakaru Oubun font no sekai
First published in Japan in 2019 by Film Art, Inc., Tokyo.
Publication rights for this English edition arranged with Film Art, Inc., Tokyo,
through TOHAN CORPORATION, Tokyo.

Seven Seas press and purchase enquiries can be sent to Marketing Manager
Lianne Sentar at press@gomanga.com. Information regarding the distribution
and purchase of digital editions is available from Digital Manager CK Russell
at digital@gomanga.com.

Seven Seas and the Seven Seas logo are trademarks of
Seven Seas Entertainment. All rights reserved.

ISBN: 978-1-64505-639-3

Printed in Canada

First Printing: November 2020

10 9 8 7 6 5 4 3 2 1

READING DIRECTIONS

This book reads from *right to left*, Japanese style.
If this is your first time reading manga, you start
reading from the top right panel on each page and
take it from there. If you get lost, just follow the
numbered diagram here. It may seem backwards at
first, but you'll get the hang of it! Have fun!!

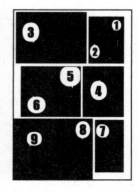